The
OTHER SISTER

DIANNE DIXON

Published by Sourcebooks Landmark, an imprint of Sourcebooks, Inc.
P.O. Box 4410, Naperville, Illinois 60567-4410
(630) 961-3900
Fax: (630) 961-2168
www.sourcebooks.com

Library of Congress Cataloging-in-Publication data is on file with the publisher.

Printed and bound in the United States of America.
VP 10 9 8 7 6 5 4 3 2 1

ALSO BY DIANNE DIXON

The Book of Someday

For Elizabeth, Christi, and Stephen.
With love.

The lotus comes from the murkiest water
but grows into the purest thing.

—Nita Ambani

Part One

RHODE ISLAND

Prologue

IN THE GLASS-WALLED BALLROOM OF A NEWPORT, RHODE ISLAND, mansion, a swarm of butterflies had just been released—and in the same split second, a bridal bouquet of lavender roses was thrown into the air.

Ali, the maid of honor, stood at the bottom of a curving flight of stone stairs in a shimmering, sage-green gown. She was so incredibly beautiful that even with the spectacle of the butterflies and the bouquet, everyone's attention was on her.

A bridesmaid wearing a pale-pink dress scrambled to grab the falling flowers. No one noticed, including Ali.

While the wedding flowers grazed the bridesmaid's straining fingertips and sailed away, Ali was in the midst of a kiss. At the end of the kiss, Ali stretched out her hand with a quick, effortless gesture.

The bouquet dropped directly into her open palm, its slap on her skin startling her, making her laugh. In response to this charming accident, the bride and the wedding guests whistled and applauded.

But Ali was suddenly nervous. Leaning over the stair rail, scanning the faces in the crowd, searching for someone. Matt, the man she'd been kissing, told her, "I know what you're thinking. Don't do it." He wrapped her fingers around the base of the bouquet. "Hang on to this. It's proof. You'll be the next one to get married."

"I'm not even engaged," Ali said.

"Not yet." Matt put his lips on her shoulder, bringing them up along the length of her neck, very slowly.

The bridesmaid in the pink dress moved closer to the bottom of the stairs, closer to Ali—arms crossed, gaze lowered. Her fingernails dug into the soft flesh in the crooks of her elbows.

When the bridesmaid finally raised her head, her angry gaze was fixed on Ali.

Ali clearly understood the message that had been sent. The bridesmaid was her sister. Her twin, Morgan.

For anyone who happened to see it, the poisonous look that went from Morgan to Ali was a disturbing glimpse into the darkness that can cling to the underside of love.

For Ali and Morgan, the darkness was directly connected to the fact that their twinness wasn't identical. Ali's eyes were sparkling, changeable, sometimes brownish green, sometimes golden brown. Her glossy hair was caramel colored, and her body was voluptuous. Morgan's shape was narrower, the body of a fencer or a long-distance runner. Her eyes were simply, and always, brown. Her hair, a quiet ash blond. Compared to what her sister had received, Morgan had always felt that what she'd been given wasn't enough.

In her pale-pink bridesmaid's dress, Morgan was staring up at the bridal bouquet. Asking *Why?* in a voice that was almost soundless.

She let several seconds pass. Eventually, when she understood Ali wasn't going to answer her question, or let her have the bouquet, Morgan turned and walked toward the crowded dance floor. As soon as she got there, her attention went straight to the handsome groom. He was slyly grinding close and slow with his laughing bride.

~

The guests had scattered; the band had gone home. It was just before midnight, and the bride was in the ballroom, where the only light was coming from a satin-shaded lamp on a table near one of the glass walls. She was there with her family. They were cheering as she held up a champagne glass and announced, "Here's to my new life! May it be as fabulous and happy as the one I grew up in!" The groom sat next to her, saying nothing.

Ali was in one of the mansion's guest rooms, excited and happy, taking a handful of unlit sparklers and a gift bag stuffed with tissue paper from an open suitcase on her bed. The bridal bouquet of lavender roses was lying on her pillow.

Morgan was in the shower, surrounded by a thunder of water. Ali called to her, "Don't wait up! Matt and I will be doing some major celebrating."

Ali had traded her wedding finery for a plum-colored linen shirt and a pair of jeans and was heading toward the door, holding the sparklers and the gift bag. As she passed Morgan's bed, she noticed the plain cotton pajamas Morgan had neatly laid out—and that the book on Morgan's bedside table was a dog-eared romance novel.

Instantly, Ali's happiness was flattened by guilt, by a grinding sense of obligation planted in her years ago. When she was a little girl on her way to birthday parties and sleepovers. When her parents' constant refrain was *"What about Morgan? You wouldn't want her going off and leaving you all alone. Be a good girl. Take care of your sister."* That lifelong guilt about Morgan's loneliness was what had made Ali agree to share a room with her this weekend, instead of being where she wanted to be, with Matt.

Ali opened the book on the bedside table. On the inside cover, her sister had written her full name: Morgan Marie Spencer. The same way she'd written her name in every book since she was six—like she was relentlessly hanging on to being a child.

Ali glanced toward the closed bathroom door, thinking, *Everybody in the wedding is staying in this mansion tonight. The place will be full of parties. You're twenty-seven, Morgan. All grown up. Go out… Have some fun.*

But the truth was that Morgan had nowhere to go. She didn't know how to find her own fun. She'd stubbornly refused to learn.

Ali tossed the romance novel onto the bed. "I don't feel sorry for you, Morgan. It's your own fault you're alone."

Yet, just before Ali left the room, she moved the bouquet of lavender roses from her pillow to Morgan's.

In years to come, seemingly random events taking place in the mansion that night would lead to brutal, unexpected violence—and to the discovery of something so bizarre it would be heart-stopping. No one could have known this.

But if Ali had a choice, would she have wanted to know? Would she have appreciated advance notice on the identity of the person who would someday shatter her life? What would be less painful? To find out it was a stranger? Or someone close? Someone she'd slept beside or danced with? Maybe even somebody she loved.

Was it for the best that, in a future place and time, things happened exactly the way they did? Hitting her out of the blue. Without warning.

Ali

A LI HAD ARRIVED AT THE FARTHEST EDGE OF THE MANSION'S rolling back lawn, where the grass gave way to a sandy bluff overlooking the ocean. Matt was there, spreading a white tablecloth under a small, wind-gnarled tree. Setting up a picnic borrowed from the wedding feast. A bottle of wine, a pair of engraved forks, and a gold-rimmed plate containing a single slice of wedding cake.

The minute Matt saw Ali running toward him, he jumped to his feet, reaching out, catching her, and lifting her up.

The warmth and strength of Matt's embrace, the clean, fresh smell of his skin—to Ali it was like being carried into heaven. "Am I late?" she whispered.

"No worries. We still have four minutes till midnight. It's still our anniversary."

In the light from the half-moon, Matt looked like a blue-eyed, fair-haired angel. He took Ali's breath away as she told him, "I can't believe it, the anniversary of our first date. Exactly one year ago."

"Before that night, I'd never gone out with a girl as wonderful as you."

"As wonderful as me…?" All Ali could think about was Morgan—the drab cotton pajamas and the dog-eared romance novel, how alone Morgan was at that moment. It wracked Ali with guilt when Matt said, "You're so loving, so giving."

"Am I?"

"Yeah. You make me wake up every morning wanting to be a better man, just to be worthy of you."

Matt leaned in for a kiss. There was nothing Ali wanted more, but she flinched and pulled away.

"Al, what's wrong?"

She didn't know how to explain without sounding crazy—because there was no uncrazy way to say *I'm being hit by a horrible ache that belongs to Morgan, the misery of my sister's loneliness.*

"Ali, what's going on?" Matt gave her a gentle shake.

"Maybe we should put this off, our celebration, till tomorrow. We could do it after we get back home." She tried to slip out of Matt's embrace; he didn't seem to notice.

He nestled her closer against his chest. "To be with you, Al...it's the only thing I'll ever need for the rest of my life." Matt glanced toward the feast beneath the tree, then looked up at the sky. "I brought you cake and champagne. And the moon. Because anything less wouldn't have been enough."

"I got you a present, too. Hope you like it." Ali suddenly remembered what was in the bag she'd brought with her. The thought sent a blush across her cheeks. "It's a gift I autographed. *Very* personally."

Ali's blush made Matt laugh. "Can't wait to see what it is." His laughter stopped, leaving behind an enigmatic smile. "But I want to open my present later. Right now, there's something more important we need to do."

The sparklers Ali had brought with her from the mansion were still in her hand. Matt took them from her and planted them in a wide circle in the grass.

He lit the sparklers carefully, one by one. Surrounding Ali in a cloud of fairy-tale light. Light that danced across the wine bottle. And the china plate with its single slice of wedding cake. Light that danced across the diamond ring that Matt was slipping onto Ali's finger as he asked, "Alexia Spencer, will you marry me?"

For a moment, Ali was speechless. Then she said, "Yes. Yes. I'll marry you. And I'll spend the rest of my life loving you. You're everything I'll ever want."

For a while, Ali and Matt simply held each other, sharing intimacy that was quiet and sweet.

Then as they were enjoying the wedding cake and the champagne, Ali said, "Our life together is going to be fantastic."

Matt grinned. "Tell me about it. Every detail."

"Well, as you know, one of the nicest parts will be my restaurant." Ali put down her champagne glass, eager to tell Matt the news. "By the way, I have a new idea for the layout—simple, welcoming. Totally unpretentious."

"Even if we make it unpretentious, the restaurant's an expensive proposition, Al." Matt's grin was gone. "You're about to marry a thirty-year-old, first-year assistant professor of English. It might take a while before we get this thing off the ground."

Ali knew Matt wanted to be her hero. And every time they talked about the restaurant, it made him nervous. Because teaching—the career he loved—could never provide him with enough money to make all her dreams come true. In a rush of protectiveness, Ali laced her fingers into Matt's. "I don't care about having piles of cash. I never have."

"It's easy to live without a lot of money only if you've never had a lot of money," Matt told her.

"What does that mean?"

"Nothing." He shrugged and looked away. "I'm just babbling."

Ali wondered if it was true, wondered if there wasn't something more to what he'd just said, but she didn't push him. There were parts of himself that Matt kept private, things Ali could only guess at. Hurts that she assumed were connected to losing his parents when he was still a teenager. And having no other family. His grief at being left completely alone in the world.

Ali cuddled close, wanting Matt to feel how much he was loved, believing that someday, their love would make him feel safe enough to open up and tell her everything.

Matt, meanwhile, had turned his attention toward the soft glow coming from the mansion's windows. "That house is enormous. How many bedrooms do you think it has?"

Ali cuddled closer, loving how warm Matt's skin was. "I don't know, dozens?"

"And I'm not the only guy staying here tonight who's in love with you, am I?" There was the slightest flicker of a frown in Matt's expression.

Ali was puzzled. "What are you talking about?"

"That guy. You know the one, the ginger-haired hulk."

A wave of heat rose in Ali. Embarrassment, discomfort. For an instant, she was back at the wedding reception...*in her sage-green gown. Dancing way too many dances with a partner who wasn't Matt. Experiencing a familiar surge of excitement. The one that had always been there every time that handsome, ginger-haired man touched her.*

"You mean Levi?" Ali said.

"Yeah. Levi. The guy you were all over the dance floor with. What's the story with him?"

Ali shook her head, trying to clear it. "Um...we've known each other forever."

"And that's it? That's all there is to tell about Dancin' Levi?" On the surface, Matt's tone was playful; below the surface, Ali heard something that sounded like jealousy.

She quickly put her arms around Matt and hugged him. "I've known Levi since second grade. We went all through high school together, and college."

"What about now? What's his story now?"

"He plays professional hockey. He's a goalie. And we see each other every once in a while, mostly at the weddings of people we went to college with. Levi and I are friends."

"Was it ever anything more than that?"

"No. Not really."

Ali hugged Matt again—tighter than a moment ago. She'd just told him a lie, put a sliver of distance between them. And she wanted to be close again.

~

Later, when the two of them lay down together in the grass, a breeze lifted the gauzy linen of Ali's shirt. Matt slipped his hand between the billowing fabric and Ali's skin, moving with delicious slowness, letting his fingers come to rest low on her belly. There was lust in the way he touched her. There was also a hint of a question.

The lie she'd told about Levi was still fresh. It made Ali hesitate before she said yes to Matt.

When his hand slid beneath the waistband of her jeans, it sent a delicious shock through Ali, like fireworks. Yet she pulled away a little.

"What?" Matt asked.

"Nothing," Ali said.

There was a flicker of worry in his eyes—and a flutter of guilt in Ali. "Kiss me," she whispered. "Please."

Matt did as he was asked. He kissed Ali deeply, and for a long time. Then he slipped out of his clothes and helped Ali out of hers.

But just as he leaned in to kiss her again, something stopped him. A fierce gust of wind rushed across the mansion's lawn. Toppling the champagne bottle and smashing the wineglasses. Scattering Ali's and Matt's clothes. Spilling the contents of the tissue-stuffed gift bag. Spiraling everything into the air, flying all of it toward the edge of the bluff.

Matt grabbed for the gift bag.

Ali instinctively chased after the clothes.

Shivering in the wind, she was pulling on her shirt and jeans, facing away from Matt, when she heard him say, "Sealed with a kiss. Great card!"

"What?" She had no idea what he was talking about.

Matt held up a small card inscribed with the words *Sealed with a Kiss*. He was also holding a blue box tied with a black velvet cord.

Ali reeled. Like she'd been gut-punched.

The minute she caught her breath and could see straight, she grabbed the box and the card, and with her shirt half-open and her jeans pulled on in a rage, she started running.

Matt, struggling into his clothes, called out to her to stop.

Blind with anger, Ali poured on the speed. Sprinting toward the mansion. Asking a furious one-word question.

Why?

Morgan

A LITTLE WHILE AGO, WHEN SHE THOUGHT SHE HEARD ALI SAY
she was leaving, Morgan had shouted, "Wait! I need to tell
you something!"

But Ali never came in to talk to her. And Morgan realized that the
noise of the shower, echoing off the marble walls of the bathroom,
had probably drowned out everything she'd said. Now she was worried about what would happen when Ali opened that pretty gift bag
and discovered what Morgan had added to it.

Morgan stepped out of the shower and wrapped herself in a towel.
Along with the worry about the gift bag, she'd also been hit with
the reality of the empty night that was ahead of her. Morgan was the
queen of loneliness, alone at a wedding. And it wasn't the first time.
It hurt so much she couldn't move.

When she finally left the bathroom and walked into the bedroom, Morgan was startled to see that someone was there. A smiling, brown-skinned maid, turning down the beds, saying, "Sorry to
frighten you. I thought nobody in here. I saw your friend when she
leave. She very pretty, your friend."

"She's not my friend." Morgan bristled with irritation and a possessive kind of pride. "She's my twin sister."

"Twin?" Surprise darted across the maid's face. "Why you no look
like her?"

Morgan's stomach went achingly tight. The maid's comment, the
look of surprise, were pinches that had been stinging Morgan for a

lifetime. Everyone—from her kindergarten teacher to a plumber who'd asked her out to dinner last year and handed her a hot dog—everyone always had the same reaction. *"You two are so completely different"* was what they'd say. But Morgan knew what they meant was *"You're so ordinary. How could you possibly be a twin to somebody as spectacular as Ali?"*

Caught between resentment and heartbreak, Morgan explained to the maid, "We're not identical twins. We're fraternal. Two separate people who shared a womb."

"I saw on TV about twins who are the same," the maid said. "They have each other's thoughts. Have each other's pain. Is it like this for you and your sister?"

"Sometimes. Not always." Morgan took a quick, wistful breath. "It's sort of like listening to AM radio out in the country. You can't quite hold on to the signal. You never know when you're going to have it or when it will go away."

The maid, finished with the beds, walked toward the door. "Even so...you are lucky. You have a sister who is very nice, so pretty. You must love her very much."

"Yes," Morgan said and left it at that. She didn't say the rest of it aloud, the ugly complicated truth: *I love my sister. I'd kill and die for her. And at the same time, I'm furious that she even exists...because she makes me invisible.*

The maid gave Morgan a cheery wave as she left the room. Morgan didn't see it. She'd taken her phone from a desk near the bathroom door, pressing a number in her contact list, thinking about how unfairly she'd been treated by Ali today.

The call was picked up on the first ring.

A smoky, ambiguously genderless voice said, "Hello, friend."

And Morgan replied, "Hi, Sam."

Morgan didn't know the person's name—it had never been mentioned. And since she wasn't certain if it was a man or a woman, somewhere along the line, Morgan had given this mysterious creature an identifier that would work for either sex—Sam.

Theirs was a relationship that had started in anonymity and, to a certain extent, stayed that way. A little over two years ago, when Morgan was in a department store, a text had appeared on her phone: What're you doing? I have a question. Got a minute?

Morgan, who had recently landed a job as a temp, assumed the text was from her new cubicle mate, wanting to ask a question about work. But it quickly became apparent that Morgan was texting with a stranger. That's when she wrote: You have the wrong person.

Instantly a text came back: Sometimes the wrong person can turn out to be the right person.

The message rattled Morgan, scaring her a little. It was too vague, too mysterious. She had hurriedly shut her phone off. But she couldn't get the unusual exchange out of her mind. Late one night, she dialed the number the texts had originated from, curious to hear who would answer, planning to hang up immediately. But that smoky, ambiguous voice at the other end of the call had fascinated her. They ended up talking for over an hour. The person Morgan would come to think of as Sam was unlike anyone she'd ever talked to. Sam welcomed her with compassionate questions and listened to her with total acceptance, never a shred of judgment or criticism. Their interaction had been remarkable—and addictive.

To Morgan, it had been like cool water on parched earth.

By the time their first call had ended, Morgan was captivated. As their calls continued, she learned that Sam lived in Watch Hill, Rhode Island, and enjoyed a wide variety of music. (Beethoven was playing in the background just as often as songs from a group called Pink Martini.) Sam mentioned looking forward to daily swims and had an interest in Greek mythology. Meditation and a small amount of Napoleon brandy were part of a mellow daily routine.

From this information, Morgan had created a fantasy about Sam. Sam was male. Young enough to be handsome and desirable. Old enough to be wise and tender. In Morgan's mind, Sam had an athletic body, sandy-brown hair, and sea-green eyes.

In one of their earliest conversations, Sam asked her, "Do you have any idea what a beautiful woman you are? What a beautiful soul you have?"

Sam's vision of Morgan was why she had never asked Sam's gender or name or marital status. She didn't want to risk knowing too much, shattering the dream. Sam was precious to her—a place where she felt safe, accepted. And desirable.

On some small but important level, Morgan had fallen in love with Sam.

Now Sam was asking, "How are you tonight?" Sam never used Morgan's name. As far as Morgan knew, Sam didn't know what it was. And, after all this time, Sam had never asked.

"I'm hurting," Morgan told him. Just saying the words brought her to tears. She slid into a sitting position at the side of the desk, her back against the guest room wall. "I'm at a wedding and I'm alone."

There was a short silence. "Is that what hurts the most, being alone?"

"I guess so. But what hurts almost as much is not ever being able to get what I want." Morgan's thoughts were on something very specific. A walk she'd taken on a warm summer afternoon a little over a year ago...

Her hair was freshly washed, she was wearing a new dress, the sun was warm on her bare arms and legs—and she felt pretty. She came around a corner and narrowly avoided a collision with a man who was at the curb, crouched beside his car, inspecting a flat tire. He looked up and smiled at her. When he got to his feet, he said, "Can I borrow your phone? I left mine at work, and I need to call the auto club." Morgan nodded, couldn't speak. His height, the spectacularly blue eyes, and his incredible good looks had her

*tongue-tied. After he made the call, he said, "You saved me. I owe you."
He pointed to the ice-cream store across the street. "How about I buy you a
cone...double-dip chocolate?"*

*Morgan, who didn't particularly like ice cream, told him, "That would be
perfect." And they'd sat side by side, eating jumbo cones on a bench in front
of the ice-cream store, while he waited for his flat tire to be replaced. Morgan
couldn't take her eyes off him.*

"I'm a teacher," he'd said. "How about you?"

*"I work in an art museum." She wanted to tell him so much more, but
the flat had been fixed, the ice cream was gone, and he was saying, "Time to
hit the road." He was already halfway to his car. Morgan frantically tried to
think of something to say. He was so good-looking—and good-looking was
her idea of the perfect man. She desperately wanted the chance to get to know
him and was sure she'd fumbled it. Then, miraculously, he turned back to
her. "I'm not quite ready to say good-bye. Are you?"*

"No. Not even close." Morgan's heart was racing.

"When I ran into you," he asked, "where were you headed?"

*"To meet my sister. She gets off work in a little while, and we're going
to see a movie."*

*He was holding open the passenger door of his car. "How about I give you
a ride?" Morgan had never been so happy. She actually thought she might
faint. It only took them a few minutes to arrive at their destination, the local
Williams-Sonoma store where Ali worked. And as he brought the car to a
stop, he told Morgan, "I live on pasta. It's the only thing I know how to
make. Maybe I should branch out, get myself a cookbook. What if I come in
with you and pick one up?"*

*Morgan nodded, thrilled, already picturing their future together. Within
moments of entering the store, Morgan introduced him to Ali. That's when,
with an awestruck look on his face, he had stepped around Morgan, holding
his hand out to her sister, saying, "Hi. I'm Matt."*

"I never get what I want," Morgan told Sam. "Not even something as small as catching a bridal bouquet. I wanted it so much...not because I thought I'd get married, but because it was pretty. My sister saw... She knew, but she kept it. And all I could think was 'Why? Why won't you let me have it? You don't need it. Compared to me, you have everything.'" Morgan paused, wiping her eyes with the edge of the towel she was wrapped in.

And Sam said, "I can hear how painful this is for you."

"I know it sounds like I'm whining, and I don't mean to, but it's like I'm always being cheated."

Another silence. A peaceful, accepting void.

After a while, Morgan took a deep breath. She was feeling less frantic. "Thanks for listening."

"Always" was the soft reply. "Good night, my friend."

Morgan put her phone on the floor and rested the back of her head against the wall. *I'm alone at a wedding*, she thought, *and my twin, the person who's supposed to care about me the most, wouldn't even let me have a handful of somebody else's flowers. How can Ali be that selfish?*

It was then that Morgan saw her bed—and the bouquet of lavender roses lying on her pillow.

The rush of love for her sister, the gratitude, was instantaneous.

~

Minutes later, Morgan was wrapped in a plush terry-cloth robe. A gift given by the bride's parents to members of the wedding party. For some reason, slippers hadn't been included. In their place, Morgan was wearing pale-pink, sling-back stilettos with scarlet soles—her bridesmaid shoes. She liked them; they made her feel pretty.

She was on the terrace outside the guest room, sitting on a cushioned sofa, her feet propped up on a low stone wall dividing the terrace from a walkway that was a few feet below.

Shining in the moonlight, the scarlet soles of Morgan's stilettos had caught someone's attention. The groom's.

Ambling along the pathway below the terrace, he noticed the seductive flash of red and a woman's slender foot. In a lightning-quick move, he reached over the terrace wall and slipped off one of Morgan's shoes.

Startled, Morgan jumped up from the sofa, still wearing the other stiletto and losing her balance. Before she could fall, the groom leaped over the wall and steadied her.

With a finger hooked through the thin strap at its back, he began to swing her shoe in a lazy circle, grinning at Morgan and saying, "Hot. Very sexy."

Flustered by his sudden appearance on the terrace, Morgan grabbed the shoe from him. "These aren't mine. I mean they are, but they're my bridesmaid shoes. All the bridesmaids had them."

She sat down on the sofa, and the groom studied her, smiling.

Morgan had dated very little and slept with only two of those dates. She wasn't accustomed to being watched and smiled at by a man—any man, much less one who looked like a smoothly muscled, dark-haired movie star. The groom was making her painfully self-conscious. At the same time, she was incredibly attracted to him.

Without asking, he settled in beside her, relaxed and comfortable, draping his arm across the back of the sofa. His hand was so close to Morgan's shoulder that she could feel the heat of his skin. She was panicked. And lonely. And tantalized.

She scooted forward. Then wished she hadn't. He had set off a desire in her. She wanted him to touch her. And all she could think to do was glance toward the walkway and ask, "Where's Jessica?"

"My lovely bride is taking a stroll down memory lane with her family. I needed some air." He casually stretched his legs. His thigh brushed Morgan's.

The jolt was immediate, a thrill Morgan had only experienced in her fantasies. But underneath the thrill was something uncomfortable. Morgan knew what she was doing—what she was wanting—was wrong. But her attraction to this gorgeous man kept her where she was. Unable to move, unwilling to think.

He leaned toward her and said, "It's crazy. I do okay. I make good money, real good money. But I come from people who manage a Mighty Burger in Bakersfield. Jessica's old man was CEO of an oil company, and her mother has a painting hanging in the National Gallery. It's a big jump, status-wise. You know what I mean?"

Morgan nodded vaguely. She could barely hear his voice over the pounding of her own heart.

He stretched and then settled back comfortably against the sofa cushion. "A few minutes ago, I was sitting next to my new wife, and I realized I'd married a woman who intimidates the crap out of me." He took Morgan's hand and held on to it. "So please, just let me stay here for a little while. Be my friend for a couple of minutes?"

Only inches separated them. Morgan's every breath was filled with his scent—a light cologne and a hint of salty-clean sweat, which must have come from the dancing she'd watched him doing at the reception. His tie was loose and the top few buttons of his shirt were open. She could see the smooth skin at the base of his neck and the curling tendrils of dark softness below it.

She wanted to touch him, the man in whose wedding she had so recently been a bridesmaid. She wanted him to touch her. And she was ashamed.

Morgan's voice was shaking as she said, "Okay, you can stay. But just for a minute. Logan."

There had been the slightest hesitation before Morgan said his name. She knew she hadn't said it because she needed to. She'd said it because she wanted the feel of it in her mouth. Because, just once, she wanted to have what her sister had always had—she wanted tall and incredibly handsome. She wanted to know, if only for a minute, what it was like to have Ali's kind of man.

Logan leaned closer, leaving no space between them, his eyes never moving from hers.

Morgan was exhilarated. For once in her life, she was the winner. *He could be in bed right now with his rich, beautiful wife*, Morgan was thinking. *But who he's looking at, who he's choosing, is me.*

He was so close that his breath was on Morgan's lips as he told her, "You're every bit as hot as your red-soled shoes. But you must already know that, Megan."

The thrill dimmed. "Morgan," she said. "My name is Morgan."

His response was a shrug. "Sorry. My new wife and I kind of got married in a hurry. We barely know each other. And I only met you yesterday. I'm still figuring out all the players. And anyway, I'm a bit fucked up." He grinned. Like a mischievous schoolboy. "Let's just say I'm a little high. Wedding-day jitters."

But nothing about him seemed high, or jittery. His expression was cool and composed. He appeared to be offering her a dare, and Morgan didn't understand what its terms were. She didn't know what he expected her to do. Nothing about their encounter was making sense. Suddenly, she wanted to get away from him. "I have to go," she murmured.

The instant Morgan started up from the sofa, he pulled her back down. The grab was so fast that it left her dizzy. "Got a boyfriend waiting for you in your room? A husband, maybe?" He was making Morgan uneasy. She was anxious to get to a safer place—no sex, no heat, just two people having a casual conversation. Without thinking, she said, "No one's waiting for me. Well, not a man anyway. I'm sharing the room with my sister. The maid of honor."

"Ali? The gorgeous girl who caught the bouquet?"

What was left of the fire in Morgan turned to ashes. She knew it was irrational, but it was in moments like this that she felt crushed by Ali and hated her.

Logan sat looking at Morgan with an unreadable grin, saying nothing. She tightened the sash of her bathrobe. Nervous, babbling. Telling him things he probably already knew. "Your new wife and my sister are best friends. One of the bridesmaids dropped out at the last minute. I think the only reason I got to take her place was because I wore the same size dress she did. And I'm pretty sure Ali asked Jessica to let me fill in. Maybe not. I don't know. But anyway, my sister's not here. She's with her boyfriend. It's a big anniversary for them, and she'll probably stay with him tonight so—"

She stopped talking because the groom had leaned forward and kissed her—long and hard. A kiss that left Morgan dizzy.

He took hold of the sash on her bathrobe, waited for a fraction of a second, and then tugged. Morgan looked at his new wedding ring as he pulled the sash away, opening her robe. The moonlit ring was giving off a muted gleam. A warning light.

But Morgan was already on her back—with Logan above, lowering himself toward her. And she reached for him eagerly. It was like being swept away by magic.

Then, without warning, the magic was gone. Replaced by stomach-churning panic. "Somebody's here!" Morgan started to sit up—frantically telling Logan, "Wait! Wa—"

His hand clamped down on her mouth, shoving her back onto the sofa.

While Morgan was still trying to free herself, there was a loud noise in the guest room, and the terrace was flooded with light.

Logan vanished into the shadows, nervously buttoning his shirt, zipping his pants. Morgan scrambled off the sofa, hurrying toward the guest room's open terrace doors.

When Morgan walked into the guest room, Ali was already in there, in her rumpled shirt and grass-stained jeans. Tightly gripping the blue gift box. Her voice was rasping, furious. "Why? Why won't you ever *stop*?"

The wildness in Ali scared Morgan. "I was only trying to be nice," she told her sister. "I was trying to help. I didn't think I was doing anything wrong."

But the truth was that the item in that blue box was intensely personal, and Morgan knew, without a doubt, what she'd done was wrong.

Now Ali was asking, "Why can't you ever fucking go out and get anything of your own?"

I tried, but you took him away from me, the minute he saw you in that stupid Williams-Sonoma store. Morgan was ashamed as she said, "I only wanted to know what kind of anniversary gift you got for Matt. When I looked in the bag, I saw you'd just stuffed his present in with a bunch of tissue paper. There wasn't even a card...so I made it nice...with the blue box and the velvet ribbon. Then I wrote the note. I—"

Morgan stopped. Silenced by words she didn't have the courage to say. *I was jealous, Ali. I wanted to show you how careless you are with something I'd have been so careful with. I wanted to prove how much better I'd be at loving a man than you are.*

"I didn't blindside you. I tried to explain," Morgan told Ali. "I said I had something to say to you, when you were leaving, when I was in the shower. But you didn't come in and—"

Ali threw the blue box, and it hit Morgan full force. "This was mine," Ali hissed. "It was personal."

The box bounced off Morgan's shoulder and landed a short distance away. Now Ali threw the note at her, too. It fell at Morgan's feet, displaying the message Morgan had written with such care: *Sealed with a Kiss.*

Morgan looked away. A pair of silk boxer shorts had fallen out when the gift box hit the floor. The boxers—creamy white—were stamped across the fly with a lipsticked imprint of Ali's mouth.

The stare Ali gave Morgan was murderous. "Get your own life. Stop eating at mine like a greedy little termite."

The hurt Ali inflicted was unbearable. Morgan ran for the safety of the bathroom, where she could slam the door on her sister and lock it.

When she came into the marble-floored bathroom, Morgan was still running from Ali, and the smooth red sole of her shoe shot out from underneath her like an ice skate. Slamming Morgan headfirst into a glass shelf near the sink. Before the shelf shattered, its beveled edge plowed open a wound that traveled from Morgan's hairline to the top of her skull.

For a second or two, the shock kept Morgan on her feet, slack mouthed and stunned. Then she fell into a sea of broken glass. Landing facedown, in a pool of blood.

Ali

I N THE THREE DAYS SINCE ALI HAD WATCHED HER SISTER FALL ONTO
that spill of broken glass in the Newport mansion, Ali and
Morgan hadn't spoken to each other. Now they were in Maine, in
a little house that was old and weathered. The farm that surrounded
the house was a green-earthed, sea-swept place called BerryBlue, near
the coast. Not far from the town of Kennebunkport. Ali was sitting
across the table from Matt in the farmhouse kitchen.

"What time is it?" she asked.

"Still early," Matt said. "A few minutes before six."

Ali and Morgan's grandmother had died. After the funeral, the
mourners had gathered at the farm to talk about old times and shed
a few tears. Now that the guests were gone, Ali and Matt were sharing leftovers. It was what remained of the good, simple food Ali had
prepared for the post-funeral reception—homemade rosemary-raisin
bread spread with sweet organic butter, citrus-roasted chicken, field
greens tossed with herbed goat cheese, cranberries, and apples.

The loss of her grandmother was still fresh and the memories were
flooding in. Ali pushed her plate aside. Her voice was quiet as she told
Matt, "Grandma MaryJoy was Irish. She believed life was a celebration. She said the heartbeat of that celebration is in the kitchen. In
the joy people have when they're sharing good food and good wine."

Ali paused and smiled. "I loved everything about her, especially her
name. MaryJoy O'Conner. It sounded just like who she was. Like a
party. Remember what a great time she had at her birthday dinner

last summer at that Irish pub? Nobody in the place could believe she was ninety-three."

Matt nodded. "I'd just met her, but I was crazy about her. And her eyes, they knocked me out. They were the color of violets. I remember her dancing with the waiter, a huge grin on her face, and the band playing 'When Irish Eyes Are Smiling.'"

Ali was caught between grief and sweet remembrance. "She always said that when her time came, the only thing she wanted on her headstone was 'This is the day the Lord has made. Let us rejoice and be glad in it.' That's what she was all about...rejoicing, being glad."

Suddenly, there was an odd expression in Matt's eyes—something restless. Ali reached for his hand. "Are you okay? What's going on?" She suspected he was wrestling with ghosts from his past, the emptiness of being without any family at all. Things he didn't know how to talk about.

Matt looked around the room at the whitewashed walls, the waxed pine cabinets, and the copper-bottomed pots hanging above the old-fashioned gas stove. "This place is almost too good to be true, isn't it?"

"BerryBlue Farm is where Morgan and I had the best times of our lives," Ali said. "We spent every summer here when we were kids. The first day of vacation, Dad would always drive us up here, Mom and Morgan and me. He'd get us settled and turn around and go right back home, back to work. But he was always here on the weekends. Every single summer. Then..."

"Then what?" Matt asked.

Ali shrugged. "Then they split up. After the divorce, Morgan and I would be so sad when we first got here, but then we'd slide right back into the magic of summer at BerryBlue...sailing Grandpa's little beat-up boat, riding our bikes, picking blueberries."

"Sounds like little kid heaven." There was something in Matt's expression that seemed envious, almost cold. "Lucky you. The lovely girl who summered at BerryBlue."

Ali hadn't ever seen that kind of bitterness in Matt. It sent a shiver through her. "Talk to me. What's going on?"

Matt gestured toward the kitchen counter. "I think we're ready for dessert." He said it very quietly. Matt and Ali had been keeping their voices low because Morgan was asleep upstairs and Ali's mother was nearby, grieving, on the back porch. Ali's grandfather, the owner of the farm, was a few feet away in the living room.

As Matt left the table, Ali was aware he hadn't responded when she'd asked what was going on with him, and she knew his silence had been deliberate. There were places in Matt no one would ever be allowed to go, places that were closed and locked. Ali had recognized this from the very beginning, and it had intrigued her. But a second ago, his tone, and his attitude, had made her uncomfortable.

Matt was deftly taking a tray of sugar-crusted lemon tarts from the kitchen counter, studying them in amazement, his mood brightening. "These things are like something out of a magazine. You're unbelievable!"

There was a quality in Matt that was so guileless at that moment, so full of love and admiration, that Ali wondered if she'd simply imagined the darkness she'd just seen in him.

"When we're married, Al, you'll come up with this kind of awesome food every night, right?" As he asked the question, he kissed her.

And Ali marveled, as she always did, at how tender Matt's kisses were.

In response to his food inquiry, she gave him a teasing grin. "After we're married, the cuisine will be awesome for the first month or two, then I'll probably nose-dive right into tuna sandwiches and canned soup."

Ali playfully tugged on Matt's shirt, pulling him closer. "And speaking of getting married, guess what? I already made an appointment with Reverend Miller to talk about the wedding." She flashed an apologetic grin. "I know we have a year to make plans, and I want a really simple ceremony, but I'm excited. I can't wait to get started."

Matt stroked Ali's hair—his voice soft, full of affection. "How many kids should we have?"

"I'm not sure. What do you think?"

His answer was another kiss.

It was a moment of sweet connection between them.

But when Matt said, "I don't care how many kids we have, just as long as they're all exactly like you," the atmosphere in the room changed.

The sweetness was gone.

Morgan

MORGAN HAD SLEPT FOR HOURS, OUT LIKE A LIGHT, AS IF SHE'D been in a coma. She came downstairs staggering and groggy. And now she was in the shadow of the kitchen doorway, hearing Matt murmur to Ali, "I don't care how many kids we have, just as long as they're all exactly like you."

The tenderness in his voice, the adoration, set off raging jealousy in Morgan. It combined with her grief about her grandmother's death and sent her storming into the kitchen.

"You want your kids to be exactly like Ali?" Morgan said. "Good luck, pal. What you're asking for are little rug rats who'll be smart. And beautiful. And mean as hell."

For a minute, nobody moved. Then Ali asked coldly, "What are you doing down here?"

The simple answer was *I'm here because I needed something to eat.* But the jealousy and blame between Morgan and her sister were running too deep for simple answers. And a vindictive lie came flying out of Morgan's mouth: "I woke up and thought I'd had a nightmare. Then I turned on the light and looked in the mirror." Morgan glared at Ali, wanting Ali to see the network of cuts covering her face. "And you know what? It wasn't a dream. My face really is sliced to bits."

You stole Matt from me, Morgan thought. *And if you hadn't been screaming at me for making his present nice, I never would've gone facedown into a pile of glass. You owe me, Ali. I have the right to make you squirm.*

But Ali didn't squirm. She calmly turned her back on Morgan and began rinsing dishes in the sink, her voice flat and toneless, saying, "I'm sure you'll feel better soon."

Ali's indifference made Morgan furious. "Really? That's all you have to say? Well, fuck you!"

The loudness of her shout startled Morgan. The words *I'm sorry* were already at the back of her throat. But she didn't get the chance to say them. Matt crossed the room, blocking Ali from Morgan's view. "What happened to you was an accident," he said. "Don't even *try* to make it Ali's fault."

Matt's anger hurt every bit as much as Ali's indifference. Anxious to leave the room, Morgan turned around so quickly she almost lost her balance.

Ali grabbed her, kept her from falling.

Morgan was afraid to look at Ali, scared that this time she'd gone too far, made Ali too angry, and there would be no coming back.

"You're all right. The doctor told you…you were lucky," Ali said. "None of the cuts are going to leave scars."

Morgan could hear the caring in Ali's voice, yet Morgan couldn't let it go. She had to make her point. She needed to remind Ali of the debt she owed for always getting the lion's share and leaving Morgan with the crumbs.

"You think it'll be okay?" Morgan asked. "You really think you haven't left scars? Let me tell you about the scars you've left, Ali." Without meaning to, Morgan glanced in Matt's direction, then quickly looked away.

After taking several steps backward, to put some distance between herself and Ali, she said, "How do you think I feel, coming all the way up here and not getting to be at Grandma MaryJoy's funeral?" Morgan was upset, shouting. "Do you think that doesn't hurt, Ali? She was my grandmother, too. She was—" Morgan stopped. She was suddenly aware that her fight with Ali had brought her grandfather and her mother into the kitchen.

Her mother took a box of tissues from a shelf and put it onto the table in front of Morgan, quietly saying, "The reason you didn't go to my mother's funeral, Morgan, was because you chose not to."

Her mother's voluptuous, dark-haired, green-eyed beauty had always made Morgan feel inadequate and awkward. She was the last person in the world Morgan wanted to deal with right now. But Morgan's anger needed someplace to go, and she turned it on her mother.

"Open your eyes and, for once in your life, look at me, Mom. I couldn't go to the funeral. Everybody would've been staring at these cuts all over my face."

Her mother didn't give an inch. "You told us you were running late, and you'd meet us at the church. Then, after we left, you walked upstairs and went to bed."

No, that's not what happened. I really did go upstairs and get dressed. But my bedroom window was open, and there was a soft, warm breeze... The thought stayed trapped in Morgan's head; the words wouldn't come.

"Morgan. You deliberately missed your own grandmother's funeral." Her mother's expression was pure frustration. "What in the world were you thinking?"

Morgan didn't know how to respond.

The breeze coming through the bedroom window took me back in time to when I was five. And seven. And ten. I could feel that soft breeze on my little-girl skin as Ali and I tumbled out of the back of Daddy's car, already in our bathing suits, eager to start the summer at BerryBlue. While Grandma MaryJoy, with her beautiful smile and violet eyes, was hurrying toward us, saying, "There they are. My girls!"

Then there was that awful stab of jealousy when Ali got the first hug. Because Ali ran ahead, and I was hanging back, waiting. Wanting Grandma

MaryJoy to move Ali aside and come to me. To choose me. But it never happened. And while I was seeing little Ali getting that long-ago hug, I shouted through the open window to the Grandma MaryJoy ghost in the yard below: "I loved you just as much as Ali did. It's not fair she was your favorite."

And then I caught sight of my face in the here and now, my reflection in the mirror near the window, the disgusting web of half-healed cuts.

The humiliation of having to go out in public looking so ugly, and how sad I was about Grandma dying, and the unfairness of Ali always getting that first summer hug—all of it exploded. And I went a little bit crazy. I yanked off the black dress I was wearing and grabbed my pajamas, slamming the window shut and heading for bed. As much as I wanted to be there, I was convinced I had to boycott Grandma's funeral as a protest. To say to everybody that it isn't fair for grandparents to have favorites. It just isn't fair.

"Morgan! I asked you a question. Why did you go back to bed instead of showing up at your grandmother's funeral?"

Morgan closed her eyes. Shook her head. And said nothing. There was no way to explain. It was too complicated.

Her mother seemed to be fighting tears. "What you did broke my heart, Morgan."

Morgan let out a groan. She was embarrassed, and tired. Tired of all the ways she kept getting things wrong. Weary of not knowing how to get them right. And the weariness was making her cynical, pushing awful things out of her mouth. "Ali was at the funeral. She was Grandma MaryJoy's favorite. So me not being there to say 'bye-bye'? Trust me, the old girl won't lose any eternal sleep over that one."

Morgan's grandfather frowned, silently telling Morgan she'd crossed the line.

Her mother seemed ready to slap her. Morgan shot her a look that challenged her to do it.

But all her mother did was sigh—and walk out of the kitchen.

Morgan's grandfather took a container of ice cream from the

freezer and a spoon from one of the kitchen drawers, saying, "Let's go outside, Morgan, you and me, and sit quiet for a while."

"There's nothing to talk about, Grandpa." Morgan wanted to stop fighting, with everybody. But she was cornered and couldn't back down. "Mom knows how horrible I'm feeling because of what happened to my face. And this morning, before the funeral, it took her an hour to come up and check on me. And when she did, all I got was a couple of minutes of conversation and a kiss on the cheek."

Her grandfather's response was gentle. "Your mother probably would have put great value on somebody kissing her cheek today. She was hurting, sugar. She was about to bury her mama."

"But does that mean she can't think before she opens her mouth? Grandpa, I'm only twenty-seven, and you want to know what she told me?" Morgan did a perfect imitation of her mother's breathy, girlish voice. "'Honey, I've decided to buy a plot in that pretty cemetery where they're putting Grandma MaryJoy, so that when I die, I'll be close to her. And I'm wondering…would you like me to buy one for you, too? That way, just in case, we'd always be sure that at the end you'll have a place with…well, you know…with me, and with the people who love you.'"

Morgan's grandfather suppressed a smile. "I do see where it had its share of clumsy in it, but I don't think she meant it one bit mean."

"What she meant was she thinks there's no guy on earth who will ever want to share a life with me."

"That's not necessarily true."

"She didn't offer to buy Ali a grave."

"Well, honey, Ali has Matt and—"

That ripped it. Morgan couldn't listen to another word. She was already leaving the room. And as she left, she clearly understood that although the fight was over, the destruction was just beginning.

A fundamental part of Morgan had changed.

She'd spent a lifetime shrinking from her mother's criticism, living in Ali's shadow, and always being second best.

The funeral and its aftermath were the small, final straws that had broken something inside Morgan.

Something that wanted to do damage.

~

After Morgan left the kitchen and went upstairs into the bedroom where she'd been staying, she locked the door and sat on the side of the bed. In the dark. Thinking.

Ali got to be Grandma MaryJoy's favorite. Ali got Matt, and they got engaged. Ali got to be homecoming queen and valedictorian. Ali always gets whatever she wants…and it isn't right. Nobody should get everything they want.

For a split second, Morgan was picturing herself with Ali. At the top of a steep flight of stairs. Her hands were on Ali's back, and she was shoving her, hard. Watching Ali plummet and slam onto the ground below. Imagining the awful scream. And the sweet freedom.

When the fantasy faded, the part of Morgan that was crazy with hurt reached for the phone—scrolling to a private number Ali had called months ago. When her own phone hadn't been working and she'd used Morgan's.

"Restaurant Z. What do you want?" The rumbling voice that answered the call crackled with New York impatience.

Morgan's hands were shaking, her mouth dry. This wasn't killing Ali by pushing her down a flight of stairs, but it was close. "Is this Zev Tilden?"

"You're calling in the middle of my dinner service. Who the hell is this?"

Morgan was so nervous she could barely speak. "This is Ali. Ali Spencer. And, um, I really appreciate the chance to intern with you.

Sorry for the short notice. I know I'm supposed to be there next week, but I'm not coming. Give my place to whoever was your second choice. I get that you're a famous chef, and Z is a good restaurant, but—"

"People wait months for a reservation, and you're bailing on the chance to cook here? Are you fucking nuts?"

"My grandmother just died. I'm a little upset right now."

"Guess what? I don't give a rat's ass. You just blew the opportunity of a lifetime. You're a fuckin' rookie. Get off my phone."

As soon as Morgan ended the call, she walked across the hall to the bathroom. Opened the toilet. And jackknifed over it, vomiting in guilty bursts that burned like battery acid.

Then she felt better.

She'd made Ali pay some dues.

Ali

AFTER MORGAN'S DEPARTURE, ALI HAD STAYED IN THE KITCHEN with Matt.

Ali's grandfather went to sit on the porch outside.

And her mother came to sit at the kitchen table.

Matt filled a plate with leftover roast chicken and salad and the rosemary bread, while Ali was saying, "Poor Morgan. Don't be mad at her, Mom. It's just—"

"It's just Morgan being Morgan." Her mother changed the subject, taking a bite of the food Matt had just put in front of her and telling Ali, "This is delicious, honey. You have an incredible talent."

Ali's mother then turned her attention to Matt, holding his gaze as if trying to make up her mind about him. Finally, she said, "You understand no family is perfect, don't you?"

"Yes," Matt said. "I do."

There was something in Matt's expression that was difficult for Ali to read. And something in her mother's smile that was equally unreadable.

"You seem to be a good man," Ali's mother said. "That usually comes from having been a good boy. Is that what you've always been, Matt?"

"Not always." He quickly turned his attention to a vase of condolence flowers on the kitchen counter. "That's a really beautiful arrangement."

And Ali said, "It's from Jon and Nikki, the couple from Boston I introduced you to at the funeral. I was their kids' nanny one summer when I was in college."

That magical summer was an experience Ali had never forgotten. "Jon and Nikki took me to Europe with them. It was incredible."

"It changed everything about the way Ali cooked," her mother said.

The story, Ali's excitement, was tumbling out. "Matt, in France, in the hills of Mougins, there were freshly picked lettuces, tomatoes warm from the vine, and white wine that tasted like ripe pears. In England and Scotland, there were scones laced with currants and honey, and salmon done to absolute perfection. In Italy, rosemary and lavender and olives. And in Spain, there were flavors that danced on my tongue."

Ali stopped and smiled. "That trip made me want to cook in a way that's vibrant, connected to the earth, to make food that feeds the body *and* the soul... Wait, that reminds me. I have a new idea about the logo for the restaurant."

Her mother looked up, surprised. "What restaurant?"

"For right now, Mom, it's the one I'm opening in my dreams. But I'll find a way to change that. As soon as I can." Ali snatched a pencil and paper from the kitchen counter and began a quick sketch.

Matt reached across the table, slowing the movement of her pencil. He leaned in, his voice low so only Ali could hear. "Al, we've talked about this. I'm going to do my best. But we won't have the money for this. Not for a long time."

"Do you two want some privacy?" Ali's mother asked.

"No, Mom. It's fine. Matt's just worried I don't understand that trying to have my own restaurant is a big deal and it'll be hard." Ali looked at Matt, wanting to reassure him. "But I'm on my way. I can feel it. Things are starting to line up. Do you have any idea how many people applied for that apprenticeship at Z in New York? And I got it! I know it's only for three months, but if I impress Zev Tilden, he'll tell people and they'll listen. Who knows what'll happen? Somebody might want to back me, help me go out on my own."

"Al, it's a great dream, but there's no guarantee it'll work out that way." Anxiety was coming off Matt in waves.

"Don't worry," Ali told him. "It doesn't matter. The things I'll learn about food, working with Zev Tilden... It'll be priceless, a game changer for me." Ali snuggled close to Matt. "Everything that happens at Z will add to the momentum we already have. You're a great teacher and a fabulous writer. You won't be an assistant professor forever. And just because you met me in Williams-Sonoma selling Bundt pans and doing cooking demonstrations doesn't mean that's where I'm going to stay for the rest of my life. Together, we'll be fine."

Matt looked down. Took a breath, as if he were about to say something.

And in the silence, Ali's mother told her, "It's time you let go of this boy, Ali. At least for now. It's late, and he has a long drive ahead of him." She stood up and began to gather the dishes. "I'm glad you came, Matt, and that you were here with Ali for the funeral. It's good you understand the obligations of family."

Her mother's tone had been mild, but there was a wary look in her eyes. It was giving Ali the feeling there was something about Matt that her mother wasn't quite comfortable with.

∽

It was late, and Ali knew she should go upstairs, get some sleep. But the funeral and the blowup with Morgan had exhausted her, and she stayed lying on the sofa in her grandfather's den, watching TV. She reached for the remote and caught sight of her mother passing through the room, heading toward the back porch.

The expression on her mother's face was strange to the point of being spooky. Ali immediately got up from the sofa and hurried to an open window, one that would give her a clear view of the porch.

"Kitchen's all cleaned up," her mother was saying.

Ali's grandfather, who was sitting at the top of the porch steps, scooted over to make room for his daughter. "I'd have been happy to help."

"I know, Dad. But I wanted to give myself time to think."

Ali's mother sat down beside him. He moved a little closer and peered at her. "I recognize that look, kitten. What's bothering you?"

"It's Ali's fiancé, Matt."

Ali held her breath, waiting to hear what would come next. There was an odd tone in her mother's voice.

"I suspect there're things about himself that Matt doesn't want anybody to know."

"What kind of things, honey?" Ali's grandfather asked. "Good? Or bad?"

"That's the problem. It could go either way."

Seventy-five miles from BerryBlue Farm,
    later in that soft summer night.
Violence.
    A stifled scream.
    The smell of night-blooming jasmine.
    And a shred of amber-colored silk.

Ali

O N THE MORNING AFTER THE FUNERAL, ALI AND MORGAN MADE the two-and-a-half-hour trip from the farm in Maine to their mother's house in Providence, Rhode Island, in absolute silence—the fallout from the previous night's fight and Morgan's ugly outburst in the farmhouse kitchen.

When Ali angled her car into their mother's driveway and switched off the engine, she turned toward the passenger seat. Morgan was tapping the control buttons on the car door, repeatedly sliding the window open, then thumping it closed. "Whatever this is, I don't have time," Ali said. "I'm moonlighting at the catering company tonight, supervising a huge reception. I need to get over there and start setting up."

Morgan wasn't paying attention; she was looking out the car window, enchanted. Her smile spontaneous, and her eyes sparkling. "Ali. Look. Over there, in that shaft of light by the roses…those hummingbirds. It's like poetry. Aren't they just the most beautifully delicate things you've ever seen?"

Ali couldn't understand why Morgan spent most of her time being abrasive when, at her core, she was incredibly sweet. *There's so much that's special about you, and you're determined to bury it*, Ali thought. *You're smart. You're pretty. You could do anything you want. The world's just waiting for you to come out and play.*

But Morgan had already turned away from the window, instinctively shrinking down, going back to being small and blank.

It was like watching a self-defeating magic trick. Ali couldn't bear to look at it.

Morgan's focus had moved to their mother's gray-shingled home with its neat lawn and colorful flower beds. "You have no idea how tough it is...being forced to live in that house."

Ali didn't have the strength to get into this right now. She reached over and pressed the latch on Morgan's seat belt, sending the belt zipping into a slot near the passenger window.

Morgan ignored the gesture.

"If it's so awful being with Mom," Ali said, "why don't you stop whining about it and find a way to move out?"

"The museum where I was working...it closed. Do you think I wanted that to happen? I know I need money in order to move out, but museum jobs aren't that easy to find. And for your information, I've interviewed for one I think I'm pretty close to getting." Morgan looked back at the hummingbirds, her voice a little less sharp. "And I wasn't whining."

"You were, too," Ali insisted.

Morgan shot back with a pouty "Was not." It came out comically high-pitched, like a little kid being silly.

"Were, too." Ali said it softly, under her breath.

Morgan fought it—then gave in to a smile. "Was not."

The tension between them retreated.

And without looking at Ali, Morgan got out of the car and walked toward the house.

Morgan was happy, moving with an innocent, bouncing stride. It reminded Ali of how it used to be with her and Morgan, of how it had always been—this dance between exasperation and delight.

Ali's catering job turned out to be a book signing for a visiting novelist. The house where it was being held was huge and lavishly decorated. The guests were a cross-section of country clubbers and college professors. It made for interesting bits of overheard conversation— everything from the pros and cons of Brazilian butt lifts to the contact information for an expensive New York City call girl to the theoretical connection between Beethoven's Fifth Symphony and the rise of the Third Reich.

The author being honored was Aidan Blake, a good-looking Australian in his midforties. For most of the evening, he'd been busy chatting, autographing books, and drinking wine. And—as Ali was acutely aware—he'd also been busy watching her.

After the party got underway, Ali slipped out of her kitchen supervisor uniform into her head of catering attire: a chic, open-backed, black cocktail dress. No matter where she was in the room, she could sense Aidan Blake keeping track of what she was doing and who she was talking to. Ali was flattered. Aidan Blake was a very attractive man.

At one point, while Ali was walking past him, she overheard the party's hostess murmur, "Darling, you're an Aussie, not a Brit. Don't waste time with good manners and longing looks. Get on with it. Let the girl know what you want."

When Ali crossed his path, Aidan stepped closer, obviously intending to intercept her. But just as he was about to make his move, they both noticed that a late-arriving guest had entered the room.

In unison, they called out his name. "Matt!"

Aidan gave Ali a surprised grin. "Right, then. You first."

"I'm his fiancée."

Aidan's interest in Ali was lusty and unembarrassed, so intense it made her a little uncomfortable. She took a step back, widening the distance between them. "Your turn. How do you know Matt?"

"I had the young man as a grad student four years ago when I was writer in residence at the college where he's teaching now—"

Matt joined them, finishing Aidan's sentence. "But, more than simply being outstanding student and pretty good instructor, we were brilliant drinking buddies."

Matt give Aidan a friendly slap on the back while Aidan grabbed him in a bear hug. Both of them were tall. Both were off-the-charts good-looking. But they were polar opposites. Matt was in his thirties, golden haired and blue eyed, with the lean, graceful physique of a prep-school tennis champ. Aidan was ten years older, with hair and eyes so dark they were almost black, and a body that was rugged and muscular, like a cowboy's.

When Matt finished greeting Aidan, he asked Ali, "What are you doing here? I thought you were working a catering gig tonight."

"I am. This is it," Ali told him. "When you said you were going to a book signing, I pictured you on a folding chair in the back room of a half-empty bookstore."

"That's where these things usually happen." Matt chuckled and turned to Aidan. "I have to know… How did you manage to end up peddling your wares in a high-rent establishment like this?"

Aidan's tone was light, mischievous. "During my period in writing residence, I boffed the hostess." He leaned in close and told Ali, "She was quite taken with being taken by a Hollywood screenwriter."

Ali stepped back a little more, putting a safe distance between them. "So novels aren't what you usually write?"

"What I usually write is high-voltage crap designed to keep the hairy asses of adolescent males firmly planted in cinema seats."

"He writes action movies. Blockbusters. He's a big deal in Hollywood, very powerful," Matt explained.

"Now, however, I'm reborn as a novelist. And I want to go out and be celebrated." Aidan draped his arm across Matt's shoulders, then pointed at Ali. "But only if you come with us. I am, at least for tonight, in love with you."

Ali narrowed her eyes and shook her head, wanting him to know she wasn't playing his flirtatious game. "You guys go ahead. I need to stay and close up in the kitchen." She gave Matt a lingering kiss. "Call me. Let me know where you two decide to go." As she moved away, she looked over her shoulder and said, "I'll catch up with you."

But Ali never did catch up with Matt that night. It was as if Matt vanished after he walked out of the party.

What caused him to disappear was a single sentence: *I want to make you pay.*

Matt

AFTER LEAVING THE BOOK EVENT, MATT PARTED COMPANY WITH Aidan almost immediately. They made plans to meet later. Aidan needed to go to his hotel to see his publicist; Matt needed to stop by his office at the college to pick up a textbook he wanted to review for one of his upcoming fall courses.

Most of the students and faculty were gone for the summer, and as Matt crossed the campus, his footsteps echoed off the brick walls of empty buildings.

When he entered his office, out of habit, Matt switched on his computer. He was only vaguely aware of his surroundings. He was thinking about Ali, about the black dress she'd been wearing at the party, how it exposed the entire length of her back and how, when he'd touched the skin at the base of her spine, it had been like warm velvet.

The computer signaled the arrival of a new email. Matt clicked on it absentmindedly, with a dreamy smile.

When the email revealed itself, Matt's eyes went wide. He shuddered as if he'd just tripped over a corpse.

The message on his computer screen was:

You're not going to get away with this.

It was signed:

AKA

A monogram Matt knew well.

It put a taste in his mouth that was sour, acid, as if he'd swallowed poison. There was a pressure in his chest that had his ribs aching. It took a long time before he was able to function again. And then he wrote:

How did you find me?

After he sent the message, he sat rigid and apprehensive. For over an hour.

Finally, the computer screen lit up again.

You don't have the right to ask questions.

Matt's hands shook as they moved over the keyboard, asking:

What do you want?

He had to wait almost four hours for a response.

Matt spent those hours pacing. Worrying.

When the computer screen lit up again, the message was blunt and chilling:

I want to make you pay.

Matt's first and only thought was of Ali, of protecting her. In less than the space of a breath, he typed:

Tell me where you are. I'll come. Tonight.

He received a reply that was blindingly fast. Within a few seconds, he was in his car, heading toward I-95.

Morgan

I'M TWENTY-SEVEN AND LIVING AT HOME WITH MY MOTHER." Morgan took a jittery breath. "Sometimes I honestly think about killing myself."

Sam, the smoky voice at the other end of the call, was thoughtful, concerned. "How are things with your money problems?"

"Not good. But if this new job I'm applying for comes through, it'll be better."

"And you think you did well in the interview?" Sam waited, Beethoven playing softly in the background.

"Having somebody to talk to…somebody who listens, who hears me. It helps," Morgan said.

A slow breath, what could have been a murmur of agreement, then no other sound from Sam.

"I took your advice. When I was talking to the interviewer, I pretended I was talking to you, and I was much calmer than normal." Morgan cleared her throat. Usually she'd be uncomfortable making such a self-confident statement, but with Sam, she could say anything. "I'm pretty sure I did great in the interview."

The reply was an approving chuckle. "Later, I'll have a brandy in your honor. I'm happy for you. But not surprised."

Morgan had an unfamiliar sense of excitement and possibility. "Thank you," she said.

No response. Just silence.

In the space of that silence, Morgan had the impulse to say *I love you*—and immediately decided against it. Saying it would make her want more, would make her want to know a name, see a face. And putting a face, or a name, to this miracle of complete acceptance might destroy it. A risk Morgan didn't want to take.

"Do you think you can sleep now?" Sam asked.

To her surprise, Morgan let out a startled whimper. Out of the blue, she'd been hit with a wave of fear.

"What is it, my friend? What's happened to you?"

What was happening was the thing Morgan had tried to describe to the guest room maid at the Newport wedding—the unique connection of twinness Morgan and Ali shared, the erratic, unpredictable ability to sense each other's pain.

Morgan's mouth had gone dry and cottony. She suddenly had a pounding headache. "Nothing's wrong with me. I'm fine," she told Sam. "It's my sister. Something's happened to Ali."

Ali

ALI'S MOUTH WAS COTTONY DRY. SHE HAD A SUDDEN, POUNDING headache and was paralyzed with fear.

The fear had started only a couple of minutes ago.

When this situation began, shortly after she got home from Aidan Blake's book signing, not being able to reach Matt hadn't seemed like anything too far out of the ordinary.

She had called Matt as soon as she'd changed out of her work clothes. When he didn't call back, Ali simply called again. Then she starting watching a movie she'd recorded, a fast-paced thriller that had caught her attention. Two hours later—when Ali looked at her phone and the screen was still blank—she experienced the first prickle of worry.

Letting hours go by without returning a call was out of character for Matt. He was never out of touch with her, always in constant communication.

She made a sandwich, ate it, and wiped down the kitchen counter. She read a couple of magazines, took off her nail polish, and put on two fresh coats—all the while calling Matt and texting him.

When it was almost three in the morning and there was still no word from Matt, Ali knew something was wrong.

She got in touch with every friend she could think of, everyone Matt might have gone to or been with. *"Have you seen Matt? Has Matt called you? Have you heard from him?"* From person after person, the answer was no. Ali had tried to find Aidan but didn't know where he was staying, and when she couldn't come up with a phone number for the glamorous woman who had hosted the book signing, she had driven to the woman's house. It was locked and dark, no one home. That's when Ali called the police. And the hospitals. Nothing.

With her heart hammering, she drove to Matt's apartment and then to his office at the college. Both places were empty. It was a little after three in the morning, and there was no sign of him anywhere.

An hour and a half later, when Ali got back to her studio apartment, she had trouble holding on to the key while she unlocked the door. Matt had vanished without a trace, and Ali was paralyzed with fear. The interior of her small living space was clean and simple. As soon as she managed to get the door open, she went to the antique coatrack. In winter, this was where she hung scarves and sweaters. But it was summer, and the only thing hanging there now was a baseball cap—the one Matt had tossed there when he came into the apartment, kissing her hello, a week ago.

Ali grabbed the cap, pressing it to her face and letting out a moan. For several slow, ticking minutes, she didn't move. Then, finally, she walked to her bed and took off her clothes. She pulled on an old T-shirt and a pair of cotton shorts and lay down. She rolled onto her side, her body in a straight line from head to toe, her eyes wide and blank. *Where was Matt? What had happened to him?*

In a kind of disconnected slow motion, Ali bent her knees and brought her heels up, bringing them to rest just below the backs of her thighs. Her moaning came in a steady unbroken rhythm, like an accident victim in terrible pain.

It was then that she heard the sound of salvation. The sound of a key in the lock.

Ali saw that the door had quickly opened, and Morgan was in the room, just inside the doorway, peering into the predawn darkness, searching for her.

Morgan's expression was filled with love and concern.

As soon as she spotted Ali, Morgan took off her shoes, crossed the room, and got into bed beside her. They were lying facing away from each other, spine to spine.

Morgan pressed her back against Ali's, connecting every inch, from their shoulders to their hips. Morgan then placed the warm soles of her own feet against the cold of her sister's.

Sole to sole, back to back—this was the position Morgan and Ali had shared in the womb and had returned to throughout their years together. This was their place of strength and consolation.

Ali was crying tears of relief. Morgan was there. Her sister and her soul mate. Her thorn and comfort.

"How did you know to come?" Ali asked.

"I had a feeling that you weren't okay...that you needed me."

"Something bad has happened to Matt," Ali murmured. "He's disappeared. He's missing."

"Are you sure? Did you call the police? What did they say?"

"They asked if I'd contacted his friends, and when I said yes, they asked if I'd checked with his family. I explained that Matt's parents were dead and he was an only child... He doesn't have any family. He only has me."

"What are they planning to do?"

"They told me they'd file a report, but that people take off for all kinds of reasons, and he'd probably be back home on his own in a couple of days."

Morgan waited for a bit. "What do you think?"

"I think Matt's in trouble...and whatever it is, it's bad." Ali was trembling. For a minute, she couldn't talk. Then she whispered, "Thanks for coming."

Morgan's answer was "I'll always come."

For the rest of the night, Ali stayed in that benevolent, peculiar, joined-together position with Morgan—opposite and perfectly matched.

And while she was lying in the darkness, waiting for the light, Ali remembered the odd warning she'd overheard—the hush in her mother's voice and her grandfather's, as they'd talked about Matt:

"I suspect there're things about himself that Matt doesn't want anybody to know."

"What kind of things, honey? Good? Or bad?"

"That's the problem. It could go either way."

Matt

"I SUSPECT THERE'RE THINGS ABOUT HIMSELF THAT MATT DOESN'T *want anybody to know.*"

"*What kind of things, honey? Good? Or bad?*"

"*That's the problem. It could go either way.*"

While Ali had been remembering that disturbing snippet of conversation, Matt was sprinting through the lobby doors of a seedy Manhattan hotel. The kind of grimy place where rooms are rented for an hour, or a day, or a month. A place for transients—with bad lighting in the corridors, and carpets funky with the smell of bug spray and cheap air freshener.

At the end of one of those dim corridors, Matt had searched out a room number: the location his emailer had given him.

He understood that what was about to happen, the things that would be done to him by the people in that room, would be dreadful.

Matt only had to knock once. Before he could say a word, the person who answered the door hit him. As if they wanted to murder him.

Morgan

MORGAN, HONEY, I HAVE A NICE NEUTRAL EYE SHADOW THAT might be just what you need." Morgan's mother was in the doorway, peering into the bathroom.

Matt had been missing for almost forty-eight hours. Morgan was anxious about the toll it was taking on Ali, and she was having a hard time concentrating. She had to get ready for work. Her mother's look of concern was only ratcheting up Morgan's anxiety.

This was the first day of her new job; she'd been hired as an assistant curator at a local art museum. The job came with an income that would let her move out of her mother's house and reclaim her independence. An opportunity that meant the world to Morgan. The last thing she wanted was to show up looking like a freak.

The mirror above the old pedestal sink was giving her bad news. Instead of subtly drawing attention away from the cuts on her face, the shimmery bronze eye shadow was making her look like a bug-eyed drag queen. While her mother, in the morning light, without a drop of makeup, looked absolutely lovely.

Morgan's mother was an older, more exotic version of Ali. Their coloring was different, but their essences were identical, glowing and lush.

For a brief moment, Morgan was a little girl again, reliving a ritual that had been in all the mornings of her early childhood. *Her mother, in a bathrobe, hair loose and wild, fixing breakfast. And Morgan's father, coming into the kitchen, stopping in the middle of the room to admire his wife, telling little Morgan and little Ali, "Want to know what's beautiful in a woman, what's desirable? All you need to do is look at your mother." Little Morgan, who adored her father, took in his every word, believing it as indisputable truth.*

Then as she and Ali got older, Morgan heard her father, and everyone else, say with such excitement, *"Ali and her mother…mirror images of each other!"* When Morgan was mentioned, it was only as "Ali's sister" or "the quiet one." By the time she was in middle school, Morgan had done the math. She knew what beautiful was, what desirable was, what popular was. She had been told.

She saw that her body was long and lean, and that her mother and her sister were full and ripe. Morgan understood that she was shy, hesitant, an introverted bookworm. Her mother and sister were witty and outgoing. People gravitated to them like moths to a light show. Which is why, before her twelfth birthday, Morgan had given up and gone to live in Ali's shadow. A jail sentence that Morgan didn't understand was self-imposed. With her preadolescent logic, Morgan believed she had no choice other than being a beggar in her sister's world. Because Morgan had never been the Pretty One, the Invited One, the One Who Was Desired.

And now her effortlessly pretty, effortlessly desirable mother was asking if Morgan wanted help in patching up her bungled attempt to look beautiful, saying, "Let me run and get my makeup bag. It'll only take a minute."

"Thanks anyway, Mom. I need to get going." Morgan quickly wiped away the bronze shadow and escaped into the bedroom. The space hadn't changed since Morgan had shared it with Ali when they were growing up. Ali's cheerleading trophies and homecoming queen crown, along with Morgan's worn-out collection of fairy tales and romance novels, still crowded the shelves above matching pink-and-white twin beds.

Her mother, who had followed her into the room, stood watching as Morgan opened the closet door. When Morgan took out a silk shirt with a price tag dangling from the sleeve, she saw her mother's fleeting frown. Morgan gave the price tag a nervous yank, slipped into the shirt, and took a deep breath, knowing what was coming, hoping not to let it make her crazy.

"Honey, how can you even think about spending money on new clothes when you're so deep in debt?"

"Please, Mom... Let's not talk about this right now. It's my first day of work, and I don't want to go there stressed out, okay?" Morgan's hands were shaking as she buttoned the shirt—a gorgeous new item she'd bought with a credit card and planned to pay off with money from her new job.

As Morgan reached into the closet for a skirt and shoes, her mother sighed. "Baby, sometimes you plow through life like somebody speeding down a freeway, backward."

Needing some distance, Morgan took the skirt and shoes to the other side of the bedroom, while her mother said, "You're drowning in interest on thousands of dollars you borrowed from credit cards. Money you just gave away."

"I didn't give that money away." Embarrassment pushed Morgan's voice into a whisper. "I invested it."

"No, sweetie, that's not what you did. Don't lie to yourself."

Her mother reached for Morgan. Morgan sidestepped her, despising her for bringing up this subject. "I have to get to work."

But her mother wouldn't let it go. "You need to look at this. Learn from it. See how foolish it was, chasing after a man who barely showed an interest in you, trying to make him fall in love with you by rushing to his rescue, trying to buy his attention with money you didn't even have. Morgan, that was—"

"My personal decision! And none of your business." Morgan was angry and ashamed at how stupid she'd been. "Go away, Mom. What you're doing right now is making me hate you."

Her mother, looking wounded, not seeming to know how to respond, waited for a minute, then walked out of the room. While she watched her go, Morgan wondered what her mother had left unsaid, wondered if it might have included the word *pathetic*.

The facts her mother was talking about *were* pathetic, completely and without question.

But the way Morgan saw it, underneath the facts, there was also the truth of what had happened. She'd been torn apart in those weeks after Matt stepped around her in the Williams-Sonoma store to choose Ali. It had left Morgan crushed. Then everything changed. There was that extraordinary dinner, and suddenly the world had been full of possibility again.

It was magical… *Walking into that restaurant and discovering her blind date was gorgeous—a stockbroker—a man with golden skin that looked as if he washed it in liquid sunshine. He told her he'd been born in Spain, and every word he said carried the lilt and music of the Catalan. She was in love the minute she saw him. This was definitely a man who could erase the hurt of losing Matt to Ali. And Morgan understood she was so far out of his league that it was a joke. She wasn't Ali. She wasn't her mother. She needed some kind of advantage.*

That's why she did all those outrageous things…treating him to expensive dinners…showing up at places she knew he'd be, like those softball games and charity runs. It's why she dreamed up a million different ways to bump into him when he was coming and going from his office. And it was the reason that when she heard he was having trouble making his quotas, even though everybody said the market was crashing, she took out advances on her credit cards, borrowed all that money, and invested it in any stock he'd sell her.

She believed with all her heart that if she could stay in his line of sight long enough, he'd eventually see that she'd be kinder to him, more loyal, than any fabulous, beautiful woman he'd ever known. She would've been so grateful.

Would've loved him without limits. If he'd wanted her to, she would've dropped to the ground and worshipped him like a god.

Suddenly, the memory vanished—obliterated by the sound of the alarm on Morgan's phone.

She needed to be at work in half an hour, and she still hadn't figured out how to hide the crazy quilt of cuts that covered her face.

~

The pharmacy was small, a relic from a more genteel time.

There was a makeup counter near the entrance—frilly and old-fashioned, fronted by three tall, pink-cushioned stools. Rushing out from behind the counter, squeezing Morgan into a bone-crushing hug, was a boisterous woman with a mane of platinum-colored hair. Her name was Sherri, but Morgan had always secretly thought of her as the Big Blond. She smelled, overpoweringly, of dusting powder and peppermint. "Jesus, Mary, and Joseph," she bellowed. "Your face looks like wildcats used it for a scratching post."

"I'm starting a new job in a few minutes. Can you do something?"

"Baby doll, before I hit third grade, I could camouflage anything from a pimple to a split lip."

The Big Blond put Morgan on one of the pink stools, then swiftly went to work, launching into what Morgan knew would be nonstop chatter. "Tell that mother of yours to give me a call. She's my best friend since I'm eight years old, and I never hear from her. Y'know, the other day I was…"

The Blond's train of thought had been lost.

Her attention was on something she was seeing over Morgan's shoulder. While she continued to dab a makeup sponge along one side of Morgan's face, she let out a low, lusty whistle. "Now *that's* what I call good enough to eat."

Morgan shifted her position slightly and saw what had caught the Blond's attention. A man, leaving the store, clutching a bottle of painkillers. Morgan lurched forward, almost falling off her frilly pink perch.

Then she was gone—bolting toward the door.

∽

When Morgan ran out of the pharmacy, the man she was chasing was about to get into his car. She screamed his name.

The sound of her voice stopped him in his tracks. For an instant, he stayed motionless, with his back to her, as if bracing to take a bullet. Then he slowly turned around.

Morgan's eyes widened. She took a stumbling step backward, startled by his appearance. His forearms were covered in bloody, rake-like wounds that looked as if they'd been inflicted by clawing fingernails, and there were vicious bruises at the base and on the sides of his neck, where someone had apparently tried to strangle him.

Morgan was looking at Matt.

And he told her, "Don't say anything to Ali yet. I need some time."

Matt

IN THE DAYS SINCE HE'D BEEN MISSING, THE HORRIFYING THINGS
Matt had done had taken their toll. His reflexes were slow. And
as Morgan rushed at him in the pharmacy parking lot, she landed a
fury-filled slap, right to his mouth. It stung like hell. He grabbed her
wrists, holding her at arm's length, while she shouted, "How could
you deliberately disappear like that? How could you hurt my sister
so much?"

Matt was in acute pain, and it was hard to talk. The rasp in his
voice made him sound menacing as he said, "Settle down, Morgan."

"Where were you for the past two days?" she demanded. "Where
were you?"

The last person in the world Matt wanted to deal with right now
was Morgan. When he'd first met her, he'd liked her, but after he
really got to know, she irritated him. She was too needy, too
pushy. He was doing his best not to lose his temper. "This is between
Ali and me. I'm going to talk to her about it. I just need time to—"

"Anything that hurts my sister hurts me," Morgan insisted. "She's
my twin. We share everything. Tell me where you were!" She was
eyeing the marks on his body, the ugly scrapes on his forearms and
the bruises on his neck.

"This is something I need to work out alone," he said. "After it's
worked out, I'll talk to Ali. Then it'll be her business. At no point will
it be your business." The rasp in his voice only added to the threat in
his tone. "Stay out of it."

The sight of his injuries had stunned Morgan into silence. Matt got into his car and started the engine. After he pulled out of the parking lot, he looked up at the rearview mirror and watched Morgan running to her own car and sliding behind the wheel, obviously intending to follow him. But then he saw her check her watch and make a screeching U-turn, as if she'd suddenly remembered she was late for something important.

In the bedroom of his apartment, Matt slowly opened his shirt. It took several attempts before he could work his way out and drop it onto the bed.

As the shirt hit the bed, there was a flash of memory… *Pain, and a woman's bony, pale feet scuffling and slipping across the matted carpet of that dingy hotel corridor.*

With a gradual, reluctant tilt of his head, Matt looked down at the marks on his abdomen. They were cut in just above his navel. A pair of long, horizontal gashes, brutally bruised. Their swollen edges, red and welted; their centers embedded with threadlike trails of gritted filth.

Matt let out a roar, driving his fist into the wall, punching a hole in it. The wounds on his body were reopening other, older hurts—injuries covered over but never completely healed.

The knowledge of who had inflicted both his old wounds and his new ones, and how it had been done, was tearing Matt apart. He uncapped the bottle of pills he'd bought at the pharmacy. Then he let them roll out and scatter across the floor. He was too far gone for them to be of any help.

He switched his phone on, scanning the accumulated messages. Most of them were from Ali, each one more frantic than the one before. There was also a message from his friend Aidan, the author at the book-signing party. Breezily unconcerned that Matt hadn't shown up for their planned evening of drinking. And asking Matt to call as soon as possible about some "bloody great news."

He put the phone in his pocket; he'd deal with Aidan later.

Matt lay back on his bed, staring into space—trying to figure out a way to explain his disappearance, and his reappearance, to Ali.

Morgan

A FTER BEING ON THE JOB LESS THAN TWENTY MINUTES, MORGAN had already retreated into the emptiness of a ladies' room two floors below her office. She was pacing, repeatedly checking her phone. She'd called Ali more than an hour ago to tell her about Matt, and had been sent straight to voice mail. Ali still hadn't replied.

Deciding to calm down by splashing cold water on her face, Morgan was suddenly staring into the restroom mirror. She'd arrived at her new job looking like a complete idiot. One side of her face was a puckered patchwork of raw-looking cuts. On the other side, the cuts were streaked with muddy-looking trails of foundation and mascara. The smeary aftermath of the Big Blond's half-finished make-over, and the crying Morgan had done in the pharmacy parking lot.

She muttered, "*Shit,*" then let out a laugh that went on way too long. Hysteria trying to win a fight with misery.

When she went back upstairs, Morgan stayed at her desk, keeping her head down, devastated that she'd showed up for work looking like a train wreck. And completely bewildered that Ali hadn't responded to her phone call.

What could be keeping Ali so silent?

Ali

A LI WAS SITTING BESIDE HER MOTHER AT A GLASS-TOPPED table in a private room adjacent to a bank vault. She hadn't heard most of what her mother was saying. She was worried about where Matt was and what had caused his disappearance. Fearing the worst.

Ali was also struggling with the loss of her apprenticeship at Z in New York, the opportunity she'd been counting on to launch her restaurant career. When Ali had tried to confirm the dates and her travel plans, Zev Tilden's haughty assistant had told her that since she'd already insulted them by calling and turning down her apprenticeship, Z didn't have any further interest in her.

At first, Ali was shocked. Then angry. Then totally confused. It was a conversation that made no sense. She insisted she'd never called to cancel her apprenticeship. She asked to speak to Zev Tilden to sort things out. Tilden, in full temperamental-chef mode, announced he had a world-class restaurant to run and didn't have time for amateurs who couldn't make up their minds. Ali was yesterday's news. Someone else was already in her spot. End of discussion.

Ali was heartbroken.

And now, with Matt's disappearance, the heartbreak had doubled. Ali was having trouble paying attention to what her mother was doing—taking items out of a safe-deposit box. A sapphire ring. Then bricks of banded cash, followed by the deed to a small tract of land. The last thing lifted out was a uniquely designed portfolio made of black mahogany and shaped like a large cigar box. The clasp and lid hinges were sterling silver.

Seeing that mahogany portfolio was like being hit by lightning. For the first time since she'd entered the bank, Ali's attention was on something other than her worries.

Her mother slid the portfolio across the table. "This belongs to you now."

Ali touched the lid of the box lightly, reverently. "Wow. Mom, I've heard about this...but I've never actually seen it."

"Everything you need for your dream is in there, honey. Your roots. And your wings."

Ali's hands were unsteady as she opened the silver clasp and raised the mahogany lid. The portfolio's interior was lined with emerald-green velvet, its contents arranged between a series of brass dividers. In the center section were dozens of recipes handwritten in brown ink on ivory vellum paper. In the surrounding sections were lists of exotic seasonings and herbs, along with formulas for simple kitchen essentials like homemade baking powder. In a side section, there were swatches of fabric in a rainbow of textures and hues. And there was an assortment of color chips—some, the standard paint-store variety; others, bits of plaster scraped from the walls of old buildings.

In the long, narrow space at the bottom of the portfolio were two scrolls—a detailed drawing of the dining room and kitchen of a tiny, uniquely charming restaurant and a diagram of an outdoor garden that adjoined the restaurant's rear wall. Tucked in beside the scrolls were elegantly labeled envelopes filled with seeds, ready for planting.

When she saw the handwritten dates on the seed packets, Ali was surprised. "These are less than a month old. I don't understand. How could she have—"

"Your grandmother MaryJoy began putting this box together more than seventy years ago and never stopped. I think for a long time she believed she was piecing together a dream that belonged solely to her. She brought it with her from Ireland when she came here as a young girl. But somewhere along the line, she recognized the two of you shared the same dream…and that you would be the one to make it real." Ali's mother seemed to drift into a memory that was especially sweet. "She worked on that portfolio right up until the day she died. She wanted to give your restaurant the very best launch she could."

MaryJoy O'Conner, the Irish grandmother Ali had loved so much, had left her an astonishing gift. And for an instant, Ali was indescribably happy. Then she was immediately nervous, quickly shutting the lid on the portfolio. "What about Morgan? What did Morgan get?"

Ali's mother pointed to the deed she'd taken out of the safe-deposit box. "Morgan gets the land, the acreage Grandma MaryJoy bought years ago. She wanted to make sure Morgan would always have a home, a place of her own. The cash and Grandma's engagement ring were left to me." Ali's mother put the banded stacks of cash into her purse, then slipped the ring onto the middle finger of her right hand. Ali saw that the ring's centerpiece, the sapphire, was the same color as MaryJoy O'Conner's eyes—violet blue.

"And now, for better or worse," her mother said, "the bits and pieces of the past have become part of the future."

Ali had no idea of the destruction that would come from that deed to the tract of land and the gift of the portfolio, her tailor-made dream in a box.

Matt

H E'D BEEN WAITING ALL DAY, AND FINALLY, ALI'S CAR HAD turned into the driveway. As soon as it came to a stop, Matt ran to open the door.

In an instant, Ali was in his arms, burying her face in his shirtfront, shaking like a leaf.

"Shh," Matt told her. "It's okay. I'm back. I'm fine. Everything's okay." He leaned in to kiss her, wanting to feel her lips on his, but the kiss evaporated. Ali had pushed away from him, staring at the bruises on his face and the claw marks on his forearms.

"Ali, it's all right. There's nothing to be afraid of." His voice was calm, but his adrenaline was pumping. He didn't want to lose her.

Seeming unable to take her eyes off the angry marks on his body, Ali reached to touch them. Matt stopped her. His wounds couldn't be touched; they were too painful.

"What happened to you?" Ali looked up at him, pale and frightened. "Where have you been? You've been gone for almost three days."

"I'm not going to tell you about that." He was surprised by how matter-of-fact he managed to sound.

Ali made a little gasping sound, a whimper of surprise and hurt.

"I'm not going to discuss where I've been because what I'm telling you right this minute is more important." Matt made a point of locking eyes with Ali, refusing to let her look away. "Al, you know I'd never do anything that would harm you. And you know I'd never lie to you. That's what's important. That's what you need to focus on."

Ali's attention darted to the wounds on Matt's arms. The claw marks. The evidence that wherever he'd gone and whatever he had done were appalling. "What happened?" she asked.

Fear jackhammered through Matt. "I owed someone a debt. It's gone now. And it has nothing to do with us."

Ali moved away, bewildered by his refusal to tell her where he'd been. He understood that if he didn't tell her, he was going to lose her. He could feel it. But there was nothing he could do. Everything was being drowned out by the images flashing through his mind—*the limp body sailing backward through an open window…and the long, long time it took before there was the noise of flesh and bone smashing onto the sidewalk below.*

"Tell me where you were, Matt. Please." Ali was pleading with him.

Aware of how expressionless his voice was and how dead his eyes were, Matt could only tell her, "What happened is done. It's over. There's nothing to discuss."

Ali

THAT DEAD LOOK IN MATT'S EYES SENT CHILLS THROUGH ALI. She stared at him in disbelief. "It's done. It's over. That's all you're going to say about where you've been for the last three days?"

Matt nodded. "That's all you need to know."

Confused and scared, Ali looked around the driveway as if the answers she needed were floating in the wind.

"Ali, what happened was part of something I've been avoiding for a long time. The final part." Matt brought her toward him, cradling her face in his hands—his touch so familiar, so gentle. "Believe me. Trust me. I'm telling you the truth. Where I was doesn't need talking about. It's ugly, and there's no reason to drag you into it."

Ali understood he was asking her to listen, to have faith in him, yet there was that seed of doubt.

"I suspect there're things about himself that Matt doesn't want anybody to know."

"What kind of things, honey? Good? Or bad?"

"That's the problem. It could go either way."

In light of his refusal to talk about his disappearance, the memory of that snippet of conversation frightened Ali enough to make her jerk free of Matt and run toward her apartment.

When she reached the doorstep, she stopped, needing to give him one last chance. "I love you. If you love me, you'll tell me where the past three days of your life went." Ali wanted him to come back to her and be Matt. She wanted him to be the man she thought she knew: someone who was pure and open. "Tell me," she said again. "Please."

Matt shook his head.

Ali pushed the key into the lock and turned it, went inside.

But even after she had slammed the door on Matt, she could still see that dead look in his eyes. She could still feel him, out there, waiting.

Matt

MATT HAD HAD ABSOLUTELY NO CONTACT WITH ALI IN THE twelve days since she'd slammed the door of her apartment and locked him out of her life.

On every one of those days, Matt had thought about Ali, and longed for her. And blamed her for not loving him enough to trust his silence about what he'd done in that dingy Manhattan hotel room. It had been payback for transgressions that had taken place years before he met her. Things he promised himself he would never do again.

The memory of Ali turning her back on him because he couldn't tell her what happened in that room was tearing Matt apart. He didn't know how to survive losing her.

And now, a miracle. Ali was within his reach.

Matt was driving away from the college campus when he saw her. She was getting out of her car a few yards down the street. Looking like a dream in a simple summer dress.

It wasn't until he parked, ran after her, and pulled her to a stop that he realized he didn't know what to say. The only thought in his mind was *I want you I want you I want you.*

Ali was staring at him, puzzled, asking, "Why did you come?"

"I–I didn't. I just happened to see you. I was on my way to—" Matt was confused; Ali was standing on the steps of a church. "It's Thursday. Why are you going to church?"

Ali blinked, like she was trying not to cry. "I'm here for the appointment with Reverend Miller." She looked away, embarrassed.

"He's been my pastor since I was a little kid and he was so happy when he heard about us getting engaged. I didn't want to tell him over the phone…about the wedding being canceled."

Now Matt was the one struggling to hold back tears. "Don't call our wedding off. Please. Don't." That's when he saw the flicker in Ali's eyes and heard a catch in her breath, as though she'd just gotten unexpected, hopeful news.

"Are you going to tell me what happened when you were gone?"

She was asking the impossible. An eternity passed before Matt was able to give her a reluctant shake of his head.

The instant he did it, he was shattered by the hurt in her eyes.

The closest Matt had ever come to dying was watching Ali walk away from him. Again. And disappear into that church.

~

She was midway across the vestibule when Matt stepped into the entryway, his voice echoing under the vaulted ceiling. "Give me your hand, Ali."

Her expression was puzzled and, at the same time, brimming with love. Matt focused on the love. He put his arm around Ali, and she let him lead her into the empty sanctuary. As they walked together along the center aisle, they were haloed in light filtering down on them through slender windows of milky-white glass.

When they reached the altar, Matt knelt in front of her. He placed her hand on his chest, over his heart. "Ali, I swear, here, in front of God, that I love you, that I will die loving you, and that I have not done, and *never* will do, anything to dishonor you or the love I have for you."

Ali stayed silent. And Matt asked, "Do you believe me?"

She nodded, very slowly.

"Good." Matt took a breath.

Then he looked up at her. "There's something I need to tell you. I'm leaving the college. I won't be teaching anymore. I'm starting a new job. In California."

Ali's face was blank, as if she couldn't comprehend what she'd just heard. "But we've always talked about our life being here, in Rhode Island. It's where I grew up, where you went to college. Practically from the first day we met, we promised this would always be our home. Where we'd have our babies and raise our family." She seemed confounded. "Why would you take a job in California?"

"Al, listen to me. It's all good. It's the way for me to make enough money to give you what you want." Matt was talking fast, gripping Ali's hand—wanting this finished. "It'll take us forever to get your restaurant off the ground if all I'm bringing in is an assistant professor's salary. But doing it like this, we won't have to wait."

With what sounded like a mix of curiosity and dread, Ali asked, "What are you talking about?"

And Matt told her. "I wrote a script with Aidan Blake. We did it back when I was a grad student and he was a visiting professor. He called me, right after his book signing, to give me great news. The script's been picked up by a television network. Aidan's star power in Hollywood is attracting an enormous amount of money to the project. They're ready to start developing it as a series. Aidan wants me in Los Angeles as soon as possible. He's asked me to be his writing and producing partner." Matt's heart was pounding. "Al, this job pays huge money. It could make us rich."

Ali seemed surprised. "Do you really care that much about money?"

"What I care about is being able to give you everything you want. And I know one of the things you want most is your own restaurant."

"I want my restaurant. I do, very much. But I don't want it in California. That would be like having it in a foreign country."

Matt moved closer and whispered, "We'll never have another opportunity like this. Aidan's a huge player in Hollywood. He can take us places we've never dreamed of. This is a job I really want. Let me do it, Ali. Let me do it for you…and for me." Matt waited to discover if he'd made her believe that everything he'd said was true.

He'd kept her hand pressed tight against his chest. And as he studied Ali, while she was standing at that altar with his heart beating against her palm, Matt knew he'd won.

He could see that she'd decided she needed to love him more than she wanted to understand him. He looked into her eyes and saw Ali tell herself that the mystery of a few missing days and the shock of leaving the safety of Rhode Island didn't really matter, when measured against the happiness of a lifetime.

That was when Matt stepped back—and watched—while Ali took a terrifying leap of faith.

Morgan

THERE SEEMED TO BE TOO MUCH QUIET. "ARE YOU STILL HERE?" Morgan asked.

Sam's voice at the other end of the phone was mellow, gentle. "I'm always here."

Thank God for Sam. He was her lifeline, the only person she could really talk to. Morgan relaxed, slowed her ragged breathing.

She was alone in the park. A young couple was strolling past, laughing, arm in arm. An old woman in a red felt hat sat solitary and vacant eyed on a bench a few yards away. A very tall, very thin boy, his skin shining and so dark it was almost blue-black, was perched on a boulder near the park gate, playing a cello, making soaring music that was infinitely sad.

"Ali's going to the other side of the country. She's *leaving*. How can my sister leave me? How can she just walk away?" Morgan said.

"I can hear it in your voice, how much this bewilders you, and wounds you. Tell me why."

"Because. She made a promise to me, and she's breaking it." Morgan's attention shifted from the laughing couple to the vacant-eyed woman in the red hat.

Morgan swallowed hard. There was a knot in her throat. She was struggling to survive the hurt. "When Ali and I were little, we promised we'd never be apart. She swore she'd never leave me. And..." Morgan's voice trailed off. She knew what she was saying sounded childish, but the promise had been real for her, and she'd always believed that it had been just as real for Ali.

"What?" Sam asked. "What were you about to say, my friend?"

It was her aloneness—her fumbling inability to connect with people and the world—that was causing Morgan so much pain. But it was easier to stay jealous of her sister than to battle her way to becoming someone entirely new. "I have cuts. All over my face," Morgan told Sam. "And it's because of Ali."

The cuts were fading, but they were still there. Little wormlike welts Morgan was afraid would become a permanent mask of ugliness. The thing that would seal her fate. And keep her alone for the rest of her life.

She pressed a fingernail into one of the healing cuts. Doing it slowly, hard enough to make it hurt. When the hurt finally brought tears, she said, "It was Ali's fault that I ran…that I fell and landed facedown in broken glass. And now she's abandoning me."

Morgan noticed the old woman in the red hat was gone and that absolutely nothing remained on the bench, not even a leaf or a scrap of paper. The space the woman had occupied was completely blank. Morgan groaned. "I don't know how to be, without my sister."

And Sam, the gentle voice at the other end of the phone, said, "You have a lovely and sensitive soul. There's so much more in you that you could show to the world…so much more than your injuries."

"I'm not sure what you mean."

"Just something for you to think about, later, when you're calmer. Right now, why don't you talk to me about the wedding."

"Ali says it'll be small, just family. And it's happening fast, in less than three months. Matt has a new job working on a television series. He's flying to Los Angeles tomorrow. He'll come back for the wedding. Then Ali will be gone…to California."

The blue-black boy with the cello had started to play music that was wild and formless—swirling.

"My sister is throwing away everything, including me, for a guy who hung her out to dry, for days, while he disappeared and did God knows what to God knows who. I think that makes her a *shit*." The ache in Morgan became outrage. And she asked, "Does saying that make me sound like a terrible person?"

For a second or two, no response. Then, as always, Sam's voice was benevolent. "I'm glad we had this chance to talk. It's almost four o'clock, time for my afternoon swim."

"Wait," Morgan said. "I want to know why."

"What are you asking?"

"Why are you always here for me? Why did you talk to me, for hours that first time, after you texted…and I called?"

"When I heard your voice, I heard loneliness. It's a subject I've spent a great deal of time studying."

"Your text, the thing that started all of this…was it really an accident?" Morgan asked.

"Yes. There was someone new in my life, and I had written down their number incorrectly."

Morgan's instinct was to ask who the person was. But she didn't want to change her relationship with Sam in any way. She wanted to keep it exactly as it was—a safe, comforting mystery.

"We'll talk again soon," Sam told her.

Morgan nodded and ended the call.

The boy and his cello were filling the park with jangling, discordant sound, and for some reason, it made Morgan think about the wedding in Newport: how she'd tried to add something pretty to the present Ali gave to Matt, and Ali had screamed at her, *"Get your own life and stop eating at mine like a greedy termite."*

Self-pity welled up in Morgan, shifting her thoughts to that night at BerryBlue Farm. The night of the funeral. When Morgan was in such terrible pain, grief-stricken over her grandmother's death, and her face was raw with cuts. She'd needed Ali so much. But Ali had turned away from her, sarcastically saying, *"I'm sure you'll feel better soon."* A gesture that told Morgan, *I don't give a damn about you.*

And then, later that night, Morgan had eased her pain with a phone call. The call that obliterated Ali's apprenticeship at that fancy restaurant in New York.

Afterward, Morgan wondered if what she'd done was unforgivably wrong. Then she decided it simply had been a way of getting justice, a way of bringing things into balance.

Erasing one of Ali's dreams wasn't the end of the world. Ali already had too much. She had Matt, and an engagement ring. Did she honestly deserve more? Wasn't it only fair that Morgan had leveled the playing field a little by taking away that trip to New York?

Now Ali was planning another trip—going all the way across the country, to California. A place she'd probably never come back from.

Ali's absence would be permanent.

And Morgan had spoken the truth when she told Sam, *"I don't know how to be, without my sister."*

If she couldn't share Ali's existence, Morgan was convinced she would have no life at all—convinced that the only adventures and pleasures she'd ever get near were the ones that belonged to her sister.

Morgan believed the only way for her to survive was to stop Ali from going to California.

And the way to do it was to reach into Ali's past and arrange for an unexpected guest. A loose cannon who would annihilate Ali's wedding like a suicide bomber.

Ali

I N THE EIGHTY-EIGHT SHORT DAYS BETWEEN THE MOMENT ALI HAD
agreed to marry Matt and the morning of their wedding, her
world, and Matt's, had changed completely.

Ali had quit her job and packed up her life, said good-bye to her
family and her friends. Matt had gone to Hollywood, signed contracts,
and started work on the television show. He'd also leased an apartment fourteen miles north of Los Angeles in a city called Pasadena.
It was where the bride from Newport, Ali's best friend, Jessica, had
settled. And Matt promised Ali she would feel at home there.

Matt had also promised Ali that their wedding could be whatever
she wanted. It was her day to do with as her heart desired. But the
marriage was what was important to Ali, not the ceremony. She'd
never been one of those girls who grew up fantasizing about her
wedding, giddy about every princessy detail. Ali's dream had been
about finding a husband who was a good man, making a family and a
home with him. She had no interest in a big-deal wedding blowout.

It took her exactly two days to put her wedding together. Day
one was inviting the guests—fewer than ten people—and calling
Reverend Miller to reserve the church. And then a call, to her
mother, to decide which flowers from her mother's garden would
make a nice bridal bouquet. On day two, Ali had gone to the mall
for an hour and found her wedding dress—a simple, off-the-rack,
ivory-colored silk suit that fit perfectly and happened to be on sale.

Now here she was, in the powder room at the back of the church.

A married woman. Changing out of her wedding outfit, while her guests were gathering on the church steps with streamers and smiles, ready to send her off into her new life.

"I'm scared," Ali said.

Morgan, in a blue, knee-length dress that was a little too big on her, seemed oblivious. She was staring into the full-length mirror on the back of the powder-room door. "You knew Matt's best man was that handsome Australian. I wish you'd had the time to help me find a decent bridesmaid's dress. It would've been nice if I could have walked down the aisle looking better than this."

Morgan lowered her head and muttered, "I guess maybe you were so busy getting yourself out of town, there wasn't time to worry about the people you're leaving behind."

"You're wrong." While Ali put on the lightweight sweater and pants she'd wear on the flight to California, she thought about moments that had shaped her life. Her first Christmas. The summers at BerryBlue. That endless night when Matt had disappeared. And her wedding, which had happened only minutes ago.

In every one of those moments, in every joy, every sorrow, there was one thing that was unchangeable, constant as a heartbeat. Morgan had been there.

And tomorrow, Ali would wake up in California, a place Morgan wouldn't be.

I don't care what Matt said about Pasadena having old houses that look like they're on the East Coast. It will never be home. Home will always be here, in Rhode Island, where my sister is.

Ali was taking a small, brown suitcase from a shelf on the powder-room wall, fighting tears, saying, "I'm sorry."

"About what?" Morgan's expression was guarded.

"I'm sorry I didn't think to help you with your dress. And as far as telling you about Aidan being in the wedding, it came up at the last minute. Matt's best college professor friend was in Europe on sabbatical, and Aidan offered to step in as best man. Since Aidan's going to be a significant part of our future, it seemed to make sense." Ali's heart was aching. "I'm sorry, Morgan. I'm sorry about your dress. I'm sorry about going to California. I'm so sorry."

Morgan shrugged, her chin quivering—a gesture she used to make as a little girl when she'd been disappointed. "Too late now, huh?"

Morgan's tone was quiet, but underneath the quiet, Ali heard resentment. And it rekindled a suspicion in her. One that had hit her at the end of her wedding ceremony. When she'd turned away from the altar and noticed an unexpected guest at the back of the church.

"It's not like I'm saying you had to pull off a three-ring mansion circus, like Jessica and Logan's wedding," Morgan was telling Ali. "But it should've been something better than four people and Reverend Miller." Morgan's gaze was focused in mid-distance, as if she couldn't quite look Ali in the eye. "Wait…there were more than the four of us at the altar, wasn't there? Mom and Grandpa in one pew. And Dad and Petra the Martyred Stepmother lurking on the bench across the aisle. There were eight people."

The bitterness in Morgan's voice told Ali everything she needed to know about why that unexpected guest had shown up to witness her marriage. Ali was furious. "There were nine people, Morgan. Don't forget Levi. Why did you invite him to my wedding?"

Morgan's response was quiet, vindictive. "Your friend Levi, the hockey player, the one Matt calls 'the ginger-haired hulk'… Did it bother you to have him there?"

When Ali didn't answer, Morgan said, "Levi does have serious anger issues, especially when it involves his history with you." Morgan gave a mock frown, as if she were coming to terms with disappointing news. "But I guess he's controlling himself better these days."

The gloating quality of Morgan's next question—"Did I ruin your big day by inviting him?"—sent a shudder through Ali.

"Is that what you wanted to do...ruin my wedding?"

Morgan stared at Ali, not saying a word.

"Please tell me that's not true."

Morgan kept glaring at Ali, refusing to back down.

Ali grabbed her, shook her. "Why did you do it?"

Morgan's bravado suddenly evaporated. "I was scared. I just wanted things to stay the way they were." She gave a defeated laugh. "But it doesn't matter, does it? Nothing happened. Your wedding didn't get ruined. You're going to California. So that makes everything okay, right?"

Ali was too frustrated, too bewildered, to answer.

Morgan came closer, nervously biting her lip. "Levi asked me to give you this." She reached into her pocket and brought out a braided ring made of chewing-gum wrappers. "He said it doesn't belong to him anymore. He said you'd know what he meant by that."

Ali was trembling when she took the ring. The feel of it on her palm was the feel of passion, and regret. The weight of betrayal. She held the paper ring cupped in her hand for several long moments, thinking about crushing it.

But instead, she carefully put it into the brown suitcase, next to her wedding outfit and her marriage license. After that, she turned her attention to rearranging the rest of the suitcase's contents—making a point of not looking at Morgan.

Ali was packing her wedding shoes, arranging them on either side of her grandmother's mahogany portfolio, when Morgan crossed the room.

She glanced down at the portfolio and said, "Grandma MaryJoy's restaurant was never supposed to be in California." Morgan's tone was angry. "By moving that restaurant, you're saying *fuck you* to

Grandma MaryJoy. She wanted it here. In Providence. And you know it."

Ali did know it. She was riddled with guilt.

Morgan asked, "Did all that stuff about wanting the restaurant to be part of who you are and who our grandmother was just fly out the window because Matt slapped a ring on your finger? Grandma MaryJoy always said Los Angeles was plastic and phony. She'd hate you for putting her restaurant there."

The guilt in Ali exploded. She grabbed Morgan and shoved her into the powder room's only chair. Wanting to draw blood and break bones.

Ali could feel every muscle in Morgan bracing for the violence. They were in a place that only sisters can go—a place where love and competition and jealousy ignite like wildfire.

"Los Angeles is where Matt has the chance to make more money than we've ever dreamed of." Ali was spitting the words at Morgan. "Without that money, I'll never get any further with the restaurant than Grandma MaryJoy did. It'll never happen. If I don't go to California, the restaurant will stay nothing but a dead old woman's pipe dream. Grandma sure wouldn't have wanted that."

Ali slammed Morgan against the chair back and left her there. Both of them had tears in their eyes.

"Spin it any way you like," Morgan told Ali. "But you know you're supposed to stay here. In Rhode Island. You know that what you're doing is wrong." Morgan charged out of the chair, shoving past Ali, marching toward the door. "Someday you'll be sorry you even *thought* of going to California!"

Ali stepped in behind Morgan and pulled her to a stop. "I'll miss you, too," she said.

"Who's talking about missing anybody?"

"We both are," Ali murmured. "No matter what we've been saying, it's all you and I have been talking about for days."

"Don't flatter yourself. I don't need you."

Morgan's expression was stony. Her jaw was clenched. And she was shaking like a leaf.

Ali wondered how her sister would remain standing. When Ali wasn't there for her to push against anymore.

Within minutes, Ali was outside, in front of the church. Matt had helped her into a cab. She'd set the brown suitcase at her feet, the suitcase that contained her wedding outfit and her grandmother's portfolio.

The instant Ali felt the cab pull away from the curb, she looked over her shoulder, anxiously searching the faces of the group gathered on the church steps. Her grandfather, stately and gray haired. Her mother, as bright as a gypsy in gold bangles and layers of gauzy fabric. Her father, vaguely melancholy, with his scowling wife at his side.

When Ali's eyes met Morgan's, Morgan was blank-faced. Her arms were crossed, and her fingernails were digging into the crooks of her elbows.

Ali instinctively leaned forward, putting her hand against the cab window, wanting to call out to Morgan. But the cab went around a corner. Morgan was swept from view.

The cab was gaining speed. Rushing toward the airport.

Toward California.

It was as if Ali had just stepped off the edge of a cliff.

Morgan

M ORGAN HADN'T REALLY NEEDED IT FOR THIS TRIP; THE weather was mild. But she thought the sporty little trench coat Ali had left behind would make her look more sophisticated. Morgan had Ali's coat clumsily wadded in her hands, trying to hide the embarrassing item she'd just selected. And now the salesclerk with the pink-streaked hair and tiger tattoo was swooping in, pulling it out of Morgan's grasp, squealing, "Oh wow! You picked a great one!"

The object under discussion was a black demi-cup bra, delicately embroidered with red poppies and made of fabric so filmy it was almost transparent. Morgan was mortified.

"Are you here on business or pleasure?" the clerk asked.

"Business. I started a new job a while ago, at a museum back home in Rhode Island, and traveling's part of it so…" Morgan let her voice trail away—worried she was talking too much, sounding like an idiot.

The clerk dropped the bra onto the countertop and rummaged through the drawers below the display case. "We're the only place in Chicago that carries this brand. I'm pretty sure we still have the matching panties."

"You don't need to bother. You're probably about ready to close and—"

"No problem." The clerk smiled. "It's only eight thirty. We're open till ten."

"I was just looking. I'm not really shopping, not seriously."

Horribly uncomfortable, Morgan glanced toward the entry to the hotel boutique, thinking of running.

The clerk peeked up at her and flashed a playful grin. "This stuff is definitely for something special. What's the occasion?"

Morgan's stomach flipped.

She was thinking that the normal Morgan, the Morgan she was when she arrived at the airport this morning, wouldn't even be in a place like this—a frilly cubbyhole of a store filled with ridiculously expensive, very sexy lingerie. But the normal Morgan had been transformed by a last-minute miracle on an overcrowded plane.

Instead of having to fly to this Chicago convention seat-belted next to her sharp-tongued boss, Morgan had ended up sitting beside a friendly, talkative copier salesman from Newark, New Jersey. By the time they'd gotten off the plane, the chatty salesman, who was staying in the same hotel as Morgan and her colleagues, had managed to push past her shyness. And Morgan had done something she'd never done before—struck up an in-flight friendship with a total stranger.

Later, in the hotel, Morgan had bumped into the salesman again. When he said, "Hey, wanna join me for a drink?" Morgan was thrilled. And she realized that for the first time, she was happy Ali was gone. Happy that no one in this hotel even knew Ali existed. If he'd been aware of Ali, Morgan was convinced that instead of asking her out for a drink, the copier salesman would have shoved her aside to get to her sister.

Morgan had walked into the hotel bar excited. She was also nervous, awkward, and stammering.

It wasn't until midway through the second glass of wine that she began to relax and have fun. Then a little while later, in the low light of the bar, she noticed that her boss, Veronica, a woman with thin lips and fat calves who was constantly trumpeting her devotion to her church and her rock-solid marriage, was at a nearby table.

Nursing a bottle of ginger ale, Veronica was watching—pious and judgmental—as the copier salesman wrote his room number on a cocktail napkin, sliding it toward Morgan. The look on the salesman's face was telling Morgan (and the eavesdropping Veronica) exactly how he wanted Morgan to use the scribbled information.

Painfully aware of Veronica's scrutiny, Morgan wavered, debating whether to take the napkin or walk away and leave it on the bar. The decision wasn't easy—the smoldering look in the salesman's eyes had put a heat into Morgan, which had started low and was steadily climbing higher.

Remembering that moment of decision had Morgan lost in thought. It took her a second to snap back to the present. The pink-haired clerk was holding up two pairs of lacy, black panties. "So what's it gonna be? Bikini or thong?"

The see-through skimpiness of the underwear made Morgan blush.

"Who you gonna be wearing these for?" the clerk asked. "Your husband or your boyfriend?"

Well, Morgan thought, *maybe someday he could be both. But right now, he's a guy I said no to when he asked me to come to his room. Because my boss was looking. And because I was sure that after he saw me naked, he'd be wishing he was with somebody like Ali. But then, as I was leaving, he tucked his room number into my coat pocket and said it was in case I changed my mind. Right then, he made up for every boy who'd ever handed me a folded piece of paper and mumbled, "This is my number. Give it to your sister." So. I guess you could say I want to wear this stuff for a man who made me feel like a princess.*

"I'd go with the thong." The clerk held out both pairs of panties. "But the bikini's cool, too."

In the dressing room, Morgan had trouble keeping her balance while she tried on the bra and panties. She was anxious about having sex with a total stranger. At the same time, she was remembering the sex she'd almost had with Logan, the groom at the Newport wedding—the pleasure she'd experienced that night. The thrill.

And, in the sensual tease of the lingerie she was wearing, she was picturing a bold new version of Morgan Spencer—seeing herself knocking on the copier salesman's door, pulling out the cocktail napkin with his room number on it. Flirtatiously telling him, "I've changed my mind."

~

Her heart was banging. Morgan had stepped out of the elevator wearing nothing under Ali's trench coat but the see-through black bra and panties she'd just bought. Her clothes were downstairs in the hotel lobby, in a shopping bag from the lingerie store. She had handed the bag to the concierge and told him she'd pick it up later.

This was the most daring, exciting, moment of her life.

The cocktail napkin with the copier salesman's room number on it was clutched in her hand. When she knocked on the salesman's door, she was so exhilarated she was on the verge of passing out.

From inside the room, the salesman's muffled voice asked, "Who is it?"

"Room service." A trickle of nervous sweat raced down her back. Morgan felt giddy. Scared. Ready.

She waited anxiously for the door to open. For the space of a blink, there was complete stillness. Nothing happened. In the next millisecond, everything was happening at once.

The door handle being turned from the inside.

Morgan loosening her coat, revealing that she was unclothed except for the wisps of black fabric that were her bra and panties.

The door swinging open.

The salesman, lardy and bow-legged, a towel clutched at his waist, gaping at Morgan, caught off guard.

Morgan glimpsing movement inside the room.

A woman. In the salesman's bed. Naked from the waist up.

~

The moment Morgan had locked eyes with the woman, she'd comprehended exactly what had happened. The salesman hadn't wanted her, Morgan. He'd wanted sex. With somebody. Anybody. Morgan understood that the woman in his bed had simply walked across the bar and said yes after Morgan had said no.

Morgan also understood she'd soon be out of work.

There was no way Veronica, the thin-lipped champion of family values, could allow Morgan to go unpunished. Not after Morgan had caught her answering a booty call issued by a copier salesman from Newark.

In the time after she left the salesman's hotel room and arrived back in her own room, Morgan didn't display any emotion. She simply changed into her pajamas and lay on the bed, letting the black bra and panties stay on the floor where they had fallen when she'd stripped them from her body.

Morgan studied the bra and panties for a long time before she decided to get out of bed and pick them up. She carried them into the bathroom, held them over the toilet, and let them drop. Then she pushed the toilet's chrome lever and watched the bra and panties disappear in a rush of swirling water, vanishing like wisps of smoke.

Once they were gone, Morgan did exactly what she'd done on the day of her grandmother's funeral. She went back to bed—and gave up.

She'd put on Ali's coat and tried to be like Ali, spontaneous and interesting. Instead, she'd been fumbling and stupid. So stupid she created a situation that would cost her her job.

It seemed to Morgan that no matter how hard she tried, she would never get it right—never be able to navigate the world on her own.

She was scared to death.

All she wanted now was a place to hide.

She crossed her arms, dug her fingernails deep into the crooks of her elbows, then closed her eyes and saw her sister's face. The only way to survive was to surrender, go back to living in the safety of Ali's shadow. A place where her existence would be what it had always been—small, and cramped, and secondhand.

Morgan honestly didn't understand that she had other choices. She believed that life had defeated her by giving everything to her sister, leaving her with nothing.

It was a bitter pill to swallow. And it wasn't long before Morgan had a burning desire for revenge.

Part Two

CALIFORNIA

Ali

L IKE WATCHING A MOVIE ON FAST-FORWARD." THAT'S HOW, IN a recent phone call to her mother, Ali had described her California experience.

In the year that Ali and Matt had been there, all the things Matt promised had come true—most of them with incredible speed. Speed that had caused contact with Morgan to be sporadic. Ali thought about her sister often, but hadn't spoken to her much. The distance between them, created by their fight on Ali's wedding day, had remained unrepaired and awkward.

The apartment where Ali and Matt lived was comfortable and only fifteen minutes away from Jessica's house, making it easy for Ali and Jessica to have afternoon walks and girlfriend time. Matt's income from the television show was, by Rhode Island standards, enormous. It had seemed so enormous that when they'd discovered the perfect space for Ali's restaurant—an old, quirky, triangle-shaped building in South Pasadena—they leased it the minute they found it. Ali had named it JOY, in honor of her grandmother. A few months later, she and Matt giddily closed a deal to buy their first house.

And tonight, they were in the midst of their housewarming party.

"Careful…don't burn the place down," Ali told Matt. He was leaning around the Christmas tree, handing her a lit fireplace match.

While she put the match to the kindling, Matt gave Ali a quick kiss—and before she could kiss him back, he'd managed to hurry away.

"Where are you going?" Ali had to shout to be heard. The house was crowded with people. Music was playing in every room.

Matt's voice came to her faintly, from somewhere down the hall. "I need to talk to Aidan about changes he wants me to make on next week's script."

This had become their new normal—Matt constantly moving away from Ali. Disappearing down corridors, around corners. Obsessed with his job. She hated it. And watching him disappear from her now reminded her of the way she'd felt on her wedding day—the little, brown suitcase at her feet and the cab rushing her toward the airport, feeling like she was headed toward the edge of a cliff.

Ali quickly stepped into the hall and ran the length of it. After she caught up with Matt, she grabbed his arm and held on as if she were trying to keep him from escaping. "It's our housewarming," she whispered. "Just for tonight...can't work wait?"

"No," Matt whispered back. "I need to keep Aidan happy because I need the money I make from this show. To pay for our new home."

At the mention of money, Ali's stomach tightened. It was true that Matt's Hollywood salary had managed to fund the opening of her restaurant and cover the down payment on this house, a gracious, old, two-story Monterey colonial on a tree-lined street in west Pasadena. It was also true that the restaurant was a huge money drain—it would be months, if not years, before it turned a profit. And the mortgage payments on the house were big. Big enough to sink Ali and Matt's financial boat if anything went wrong.

There was another issue, too—one Ali hadn't yet mentioned to Matt. She was waiting for the right time to bring it up. It was something she'd started to want with her whole heart and soul. She wanted to have a baby. Soon.

Ali was talking to herself as much as she was to Matt when she said, "It was a mistake to rush in the way we did. The restaurant. The house. We should've waited."

Matt leaned in close. "Al. Tell me how much you love this place."

"I'm crazy about it. It's a dream house. I love everything, even the address, seventy-six Paradise Lane. But—"

"No buts. End of story." This time Matt stopped long enough to kiss Ali deeply before disappearing into the group at the end of the hall, all of them show-business people.

Ali was in the grip of an overwhelming sense of loneliness. And the celebration of her new California life was in full swing.

There were more than thirty guests in the house, along with truckloads of food and wine. There was fabulous music. There were garlands of white Christmas lights on every doorway, every window. And not a single piece of furniture anywhere.

Earlier in the evening, when Jessica, the bride from Newport, had walked through the front door, she'd told Ali, "Doing this party before you actually move in? It's genius."

"I know," Ali had agreed. "This way, Matt and I, as the house-warmed, get to *really* have fun because we know the housewarmers can't possibly spill anything on the brand-new furniture. Which isn't being delivered until tomorrow morning."

Jessica had let out a whoop of laughter as she went off to join the festivities. The party guests included people from Matt's television show, acquaintances Ali had made at her recently opened restaurant, and neighbors from the apartment complex that had been home to Ali and Matt since they first came to Pasadena.

One of those neighbors, a tall, good-looking Texan named Peter Sebelius, was now walking toward Ali, saluting her with a raised beer bottle. "Great house," he said. "But I'm gonna miss having you around the complex. You really class up the joint. Especially when you bring yourself out by the pool in that little green bathing suit I like so much. When's the official moving day?"

"Tomorrow. The apartment's all packed. So in the morning, all I have to do is deal with the movers while Matt's over here taking delivery on the new furniture."

Peter flashed Ali an irresistibly boyish grin. "Damn, girl. I hate to see you go."

Ali liked Peter—had liked him from the first time she met him. On a sunny October afternoon, in the apartment complex's maze-like garden area. She'd been carrying shopping bags containing the makings of a special dinner she was planning for Matt. A whistle had come from behind the low hedge surrounding the swimming pool.

The whistler turned out to be easygoing, perfectly muscled Peter Sebelius. There was a well-stocked cooler on the ground between his lounge chair and the one occupied by his bikinied girlfriend. He'd held up a bottle of beer and called to Ali. "It's Friday. Want to help us celebrate?"

Ali had chuckled. "Don't have time. I'm getting ready for a celebration of my own." She indicated the shopping bags—a bouquet of flowers peeking from the top of one, a bottle of wine and a baguette from the other. "It's our first wedding anniversary, and I'm planning a surprise for my husband."

"Too late." Peter jerked his thumb in the direction of the open patio door on a nearby apartment—someone was moving around in the bedroom, lighting candles. "Looks like he beat you to it."

Peter's girlfriend, a tough, little redhead named Liz, had given a snorting laugh. "That's not even her apartment. She lives in that building over there."

Peter had shrugged. "What can I say? I have a shitty sense of direction." Then he'd flashed that killer grin at Ali. "I'm Peter Sebelius. Welcome home." And he really had made the apartment complex feel like home—because he was so easy to talk to and laugh with.

And here he was, again, giving Ali another beer-bottle salute and telling her, "Think I'll take myself on a tour of your new house, admire your planked floors and french windows, and whatever else there is to admire."

Heading toward the kitchen, Ali blew Peter a kiss. In that same instant, she heard the sound of a lilting voice—"*Hola!*" The greeting was from Ava, a woman whose soul matched her physical appearance. Both were transcendently beautiful. Ava had dark hair, eyes that were luminous, and skin the color of golden-brown sugar. Ali adored her.

Ali and Ava had met just before the opening of JOY. Ava had been pregnant and in need of a job. Ali had given her one. Their bond was instant and unbreakable. Ava, who was from Belize and was funny and wise, had become Ali's best friend, a confidant and guide. A surrogate sister.

Ava's hug was warm as she told Ali, "Your new house, it is most lovely."

Ali immediately reached for Sofie, Ava's baby, gathering her into her arms. Sofie was six months old and had Ava's ethereal beauty. Sofie's eyes were a fascinating cinnamon color, and they danced with light. Her dark hair was silky. Her skin was golden brown. Every time Ali saw Sofie, her heart fluttered, and melted. She loved this child in a way she couldn't explain.

"I got Sofie an early Christmas present." Ali was talking to Ava and unable to take her eyes off Sofie. "It's a mobile for her playpen, a cascade of silver bells. I had it specially made. And the bells are engraved. Each one has a sprig of rosemary on it."

"Rosemary?" Ava gave a puzzled frown.

"The line from Shakespeare," Ali explained.

"Yes! From *Hamlet*." Ava's expression was bright with recognition. "'There's rosemary, that's for remembrance.'"

"My grandmother believed when a cook puts rosemary in her food, she's making a wish…wanting the love she has for the people she's feeding to be remembered." Ali ducked her head, embarrassed. "I wanted rosemary on the bells because I want Sofie to remember me."

While Ali gently handed Sofie back to Ava, Ava told Ali, "You have been with us, have loved us, from before Sofie was born. Sofie and I, we could never forget you. You are too precious to us."

Ali smiled.

"Where is Matt?" Ava asked.

"He seems to have disappeared." Ali's smile had dimmed a little. "But I keep hoping he'll be back soon."

～

The makeshift bar in the dining room had run low on wine. Ali was in the garage, gathering a few additional bottles. She hadn't bothered to switch on a light. The windows along the wall were reflecting the glow from the Christmas lights in the garden.

Just as Ali was about to go back into the house, she was startled—by Aidan. He was standing in the doorway that led to the kitchen. His body language suggesting he'd been there for a long time, watching her.

He seemed to be smirking as he said, "It's still a couple of weeks away but…Merry Christmas."

Ali was uneasy, and annoyed. "Your story conference with Matt is over?"

Aidan nodded, casually leaning against the doorframe.

"So soon? It's only been what…an hour and a half…in the middle of a party?"

"Darling girl, are you snapping at the hand that feeds you?" Aidan left the doorway and took the wine bottles from Ali. His wrist brushing against her breast. He gave no indication he was aware of it. She shot him an irritated look. He responded with a chuckle. "You're miffed. Would you care to tell me why?"

Aidan's flippant attitude grated on her. "Tonight may be a joke to you, but it's a big deal for Matt and me. It's our housewarming, in our first house—"

"And I'm deeply honored to be here."

Ali met his smile with a cold stare. "Aidan, you're not going to charm me out of this. You asked me why I'm mad, and I'm going to tell you. I'm married to a man I happen to love, and I'm really pissed that he doesn't have time to do anything but work. It's ridiculous." Ali's resentment at having lost so much of Matt to his job was sending the words flying out of her mouth, uncensored. "From the minute Matt went to work for you, there's never been time for anything but story conferences and casting sessions and rewrites and more rewrites."

"That's show business. It's the kind of game where, if you want to win, you don't treat it like a job. You make it your life."

"Matt and I barely have a life anymore, Aidan. We hardly see each other. He doesn't have time for anything…even something as simple as a broken lock. The one on our apartment's patio door hasn't worked right since the day we moved in. That was over a year ago. We're moving out tomorrow, and it still isn't fixed. Matt hasn't had the time. Because he's always at work."

Aidan cocked an eyebrow, amused. "And this is my fault?"

"Yes," Ali said.

But the reality was that she could have taken care of it herself, could have called a locksmith. She had stubbornly left the lock unrepaired, trying to make a point: Matt wasn't paying attention to their life because all of his attention had been grabbed by his job.

"It's like you're constantly swallowing him whole. You did it again tonight." Ali was glaring at Aidan. "Are you telling me that working on that script really couldn't have waited till tomorrow?"

"No. It couldn't." He flashed a smug grin.

"It actually takes twenty-four hours a day, seven days a week to produce a stupid television show?"

"Yes." Aidan's grin widened. He was playing with her.

Ali's temper flared. "Bullshit. I think you like making Matt eat dirt. In return for all that money you're giving him."

Aidan's grin vanished. He narrowed his eyes and told Ali, "You have a massive amount to learn about the entertainment industry. For any man with a serious set of balls, the rewards of show business encompass a lot more than money. Don't be naive. You're overlooking the adulation. And the power." Aidan chuckled. "And the bountiful supply of women." He kept his gaze level and cool as he asked, "Ali, my dear, what makes you think *I'm* what's keeping Matt's nose to the television grindstone?"

"Matt isn't interested in power. Or a bountiful supply of women."

"All men want power." Aidan was expressionless. Then the grin returned. "As for the joys of tearing through an endless supply of women…maybe that's just me giving voice to a load of wishful thinking."

Ali was determined not to let him see it, but Aidan had gotten to her, opened a little vein of suspicion. She didn't believe Matt was interested in power, or other women. Yet there'd been a time she would have sworn he would never give up teaching and Rhode Island for a TV series and life in California.

Suddenly Ali was the slightest bit queasy. "I need to get back to the party."

Aidan blocked her way. "You do know that almost everything I say is utter crap, don't you?"

Ali didn't answer. All she wanted to do was get away from him.

Aidan stepped aside, letting her pass.

As she walked toward the kitchen, she could still feel the practiced, Hollywood-style brush of Aidan's wrist when it had traveled across her breast. In that same instant, she heard Matt, in the living room, laughing with his show's gorgeous female star.

Aidan stepped in behind Ali and put his mouth close to her ear. "A girl from Rhode Island who probably wants babies and loves to cook is married to the producer of a hit television show and can't figure out why she's a work widow. I'd call that *Hello Kitty in the Land of the Barbies.*"

An involuntary shiver went through Ali.

She quickly wiped her hand across the place where Aidan's lips had touched her ear, wanting to wipe away the feel of the serpent's tongue.

Ali could still feel the shiver caused by her conversation with Aidan. She was in the dining room, near the makeshift bar, listening to Jessica say, "I'm going on this great ski trip to Deer Valley. One of my girlfriends, Annika, she's taking all of us up there on her husband's private jet and—"

Jessica had been interrupted, midsentence. By Aidan.

He'd appeared out of nowhere, leaning past Jessica, telling Ali, "You've given me the impression I've worn out my welcome. I'm leaving. But I'm sure I'll see you again. Soon." After that, he planted what felt like a vaguely hostile kiss on Ali's cheek and strolled away.

"Is that the good-looking Australian you told me about? Matt's boss?" Jessica asked. "Do you have some kind of problem with him?"

"I don't know. Maybe. Maybe not." Ali shook her head, trying to sort out her thoughts. "I'm not sure. Maybe my problem's with Matt."

"Welcome to the club. When I got married, *Not Sure* became my middle name. I still don't have Logan figured out." Jessica laughed her trademark tough-girl laugh. "It probably would've helped if we'd known each other more than ten minutes before we did the wedding dance. But hey, we met on a nude beach in the Caribbean. The guy had a great ass and plied me with rum and sex. I was judgment impaired."

Ali smiled.

"Which brings me back to the subject of fun," Jessica said. "The subject of *us* having fun—"

Again, Jessica was stopped in midsentence. This time by Peter Sebelius, who handed Ali his empty beer bottle and told her, "Great party. Great house. But now, unfortunately, only four beers in, I gotta roll. I'm late for the hospital Christmas bash."

Ali hadn't had a chance to talk to him. And she was disappointed that Peter was leaving. "Wait, the people we bought the house from left an old-school arcade game in the basement. Matt wanted to go one-on-one with you."

"I really wish I could, but—" Peter's phone was ringing. He glanced at it. "Liz. Again." He pointed at the phone and explained to Jessica, "My girlfriend. We're fighting, and she's righteously pissed."

Peter's smile to Ali was apologetic as he hurried toward the front door. "Gonna have to catch the arcade game later. Thanks for the invite. I had a good time."

Tracking every step of his exit, Jessica let out an admiring whistle. "That is one hot guy." She watched Peter until the door closed behind him, then gave Ali a playful shrug. "Okay, fantasy's over. I'm a married woman. Back to reality. About this ski trip... Oh, by the way, we're calling it the Perfect Ten."

"And you're calling it that because...?"

"Because it's ten women, ten days. No husbands, no kids. Nothing but snow, a world-class spa, and a ten-thousand-square-foot ski chalet that looks like it's in Switzerland." Jessica reached into the tiny, envelope-shaped purse hanging from her shoulder and pulled out her phone. "Annika sent me pictures. The whole place has just been redone." Jessica swiped a finger across the phone's screen, holding it so Ali could see photographs that could have been ads for luxury living. "Right now, we've got nine women definitely coming, and I want you to be the tenth." Jessica walked to the bar, put down her phone, and picked up two glasses of champagne, holding one out to Ali. "Here's to a hell of a good time."

Ali hesitated before she took the glass and Jessica noticed. "Damn! I *know* what you're thinking!"

Ali could feel her face reddening. "I wasn't thinking anything."

"Bullshit. You were thinking, 'What about poor Morgan? She's not invited, and it's not fair for me to go off and have fun without her.'"

Jessica was pretty much on target. For the past few weeks, Morgan had been on Ali's mind almost constantly. Something was wrong. Ali could sense it. In the few phone calls they'd exchanged, there'd been tension, a darkness in Morgan that Ali hadn't been able to get her to talk about.

"You're feeling guilty," Jessica was saying. "You're thinking that going off to Deer Valley would be wrong, just because you can't drag her along with you."

Ali began straightening the wineglasses on the bar. "Why would I be thinking that? Morgan's three thousand miles away."

Jessica shot her a knowing look. "You're running what my dad calls old tapes. I can see it."

Ali groaned. "I'm in a weird place, Jess. It's such a relief not to be looking over my shoulder every two minutes, checking to see if I should be apologizing to Morgan because I'm getting something she wants." Ali gazed up at the ceiling, feeling foolish. "But another part of me really, really misses her. It's crazy."

"Not so crazy." Jessica put her arm around Ali. "It kind of makes perfect sense. You've been her hostage since you were in diapers. Remember that story you used to tell me? About when you were little? And you ended up giving her your imaginary pony?"

Ali's smile was sheepish. "Morgan felt bad that she didn't have one. She was totally bummed about it."

"Give me a break. What kind of kid is so damn lazy they can't dream up their own imaginary friend? Sorry, Al, but the woman's a succubus. Personally, I'd—"

Jessica stopped and gasped. "Holy shit!" The color drained from her face. She was staring at something Ali hadn't seen.

Something that was lurking in the shadows just outside Ali's dining room window.

Morgan

"W HEN WHAT YOU HAVE DONE IS DISCOVERED, IT WILL CAUSE problems. You know that, don't you?" Sam said.

"Yes," Morgan answered.

"Is that what you set out to do? Create an unpleasant situation?"

"Not really." Morgan's voice was hoarse with tears. "I did it because I didn't have a choice." She was remembering...*the humiliation of standing, stranded, in the copier salesman's hotel doorway. Half-naked in Ali's left-behind trench coat. Realizing she had nowhere to go but back into Ali's shadow. Knowing that getting there would require money she didn't have. Wondering what the hell she was supposed to do. Furious that she was always on the short end of the stick. And for months, she'd stayed furious. Angry at never being the chosen one, the favorite. But then, in thinking about that concept, "the favorite," Morgan saw the answer to her money problems. The laugh she'd let out had been loud and bitter.*

"In answer to your question," Morgan told Sam, "I did what I did because it was the only way to get the money I needed."

She was recalling the ugly details of the transaction... *The thuggish girl trying to hand Morgan what looked like a dirty Kleenex, and Morgan not wanting to touch it.*

Then the girl shoving it at her. "Take it, stupid. It ain't gonna bite ya."

After the flimsy piece of paper was in her possession, Morgan stared at it, longer than she needed to. Looking at the girl was making her sick.

"Can we get outta here now?" The question came from the girl's companion, a scrawny man in a torn, inside-out T-shirt and faded jeans. His teeth

were gray, and his hair was long, bottle blond. He was leaning on the open
door of a red Cadillac.

Morgan turned her head. The girl smelled as if her armpits needed washing
and she'd tried to cover it up with cheap perfume. After she'd backed away
from the girl, Morgan asked, "Now that you've bought the land, what are
you going to do with it?"

The man bared his gray teeth and made a raucous, mocking sound.

Morgan understood this was wrong in more ways than she could count.

But all she did was sneak another glance at the wrinkled piece of paper she
was holding, a certified check. Then she put the check in her pocket.

And now here she was, listening to Sam say, "This new chapter
you're about to open…you're sure you want to go through with it?
You could simply keep the money in the bank and stay where you are."

Morgan, her chin quivering, stared into the darkness. "If it were
you, what would your plan be?"

"Why are you doing this?" Sam's voice was soft, thoughtful. "Tell
me the truth."

Morgan slumped against a tree trunk, shivering with cold. "My
sister, my twin, has everything. And I hate her for it."

"You have other choices."

Morgan's voice was dead. "No. I don't."

There was a brief pause before Sam asked, "Why?"

"Because I'm back to being 'Poor Morgan,' back to being
nobody…and I don't know how to be anything else. I never had the
chance to learn. Whether Ali meant to do it or not, it doesn't matter. For my entire life, she was so big she blocked out the sun and I
couldn't see the world around me, which is why I'm always screwing
up, getting everything wrong."

Morgan was staying in the shadows, away from the glow of the
Christmas lights. "What my sister did to me was wrong, and I think
I'm entitled to…"

"What were you were about to say? What do you want?"

"Payback."

"For what?"

"For always having to watch other people, especially Ali, get all the things I want."

"Please. Give yourself time to think. Don't leave yet. There's no reason you need to take this trip right away."

"It's too late, Sam. I left yesterday. I'm already here."

Ali

WHEN ALI FIRST SAW THE SHADOWY SHAPE ON THE OTHER SIDE of the dining room's glass-paned french doors, she thought she was imagining things.

She wasn't. What she was seeing was real. The person illuminated by the glow of Christmas lights in the garden, shivering in the night like a glassy-eyed ghost, was Morgan.

As Morgan opened the french doors and came into the room, the first thing Ali noticed was that her face was smooth, healed of its cuts. The only remaining mark was a thin, white scar near Morgan's hairline, a pale swirl that faintly resembled a tiny question mark. Yet Morgan moved with her head slightly lowered, as if the cuts were still there and she was trying to hide them.

The shock of Morgan being in California—not in Rhode Island—brought Ali joy. It also brought a stomach-dropping sense of disaster. "What are you doing here?" she asked.

Morgan was hovering between apologetic and combative. "You said your housewarming was tonight. I decided to come."

This is insane. You don't have the money to travel all the way to California for one night, for a party. Before Ali could put her thoughts into words, Jessica did it for her.

"Give me a break." Jessica shot Morgan a cynical look. "You're saying you showed up here because…what? You just happened to be in town?"

Morgan pressed both hands to her face in a defiant, self-protective gesture. "Actually, I'll be in town from now on. I'll be living here."

Ali had no idea what her sister was talking about or why she was so hostile.

"Ali needs me." Morgan was looking at the floor, while talking to Jessica. "The restaurant. And the new house. Being in a place where she doesn't have family. It's hard for her. I could tell from her emails...the few that I got." Morgan looked up—at Ali. "The only thing for me to do was come and be with you."

Confused, Ali asked, "What about the new museum, your dream job? How can you just walk away?"

Morgan blinked like she'd been jolted by a bad memory. "There was this thing with my boss, Veronica. She didn't think I was a good fit anymore. She fired me."

The old, familiar heaviness was pressing down on Ali, the suffocating weight of Morgan. "Where, exactly, are you planning to live?"

"Somewhere around here." Morgan's gaze swept the room, arrogant and calculating. Like she was playing a character in a drama no one else could see.

Morgan was clearly in trouble—losing her grip. Ali was worried. "Morgan, you were living with Mom because of all the debt you were in. What are you going to do about money?"

Morgan's smile was tight. "I have money. I paid off all my debts."

"How?" Ali asked.

"I sold the land Grandma MaryJoy left me."

"What!" Ali was thunderstruck. "Who did you sell it to?"

"Two people in a red Cadillac. They said they want to start a farm."

There was a bizarre quality in the way Morgan had said the word *farm*.

"What kind of farm?" Ali asked.

"The kind where they'll grow a little pot," Morgan told her. "Maybe cook some meth..."

And Ali exploded. "How dare you?"

"Hey." Morgan's tone was acid. "Just because you were the favorite doesn't mean you get an opinion on this. Grandma MaryJoy left the land to me. It was mine. I could do whatever I wanted with it."

Ali was so upset she was stammering. "That land has been in our family forever. It was supposed to *stay* in our family!"

Their grandmother's Irish traditions made the owning of land something sacred, and Morgan had desecrated that. Ali slapped her, hard.

Morgan came back with what sounded like a carefully thought-out threat. "I'm in a hotel right now…but only until I can find a permanent place to live. Somewhere very close to you. And Matt."

Seeing how much her sister wanted to do damage to her was scaring the life out of Ali.

"What about when you run out of money?" Jessica asked Morgan.

"I'll get a job. I told you, I was fired because of something personal. My work was fine. My boss, Veronica, wrote me a letter of recommendation." Morgan turned away from Jessica, holding out an unsteady hand to Ali. "My battery's low. I need to make a phone call."

A little dazed, still unable to sort out what was going on, Ali took her phone from her pocket and gave it to Morgan.

As soon as Morgan moved away, Jessica said, "What the hell was that? Has she lost her mi—" Jessica stopped. "Are you okay? You look like you're about to pass out."

Ali's heart was pounding. "Jess, she's different. There's something in Morgan that wasn't ever there before."

"And?"

"And it's bad… It's something sick."

Morgan

MORGAN WAS STANDING NEAR THE BAR IN THE DINING ROOM OF Ali's new home, When she broke in on Ali's housewarming, she hadn't known exactly how she was going to get the payback she wanted. All she knew was that she deserved it.

She needed something to dull the pain of going back to living a borrowed life—even if it was something small.

And Morgan had just been handed the palm-sized weapon that could bring Ali to her knees—Ali's phone. Morgan had borrowed it because she'd been scared, needing to call Sam. But that call was forgotten the instant Morgan switched on Ali's phone and saw the trail of texts. Flirty exchanges between Ali and Levi, the ginger-haired hockey player.

There were messages from Levi like: **Thinking about your mouth. Wanting my tongue in it.** Followed by Ali's reply: **You always were an epic kisser.** And a different message from Levi saying: **Where are you?** To which Ali responded: **In the dark, in bed.** Levi immediately asked: **Alone?** And Ali's comeback was: **Completely alone. It's just you and me.**

The messages, which were suggestive but never explicit, had been going on for several months. The most recent was only a few hours old—from Levi: **Hey, Pretty Woman. Texting you all day. No reply.**

At the sight of that greeting—*Pretty Woman*—Morgan instinctively put her hand to her face. The place where the cuts had been. The place where bitterness still lingered over Ali's contribution to the fall that made Morgan feel so ugly.

As Morgan read the end of the most recent text from Levi, she saw it said, **Don't make me crash your housewarming and cause a scene just to get an answer from you. Could do it. Don't forget…am on my way into LA with a buddy who plays for the Kings. xo**

Morgan looked at that little *xo* and knew exactly what to do. Levi had somehow managed to restrain himself at Ali's wedding, but he was still a hothead with anger issues who'd been in love with Ali since high school. And from the looks of things, the heat had been turned way up. Now that Ali was apparently having an affair with him, he'd be a powder keg.

The way this could play out had Morgan in an adrenaline-fueled fantasy.

Levi's fist slamming into Ali's front door.

The door almost breaking off the hinges…banging open.

Startled guests scattering.

Levi marching into the house. Shouting that he'd warned Ali not to ignore his texts.

Levi telling Matt, and every one of Ali's friends, that Ali is his lover, the woman he's sleeping with.

Ali, disgraced, humiliated.

Matt, furious. Dragging Ali to the front door, shoving her through it. Telling her he never wants to see her again.

Ali, gone. For good.

Matt, heartbroken…collapsing into Morgan's arms.

Morgan comforting him.

Ali locked out of Matt's life. Begging for forgiveness that will never come.

Morgan couldn't stop smiling. Ali's texts with Levi had handed her the gasoline *and* the matches. All she had to do was set the fire by sending a text of her own. But just as Morgan was touching her finger to the screen, Ali tapped on her the shoulder, saying, "We need to talk."

Morgan quickly hid Ali's phone. Slipping it in among the house-warming gifts stacked at the end of the bar. Then she turned around and calmly asked Ali, "How long have you been cheating on Matt?"

Ali's eyes widened. It took her a while to pull herself together. "What're you talking about?"

This was something Morgan had never experienced—having the upper hand, the power to take Ali down. It felt good.

Walking tall, Morgan moved in, leaving only inches between her-self and her sister. "Save your breath…*Pretty Woman*."

Ali was stunned. "You read my texts?"

"That's how I found out your old friend Levi calls you Pretty Woman. That's how I found out a lot of things."

Ali lunged toward Morgan. "Give me my phone."

"Too late!" Morgan ducked out of reach and held up both hands, fingers spread. Showing that the phone was gone.

Ali was paper white. She seemed to be having trouble swallowing.

"Does Matt know about your little affair?" Morgan asked.

"It's not an affair. Levi and I have just been…"

While Ali was trying to finish her sentence, a tall woman in a skintight dress had hurried over and steered her toward the other side of the room, saying, "Come meet my husband. He absolutely loves your restaurant." As Ali was dragged away, she looked back at Morgan. Frantic.

As soon as Ali was out of sight, Morgan slid her fingers in among the housewarming gifts, probing the edges of an enormous Tiffany's box. The instant she felt the phone's shape, she closed her hand around it and moved like lightning.

She only had a few seconds to send a text that would piss Levi off, something that would make him angry enough to crash the party and cause a scene—expose Ali's slutty secret in front of a house full of peo-ple. Bring Ali to her knees and give Morgan the revenge she deserved.

Morgan switched on the phone, trying to stay calm and focused. When the screen lit up, there was a new message: **Missed my plane. Running late. Apologies to the hot hostess.**

Ali's voice, and Jessica's, were coming from somewhere nearby. Morgan only had a split second to get this done. Her fingers were flying. In the blink of an eye, she'd typed **Go screw yourself, you pathetic asshole**, hit the Send button, cleared the screen, and jammed the phone into the pile of gifts, somewhere near the Tiffany's box.

Ali and Jessica had arrived at the bar. Jessica was saying, "I want to pick up Logan at the airport and get him back here as fast as I can. He's been in meetings at the corporate office in San Francisco all week. I just need to grab my phone before I head out. I left it here... next to the present I brought you." Jessica reached in behind the Tiffany's box and pulled out a phone.

Jessica looked at the screen, frowned, and then put the phone to her ear. "Shit, I missed a voice mail from Logan." After listening for a moment, she told Ali, "He didn't catch his damn plane... He's not going to get back in time... Says he sent you an apology text." Jessica lowered her voice. "I think I'll hit the road. I want to be in bed, and ready, when he finally walks in. He's been gone a week... I'm a little horny."

While she watched Ali walk Jessica to the door, the air went out of Morgan. She wasn't going to have what she wanted. She'd texted the wrong person.

The "apologies to the hot hostess" text had been from Logan. Morgan's "Go screw yourself" message went to Logan, not Levi.

There wouldn't be any infuriated hockey player roaring through the door, outing Ali as a cheating wife. Ali was safe.

Morgan held on to the bar with both hands, dizzy with relief. *Payback was what I wanted. Why am I glad I didn't get it? It's like I'm going crazy.*

The room started to spin. *I love Ali. I don't want to hurt her but I need to. I need to make her pay for having everything and leaving me with nothing.*

Morgan had to call Sam. She was out of control.

AFTER THE HOUSEWARMING CELEBRATION ENDED, MATT HAD offered a ride home to one of the cast members from his show, someone who'd had way too much to drink.

Ali had gotten into her own car, preparing to head back to the apartment. As she drove away from the new house, she was distracted—upset.

She didn't notice that someone was parked at the curb. Watching her.

Ali was only vaguely aware of her arrival at the apartment complex. Her mind was still on Morgan's sudden, disturbing move to California.

Pulling into the underground garage, Ali narrowly missed sideswiping stacks of moving boxes that were lined up at the edge of her parking space, in front of a closet-sized storage room.

Getting out of the car, she stumbled over a pile of odds and ends. Old books and clothes. A few pots and pans. And a small, brown suitcase, the mud-colored wedding gift from her stepmother, an item Ali had never liked. It irritated her to see that suitcase, and the other things, still in the garage. Days ago, she'd asked Matt to drop them off on his way to work. To make sure he didn't forget, she'd even put a hand-lettered sign on top of the pile: "For Salvation Army."

Wondering what else Matt had overlooked, she did a fast check of the storage room and then ran for the elevator. She hated this parking garage with its gloomy shadows and its constant echoes and creaks. It gave her the shivers.

By the time Ali got upstairs and opened the door to her apartment, there were only two things she wanted to do: take a hot shower and drop onto her bed, the one functioning piece of furniture that remained in the apartment. The rest of the furniture, most of it from IKEA, had been given away to various neighbors.

The apartment was stuffy and almost eerily quiet. Ali had flipped the wall switch beside the front door, then remembered that there was no overhead lighting fixture in the living room and that all the lamps were already packed. After she shut and locked the door, she had to thread her way through a forest of moving boxes in darkness and silence.

Just as she was stepping into the bedroom, the silence was broken by a peculiar tapping sound. Coming in erratic bursts. Abruptly stopping before starting again.

Whoever, or whatever, was making the noise was only a few feet away. On the other side of the darkened bedroom.

Ali began a slow, nervous retreat.

A new round of rattling started up—faster, louder. Terror hit. And Ali collapsed, landing on her knees, her teeth chattering. "Who… who's there?"

No answer. Another burst of rattling taps.

Then Ali saw the far wall of the bedroom—the sliding glass door that led to the patio. The door was rattling. The wind was blowing, and the lock was loose. The lock Matt had never fixed, the symbol of his preoccupation with his work. The lock that Ali had refused to fix because doing it herself would've meant letting Matt get away with ignoring his responsibilities.

In the midst of her fright, Ali was ragingly angry. If Matt had been there, she would've wanted to hit him with a tire iron.

When she caught her breath, she stormed across the darkness of the bedroom and grabbed the handle on the sliding door, shoving at the lock, trying to force it to catch. But it was badly bent and wouldn't fall into place. She banged it with her fist and screamed the word *damn*.

Ali was furious with Matt—scared about what was going on with Morgan.

And above all, Ali was tired and needed to sleep.

Stepping away from the sliding door, she tapped the switch plate on the wall and used the weak glow from the outside patio bulb to illuminate the way to the bathroom. Once she got there, she pulled off her clothes and didn't bother to turn on the lights. She was too exhausted.

She went straight into the shower, letting the hot water pour over her for a very long time.

$\sim$

Ali's eyes were heavy, her body loose and relaxed. She came out of the dark of the bathroom into the semidarkness of the bedroom, lazily running a towel over her wet hair and face.

She never saw the man who grabbed her.

But as she was being slammed to the floor—as he was forcing her legs apart—Ali saw the unlocked sliding door. The wind wasn't rattling it now, and it was wide open.

Matt

"T HIS WHOLE THING IS UNBELIEVABLE." MATT'S EYES NERVOUSLY shifted from the uniformed police officer to the front door of the apartment, then back again.

He was thinking that the cop was incredibly young. *She looks like a high-school girl playing grown-up. With her shiny, new badge, and that big black gun riding way up high on her hip. The badge says "R. Yamanaka." Wonder what the R is for. Rosie? Rachel? Why the hell am I standing here letting myself be interrogated by her? Why the hell didn't I—*

"Sir? Is there anything else you can tell me about what happened?" Officer Yamanaka was now resting her hand on the butt of her holstered firearm.

There was something in her eyes, the way she was looking at him. What was it? Accusation? Disgust? He knew he had to be imagining it, but she seemed to be staring at him like he was transparent, like she was seeing what he was remembering… *Another night, in another place. A girl crumpled on the floor, a knife wound running the length of her back.*

Matt's knees buckled. He dropped into a sitting position, perched on one of the sealed moving boxes.

"Sir," Officer Yamanaka said again. "Is there anything else you can tell me?"

"I told you everything. After the party ended at our new house, Ali came back here, and I gave a ride home to one of our guests who'd had too much to drink. It took about half an hour. Then I came straight here, parked the car, and came upstairs. When I walked in, I called out to Ali, saying how glad I was this would be our last night in the apartment and I couldn't wait to get into bed, to hold her. Then when she didn't answer, I went looking for her. I found her in the shower, crouched under a stream of scalding water. She was scrubbing her skin raw, rocking against the shower wall and crying. She was—" Matt stopped himself abruptly. "Like I said, I told you everything."

Matt knew that wasn't the truth.

He hadn't told the attractive young cop everything.

He hadn't told her how guilty he was.

Ali

ALI'S RAPE HAPPENED SHORTLY BEFORE MIDNIGHT. SHORTLY before dawn, detectives and uniformed police officers were wrapping up their investigation of the crime scene.

Ali had just gotten back from the hospital, where a doctor had examined her and sent evidence of the rape to the police lab. Now she was in a blue bathrobe, sitting on the bed with her back against the headboard and her knees drawn tight to her chest. Matt was beside her.

A stocky female detective, who had skin like leather and eyes that were drowsy and empathetic, said, "And nothing out of the ordinary in the days leading up to the rape? Unusual phone calls? Text messages?"

"There weren't any messages that were out of the ordinary," Ali said.

The mention of text messages had given her a little zap of guilt, even though what she'd said was true. The messages she didn't want to discuss weren't out of the ordinary. They were an everyday routine that had started when Matt disappeared into his work and Ali was hopelessly lonely. The messages had been delicious, flirtatious conversations with her old friend Levi.

The texts had continued right up until the day before yesterday— when Ali put a stop to them, because she loved Matt and knew what she was doing with Levi was wrong.

"You're sure you've told me everything you can remember about the man who attacked you?" the detective asked.

Ali was still thinking about the text messages. They'd started a few months ago, right after Ali and Matt's first wedding anniversary. Ali was looking at the patio door. Looking at the broken lock. Remembering the details of her anniversary.

∿

Matt hadn't come home until the early hours of the morning. The special dinner she'd prepared was on the coffee table in the living room, untouched. Ali was in bed. The drapes on the patio doors weren't quite closed, and the broken lock was highlighted by the strip of light peeking through the slit.

Ali pretended to be asleep when Matt came into the apartment. "I know you're awake," he said.

"And I know it's after midnight. It's already tomorrow. You missed our anniversary." She was weary, worn-out from being alone and lonely.

"Ali, I would've been here if I could. We got notes from the network. The script needed a total rewrite. I had to stay till it was done. I didn't have a choice."

Ali rolled away from him and refused to speak. Matt sat on the side of the bed, looking exhausted. "Al, this job is all about you. It's me stepping up and giving you what you needed—the restaurant, the new house."

"I never asked you for those things. I could have waited." Ali was thinking that what she really needed was a baby.

Matt was insistent. "I didn't want you to have to ask. Or wait. Ever."

"This is crazy. It's like you're killing yourself trying to make up to me for something you never did wrong in the first place."

There had always been a quality in Matt that Ali didn't understand, a secret she couldn't quite name, and she knew what she'd just said had touched a nerve. Matt had winced. The only thing that wasn't clear was the nature of the secret he was keeping. And as much as she wanted to ask what it was, Ali didn't know how. She should have asked a long time ago, at the beginning of their relationship. And now the silence had gone on too long.

Which is why her only question was, "Can't you back off, just a little, on how much time you spend at work?"

"Al, I'm holding on to this job by my fingernails. And we're too far in debt for me to slack off, even for a minute."

"What do you mean…holding on by your fingernails?"

Matt seemed to be hurting as he said, "There's a writing team on my staff, Jacobs and Karel. Jacobs quit last week. But Karel asked to stay. Aidan's away, working on his new movie, so I talked to our co-executive producer. Want to know what he said? He said Karel was an outstanding writer, but he's expendable. The idiot said good writing isn't what we need. What we need is someone who can keep the banter coming." Matt gave a bitter, mystified laugh. "I have a PhD in English literature, and I work for a man whose holy grail is banter."

"I wish you'd never talked me into coming to California," Ali murmured. "I wish we'd stayed home." Matt crawled into bed beside her and cradled her as she asked, "Do you think we could ever go back?"

"Go back?"

"To Rhode Island. To you being a college professor."

Ali could sense the ambivalence in Matt. It unnerved her. "Tell me you love me," she said. "Tell me everything's going to be all right."

"I love you, Ali. Everything's going to be all right." Matt moved closer and put his hand on the flat of her belly, trailing his fingertips in slow circles.

Ali's quiet moan was the sound of want—the wanting of a child. It was also the sound of unhappiness. There would be no way to have a baby for a very long while. The restaurant, still in its infancy, had left Ali without the time or the money for anything else. By rushing her into making the restaurant a reality, Matt had taken a baby away from her. By bringing them to California, he'd created a life where he'd vanished into his job and left Ali feeling completely abandoned.

As she was drifting into sleep that night, she'd gazed at the broken lock on the patio door. The lock she'd stubbornly left unrepaired to show Matt he wasn't paying enough attention to her. And she had been consumed by a single gut-wrenching thought—*I'm unprotected.*

The same thought had been in Ali just a few hours ago, while the rapist was slamming her to the floor—breaking her open, shattering her.

Ali's voice was hollow as she answered the detective's question about the man who had attacked her. "All I remember are the clothes. Only his clothes. I never saw his face."

"Why is that?"

"It was dark. I'd been drying my hair and, at first, the towel was over my head. Later, it slipped a little. I saw the shirt he was wearing, and the jeans."

"Describe them for me one more time." The detective checked her notepad. "I want to be sure we got everything."

"The jeans were just regular jeans, I guess. But his shirt was like an old-time cowboy shirt…satiny…with snap buttons. They were black. The pocket and the cuffs had black edges."

"Anything else?"

Ali touched the sore place on her hip. "His belt buckle. It was big, in the shape of a horseshoe." Her eyes widened. "Wait. Shoes. I saw his shoes!"

The detective looked up from the notepad. "What kind of shoes?"

"Cowboy boots. When he left, when he walked away, he almost stepped on me. The boot was dark, like maybe an eggplant color, and it was bumpy. It could've been alligator. Or ostrich. Something like that."

"Okay. Good." The detective flipped back through several pages, scanning her notes, before she asked, "And the attack itself—"

Ali had a quick, involuntary intake of breath.

"Don't worry. I'm not going to make you talk about it again. I just need to clarify one thing. When the rape was over...that's when the attack stopped? Afterward, he didn't make any attempt to hit you? Choke you? Harm you in any other way?"

"No," Ali whispered. "It hurt so much. But it happened fast. Fast. And ugly."

There was wildness in Matt's eyes as he told the detective, "It's my fault. I wasn't here to protect her."

The detective studied Matt for a moment, then asked Ali, "Anything else about the man who hurt you? Perhaps something he said?"

"I don't think he said anything. No, I'm sure. He didn't. I never heard his voice." Ali frowned, puzzled by the information she was about share. "But I remember his breath. It smelled like mint but was still kind of sour...like maybe he'd just put a breath freshener in his mouth."

"Do you remember if he was wearing any jewelry? A watch? A ring?"

"I don't know... I guess he could've been wearing a watch. I don't remember."

The detective closed her notebook. "Okay. I'll let you get some rest." She reached out and patted Ali's shoulder. "What you're going through right now is awful, but it gets better. I promise."

Ali shook her head. "You couldn't even imagine what I'm going through."

"I don't have to imagine. I know." The detective held Ali's gaze for a beat, then walked out of the room.

The instant the woman was gone, Matt moved closer to Ali. She shot away, repulsed by the thought of being touched. "Don't come near me, Matt. I don't think I ever want anyone to come near me again."

Matt's voice was thin, ragged. "Please. Al—" That's as far as he got. A shout was echoing in the living room.

Peter Sebelius—calling Matt's name, and Ali's.

Ali was immediately in a panic. "Don't say anything! Don't tell him. I don't want anybody to know. Ever." She grabbed Matt's arm hard enough to leave marks. "Promise. Promise you won't tell anybody."

It was as if something inside Matt was shifting, compressing. Ali saw unexplainable darkness in him as he said, "I won't breathe a word. I promise."

Ali kept looking at Matt's eyes, wanting to see into his soul, into whatever the darkness was. But finally, she understood it was impossible. She let go of him, and he walked away.

Then the thought came again—*I'm unprotected.*

Ali quickly got out of bed and went to the doorway to watch what was happening in the other room—to be sure Matt was keeping his promise.

Peter Sebelius was just inside the apartment doorway. Wearing hospital scrubs, a stethoscope draped around his neck, telling Matt, "I saw cops leaving here. What happened?"

"Nothing," Matt said. "No big deal." He had crossed the living room and was standing directly in front of Peter, keeping him from coming any farther into the apartment.

"A bunch of cops at six o'clock in the morning? That's more than 'no big deal.' Are you guys okay?"

"Just a prowler. Somebody tried to break in."

It was apparent Peter didn't believe Matt's story. "You're sure everything's all right? Nobody's hurt?"

"Yeah. We're both fine." Matt flashed a tense smile. "Hey, man, you have circles under your eyes like somebody punched your lights out. It must've been a long night at the hospital. Go get some sleep."

"Actually, I'm on my way back to work. Just got a call to come in on an emergency consult. A newborn with a severely deformed hip." Peter still sounded concerned as he went out the door and said, "I'll check in with you later."

Ali edged into the living room, positioning herself behind a stack of moving boxes so that she was out of sight but could see into the hallway.

Peter was heading toward the elevator that would take him down to the garage. As the elevator doors opened, he stopped short and looked back at Matt. "Wait. You won't be here later, will you? You guys are moving today. I forgot."

Ali had forgotten, too. The movers would be arriving in an hour, and there was no way she could stand being in this apartment for another minute. And with every fiber in her body warning her not to do it, she told Matt, "Call Morgan."

Morgan

HER RINGING PHONE STARTLED MORGAN OUT OF A DEEP SLEEP. In a stuffy motel room. She was disoriented, groggy. Groping into the folds of the blanket, pushing aside crumpled tissues and wrinkled magazines.

She finally found her phone and mumbled, "What? Who is it?"

"It's Matt."

At the sound of his voice, the bleakness of his tone, Morgan immediately tried to wake up, but she'd taken a sleeping pill last night. Her brain felt heavy, foggy.

"Morgan, I apologize for calling so early. I need a favor."

"Sure. What do you need?" Morgan sensed something was wrong but couldn't think straight. She was struggling to clear her head.

Matt told her, "The movers will be here at seven. We're all packed, but Ali's exhausted. She needs to go over to the new place, get some rest. And I'm wondering if you could—"

"Wait a minute. You woke me up at the crack of dawn because my sister needs a *nap*? You've got to be—" Morgan stopped speaking. She was so angry she could spit.

"Morgan, I want to take Ali to the new house right away. She really needs to get out of the apartment," Matt said. "Somebody has to be here to deal with the movers. Please. We need your help."

There was a quality in Matt's voice that was so strung out and desperate that it sent Morgan stumbling out of bed, groping for her clothes. "Okay. Okay. I'll do it."

After the move was over, Morgan stopped in the late afternoon to pick up a pizza. Then she went straight to Ali's new home.

The heat from the pizza box was burning her hand as she entered Ali's kitchen. She needed a place to set the box down as fast as possible. But all the countertops were covered with packing containers and stacks of dishes and cooking utensils. The only open space was a chair seat—empty except for a neatly folded, crayon-yellow apron.

She moved toward the chair, still enjoying the high-flying sense of elation from earlier in the day, when one of the movers had assumed Morgan was the Mrs. Easton listed on the work order and said, "Your husband's a lucky guy. A lot of women have no idea how to organize a move."

Morgan was thrilled by the compliment. She really had brought organization to Ali's chaos. Wading into the maze of jumbled moving boxes, quickly labeling them. Sealing them. Lining them up in tidy rows. She'd let herself dream she was a happy, young wife, moving to a beautiful new home—*the kind of wife who really appreciates my husband, and our love—not somebody like Ali, who has life handed to her on a silver platter and takes it all for granted.*

Morgan had completed Ali's move feeling proud of the meticulous way she'd managed every little item. Right down to washing out the inside of the refrigerator and getting the Salvation Army to pick up a pile of odds and ends in the parking garage—details Ali had obviously overlooked.

She had walked into Ali's new house with a sense of efficiency and purpose. And as she put the hot pizza box on the chair, on top of the apron, Morgan was startled by what sounded like a polite but firm criticism. "If you please…do not do that!"

Ava, the stunningly beautiful woman who worked at Ali's restaurant, was kneeling in front of the kitchen's center island, lining the cabinet shelves underneath it. She rushed to the chair, lifting the pizza box away from the apron. "The grease. It will stain." She indicated the oily splotch on the bottom of the box.

Morgan's fragile bubble of happiness was instantly annihilated, replaced with something more familiar—hurt and defensiveness. "I put a pizza box on an apron. Isn't catching stains what aprons are for?"

Ava slid the pizza box onto the stove top, then picked up the apron. Shaking it out. Holding it so Morgan could see it was embroidered with the name of Ali's restaurant, JOY, and with the date of the restaurant's opening. "This is not used for cooking. It is precious to Ali. The only one there is. Her husband had it made for her special, as a present."

"Of course he did." Ava and the apron had sucked Morgan back into being nothing more than Ali's bumbling sister. And she was already halfway to the back door. Her face flushed and hot. Her fingers roaming the places where the cuts had been—the invisible traces of ugliness.

Morgan was almost out the door when she was stopped by the sound of bells and a tiny, delighted laugh. Morgan suddenly realized that Ava's baby was in the room, with a cascade of miniature silver bells dancing above the rim of her portable playpen.

The baby and the playpen, the coziness of it, triggered a wicked stab of jealousy in Morgan.

Ava, someone Morgan had only met once, was completely at home in Ali's house, while she, Morgan, was a stranger here at 76 Paradise Lane.

Morgan looked from the baby to Ava, her jealousy resentful and possessive. "Very cozy. But I'm confused. At the housewarming, I thought I heard somebody say you were one of my sister's restaurant workers."

"I am. But I am also her friend." Ava calmly went back to lining the cabinet shelves. "Ali's husband called me today and said she was not well." Ava stopped to gaze at her dark-eyed, strikingly lovely baby. "I told him Sofie and I will come and make the kitchen ready."

Morgan saw how easy Ava was in the way she moved, perfectly comfortable in her own skin. Morgan envied that. And immediately wanted to get rid of Ava. "It's nice you're available to be hired on such short notice, but—"

"There is no hiring here. No money involved." Ava's tone was mild. "Ali is my dear friend. A sister of my soul."

Hearing Ava refer to Ali as a sister grated on Morgan and turned her bitchy. She wanted to put Ava in her place. "All I can tell you is…I'm sure they plan to pay you…like any other worker. I'll remind Matt to write you a check." Morgan gestured toward the entryway to the dining room. "By the way, where is my brother-in-law?"

The expression in Ava's eyes had changed, but her tone remained agreeable. "Your sister's husband is upstairs. In the room that will be his study. The workmen are installing the cable for his television and computers. There have been people here all day…movers, locksmiths, electricians. Do you want me to tell him you are also here?"

Ava's refusal to be rattled was only hardening Morgan's determination to win. "I have a few things from the apartment in my car. Towels and the vacuum cleaner, some other stuff. Why don't you…" Morgan was about to tell Ava to run out and fetch the items but changed her mind. It would only prolong Ava's time in Ali's house.

"You know what? While I get everything and put it away, why don't you finish up in here? Then you can leave, Ava. My sister wants it to be just us in the house this evening. Just family."

Even as the words came out of her mouth, Morgan was

ashamed—her arms crossed, her fingernails digging into the crooks of her elbows.

She was acting like a scared little shrew. She wanted to be something so much better.

~

While Morgan took the vacuum cleaner from the trunk of her car, along with other items from the apartment, and put them away in Ali's house, Ava quietly departed.

When Morgan came back into the kitchen, the phone was ringing. She reached for it, inadvertently hitting the speaker button. The call was in the process of going to voice mail—Jessica saying, "Ali, I've been calling all day. Why aren't you answering? Anyway, just want to tell you I had a blast last night at your housewarming. Wish I hadn't left early. Logan's flight ended up getting totally canceled. He was stuck in San Francisco all night. I never did get laid."

Morgan reached for the receiver, intending to answer the call, while Jessica was chirping, "You know my number. Use it. I want to come help unpack and decorate." By the time Morgan picked up the phone, Jessica was gone. Morgan was relieved. She didn't like interacting with women like Jessica; they were always moving too fast. Morgan could never find a way to keep up.

After deleting the message, she made a word-for-word note of Jessica's call, planning to use it as an excuse to go upstairs and talk to Ali. But before she could do it, Matt walked into the room.

He looked exhausted. He passed Morgan without speaking to her, going directly to the refrigerator and opening it. The only thing inside was a serving tray containing a slender bottle of mineral water, a dish of lemon slices, a chilled bowl of the signature pear-ginger soup from JOY, and a lightly dressed jicama salad. There was also creamy rice pudding, sprinkled with cinnamon and spooned into a delicately enameled yellow cup.

Matt picked up the tray. As the refrigerator door swung shut, he said, "Ava brought this from the restaurant for Ali. I'm going to take it up to her now. She hasn't eaten all day."

Morgan was about to say "But I brought pizza" and could hear how silly it would sound. Pizza wasn't exactly in the same food league as the offerings on the tray Matt was holding. But Morgan needed to include herself, to regain her footing in Ali's life.

"Wait! Bring the tray over here." She grabbed the pizza box, snatched two paper plates from the kitchen counter, and put them on the table. "We'll all eat together. There's no reason Ali can't come downstairs to enjoy her fancy gourmet treat. You and I can share the pizza." Morgan hurried across the kitchen telling Matt, "I'll run upstairs and get my sister."

He stopped her. "Leave Ali alone, Morgan. She isn't feeling well. She needs to rest."

Morgan felt criticized, rejected—and it hurt. "Why the big need for rest? Ali was perfectly fine yesterday. Throwing a party and texting old boyfriends. How come today, out of nowhere, she's too weak to sit at a dinner table? Or even pick up the phone when it rings?"

Matt wasn't listening. He was already leaving the room. "Ali has the flu, Morgan. She came down with it late last night. We appreciate everything you've done. Now it's time for you to go." The look on Matt's face said he wasn't interested in any further discussion.

Watching him climb the stairs, Morgan was nursing a hurt that was killing her. Without coming out and saying it, Matt had told her the same thing she'd just told Ava: *You're not wanted in this house.*

Morgan was scared. And outraged.

She listened to Matt's footsteps crossing the hallway on the second floor, going into and out of the master bedroom. When she heard him enter his study and close the door, she ran for the stairs. To plead with Ali to take her back. Love her. And make her safe again.

~

The pizza receipt landed on the floor at the foot of the bed. It wasn't what Morgan had intended. She'd opened the door in such a rush that the receipt had gone flying out of her hand. As if she'd thrown it at Ali. When what she wanted to do was simply show it to Ali— show her that Ava wasn't the only one who had thought about taking care of dinner.

The receipt ended up a few feet from the chair where Ali was sitting. She looked down at it. "What's that?"

The tone in Ali's voice was strange, empty. Morgan ran across the room, bending down and grabbing the crumpled slip of paper, telling Ali, "It's nothing. It's a receipt for the pizza I bought. For your dinner, but—"

"Not now, Morgan." Ali's voice had abruptly turned ice-cold. It startled Morgan, kept her silent.

The chair Ali was in was close to the window. The tray Matt had taken from the refrigerator was on a nearby table, the water glass half-empty, the food untouched. Behind Ali, the wall was a delicate robin's-egg blue. The furniture and bedding that surrounded her were brand-new. White and pillowy. Like mounds of freshly whipped cream. Against that backdrop, Ali's ankle-length nightgown—long-sleeved, high-necked, and dolomite gray—looked like a storm cloud, in the blue and white of a summer sky. The gown's somber cut and color only emphasized how deathly pale Ali was.

Still crouched on the floor, clutching the receipt, Morgan was thinking about this morning, when Matt called with the story about Ali having the flu. And suddenly she knew it was a lie. Whatever was wrong with Ali had nothing to do with a cough or a fever. "Tell me," Morgan said. "I want to know."

Again, an ice-cold response. "Go away. I'll pay you for the pizza later."

"I didn't come up here for pizza money. And I'm not going anywhere till you tell me what's wrong." There was only one emotion in Morgan now—heartfelt concern for her sister.

Ali's reply was a growl. "Get out." She sounded like she'd been scalded—all softness burned away. All the tenderness gone.

It was a moment of pure terror for Morgan. And the terror came out as a fear-filled rant. "You're telling me to *get out*? After all the grunt work I did for you today, that's what you have the nerve to say? How dare you? You treat strangers, and their babies, like they live here, like they're members of your family. And you tell *me* to get out?"

Ali looked away, expressionless.

What Morgan was seeing was tearing her apart. Ali had moved on. Moved up. Into a big house and a new marriage and a friendship with someone who was "a sister of her soul." Ali had escaped into a new world, had left Morgan locked out, abandoned.

Choking on tears, Morgan shouted, "Fuck you while you sit up here in the guest room of your own house like some kind of visiting queen. Go to hell, Ali. You're nothing but a spoiled, selfish bitch!"

While those words were being said, Matt ran into the room, crossing it in a blur—grabbing Morgan and throwing her out into the hallway.

She hit the wall, bounced off it, and fell to the floor. It took her a while to catch her breath. When she went back into the bedroom, her arms were crossed. Her fingernails, deep in the crooks of her elbows, were drawing blood.

Morgan looked at Ali. Then at Matt. "I hope whatever's wrong with my sister is something awful. You two deserve it."

Matt

MATT LISTENED TO MORGAN'S FOOTSTEPS ECHOING DOWN THE stairs.

The glare Ali was giving him was murderous. "Don't...ever again...even *think* of laying a hand on my sister."

The hostility in Ali startled Matt. He didn't try to touch her, didn't even look at her as he said, "I was trying to protect you. Protect my family. It's what I'm supposed to do."

His voice was a whisper. One part of Matt was there in the room with Ali, while another part of him had traveled back into the brutality of his past, bringing tears to his eyes. He quickly wiped the tears away, hoping Ali hadn't seen them.

If she had, she was ignoring them. She'd walked away from Matt, crossing to the bed and sitting on its edge. He didn't quite know what to do. It took him a long time to decide to go and sit next to her. As soon as he did, Ali stood up and went to the other side of the room.

"We need to talk about what happened to you," he said.

Ali touched the place where her attacker's horseshoe belt buckle had bruised her hip. "What do you want me to say?"

Matt shook his head, not sure how to answer.

From downstairs, there was the sound of the kitchen door banging shut—and Morgan's car leaving the driveway, tires screaming.

Matt could hear the baffled sorrow in Ali's voice as she asked, "Do you know what I figured out while I was sitting in here today, thinking about my rape?"

"No." He'd cringed when Ali said the word *rape*.

"Just because I don't want anyone else to know what happened to me," Ali said, "doesn't mean I don't know what happened. I was *raped*. And you know what I figured out about that?" Ali's words were slow and detached. "You should've fixed the lock. And you should've been in the apartment with me. Instead, you were busy taking care of one of your coworkers…giving her a ride home because she had too much to drink." Unblinking, Ali looked directly at Matt. "What happened to me was your fault."

A fragment of memory raced into Matt's mind—a horrible secret he'd never forgotten. *He'd jammed a girl who trusted him into a boxlike space that smelled of garbage and piss. Then, later, there had been that angry voice warning him, "You're a fuckup and a lightweight. No woman will ever feel safe with you."*

Matt lowered his head. Not wanting Ali to see in his eyes the memories of the other things, awful things, that were also his fault.

*Three hundred twenty-three miles from 76 Paradise Lane,
two days later, a week before Christmas.*

Fury.

*Droplets of crimson-red blood on a blanket of snow.
And the letter* L.

Matt

THE KNOCKING HAD STARTED AGAIN. A SOFT FEMALE VOICE WAS saying, "Are you in there? They want you at the run-through. You need to get down to the stage right away."

Matt ignored the woman on the other side of the door and stared at the framed photograph on his desktop—the picture of Ali, taken in Newport, minutes after he'd proposed to her. The backdrop was the night sky. The lighting was the iridescence from a dozen glowing sparklers. Ali. Showing off her engagement ring and blowing a kiss to the camera.

After Matt had driven Ali to her restaurant a little while ago, he had come directly here, to his office. A room where every wall was lined with shelves crowded with books. There was only one exception—at the back of the room, on an inaccessible bottom shelf, there was a solitary row of scripts from his television show. That half-hidden row of scripts was the sole indication that Matt's office was on a Hollywood production lot, not a college campus.

From the moment he sat down at his desk, he'd been blank, numb. The worry over Ali's rape and all the things he'd done wrong were keeping Matt deaf and blind to what was going on around him. Ringing phones. Emails accumulating on his computer. And those persistent knocks on his door.

The knocking stopped, and for a few seconds the office was silent. Then. Out of the blue. A thundering boom. Somebody on the other side of the door had banged a fist against it.

The door flew open, and Aidan stormed into the room. Frowning at the bookish decor. "Professor, I've come to remind you...we have a television show to run. Get your high-class ass in gear."

Matt didn't say a word. He didn't have the strength.

Aidan dropped onto the sofa, lit a cigarette. "Right, then. Let's discuss what I'm assuming is your disappointment in our less-than-illustrious show." He put his feet up on the coffee table in front of the sofa. Casually directing the cigarette smoke, and his words, toward the ceiling. "The stories are crap. The dialogue is crap. That's because most of the writing is supervised by a co-executive producer who's a world-class creator of crap. An individual neither of us would wipe our literary boots on. However—"

There had been another knock at the door, a timid one.

And Aidan shouted, "For fuck's sake, you little rabbit, just open the bloody thing and say what you've come to say."

The door inched open. The person peeking into the room was barely five feet tall. Very slender. With a captivating smile, eyes that were piercing green, and hair that was curly and strawberry blond. She looked like a remarkably attractive elf.

This was the same woman who had knocked earlier to say that Matt was wanted downstairs. And now, as she caught sight of him, she seemed flustered, at a loss for words.

Aidan laughed. "Open your little rosebud mouth, Danielle, and tell us what the hell you want."

Danielle was looking at Matt as she said, "The run-through for this week's show... They need you downstairs." She glanced at Aidan. "Both of you."

As she left, her focus was on Matt. The look she gave him was full of concern. It was evident that she was worried about him.

Matt didn't care.

Blowing smoke rings and watching them float toward the ceiling,

Aidan said, "What I need you to remember is that the crap on our show is extremely *popular* crap. Crap that's about to make a lot of people rich, including you."

For the first time since he entered the room, Aidan looked directly at Matt, and he seemed shocked. "Bloody hell. What's going on? You look like a man who's fallen into his own grave." Aidan rapidly stubbed out his cigarette.

"It's Ali," Matt said.

At the mention of Ali's name, Aidan leaned forward, elbows on his knees, hands tightly clasped. "What about Ali?"

"I can't give you the details. I promised her I wouldn't."

"Why would she specifically not want *me* to know?"

"She doesn't want anyone to know." Matt's jaw was tight. A muscle in his cheek was quivering.

Aidan glanced away, looking uncomfortable.

"The thing that happened, happened four days ago. She says she'll never forgive me, Aidan. Says she expects me to pay for it for the rest of my life."

Aidan's body language was tense, his tone cautious. "So we're talking about something *you* did to her?"

"Let's just say I made it possible."

"In what way?" Aidan lit another cigarette, a slight tremor in his hands.

Matt came around the desk to a chair directly across from Aidan. "It's like this…like a good-looking woman walking down a sidewalk in a tight, red dress. And a guy behind the wheel of an SUV takes his eyes off the road, for a split second, to look at her. And in that split second, a kid chases a ball into the street and the guy runs him over. The guy in the SUV did the damage. But the woman in the red dress made it easy for him to do it." Matt took a shuddering breath and said, "I made it easy for unforgivable damage to be done to my wife."

For a long beat, Aidan appeared to be struggling with what he wanted to say. Then he told Matt, "If you contributed to whatever it was that hurt Ali, maybe you do owe her...for a while. But if what happened wasn't a thing you planned, or a thing you wanted, at some point it's only right she calls the debt settled and lets you be free of it."

"I don't deserve to be free of it." Matt wasn't thinking only about Ali's rape; he was thinking about the other crimes, the ones he'd worked so hard to hide.

He was thinking about those steely fingers closing around his throat, trying to strangle him—the deadly fight in that Manhattan hotel room.

Aidan, meanwhile, was doing a one-handed shuffle of his lighter and cigarette pack. His movements, fluid and distracted, like a preoccupied gambler palming poker chips. "It sounds as if the only thing that really happened was you made a mistake. That's what human beings do. Isn't it?"

"It's bigger than that," Matt said. "Some debts can't ever be forgiven. They don't deserve to be."

"Your theory is complete rubbish." Aidan pocketed his cigarette pack and lighter. "Not being able to forgive is the only thing that's unforgivable." He waited for Matt to say something. Matt stayed quiet. Aidan stood up, ready to leave. "I'm hoping, for all our sakes, Ali's a better human being than you're giving her credit for."

Then, as Aidan walked out of the room, he told Matt, "Get yourself downstairs. We have work to do."

Matt didn't move. He was paralyzed by guilt. And by the disturbing worry that, soon, the secrets he'd tried so hard to keep buried were going to catch up with him.

Ali

LI HAD WALKED THROUGH A FRONT ENTRYWAY FLANKED BY glass panels etched with the word JOY. The irony hit her like a slap.

She wobbled a little. Then steadied herself by leaning against a pillar near the reception desk.

Ava was a few feet away, folding napkins at the antique pine sideboard that ran along the restaurant's north wall. Ali was surprised to see that the dining room was almost empty. Only three customers—a regular named Mr. Wallace, who had thinning hair the color of dried orange peels, was at one of the smaller tables where he'd barely touched his plate of eggs and was hunched over a smudged résumé, and two women in expensive yoga gear were at a table in the middle of the room, chatting over coffee and sharing a scone.

It had only been four days since Ali was attacked; she was in a haze of pain and confusion. For a moment, she wondered why the restaurant wasn't full. Thinking it was time for the breakfast rush. Then remembering it was already midmorning.

She let go of the pillar she'd been leaning against and began her trek across the dining room. Matt was outside in the car. Ali had asked him to drive her to the restaurant before he went to his office. And he was still there, at the curb, on the other side of the plate-glass window. From the minute she left the car, she was aware that he hadn't taken his eyes off her, yet she'd continued to walk away, refusing to acknowledge him.

Ali was halfway across the dining area now, her gaze meeting Ava's—and she understood Ava's gasp. It was in reaction to the haunted look in Ali's eyes and the hesitant way she was moving, as if some essential piece of her had been blown apart.

"In the name of the Blessed Mother, what has been done to you?" Ava swiftly put her arms around Ali, shielding her from the customers' curious glances. Ava's embrace was light and at the same time fiercely protective.

~

Strength and protection were gifts Ava had given Ali from the moment they'd met. When Ali had been in the walled garden at the back of her soon-to-be-opened restaurant. She was aching and blistered from working alongside the construction crew—day and night, for months—transforming a crumbling, quirky, century-old space into a tiny, beautiful, twenty-first-century restaurant.

Ali was shouting "Roses! We agreed on yellow roses!" while a Hispanic landscaper, pretending he didn't speak English, was delivering a river of red geraniums.

"No! No! You said you'd bring yellow roses!" Ali snatched up the geraniums, trying to give them back to the landscaper. As he blithely sidestepped her, they were interrupted by the sound of a woman's voice, saying a single word: "*Hola!*"

That voice stopped Ali and the landscaper in their tracks. It had music in it, like golden bells.

The woman to whom it belonged was standing in the doorway of the restaurant kitchen. She was young. Slender. Her dark hair gathered into a waist-length braid. Her eyes were luminous, and her skin was the color of golden-brown sugar. The fabric of her bright-pink dress was floating and silky. A silver cross hung from a length of magenta-colored ribbon loosely tied around her neck. She was pregnant. Her folded hands resting lightly on the swell of her belly.

When she called out her initial greeting, she had been addressing Ali. Now she was talking to the landscaper, engaging him with a sly grin, "*¿Le cobraste por las rosas? Bueno. Llevarás algo de dinero extra a tu casa.*"

The landscaper was laughing. "*Sí. Mucho dinero.*"

She scowled and whispered something in his ear. He immediately began to gather up the geraniums. "So sorry! I bring roses. Quick. Many, many roses. All yellow!"

The woman turned to Ali, serene. "He was trying to cheat. Taking money for expensive flowers and giving cheap ones." Her expression was impish. "I whispered to him that you are my sister-in-law, and if those lousy geraniums don't turn into roses real fast, my brother will arrive. And bust him open. Like a piñata."

Ali's laugh was cut short by a loud cannon-like bang from the restaurant's interior.

Both Ali and the woman rushed toward the kitchen door. As they ran, the woman told Ali, "My name is Ava. I see you have a restaurant coming here, and I need a job."

"Have you worked in a restaurant before?"

"Yes. I have food as part of me. In my country, in Belize, from when I was a girl, I helped with the cooking for a house full of people. I know good food. I know how to run a good kitchen."

At this point, Ali had disappeared through the kitchen doorway, wailing, "Jesus God, I don't believe this!"

A pipe in a brand-new wall had burst. Cold, slimy water was snaking around her ankles—and Ali, who hadn't slept for days, was in tears.

Ava, on the other hand, was tranquil. Wading through the dirty water, going toward the archway that separated the kitchen from the dining area—toward the earsplitting noise of pounding hammers and screaming drills. When Ava stepped into the archway, she called out two short sentences in fluent Spanish.

Forty-five minutes later, the restaurant's Latino construction crew had the broken pipe fixed and the kitchen floor clean and dry. The landscaper had returned with forests of yellow roses and was planting them in the walled garden. And Ava had made buttermilk biscuits and hot coffee.

The biscuits were featherlight, warm in Ali's mouth, melting with honey. The coffee, which was strong and bold, had been gentled with steamed milk and a dusting of cocoa powder. It was the first meal Ali had eaten all day. It tasted like heaven. When she'd finished, she sighed and told Ava, "Thank you."

And Ava said, "Please, you have a restaurant coming here... May I have a job?"

Without a flicker of hesitation, Ali answered, "Of course."

It had felt right to say yes to Ava. She'd come like an angel, bringing peace to chaos.

Now, the dream had come true, the restaurant was a reality, and Ava was once again acting as Ali's angel—nurturing her, protecting her.

Ava looked into Ali's eyes, seeing the pain. "I want to know what has happened. Come. We'll go into Sofie's nursery and close the door. And we will talk."

Sofie's nursery was an area in the kitchen that had originally been a large, walk-in pantry, with an arched window at one end. Ava had completely transformed it, painting the walls the color of Meyer lemons and covering the floor with a buttery-green carpet. In place of the pantry's heavy metal doors, Ava put sliding panels of woven bamboo that had the muted, ethereal gleam of sea glass. Then she'd furnished the little room with a playpen and a rocking chair, a crib, and shelves of baby toys. There was nowhere in the world Ali would rather be, but she told Ava, "I can't go, not right now."

Ali was groping for a chair at the nearest table, too weak to take another step. Ava went to the sideboard to pour a cup of coffee.

Ali's thoughts were on Sofie, the child who was so much like Ava. The child Ali dearly loved.

The first time Ali saw Sofie had been in the restaurant kitchen, early on a June morning. The door to the walled garden was open. The yellow roses were in full bloom. The air was cool and misty. And suddenly there had been the sound of music in it. The sound of that melodic greeting—"*Hola!*" And Ava was there in the doorway. Haloed by the morning sun and holding an oval basket. The small, exquisite ark in which her new baby was being carried into JOY.

Ali had raced across the kitchen and hugged Ava, delighted and surprised to see her. "You gave birth a week ago. You should be home, resting."

Ava's smile was radiant as she glanced down at the basket. "I am home. And this is my Sofie."

Ali looked into the basket, saw Sofie, and her heart melted. When she laid her finger on Sofie's arm, it was as soft and warm as a sun-ripened peach. "I don't want to ever take my eyes off her."

"You will never have to. Sofie will be yours to see whenever you want." Ava put Sofie's basket onto the wooden table at the far end of the kitchen and then slipped into a clean apron. "We are not here to visit. I am here to work."

In response to Ali's puzzled look, Ava asked, "Why are you surprised by this? Of course Sofie will be here, with me, every day. I am her mother. How can I teach her the things she needs to learn from me if I am not with her?"

"Are you having trouble finding a day-care provider?" Ali asked. "Because I could help you look for—"

Ava's laugh was lighthearted. "There is no problem with the finding. My landlady is a day-care mother...and she is in the apartment downstairs from me. Her name is Marcie. She is a very good person. Very nice." Ava lifted Sofie from the basket, cradling her close to her breast. "But this is my baby. She is my flesh. My heart."

Ava gazed down at Sofie, then looked at Ali with a potent mix of tender love and unwavering determination. "Marcie is a Baptist from Kansas, and I am Catholic from Belize. She cooks tuna, in a casserole. I make green corn dumplings and tamales." Ava flashed a rascal's grin. "Sometimes, like my grandmother's way, with chicken feet in the tamales." After a quick beat, Ava asked, "Do you understand what I am saying?"

Ali nodded and held her arms out. Ava transferred Sofie into Ali's embrace.

The kitchen had filled with cooks and waiters arriving for work, calling out their morning greetings in Spanish, and someone had hit the power button on the sound system. The room was alive with the rhythms of Latin music, the whoosh of the gas burners on the stoves, and the sharp smell of red peppers being thrown into hot pans.

"My friend Marcie and I do not put the same tastes into our children's mouths," Ava said. "We do not sing the same songs into their ears. If Sofie spends more time each day with Marcie than with me, she will grow up strong and fine. But she will be more from Kansas than from Belize. She will know more of the heart of Marcie than of me."

Ali kissed Sofie on the crown of her head and returned her to the basket on the long wooden table. She made sure that Sofie was facing the open kitchen doorway. On the other side of that doorway was a sea of yellow roses.

There was no more discussion. It was decided. The energy of Ali's restaurant kitchen and the serenity of its walled garden would become the fragrant, lyrical landscape of Sofie's babyhood. And Sofie would become a permanent part of Ali's heart.

"Being with Sofie will do you good," Ava was telling Ali. "But first we must talk." Ava put a cup of coffee on the table where Ali could reach it. "You are my dear friend. And something is terribly wrong. Let me help you."

Ali understood that Ava was offering unconditional love and acceptance. There was nothing she couldn't say to Ava, nothing she couldn't tell her. But Ali was too shredded to tell her story and explain what it had left in its wake. She only had strength enough to say, "I'm not a good person. I always thought I was, and I'm not."

Ali was talking about her anger toward Matt. She knew it was wrong to insist the rape was entirely his fault. But her anger was the only thing that was keeping her sane.

Ava seemed to know Ali didn't have the courage to clarify her comment about not being a good person. And to Ali's relief, Ava didn't ask any more questions. She put her hand over Ali's, and they sat together. Peaceably. Until Ava said, "What is it that has befallen you?"

Thinking about being attacked on the floor of her darkened apartment, Ali said, "It was the worst thing that'll happen to me in my entire life."

She had no idea that the worst was yet to come.

Morgan

MORGAN'S TEETH WERE CHATTERING—HER FEET FELT LIKE blocks of ice.

She hit the ignition switch, turned up the heater, and huddled into her coat. She hadn't expected a California winter to be so cold. An old man in a bulky jacket, the same person who had gone past the car earlier, was coming back toward it. He must've finished his morning walk and was heading home.

As soon as he got alongside the passenger door, he leaned down, jerky and arthritic. Tapping the window, squinting in at Morgan. "You been here a mighty long time. You got engine trouble?"

Fighting a skull-splitting headache, Morgan strained to reach across the passenger seat and lower the window. "I was…um…waiting for a friend."

"Is that so?" The old man scanned the emptiness of Morgan's car, checked the emptiness of the street, then looked at Morgan with suspicion. "Sorry you're sittin' in a parked car, all alone on Christmas Day. But you best go on home. Get out of the cold."

What she was being told was that this old man's next move would be to call the police. Morgan closed the window and shifted the car into Drive. While she pulled away from the curb, she watched the old man, and the front yard of Ali's house, disappear into the distance.

Morgan had been parked outside Ali's home since dawn—her eyes half-open, hair uncombed, her lips cracked and dry. Even though she was steadily drugging herself with sleeping pills, she hadn't slept in days. The only thing that had kept Morgan awake enough to make the drive had been her anger, and her hope.

After standing by and letting Matt shove Morgan through a doorway, bouncing her off a wall like sack of garbage, Ali hadn't called or texted. Hadn't reached out to Morgan in any way.

Morgan had come here half hoping for Ali to look out the window, see her, and invite her in for Christmas. She'd also come half hoping to find a way to hurt Ali for allowing her to be tossed through that doorway—then abandoning her.

But what to do? Take a can of spray paint and scrawl *Bitch* across Ali's pristine front door? Or maybe stand in the yard with a bullhorn, broadcasting to the neighbors who Ali really was: a cheating wife and a sister who was cruel and disloyal?

Or should it be something bigger? Something that would put a final stop to the endless battle between herself and her twin. Should she set fire to 76 Paradise Lane? Burn it to the ground with Ali in it?

Morgan drove away from her sister's home and into the void that was Christmas Day, with no idea what she should do. Or what she wanted to do. Or what she might do without meaning to.

Ali

ALI CAME OUT OF A DEEP SLEEP, EYES WIDE, FRIGHTENED BY A dream.

Snow-white silk pajamas. A room made of white tiles. Clear water in a crystal bowl. Transforming into blood, rumbling like a volcano. And the blood spinning into a dark, thick funnel. Splattering, heavy and wet, onto the white silk of the pajamas.

It was the soaking, sticky feel of the blood that woke Ali. Leaving her bolt upright in bed—screaming.

When the scream was gone, she lay down again. Shivering. The dream was how she saw herself. Bloodied, torn apart, and dirty. It was the reason she was so adamant about keeping the rape a secret. She'd always been the golden girl, shining and perfect. And she was afraid if anyone knew what had happened, she'd be seen as tarnished, less wholesome, less lovable.

Other than her one trip to the restaurant, Ali hadn't left the house in the three and a half weeks since the attack. She'd stayed hidden, letting all the phone calls go to voice mail and then having Matt return the calls with a rehearsed story about Ali having the flu, which was always followed with a quick good-bye.

After almost a month of hiding, Ali was incredibly lonely, staring at the phone, wanting it to ring. Wanting it to be Morgan. From the moment she left Ali's house the day after the rape, Morgan had maintained an unbroken silence. She had cut Ali off completely, something she'd never done before.

Having that silence still there, on this particular morning, was killing Ali. She had truly believed this was when Morgan would come back. Because it was Christmas. Ali and Morgan had never had a Christmas morning when they didn't communicate with each other—and Morgan had never spent Christmas on her own, away from family and Rhode Island.

Ali knew without a doubt that her sister was as lonely as she was. She could feel it in her bones. Yet she continued to lie in the middle of her bed, unable to reach for the phone.

For the first time in their lives, Ali didn't have the strength to rescue Morgan.

The rape had put Ali emotionally underwater and held her there. She was in the process of drowning.

～

Ali finally came downstairs a little before noon, wearing red-and-white polka-dot pajamas and with her hair gathered in a loose ponytail. She was wandering through half-empty rooms where the furniture, most of it factory new and still mummy-wrapped in plastic, was scattered at crazy angles. Chairs and tables abandoned where the strangers who delivered them had left them.

Her reflection in one of the curtainless windows startled her— showed how vacant she looked. What happened that night in the apartment had drained the life out of her.

Today is Christmas, and it's so different from last Christmas, she thought. *Our first Christmas as a married couple. It was like being in heaven. Matt and I were in the apartment, and it was still dark when I woke up. Matt had gotten out of bed to light dozens of cream-colored candles. He put them in every room. On every shelf, every tabletop. In every corner. He made cranberry waffles shaped like Christmas stars and brought them to me on a tray, with a pitcher of warm maple syrup that smelled like home, like the holidays.*

We had breakfast in bed—and I told him, "I'm in love with the most magnificent man in the world." When we got out of bed, we went into the living room and sat on the floor, surrounded by the tree lights and the flickering candles. Matt gave me a silver charm bracelet. The charms were tiny kitchen things…little whisks and spoons hardly bigger than eyelashes. It was the most beautiful present anyone ever gave me. Matt and I stayed beside the Christmas tree all morning. Nestled in each other's arms. Letting our kisses carry us into sleep…our lovemaking drowsy and tender.

Ali was looking around the cold, lifeless living room of her new house, the place she and Matt had been so eager to leave their cozy apartment for—and she was grieving for what had died.

∿

Ali's wandering trip through the house eventually led her into the kitchen. Matt was there, shaved and showered, briskly taking plates and napkins to the table.

The light in the room was too bright; she ducked her head and put her hand over her eyes. Matt pulled the cord at the side of the kitchen window, dropping the shade, and then went back to setting the table. He didn't look at Ali. And she didn't look at him. In the weeks since the rape, it had been nothing but distance between them.

When Matt spoke, it was in a monotone. "After we eat, we could go in the living room and have a fire…might make it seem more like Christmas."

Ali's shrug was vague. "Yeah. Maybe."

"I got a tree yesterday." Matt's face was blank. "I was going to surprise you, but then I realized I didn't know where the decorations were." He had moved to the kitchen counter and was making sandwiches.

Ali sat at the table. Absentmindedly turning her wedding ring in a slow circle—it felt cold and heavy on her finger. After a while, she glanced at Matt and at the sandwiches he was preparing. "Until I woke up this morning, I'd forgotten that today was Christmas. I should've asked Ava to send some food over from the restaurant."

And Matt said, "It doesn't matter. I've never minded having peanut butter and jelly on Christmas."

Ali blinked, surprised—wondering, *When, and where, were peanut butter sandwiches what you ate for Christmas dinner?*

She knew Matt's parents were dead and he was an only child, and that he didn't have any family; she'd known it from the beginning of their relationship. She'd explained it to the police the night Matt disappeared after the book signing in Rhode Island. But Matt had always described his childhood as "normal, average, middle class." How could a Christmas meal of peanut butter sandwiches fit into that picture?

If it had been three and a half weeks earlier—if it had been before the rape—Ali would've cared about the answer. But her closeness to Matt was steadily eroding, and her thoughts had already moved on. She was inside a flash of memory...*being attacked on the floor of the apartment, inches away from that broken lock on the patio door.*

Matt dutifully continued making sandwiches. And Ali was furious with him for not fixing the lock. She couldn't let go of it. Her only way to deal with chaos of the attack was to turn it into an explainable event. Something manageable that could have been prevented with a couple of screws and a power drill.

Ali sensed Matt waiting for her to talk to him. She continued to sit, wordlessly, at the kitchen table. Turning her wedding ring around and around on her finger.

Finished with the sandwiches, Matt stared into an undefined mid-distance. "I'm sorry."

Ali said, "I know," and went back to steadily turning her ring.

There was a long space of nothingness.

Then the ring slipped off her finger, clattering onto the table.

Matt winced. As though the sound of Ali's wedding ring hitting the table had caused him physical pain. "I don't know what to do, Al. I don't know what else to say. I'm sorry."

Ali's response was, "I'm sorry, too." But even as she said it, she wondered what it meant. Was she was sorry about how much she and Matt were hurting? Or sorry because she was so dangerously close to wanting their life together to be over?

Matt moved to the sink and stayed there, staring out the window.

Ali picked up her wedding ring, holding it in her hand, weighing her decision. Eventually, she slipped the ring back onto her finger. "I love you," she whispered.

Her voice got stronger as she said, "I want to forgive you. I just don't know if I can."

Matt's gaze never left the gray winter landscape on the other side of the window. "I understand."

The look in his eyes was so clearly from some other place and time, it made Ali shiver.

◠

Wanting to escape the deadness that had been in Christmas Day, Ali got up early the next morning and did what she hadn't done in weeks. She went to work.

The restaurant was on a holiday schedule, open only for breakfast. The mood was festive. The dining area of the gracious old building was glorious—its glossy black-and-white floors and hammered tin ceiling washed in clear winter light streaming through the plate-glass windows hung with lace curtains the color of whipped cream. Some of the tables were marble topped; others, farmhouse plain and covered in white tablecloths—all of them accented with tiny crystal vases brimming with holiday greenery. The air smelled of oranges and coffee and cinnamon.

It was as if Christmas had come alive in one of the drawings from MaryJoy O'Conner's portfolio.

JOY was packed with customers. The most demanding ones were monopolizing a table in the center of the room—a pair of teenage girls and two small, unruly children.

Rushing between the kitchen and the dining area, filling in as a waitress, Ali had been trying to gently encourage the two girls to pay their check, which had been on the tabletop for over an hour. The girls had refused to budge.

Ali was ready to scream. Ava, who was dealing with a long line of people waiting to be seated, shot a scowl in the direction of the teenagers, silently telling Ali, *They need to go.*

The two small children had started squealing and throwing food at each other, sliming the floor with scrambled eggs and marmalade. The girls were chatting and texting.

Before she could stop herself, Ali marched over to the table and stripped away the plates, the centerpiece, and the tablecloth. Then she grabbed a wet towel, dropped to her knees, and began to clean up the mess on the floor. When she finished, she gave the teenagers a withering look and growled, "Out. This instant. Breakfast is over!"

One of the girls immediately shouted to Ava, "This grinchy woman who's our waitress is a total nightmare. If I were you, I'd get rid of her. It's like she thinks she owns the place."

The absurdity of that statement released the tiniest bit of pressure and made life bearable again. Bringing Ali a surprise—the sound of her own laughter.

She was enjoying the moment, unburdened. And completely unaware of what was happening on the other side of the front window.

A beige Honda was driving past the restaurant at a crawl. Repeatedly making U-turns. Then coming back again.

The grim-faced driver was Morgan. And her attention was locked on Ali.

~

Morgan's strange surveillance continued to go unnoticed by Ali and ended after the restaurant, on its holiday schedule, closed early.

Ali was in the kitchen with Ava. Bundling Sofie into her stroller. Getting Ava and Sofie ready to go home.

Just as Ali and Ava were saying good-bye, holiday visitors arrived— Jessica and Logan, coming in through the door to the walled garden, bringing Christmas presents and excitement.

Within minutes, Ali was preparing an impromptu brunch. She invited Ava to stay. And, in what seemed like no time at all, a party had happened. The room was loud with laughter and cooking clatter.

Jessica was using a soup ladle as a gavel, banging it on the wooden table at the far end of the kitchen, shouting, "Hey. Hold it down. I have something to say!"

Sofie, now seven months old, was in her high chair, keeping up a nonstop stream of baby jabber. Ali was busy making brioche French toast and lemon-ricotta pancakes. Ava was working on fresh fruit for a salad. And Logan, who'd been asked to fry thick-cut strips of applewood-smoked bacon, was at the griddle.

"Will somebody *please* listen? I have an announcement." Jessica raised her voice. "Delivering Christmas presents isn't the only reason Logan and I came here today!"

"It'll have to wait, Jess." Ali held up a stoneware platter stacked with French toast and lemon pancakes. "Brunch is served!"

This, for some reason, made Sofie giggle. Ava leaned over and tickled her. Sofie giggled again.

Ali asked if the bacon was ready, and Jessica handed over a bacon-filled plate, telling her, "I want you to know this is Logan's signature dish. He only makes it for very special occasions."

"*Bacon* is a signature dish?"

"Absolutely. And his backup showstopper is buttered toast."

Ava passed between Ali and Jessica, bringing the fruit salad to the table, playfully saying, "You are a lucky woman, Jessica, to have such a talented husband."

"I am a very lucky woman." Jessica took a dramatic pause. "Which brings me to my big announcement. Frying bacon and burning a piece of toast aren't my husband's only talents. It turns out he's pretty good at making babies, too."

The lightheartedness in Ali suddenly dimmed. She was startled, envious. "Jess. You're pregnant?"

"I've been trying to tell you for days. I called a hundred times, but all I got was voice mail."

"I've been a little distracted." A moment passed before Ali realized she'd stopped talking, and when she said, "But, Jess, I'm so happy for you," it was an awkward combination of gladness and jealousy.

Jessica only seemed to hear the gladness; she was glowing with delight. "I'm three months along. We didn't want to make the announcement till we were sure everything was okay. And it is!"

"Many, many congratulations." Ava clapped her hands.

Ali was fighting tears, forcing a smile.

Ava clapped her hands again. Sofie spontaneously did the same.

Everyone laughed. And Sofie crowed with delight.

Ali went to one of the refrigerators and brought out a bottle of champagne, taking longer than she needed to, waiting to get her emotions under control. A baby was something Ali wanted desperately and couldn't have, because it had been pushed aside by the opening of the restaurant and then buried by the trauma of that night in the apartment.

Ali was truly glad for Jessica, and infinitely sad for herself, as she called out, "Let's drink to the new parents and their new baby!"

Ava embraced Jessica, saying, "You must be very happy."

"We're so excited we're practically delirious!" Jessica was beaming, looking at Logan.

Following the direction of Jessica's gaze, Ali expected to see that Logan's enthusiasm was as bright as Jessica's. But it wasn't.

He seemed uncomfortable and trying to play it off as a joke. "What's the big deal? All I did was what my wife told me to do. I got her pregnant."

"How does it feel," Ali asked, "knowing you'll have somebody looking up to you, following in your footsteps for the rest of your life?"

Logan shrugged. "I guess I've never thought about it."

Jessica put her arm around him, gave him a teasing grin. "I think the boy's finally admitting it. All he thinks about is sex."

Logan stepped away from Jessica. "Okay, enough. I've done my time in the hot seat." He picked up an empty plate from a stack on the table and began piling food onto it. "My wife's knocked up. Nothing more to discuss."

Logan's flippant attitude grated on Ali. While she was filling three flutes with champagne, she said, "Are you kidding? There's a *lot* more to discuss."

"Like what?" Logan asked.

"Well…for instance, are you guys going to find out if it's a girl or a boy? Or will you hold out for the surprise?"

Logan passed a glass of champagne to Ava. There was a clumsy silence. He was obviously waiting for Jessica to answer Ali's question.

"The mother-to-be plans to stay uninformed and surprised," Jessica announced.

Not liking the way Jessica was being treated, Ali glared at Logan. "And what about the Bacon King? What are your plans?"

"What plans do I need?" Logan seemed annoyed.

Jessica sounded mildly exasperated. "For Christ's sake, Logan…all kinds of plans."

"Like what?"

"I don't know…like are you going to make a video of our baby being born?"

"And then what? Show it later at parties?"

"Don't be a dope." Jessica gave him a frown. He walked away. Jessica looked at Ava, eager for information. "What do you think we should do? Did Sofie's father shoot a birthing video?"

"It was not possible. He was not with us." Ava's tone was matter-of-fact.

Ali put down her champagne glass, listening closely. Ava was an obsessively private person. This was the first time Ali had ever heard Ava mention Sofie's father.

"Where was he?" Jessica asked.

"In the Marines," Ava said. "In Afghanistan."

"Oh. Is he still deployed? Has he had a chance to see her yet?"

Ava smoothed the skirt of the yellow apron she was wearing, each of her movements restrained and deliberate. "He did not see her. And now he is no longer alive."

Ali gasped. "Ava, I'm so sorry to hear that." Then she murmured, "Oh my God, he never got to hold his only child."

"I thought that, too. For a time." Ava glanced down, carefully folding her hands. "But I discovered he had already had three children to hold in his arms. And a wife."

Ali didn't know what to say.

Ava's expression was serene. "Sofie and I are alone. But we are fine." She turned to Ali. "In fact, we have just received some very good news. There is to be a master cooking class in the Napa Valley. One of the students has unexpectedly declined." Excitement crept into Ava's voice. "I have been accepted to attend in her place."

"Ava, that's fantastic!" Ali said.

"When I begin, in a few months"—Ava lifted Sofie from her high chair and cuddled her—"will you watch after Sofie for me while I am gone?"

"Yes, of course." Ali's response was enthusiastic, eager. "I can keep her for as long as you want."

"It will be for two days only."

Jessica reached out to stroke Sofie's hair. "What a precious little angel. If you were leaving her with me, I wouldn't care if you never came back."

Jessica looked from Sofie to Ava to Ali and said, "I love you guys. Let's make this a tradition. No matter who else comes or goes, the four us…Ali, Ava, Sofie, and me…Christmas brunch, here at JOY. Same time next year. Promise."

Ali raised her champagne glass. "Same time next year. The four of us. I promise."

Same time next year. The four of us. Ali had made a vow that would be impossible to keep. In a matter of weeks, one of the four would be dead.

Less than a mile from JOY,
two days after Christmas.
Terror.
White cotton, ripped and torn.
And a woman's green eyes—so very wide open.

Ali

ELEGANT STONE WALLS, LUSH GREEN LAWNS, AND IRON GATES were on the other side of the truck's window. Ali and Aidan Blake were driving through an upscale neighborhood on the western edge of Pasadena, on a street called Patrician Way.

Aidan shot her a look that was undisguised, unembarrassed lust.

It touched a nerve that had been raw in Ali ever since the night of her attack. Determined to sound controlled and businesslike, she told Aidan, "I appreciate you giving me this ride. But—"

Aidan cut her off. "No worries. Matt had meetings all morning and I didn't. Which is why I took the liberty of taking his place. I'm more than available."

He shook a fresh cigarette from the pack in his lap. After he lit the cigarette, he blew out a long stream of smoke. "Will you want me to come and collect you later?"

"No. All my car needed was an adjustment to something in the computer. It'll be ready right after lunch. My friend Jessica can take me to pick it up."

Ali moved closer to the truck's passenger door, wanting to be as far from Aidan as possible. There had always been something about him that made her nervous.

Aidan studied the expensive homes they were passing. "Whatever your friend Jessica does for a living, she must do it very well." When Ali didn't answer, he gave her a slow, sidelong look. "Or is it that your friend doesn't do anything? And it's whatever her husband does that's going so brilliantly?" Aidan nodded, indicating the spectacular array of houses. "Makes you the slightest bit jealous, does it?"

"No," Ali said.

"That's good. You being jealous would be a fucking waste of energy." He finished his cigarette and stubbed it out. "If this television show Matt and I came up with is only a fraction of the hit everyone's expecting, it won't be long before you'll be taking up residence in a neighborhood twice as posh as this one."

She scowled at him. He was goading her, annoying her. "Posh isn't who I am. I want kids…and I'm happy with the house I have, a place that looks like a home, not a hotel."

Aidan chuckled and returned his attention to the road.

Ali was uncomfortable with how male Aidan was. In every way. From the deep rumble of his voice to the rough handsomeness of his face to the authority with which he was maneuvering his massive, gleaming F-250 through the hairpin turns leading toward the top of the hill. She was uncomfortable because he was a man she didn't really know, and she was in a confined space with him. The awfulness of her attack was still too fresh. She desperately wanted this trip to come to an end. Without warning, Aidan brought the truck to a screeching stop. Ali gave a startled shout.

Aidan's reaction was a belly laugh. "No need to scream. You're as safe as in your mother's arms." He grinned, amused that he was making her nervous. "Look." He gestured toward the numbers on a copper mailbox just outside the truck's passenger window. "This *is* the address you asked to be delivered to, right?"

Ali reached for the door handle, ready to bolt. Then out of nowhere—so fast it confused her as to whether or not it had actually happened—Aidan kissed her. The kiss was warm and firm. It terrified her. Ali scrambled out of the truck, slamming the door, shooting him a lethal glare through the open passenger window.

It wasn't until after Aidan had driven away that she discovered the taste of his cigarettes on her lips. It made her feel dirty, violated.

Ali was trembling as she walked up the driveway toward Jessica's house, trying to make sense of Aidan Blake. Was he was simply an idiot, an adult with the crude impulses of an adolescent? Or was he something much worse?

～

"It's like you've been hit in the head with a hammer. No matter what I say, you're only half listening to me. Where are you?"

"I'm listening to every word, really. I was just thinking about... um...being in California," Ali lied. "I'm not you, Jess...the tall blond with yards of style. I'm not sure I fit in." She wasn't ready to talk about what had been preoccupying her—Aidan Blake and his unwelcome kiss.

"You were born for California. Everyone is," Jessica said. "It's paradise."

Ali and Jessica were having lunch: curried shrimp salad served on wafer-thin coral-colored plates paired with sea-green linen napkins. The salad had been accompanied by a perfectly chilled white wine for Ali and sparkling water for Jessica, served in stemware the color of dusty-pink rose petals.

The view from the patio was breathtaking—sweeping from the hilltop where Jessica's house was located across the downtown Los Angeles skyline, all the way out to a hazy strip of the Pacific Ocean, glittering in the distance.

"Just look at this. We're having lunch outside, Ali. In *January*. Try that back in Rhode Island. You'd be freezing your ass off." Jessica laughed her bawdy, tough-girl laugh, a raucous guffaw that belonged on a fun-loving waitress in a biker bar.

Hearing that familiar laugh, Ali relaxed, felt safer. "Want to know something, Jess? One of the best things that ever happened to me was you showing up as my college roommate."

"Damn straight," Jessica agreed.

After that, they scooted their chairs back from the table, and Ali let herself enjoy the rest of the afternoon.

She talked to Jessica for hours—about Jessica's pregnancy and old friends and Rhode Island and what it was like to be married.

"All I thought about was *getting* married," Jessica said, "never about *being* married. But, hey, I was lucky. I landed a California boy who makes a ton of money in health care and loves me like crazy." She stopped to refill Ali's wineglass. "Did I tell you Logan got a big promotion? I'm a little pissed that now he's spending so much time in his company's regional offices…traveling all over the state instead of all over me but…" Jessica gave an apologetic giggle. "But enough about me. What about you? What did you focus on in the beginning, the wedding or the marriage?"

Her marriage, Matt—the jumble of blame and disconnection—it was too painful to discuss. Ali took a deep breath. "What I thought about was how great it would feel to finally be taken care of. I wanted it so much…to be protected, looked after. I was tired of always being the one taking care of somebody else."

"So. How sweet is life without the human ankle monitor?"

Ali's shrug said *Go ahead, tell me I'm crazy*, and at the same time, she was trying not to cry. "I haven't seen my sister, haven't heard a word from her, since the day after my housewarming. And I miss her."

"I can't believe you said that!" Ali's comment had Jessica choking on the sip of water she'd just taken. "Maybe it's because I'm an only child, but from how I see it, the hold Morgan's got on you is totally nuts."

"Jess. Morgan and I were born eight minutes apart. A few hundred seconds, at the very beginning of my life, was the only time I couldn't actually feel Morgan's breath on the back of my neck."

Jessica arched an eyebrow. "And you're offering this up as a good thing...or a bad thing?"

"I guess what I'm talking about is something that's in a photograph my mom has of me when I was a baby, taking my first step. I'm half tipped over, with this look on my face that's sort of scared and sort of crazy determined, all mixed together. And it's because Morgan's right behind me, trying to take her first step, too. She's grabbing on to the back of my shirt. And you can see how much I feel her being back there, weighing me down. Making me know I'm going to fall... at the same time making me know that I can't fall, because I'm not allowed to. Because I'm the stronger one, and she needs me...she needs me to keep standing up...for both of us."

Jessica's Salvadoran housekeeper had cleared the lunch plates and was now bringing out a tray filled with miniature, intricately frosted cupcakes.

Jessica waited until the housekeeper went back into the house before saying, "That sister of yours isn't a little kid anymore. Shake her loose. Make her stagger through life on her own. The same way the rest of us have to."

"It's not that simple, Jess. I can't just 'shake her loose.' I owe her."

"Bullshit." Jessica yawned and popped one of the cupcakes into her mouth. "You haven't run around deliberately shoving her into the shadows. No crime. Therefore, no guilt." She waited for Ali to agree, and when she didn't, Jessica said, "Okay. So you think you're on the hook for how shitty her life has been. But do you honestly believe you can run up a debt to another person that's so monumental it can't ever be repaid? Shouldn't there be a time, after you've done your absolute best, when you get to slap an expiration date on the damn thing and be done with it?"

Ali was remembering the last glimpse she'd had of her sister—
the devastated look on Morgan's face as she was tossed out into the
hallway of Ali's new house. "If there is an expiration date, Jess, how
could I ever be heartless enough to use it?"

Just as Jessica was about to answer, both she and Ali were surprised
to see Logan coming across the patio toward them. The instant he
arrived at the table, Jessica gave him a kiss—and he told Ali, "You're
looking good. As always."

"Hey, aren't you supposed to be on a plane to San Diego?"
Jessica asked.

"I'm on my way to the airport. Forgot my laptop."

Jessica quickly headed toward the house. "You left it on the
dresser. I'll get it. Grab some wine and say hi to Ali."

Logan relaxed into the seat Jessica had just vacated. Ali scooted her
chair an inch or two farther from the table. For a second time in the
same day, she was alone with a man who made her uncomfortable.

Her initial introduction to Logan had been at the wedding in
Newport. Since moving to California, Ali had only interacted with
him a few times, and never without Jessica. She was trying to think
of something to say—all she could come up with was "This view
is spectacular."

"That's what I was thinking." He looked at her and smiled. "Where
have you been keeping yourself? What is it with you and that husband
of yours? You're like hermits. All of us should get together."

"Well, it'll be a while before we can plan anything…"

"Right. Jess mentioned that Matt's job has him pretty busy. She
says you told her a lot of nights he doesn't get home until one or two
in the morning." Logan chuckled. "Hard to believe he never takes
any time off to go a little nuts, have a little fun."

There was an undercurrent of sexual innuendo in what Logan had
just said. Before she'd been slammed onto the floor by her attacker, it

probably wouldn't have bothered her—but now, Logan's comment made Ali's skin crawl.

He was stretching his legs out, casually crossing them. He rocked his heel and tapped Ali's ankle with his foot. "Not exactly a fan of mine, are you?"

"I guess I don't know enough about you to be one. The most time I've ever spent with you was at your wedding. And that was what? Maybe an hour or two?"

Ali didn't like Logan. He was too arrogant, too self-involved. And there had been talk that at his Newport wedding, someone thought they'd seen him on one of the mansion terraces, "going for it" with a woman who wasn't Jessica. It was only a rumor, but the minute she'd heard it, Ali's instincts about Logan made her believe it was true.

"So what are you guys chatting about?" Jessica asked. She had returned with the laptop.

Logan pushed away from the table. "We were talking about Ali's opinion of the view out here."

Jessica slipped her arm around Logan, saying to Ali, "We were so lucky to get this place. We—"

Logan had taken the laptop from Jessica, telling her, "Gotta go." Crossing the terrace, making his exit, he added, "I'll call you tonight."

Jessica watched Logan until he disappeared from view, tracking him like he was a wilderness she was trying to map. Then she asked Ali, "Okay, where were we? What were we talking about before he interrupted us?"

"A million different things. Morgan. And marriage. You were telling me about living in California...that it's been paradise."

"Yeah. It has been. Pretty much." A frown flitted across Jessica's brow.

"What do you mean...pretty much?"

Jessica sat at the table, picked up her glass, and took a swallow of water. "It's just that, right after we bought this house, something really sick happened."

Ali was startled by the sudden shift in Jessica's mood. The playfulness was gone, replaced by something worried and tense.

"There were rapes," Jessica was saying. "A bunch of them."

The word *rape* cut into Ali like a razor.

"And the thing that made it truly creepy? All the victims seemed to be describing the same guy. His trademark was a name he called all the women, the name of a summer wildflower. And he always took their underwear." Jessica shuddered. "When one of the attacks happened a couple of blocks from here, I went totally bonkers...started collecting articles from newspapers, downloads from the Internet. Information about assaults that occurred all over the state. Anything that sounded even vaguely similar to the local ones."

"Why did you do that?" Ali couldn't believe the weirdness of this conversation.

"I don't know." Jessica seemed lost in thought. "I really went off the deep end for a while. Logan was ready to have me committed. All the stuff is in a file folder I have somewhere."

Ali was on the edge of her seat, her heart pounding. "Did they find out who he was? Did they ever catch him?"

"I don't know. After a while, I told myself I needed to stop thinking about it." Jessica shook her head, sounding bewildered. "I'm sorry. I don't even know why I told you all of that."

Aidan Blake's cigarette-sour kiss and now this unnerving story from Jessica. It was too much.

Ali had to grip the arms of her chair to keep herself steady.

She felt like Alice, plummeting down the rabbit hole.

Morgan

MORGAN FLATTENED HERSELF AGAINST THE LIVING ROOM WALL. Hoping they hadn't seen her.

But they must have heard her moving around. The walls were thin in her new home—the rear half of an old Craftsman-style duplex on Garfield Road in South Pasadena.

Now the people outside were knocking again. Harder. Louder.

Morgan edged toward the door, painfully aware that when she opened it, the people on the other side would see how undone and pathetic she was. The whole place was visible from the front door. The empty living room. The bedroom with nothing in it but an air mattress, a TV, and a shadeless lamp Morgan had found in the back of a closet. The kitchen, with its chipped Formica-topped table and chrome-legged chairs, castoffs the former tenant hadn't bothered to throw away.

Just before she opened the door, Morgan stopped, looked over her shoulder, nervously catching his eye and saying, "Shhh." Then she swung the door open and faced the tanned, athletic-looking couple on the porch.

The man was clutching one of Morgan's signs.

A few weeks ago, when she'd put up those signs, she'd been fervently hoping somebody exactly like these two would appear. When nobody did, she was terribly upset. But now that somebody was finally here, Morgan wanted them to go away.

"This is the right place, isn't it?" The man held up the sign. Morgan wasn't seeing it.

She was back in the moment when it all began...*walking home from the grocery store in the early evening. Taking a shortcut down a tree-lined alley. She knew she was being followed; she could feel it. Her pulse was racing. She was picking up the pace, breaking into a run. So was her pursuer. The end of the alley was only a few yards away. It might as well have been miles. She'd never make it. He was gaining on her so fast she could hear his panting breath. She had to find a way to save herself. She stopped and whirled around to face him—pleading. "Don't hurt me. Please don't hurt me."*

And out of the blue, she was laughing, hysterically. Collapsing. Weak with relief. Seeing that she wasn't being stalked by someone trying to hurt her. She was being followed by a small, biscuit-colored dog.

The dog was looking up at her expectantly, tail wagging, vulnerable and sweet. The moment of fright had passed. And now all Morgan wanted was to get home, close the door, and go back to trying to survive the pain of being locked out of Ali's life. Heartache was the only thing she had room for.

For several blocks, Morgan determinedly shooed the dog away, and he happily ignored her. Which eventually left Morgan with no choice but to talk to him.

It was the end of the weekend, and other than a brief thank-you to the clerk who'd bagged her groceries a few minutes ago, the dog was the only individual Morgan had spoken to since leaving work on Friday. At first, she said things like "Go away" and "Get out of here." Then, while he waited patiently for her to unlock the door to her duplex, she explained, "I'm not crazy about animals. I never have been. Go hook up with a nice PETA person." But he followed her into the house, gazing at her with those big, brown eyes... begging her to take care of him.

She went into the kitchen to put down the grocery bags, and the dog went with her. She kept talking to him; he kept listening. She reminded him that she expected him to leave. He lay down at her feet and gave a little sigh.

Morgan had a pang of concern, wondering if he was hungry, and wondering what she had in the kitchen that she could feed him.

As she kneeled to stroke his head, surprised by how soft and warm his fur was, she told him, "I've never been responsible for taking care of anything that was alive, anything with feelings. The whole idea makes me really uncomfortable."

In response to that news, he licked her hand.

And Morgan told him he could stay...but only until she found him a good home.

The next day, she had put up "Dog Found" flyers with the dog's picture and her phone number, hoping his owner would come for him. A week later, she switched to flyers that announced "Free Dog to Good Home." She'd done it because, as she'd already explained, the idea of being responsible, being the leader, made her uncomfortable.

But now she'd gotten to know him. They were friends, and things were different. Morgan wasn't sure what she wanted to do.

The man on her porch was reading aloud from the sign she'd posted. "Healthy dog. Free. To good home."

Morgan was panicking a little.

The man craned his neck, trying to see into the house, while the woman asked Morgan, "Is there a problem?"

As if sensing Morgan's distress, the dog had appeared out of nowhere. Resting against her leg, warm and loyal—making her think about how nice it was to come home to him. How her spirits lifted every time she walked in the door and saw how happy he was to see her. How she wasn't so lonely anymore.

The people on the porch exchanged impatient glances.

Morgan was about to say, *Maybe those signs were a mistake. My dog depends on me. He needs me.*

She bit her lip, thinking about money. About the job she'd managed to find at a local museum known for its collection of fine art and rare historical documents. Her new boss, Mr. Dupuis, a dapper gentleman in a well-tailored suit, had hired Morgan for a position that came with an extravagant title and an extremely small paycheck. She was thinking about the price of dog food. And vet bills. And leashes and chew toys. And pooper-scoopers. And dog groomers. She was thinking about how much work it was to take care of another living thing—how much easier it was not to have to.

"We can take him right now, if that helps." The man was enthusiastically reaching for the dog.

Morgan blocked him—remembering how things were before that walk home from the market. How dead the duplex had been. And how, from the moment the dog arrived, he'd lit up the place with energy and life. How he'd transformed three desolately empty rooms into a cozy place where Morgan was loved.

Morgan swallowed hard. This was a turning point. A decision that would, on some level, define who she was as a human being.

She glanced away, then looked back at the man on the porch.

Her voice cracking as she said, "Okay."

Ali

BEING HIT WITH A LEAD PIPE. THEN BEING HIT AGAIN. NOT knowing how you're still standing. And the only thought in your head is *Please God, don't let this be true.*

That's was what it was like for Ali, holding the phone to her ear, in the darkest part of the night—listening to a woman named Marcie say, "Well, I guess I've told you everything. I should probably let you go."

Ali was staring at nothing, continuing to hold the phone until, at some point, it dropped to the floor.

Matt, who'd been sleeping in the study since Ali's attack, appeared in the bedroom doorway, worried. "It's the middle of the night. Who was that?"

Ali slowly shook her head. She couldn't remember the woman's name. Couldn't remember anything except the incomprehensible story the woman had just told her.

"What's going on?" Matt asked.

Ali looked up at him. Dazed. "Ava's dead."

Morgan

A FTER THE MAN ON THE PORCH HAD TOLD MORGAN, "WE CAN take him right now if that helps," and Morgan had said, "Okay," there had been a moment of indecision before Morgan rapidly added, "I'm sorry. There's a new plan. Things have changed."

Now, four months later, Morgan was contentedly curled up on her sofa with the dog lying beside her. She was on the phone with Sam, telling him, "That's when I felt everything about me go in a different direction."

"In the beginning, why do you think you were so afraid of keeping the dog?" Sam asked.

"I'm not sure. It seemed like such a huge change. The idea of taking care of somebody else was scary. Like I'd have to become a completely different person."

"Change is never easy," Sam said. "And, as much as you always resented being the one who was taken care of, you probably sensed what hard work it was to be the person doing the caretaking."

"What do you mean?"

"You've often talked about your sister having the easier life… because she's the strong one. When the dog followed you home, asking to be dependent on you, you knew it would change everything. You'd have to step up and be the leader. You understood the responsibilities it would bring. The same ones that were on your sister when you made it her duty to take care of you."

"Maybe," Morgan said. "All I know is that I'm glad he's here."

The dog had nestled in, warm and so close that Morgan could feel the comforting beat of his heart.

"What did you name him?"

"He followed me home from a Ralph's supermarket and…" Morgan smiled. "The truth is, he kind of looks like a Ralph. And that's what I named him. Ralph."

There was a soft chuckle from Sam, followed by a brief silence and a change of mood. "So deciding to keep Ralph was the tipping point?"

"Yeah. That's when I had the courage to step up and be different. But I'd known for a long time that I needed to change, and what made me realize it was something that happened between me and Ali."

Morgan took a deep, trembling breath. "Just before Christmas, on the night Ali moved into her new house, her friend Ava was there with her baby. When Ava told me how close she and Ali were, like sisters, I hated it. I felt like I'd been erased from Ali's life. I don't think I've ever been so sacred or angry. By the time I got upstairs, I was totally out of control." Morgan's voice went quiet with shame. "The minute I saw Ali, I knew something was wrong. She didn't want to explain it, and I was so caught up in needing her to pay attention to me, I didn't take the time to find out what was going on with her."

Tears filled Morgan's eyes as she said, "A few minutes later, something happened that made me furious, and I told my sister I hoped whatever was wrong with her was really terrible…and I knew in my bones that it was."

"What made you so angry?"

"I came into the room expecting Ali to put aside her own problems and focus on mine. When she didn't, it made me mad. I screamed at her that she was a selfish bitch. Matt was the one who threw me out of the room, but I was furious with Ali…for being a traitor. The way I saw it, I was the victim. She owed it to me to defend me, do something, not just stand by while I got tossed out into the hallway.

So to punish her, hurt her, I told my sister I hoped whatever was wrong with her was something terrible."

Humiliated by the memory, Morgan closed her eyes. "As I was screeching my car out of Ali's driveway, I remembered what I saw when I first came into her room...the haunted look in her eyes... how pale and shattered she was. And I caught a glimpse of my face in the rearview mirror. I looked like a bitter, selfish witch. I was everything I didn't want to be. I wanted to be kind and generous. I wanted to go back into that house and take care of my sister. And I didn't have a clue how to do it... I didn't even know how to take care of myself. The one thing I knew for sure was that I needed to change. The problem was that I didn't know where to begin.

"When Ralph came along, it gave me a place to start." Morgan wiped away a tear. "But the change had been waiting to happen ever since that moment in Ali's driveway when I realized how much I loved her, and how much I'd let her down because I'd spent my life refusing to grow up. That night at her new house when she was so broken and vulnerable...without even realizing it, Ali changed my life."

"And what about Ali?" Sam asked. "What about the revenge you used to say you wanted?"

"Sometimes I still wonder if a moment of payback would close out my old story with Ali and make it easier to start a new one." Morgan had a little stab of heartache as she said, "But it's too late now. Ali's gone."

"Gone?"

"It's been six months and I haven't heard a word from my sister." Sam's voice was soft with compassion. "Why don't you call her?"

Morgan wiped away a tear. "I think I've finally crossed the line with Ali. She doesn't want me anymore."

There was a benevolent silence. Then Sam said, "You're wrong. In the time that we've been friends, I've gotten to understand who you are. Underneath all your frustration and insecurity, you're someone quite special. Your sister knows that."

Morgan shook her head, disagreeing. "I'm different with you than I am with her, Sam. Ever since I was born, right from the start, I've been invading Ali's life…like a hermit crab grabbing somebody else's shell…just moving into it without asking and living there. Maybe she's glad to finally be rid of me."

"Tell me about your new shell," Sam said. "The home you're building for yourself."

Morgan's spirits immediately lifted. Her house had been transformed; she loved it now.

"It's pretty," she told Sam. "And that's because of you. Do you remember the conversation we had when I moved in here?"

"Yes. You told me the place was ugly and dingy, and how discontent it made you."

Morgan gave an embarrassed laugh. "I was expecting you to sympathize with me…but you said, 'If it's ugly, make it beautiful. You're a curator at an art museum. You understand color and form and proportion. You can use what you know to work magic.'"

"Was I right?" Sam sounded pleased.

"Yes. It surprised the heck out of me. You were unbelievably right."

"How did you get it done?"

Morgan pulled Ralph close and grinned. "A lot of the credit goes to Ralph. On the weekends, I started taking him to the park to play. And on our way there, we'd pass this little store, a place I wouldn't even have noticed if Ralph hadn't dragged me in. It turns out that the owner keeps a dish of dog treats in the doorway. Once Ralph and I were inside, I discovered the shop has a back room with really cheap, really great secondhand furniture. It's where I got most of the things for the house."

Morgan leaned forward, her eyes dancing. "When you said it, I didn't believe it. But it turned out to be true. Sam, I *do* have a flair for decorating."

"Tell me what you've done." Sam sounded eager, interested.

Morgan looked around her home, excited about what she'd accomplished. "I outfitted the living room with a great-looking slip-covered sofa and a matching chair, and pine tables that I decorated with stacks of books and magazines. Then I found some really nice throw rugs and scattered them on the floor. And for a pop of color, I added a display of flowering plants, in quirky containers, that I tucked into a corner.

"And for the bedroom, I found an old four-poster bed and layered it with a down-filled comforter and oversize pillows. On either side of the bed are two wooden chests, where I have photos of me and Ali, along with my knitting projects and a pair of mini speakers." Morgan paused and chuckled. "Sam, I think I must've caught the music bug from you. Ralph and I have music playing day and night."

"What's on your playlist?"

"Right now it's Billie Holiday and Yo-Yo Ma. And Charlie Haden."

"That's wonderful!"

Morgan was truly happy. Happy being connected to Sam. And happy to have Ralph—delighting in loving him.

Looking around the room, Morgan was thrilled. She'd started with something bleak and empty and had made it warm and welcoming.

"Sounds like much has changed," Sam said.

"Almost everything," Morgan agreed. "And, Sam...I even have someone I'm dating."

His name was Ben Tennoff. He was a cousin of one of Morgan's coworkers at the Pasadena museum where she had recently started working. The woman had set Morgan up with Ben because he was single and thirty and wanted to get married.

Tonight would be Morgan's third date with Ben, and the memory of their first date was making her smile…

The minute she opened the door, Ben Tennoff handed her a bouquet of flowers. Peach-colored lilies that were absolutely beautiful.

Taking the flowers with one hand, Morgan already had her other hand on her face. And then felt silly—realizing she was trying to hide cuts that weren't even there anymore.

With a sweet smile, Ben reached out to her, moving her hand away from her face. "You're pretty," he told her. "Just the way I imagined you'd be."

Morgan had never met a man like Ben Tennoff. A man so effortlessly compassionate.

He was nice looking, but a long way from knockout gorgeous. Ben was medium height. His face was round. He was wearing glasses, and his modest, side-parted haircut made him look like a guy who collected comic books and ate Sunday dinner with his mother.

Morgan saw intelligence and playfulness in his eyes. "I'm Morgan," she told him. "I'm glad to meet you."

She was hoping that Ben was as decent as he seemed.

And he was.

They had dinner in a South Pasadena restaurant called Shiro. Feasting on crisp-skinned, perfectly fried catfish accompanied by a light soy sauce and topped with mounds of fresh cilantro.

All through the meal, Morgan and Ben talked…nonstop. Ben was one of the most genuinely charming people Morgan had ever encountered.

He was a high-school history teacher who loved animals and was interested in learning about opera. And he told wonderfully funny stories about his students and some of the blunders he made when he first started teaching.

The way Ben looked at Morgan—the way he touched her arm each time he leaned toward her—made her feel interesting and pretty.

After dinner, Ben took Morgan to his favorite bookstore—Vroman's, on Colorado Boulevard in Pasadena. He introduced her to a friend of his who worked there, a chatty girl named Clio who complimented Morgan on her dress and told her what a great guy Ben was.

On their way out, Ben bought Morgan a book about the early days of South Pasadena, which contained a grainy photo of her duplex when it was home to a young flapper who became a famous poet.

And at the end of their date, while Ben walked Morgan to her door, he kissed her hand and told her, "You're lovely."

Morgan was too happy to speak, or breathe. She understood Ben Tennoff meant what he'd just said. And she was thrilled.

It had been the perfect first date—from the moment she'd opened the door.

And here she was again, opening her door to Ben—for their third date. He was holding a large canvas tote and a giant bag of popcorn. His eyes sparkling with anticipation. "I hope you enjoy surprises."

Being playful and lighthearted wasn't something Morgan had much experience with before meeting Ben. She was starting to like it. "What's in the tote bag?"

Ben gave her a slightly bashful kiss on the cheek. "Remember you told me you'd never seen *Sideways*?"

Morgan nodded. "And you told me I'd missed out on a really funny movie about love and wine."

"Well, I think a girl as great as you should never have to miss out on anything." Ben walked into the living room, put the tote and the bag of popcorn on the coffee table, and quickly unpacked the tote's contents. "So I rented *Sideways... That's* what's on this DVD. And then I made a trip to the Cineplex to buy this empty popcorn tub and this pair of concession-stand drink cups." He looked at Morgan and winked. "Since this is your first time viewing the film, I wanted to provide you with the complete moviegoing experience."

Morgan was realizing all the wonderful ways in which her life had changed. Thinking how nice it was to have a boyfriend. And how beautiful her house was. And how well she was doing at her new job. And how, in taking care of Ralph, she had found laugh-out-loud happiness.

Ben piled a mountain of popcorn into the empty Cineplex tub and filled the concession-stand drink cups with an excellent merlot, telling her, "Sit down. Get comfortable. There's just one more thing I have to do."

And Morgan watched Ben write her name on the side of one of the cups, drawing a heart around it.

〜

When Ben was leaving—after they'd shared the movie and the popcorn and the wine—he told Morgan, "I'm happy we found each other. I like you a lot."

"I like you," Morgan said. "Very much."

Ben leaned in toward her, smelling clean, like freshly laundered linen, his kiss warm and caring.

His car was parked in front of her duplex. While Morgan watched him walk down the path that led to the curb, she was thinking what a truly terrific guy Ben was.

But then she noticed that he was a little pigeon-toed and had the slightest amount of fat around his middle.

Morgan closed the door more quickly than she'd intended, before Ben had even gotten to his car.

He's the nicest guy I've ever met... I really like being with him. But it bothers me that he's not better looking and more sophisticated. More like Ali's kind of man.

Having this thought made Morgan ashamed of herself.

A lot had changed in her life, but not everything.

There were places in her that were still painfully unresolved.

Ali

"THE APARTMENT IS EXACTLY LIKE SHE LEFT IT." THE WOMAN saying this was named Marcie.

The space Marcie and Ali were in was small. A miniscule living room and galley kitchen. At one end of the living room, the entry to a bedroom and bathroom. A standard, low-rent, cookie-cutter layout. And it was taking Ali's breath away. This was a place that could have belonged only to Ava.

Two of the living room walls were lime green; the third was sunflower yellow. The window shutters and the woodwork were meticulously enameled in white. And on the fourth wall, filling it completely, was a vibrantly colored, hand-painted mural. A dreamscape. A rain forest with sweet-faced monkeys in jewel-studded masks tumbling and dancing while birds feathered in the colors of the rainbow swooped above their heads.

"Isn't that the most incredible thing you've ever seen?" The question came from Marcie, the person who had called Ali with the news of Ava's death. Marcie was the neighbor Ava told Ali about, the landlady from Kansas.

"It's…" Ali was searching for the right words. She couldn't find anything that even came close to what she was thinking. She eventually settled for "It's wonderful."

Marcie's tone was hushed, reverent. "Ava painted it when she was pregnant. While she was waiting for Sofie."

Ali gave a tense nod. Marcie cleared her throat. It was obvious they were both feeling awkward.

"I've never been here before," Ali said.

"Well, Ava didn't ever have company over, like most people do. She was real private. But real friendly, too. I loved it when she'd come down to my place to visit." Marcie looked around the room, lost in thought. "After I first rented this unit to her, I never was in here again until she…until she passed away."

Marcie had already given Ali the facts of what had happened. Ava was on the stairs, going up to her apartment after leaving the laundry room. "A blood clot," Marcie had said. "And in a split second her life was over."

Ava and Ali had truly loved each other, had known each other's hearts. And Ali instinctively understood what Ava had experienced at the moment of her death, when the blood clot hit. The jolt of surprise at death coming so suddenly, and so soon. The rush of love for life and for Sofie. The fervent prayer that Sofie would be safe, cared for. And then a sense of peace. A sense of going home, surrounded by angels.

Ava was gone—and Ali missed her with every fiber of her being.

Ali's heart had been aching during Ava's cremation, and when her ashes were scattered in the walled garden behind the restaurant. Right up until the end, Ava had remained intensely private. There had been no funeral, no fuss. No one there but Ali and Matt. It was what Ava had requested in the handwritten will found in the drawer of her bedside table, tucked away with her green card and Sofie's birth certificate.

"So. How's Sofie?" Marcie was straightening a seat cushion on a nearby chair. "Is she good?"

She's more than good, Ali thought. *She's a little bit of heaven. She has the same spirit, the same magic that Ava had.*

"Everybody who meets Sofie falls in love with her," Ali told Marcie. "The restaurant staff's crazy about her. And all the suppliers—the linen delivery, the produce people—they all want to spend time making her laugh and singing to her. And there's this old man who always wears a starched white shirt and a plaid bow tie. He has a bookstore across the alley from the restaurant, and he closes his shop at noon, every day, just so he can come for an hour to hold Sofie on his lap and tell her about cows that jump over the moon and little lambs with fleece as white as snow." Ali sighed. There were too many emotions. They were too complicated.

Every minute of every day, Ali struggled with the pain of losing Ava. In addition to Ava's loss, Ali was also struggling to understand Matt's hostile reaction when he heard the news about Sofie's future.

After Ava's cremation, after they'd scattered her ashes in the walled garden, Ali had told Matt, "Ava's landlady has been taking care of Sofie for the past few days, but now Sofie is coming to stay with us."

The color drained from Matt's face. "When?"

"Now. This afternoon."

"No." Matt looked horrified. "This is a bad idea, Ali."

"Why?"

"Because I fucking said so!"

Ali was stunned. Matt had never talked to her like that, ever.

The next thing she knew, he walked out of the walled garden, got into the car, and drove away. Ali had to call Jessica for a ride home. From that day to this, Matt and Ali had been cut off from each other. And Sofie was the wall between them.

"Yeah, Sofie's real special…a real good baby." Marcie was folding her hands, then unfolding them, nervous, uncertain. "You know Ava had Sofie on formula, right? Jeez, of course you know. You've been taking care of her for how many months now?"

"Almost five." Ali fiddled with the strap on her purse. "Sofie's first birthday is in a few weeks. I should've come sooner." But Ali knew there was no way she could have done that. The agony of her rape, the rapist still being on the loose, her shredded relationship with Matt—all of it was emotional quicksand. It had taken Ali a long time to begin to pull herself out, even a little.

"Gosh, I wasn't saying I thought you should've gotten over here sooner. That wasn't what I meant." Marcie's voice faltered. "I was just trying to say Ava was a good mom…wanting Sofie to eat all organic and everything. It about broke Ava's heart that she couldn't nurse. Her milk just never came in right and—" Marcie rolled her eyes. "Oh for goodness' sake, I'm talking too much. It drives people crazy."

"It's okay." Ali's smile was sincere. "I don't mind."

Marcie went into the kitchen, to a shelf where there was a row of drinking glasses, each of them a different iridescent shade of peacock green. She filled one with water and gave it to Ali. "I feel like I know you. I guess it's because Ava used to tell me about you all the time. She really loved you."

"I loved her, too." As she said this, Ali was remembering Ava… *in the doorway of the restaurant kitchen, gazing out at Sofie with such love. While Sofie cooed in the sunshine of the walled garden. While she napped in its gentle breezes.*

And Ali was recalling something else, too… *A particularly beautiful Saturday afternoon. The yellow roses were in full bloom around the garden walls. Several months earlier, she and Ava had laid out a series of winding, gravel pathways and filled the spaces between them with purple basil and dusty-green sage. With the sturdy splendor of rosemary and the delicate silver of Spanish lavender. On that Saturday, Ali and Ava were getting the garden ready for the mild California winter. They were just finishing their work, the scent of herbs and the feel of the damp earth still on their hands, as Ava touched her open palm to Ali's saying, "Where our sweetest first memories are made…that is where we put down the roots of home."*

Ali had been looking at Sofie when she told Ava, "I hope that for Sofie, this garden will always be home."

The memory spurred a twinge of guilt in Ali: *Be careful what you wish for.* Had she, in loving Sofie so much, wanted Sofie all to herself? Without knowing it, had Ali wished Ava was gone?

She pushed the thought away. It was too awful.

Ali saw that Marcie was waiting restlessly. The time had come. They needed to get down to business. Ali was apologetic. "I'm sorry it's taken me so long to get over here to pick up Sofie's things…" Her voice trailed off. She started again. "I guess now there's really no point in doing it. Sofie has probably outgrown all the clothes."

"Yeah. But she might like having some of her toys." Marcie flashed Ali an encouraging grin. "There's this one little teddy bear she was crazy about. I bet she'd be real glad to see him again."

Not wanting to break down, Ali was trying to focus on what needed to be done. "I brought boxes… I forgot them in the car."

"No problem." Marcie indicated a stack of grocery bags piled near the door. "I already packed up all the baby things for you."

Ali was looking at the beauty Ava had left behind. The rain-forest mural and the wood-framed photographs lined up on the window-sill, and the rows of books neatly arranged in a series of low, coral-colored bookcases.

"I still can't bring myself to do anything about her stuff," Marcie said "God knows I need the rent on this place, but I just can't clear it out…can't stand the thought of anybody else being in here." Marcie went to one of the bookcases, signaling she wanted Ali to join her. "Come take a look at this. You're not gonna believe it."

The bindings on the books were faded and cracked. When Ali leaned in to look closely, she was surprised. She saw names that included Dickens and Brontë, Shakespeare, Victor Hugo, Dostoyevsky, and Jane Austen.

"It's how she learned English," Marcie said, "by reading all this fancy, old-fashioned stuff. That's why it sounded so pretty when she talked." Marcie took one of the framed photographs from the windowsill. A picture of a teenaged Ava, in a kitchen garden, wearing a school uniform. "Ava went to Catholic school for a couple of years." Marcie pointed to the other person in the photo, an elderly nun whose face was luminous. "That's Sister Pierre. She gave Ava all these books. She was from France, and she was in charge of the school's kitchen. That's how Ava learned to cook."

"Sounds like you and Ava were close...like you spent a lot of time together." Ali was jealous. Ava belonged to her—Ali's surrogate sister after Morgan stormed out of Ali's life.

Marcie sounded worried that she'd offended Ali. "We were pretty good friends, but it wasn't the same as how she felt about you. Ava adored you. She told me you and she had the same soul. That's why I wasn't surprised, after Ava was gone, when I found the papers she'd made out just after Sofie was born, her will, where she said she wanted you to take care of Sofie if...if anything ever happened."

The loss of Ava was hitting with full force. Ali had a painful tightness in her throat. "Were you with her when she died?"

Marcie drew an unsteady breath. "Like I told you...she was on the stairs out front. I don't think she'd been there very long. By the time I found her, she was already gone."

"I still can't believe she's dead." A new wave of grief swept through Ali.

"Did you know she'd met somebody?" Marcie asked.

"No."

"I think Ava was keeping it a secret until she was sure it was going somewhere. The only reason I knew is I ran into him a couple of times when he came to pick up Ava." Marcie's smile was wistful. "When I got nosy and asked, Ava said she thought maybe she was falling in love with him."

Marcie dabbed at her eyes. "It's why she started taking the pill. And that's what killed her...being in love. That blood clot from the stupid birth control pills went into her lungs, and she was dead. Just like that." Marcie shook her head, then said, "Kinda gives you the shivers how easy it is for the people you love to just be...gone."

"Yes," Ali agreed. She was thinking about all the people who were suddenly gone from her. She was thinking about Ava. And her grandmother MaryJoy. And Morgan. And Matt.

Ava and her grandmother would never return, and Ali wished they could.

She knew Matt and Morgan could return, and she wasn't sure how she felt about it.

She wasn't sure that when they came back, if they came back, they would be people she still loved.

Matt

T HIS IS UNFAIR, MATT. IT'S NOT LIKE I'M ASKING FOR THE MOON."
Matt understood why Ali had kept her voice low—because she didn't want to wake Sofie—but she'd made no attempt to hide her anger.

They were driving away from a dinner party hosted by one of the actors on Matt's show. Sofie was asleep in her car seat. The argument, which had started during the party, was boiling over now. Matt tightened his grip on the steering wheel. "I didn't say you were asking for the moon. I'm simply telling you I don't think I can make it."

Matt switched the radio on—thumping hip-hop. Ali slapped the power button and shut it off.

"Matt, since Sofie's been with us, you haven't gone to even one of her pediatrician's appointments."

He could feel Ali looking at him, trying to get him to look back. He kept his attention on the road. "Give it a rest, Al." It was a warning.

Ali lunged toward him and was yanked back by her seat belt, her words coming out choked and clipped. "Don't bother to give me the 'I'm too busy at work' speech." She angrily loosened the seat belt. "Every time I go to the pediatrician's office, there's a waiting room full of parents, and plenty of them are fathers. I doubt they're all unemployed."

Without giving Matt a chance to respond, she added, "It's not that off the charts. It happens all the time. Kids go to doctor appointments with their parents."

"We're her temporary guardians." Matt was jaw-clenched, pounding-headache angry.

It was obvious Ali was equally angry—ready to scream at him or hit him, or both. He told her, "I know you're in a tough spot, Al. You and I haven't been the same since…" He couldn't bring himself to say the word *rape*. "Ali, it isn't just what happened to you or what's going on with us. It's this thing with your sister. You being cut off from Morgan. That's not doing you any good either."

The mention of Morgan brought a quick silence. Afterward, it sounded like Ali was fighting tears. "I don't know how to get it all done," she said. "I don't know how to take care of myself, and Sofie, *and* Morgan." Ali looked exhausted. "When Morgan's around, she leans her entire weight on me, expects me to be her rock. Right now, I need a rock…somebody I can lean on."

"Then lean on me." Matt said it with gentleness and tenderness. There was nothing he wanted more than to have Ali lean on him—and be close to her again.

"What good would it do…to lean on you? I'd just fall flat on my face. You wouldn't be there. You'd be at work." She'd said it sarcastically, with disgust.

His feeling of gentleness had vanished—Matt was aggravated now. "Ali, there's no reason for me to play daddy at a doctor's visit for a kid who'll probably be gone before it's time for her next appointment." The left turn he made was deliberately hard; the car rocked. "We're her *temporary* guardians."

He wished he could tell Ali why he was so unwilling to be responsible for Sofie. But there was no way to explain without telling the truth about the things he'd done and exposing secrets that could cost him Ali's love.

"Maybe we're her temporary guardians for now," Ali snapped. "But I won't let it stay that way. It'll be permanent. Just as soon as I can get all the legal stuff worked out."

Ali's tunnel vision about the issue of Sofie terrified Matt. Ali was pushing him into a place he didn't want to go—not again. He had to stop her. "Al, you need to put the brakes on this. We're not ready for it."

"Not ready for what? Not ready to do what's obviously the right thing?"

Why didn't she understand that he was trying to warn her? Why wouldn't she listen? Matt's anger exploded. "There's nothing obvious about it. It's complicated as hell!"

"Not to me," Ali shouted.

Matt had to let several minutes pass before he could get his temper under control. "Ali, ever since you were—" He stopped, then said, "Ever since that night when you were attacked, we've been cracked up. To take on this kind of responsibility out of nowhere, out of the blue, it seems like the straw that's going to break us."

Ali's determined expression left no room for negotiation. "I want Sofie. I want to be a mother. I'm going to be *her* mother. I expect you to step up and be her father."

Matt felt goaded—and was pushing back. "You *expect*?"

She stared him down, silently telling him, *You owe me this.* He was too upset, too guilty, to tell her he didn't.

"Sofie belongs with me," Ali said. "It's what Ava wanted. It's what I want. And I won't let you try to stop me."

Ali was shoving them into a corner they might not be able to get out of. Matt sensed the color draining from his face. He glanced up at the rearview mirror—looking at Sofie, in her car seat.

When Matt looked back at the road, he was seeing another little girl from a very long time ago. Dancing in a flower-sprigged dress. So breakable. So defenseless.

And he murmured, "I can't do it again."

Ali gave him a curious look. "Can't do what?"

"I can't have this fight right now."

"No. That isn't what you meant." Ali was scrutinizing him, trying to see what he was hiding. "You were talking about something else. I heard it in your voice."

His laugh was hollow. "That's impossible, Al. You haven't heard a word I've said, or noticed anything I've done, for months."

Matt turned the car onto their street, Paradise Lane, his pulse racing like he was hurtling toward a brick wall.

Ten miles from Paradise Lane
  at the beginning of spring.
Brutality.
    A vicious punch.
    A terrified moan.
    And a diamond stud. Falling into soft, new grass.

Matt

BEFORE HE COULD GET TO THE DOOR, THE PHONE RANG. THE voice at the other end of the call was coldly impersonal: Matt needed to report to the soundstage immediately.

Matt's heart skipped a beat. Whatever this was, it was trouble.

When the call came, he'd had his car keys in his hand, was seconds away from leaving his office. Sofie was scheduled for another routine checkup today. He'd decided to be there and make it a surprise for Ali.

Ever since the fight they'd had in the car about Sofie, Matt and Ali had stayed sealed off from each other. Ali, with Sofie never more than an arm's length away, spending the majority of her time at the restaurant; Matt almost always at the studio. What he had been hoping for this afternoon was to find his way back to Ali. All day, all he'd thought about was walking into that pediatrician's waiting room and putting a smile on Ali's face.

Now, the only place he was headed was back to work, because there was an emergency on the set of his show. The series, called *Darling*, followed the exploits—in and out of the bedroom—of a glib sleuth for hire named Jake Darling. A recent ratings spike had turned Seth Kates, the actor who played Darling, into one of the hottest stars on television.

When Matt arrived on the soundstage, the only illuminated space was the lavish set that was the interior of Jake Darling's private jet. Seth Kates was there, sprawled on one of the set's oversize leather lounge chairs, playing a game on his cell phone. Aidan Blake was nearby with two high-ranking network executives. A tall, hawkishly attractive woman. And a man with peculiarly small ears that were several shades lighter than his face.

Aidan gave Matt a tense smile, confirming what Matt already suspected—whatever the trouble was, it was serious.

Matt gestured toward the darkened soundstage, then shot Aidan a questioning glance. "We're scheduled for a full day today. Why are we shut down?"

"On his way back from the lunch break, our boy Seth announced he wants to leave the show at the end of this season," Aidan said. "We sent everyone home till we can get things worked out."

"I'm not interested in working anything out." Seth didn't look up from the game he was playing on his phone. "All I want is for everybody to join me in celebrating my freedom."

Aidan yanked the phone away from Seth and tossed it to Matt. "Before he got this part, he was a fucking out-of-work Pilates instructor living in his Subaru, and now he's a television star with more money in the bank than he knows how to count. So, you might ask yourself, what could the man's problem possibly be?"

The game noises stopped as Matt switched off Seth's phone and looked at the others, waiting for the answer to Aidan's question. The network executive with the tiny ears spoke up. "It seems Seth sees himself as a movie star."

Seth gave Matt a patronizing squint and held out his hand, demanding his phone. The hawkish-looking female executive reached in and slapped his hand away. "The show's called *Darling*. You're Jake Darling. No you, no Jake. No Jake, no show." She gave Seth a glare cold enough to freeze him. "Do you understand the world of hurt you're about to create?"

"Have you ever heard of the saying 'strike while the iron is hot'? Well, my iron is sizzling."

Matt's stomach was in a knot. "If this show shuts down," he told Seth, "it will put a lot of people out of work."

"*Hundreds* of people," the female executive added. "Writers, crew, wardrobe, makeup. They'll all be unemployed because of you, you selfish little shit."

"It's just money." Seth's statement was accompanied by a wave and a careless grin.

Matt was fighting not to grab Seth and choke him. Without the weekly paycheck from *Darling*, Matt had no idea how he and Ali would survive. Their finances were stretched to the limit. The restaurant was slowly moving into the black but was still a money drain. The mortgage and maintenance on the house took a huge bite out of the bank account every month. And now, with Sofie, there even more expenses.

Matt was gritting his teeth when he said, "Do you know what kind of bastard this makes you?"

"Did *you* know there was a time when Einstein was all sick and sad because he got bumped out of his steady gig as a high-school math teacher?" Seth yanked his phone away from Matt, stuffing it into a designer messenger bag. "The guy responsible for that particular job loss, was he a bastard? Or was he the hero who paved the way for our pal Albert to stay hungry and keep scrambling till he came up with E equals MC squared?"

Seth swung the messenger bag over his shoulder, winking at Matt. "It's always about the Next Thing. All about keeping the wheel turning, baby. All about change." As he walked away, he said, "If things don't change, you got no chance to grow. And without the chance to grow, there's no point in being alive."

The only clear thought in Matt's head was—*This must be what it's like to have a heart attack.*

"What are we going to do?" he asked.

"Not much we can do," Aidan replied. "Most of the time, what these idiots want is more money, but we've talked to his agent. Money isn't the issue with this guy."

The female executive picked up her purse. "We could tie him up in court. But as long as he refuses to come to work, we've still got no show."

The two executives and Aidan were leaving the set, heading into the gloom of the unlit soundstage. The female executive was muttering, "If we don't find a way to convince that asshole to stay put, we're completely screwed."

Matt heard Aidan's voice float toward him out of the darkness: "Hey, Matty boy, want to join me on a two-day drunk in Cabo?"

Matt didn't bother to answer. He just waited until the steel doors at the other end of the building banged shut. Then he lowered himself into the lounge chair where Seth Kates had been. And Matt sat there, not moving a muscle. Like he'd been turned to stone.

The house Matt came home to later that night was a very different place from the one he and Ali first moved into. With Sofie's arrival, Ali had come out of her emotional fog and had started to take an interest in 76 Paradise Lane. There were pictures on the walls and fresh flowers on the tables. The furniture, most of it casual and upholstered in simple ivory twill, was beautifully arranged. The chairs had pretty baskets next to them, filled with craft projects and baby toys.

Matt found Ali in the kitchen. A mellow light was coming from small, parchment-shaded lamps spaced at intervals along the soapstone countertops. The room was peaceful, inviting.

Sofie, now fifteen months old, was playing on the floor, entertaining herself with a flow of giggles and toddler jabber.

Matt's attention was on Ali. She was setting the table for dinner. It looked as if she'd just gotten out of the shower. Her skin was clean and fresh, her hair coiled at the back of her head and pinned up, curling tendrils clinging to her temples and the sides of her neck. And Matt wanted her. In the same blind, urgent way he'd wanted her the night he'd proposed to her on that windblown bluff in Newport.

He impulsively reached for her, then quickly pulled back. He saw the look in her eyes and remembered the visit to the pediatrician. The Seth Kates crisis had erased it from his mind. His instinct was to ask how the appointment went, and he understood it wouldn't do any good. It would only open the door to a fight.

Ali didn't want him the way he wanted her. She didn't want him at all. She was disgusted with him.

Matt turned and walked away. Tired of failing. Tired of being shut out. Tired of scratching to find a way in. He was ready to give up on Ali, ready to give up on everything.

Then, just as Matt was leaving the kitchen, Sofie let out a happy shriek. It startled him; he turned to look in her direction.

Since she'd come to live in this house, Matt had done his best to avoid Sofie. He wanted to keep his distance. Because of his past and the sins that were buried there, sins against vulnerable little girls and helpless women. Places he didn't want to go again.

But the truth was that as much as Matt had tried to wall her off, Sofie had slipped through his defenses and charmed him—just as she charmed everyone who came in contact with her.

And this was the moment Matt knew he'd lost the fight. Sofie had made her way straight into his heart. Eagerly holding her hands up to him, eyes bright—saying: *Da.*

Matt's surprised gaze met Ali's.

In the stunned silence that followed, Sofie again held her hands up and reached toward Matt, her face lit with pure adoration. And again, she uttered that single, soft syllable. *Da.*

It was as if Matt, who'd been so cold and alone lately, was being warmed by a shaft of sunlight. What he was seeing in Sofie was unconditional love. The kind of love Ali had for him before her attack, before she'd armored herself with such sharp edges.

Sofie, as she held her hands out, was giving Matt what he was desperate for. She was giving him hope.

And that changed everything.

~

Over the next few weeks, a thread of tenderness began to reconnect Matt and Ali. Sofie's smiles and happy embraces drew Matt like a magnet, and Ali seemed pleased by how willing he was to be drawn.

This morning, as he did every morning before he left for work, Matt was making a little ceremony of saying good-bye to Sofie. She was in her high chair in the kitchen, just finishing her favorite breakfast—warm oatmeal, with golden-brown plantains that Ali had sautéed in butter.

The room was sunlit. And full of happiness.

Sofie was bouncing with anticipation as Matt placed her plump, little hand on his freshly shaved cheek.

And because he didn't know any nursery rhymes, he was doing what he did every morning to put that grin on Sofie's face. He was serenading her with classic rock. Today it was a full-on Joe Cocker–style rendition of "You Are So Beautiful."

Sofie was cooing with delight.

Ali was nearby. Glowing and contented.

When he finished singing to Sofie, Ali leaned close and kissed the spot on Matt's cheek where Sofie's hand had been. "Thank you," she said.

There was lump in his throat, gratitude and wonder, as he told her, "We're becoming a family, Al."

The joy, this feeling of connection, was more powerful than anything Matt had ever experienced.

He was already looking forward to tonight, to the three of them being together.

The demands of the television show didn't make it easy to do, but Matt had started coming home for dinner. Every night. He always had to head back to work the minute their meal was over—a forty-minute drive each way—but it was worth it.

Matt was winning his wife back—and falling in love with his daughter.

~

Every now and then, there were rare nights when Matt didn't have to put in late hours at the studio. He cherished them.

Tonight was one of those quiet, peaceful nights.

Matt was in his study. With Sofie in his lap, drowsy against his chest, her eyes heavy, her breathing soft and content. He was reading aloud to her from a script he was editing.

Out of the corner of his eye, he noticed that Ali had slipped into the room and was curled up in her favorite chair. Matt put down the script.

Sofie sighed and tucked her thumb into her mouth, drifting off to sleep.

Ali studied the two of them for a while.

Then she said, "I love you." Words Matt thought he'd never hear again.

It was salvation from a living death.

And he didn't want to disappoint Ali—couldn't risk losing her.

Which was why, although he was rapidly running out of time, Matt didn't tell Ali about the large ax that was waiting to fall.

Matt's television show, the source of his income, was about to be canceled. Each passing day had become a deathwatch—everyone hoping for a last-minute reprieve, while bracing for catastrophe.

Only two more episodes of *Darling* were in production, and Seth Kates had still refused to renew his contract. Matt was about to be unemployed. The money he'd been making was impressive, compared to a teacher's salary. But by Hollywood standards it wasn't much. And Matt had been living by Hollywood standards.

The monthly expenses drained every penny. He was on a collision course with disaster.

The dialogue in Matt's head was relentless: *I'm finished in television. I've got no track record. No power. The network thinks I'm Aidan Blake's charity case, an egghead who got lucky. And I can't go back to teaching. I only had the assistant professorship for a year before I ran off to Hollywood. On paper, I look like a flake. A failure. How will I ever find another job?*

There were times, during those weeks of waiting, that Matt's heart hammered so hard he thought it might actually tear him to pieces.

Searching for a way to calm down, he started going to the empty soundstage after shooting had wrapped for the day. He went onto the darkened set and stretched out on one of the leather lounge chairs in Jake Darling's private jet, always the same one. Its plush leather molded itself to his body like a gloved hand and made him feel protected. But it was protection that came with a touch of mockery. The luxury of a Gulfstream jet was the ultimate symbol of money, the thing Matt was desperate for.

And then the day came when, in less than a week, Matt would be out of work. A failure as a husband and provider, and as a father. It wasn't just Ali depending on him; Sofie was depending on him, too.

As Matt lay in the dark in that plush leather chair—for what he suspected was the last time—he let out a wailing moan.

Matt had made promises to women he loved, important promises. He was tormented by how many of those promises he hadn't been able to keep—and how many women he had harmed.

He was remembering something that happened years ago... *Lying in the dark, surrounded by the smell of garbage—with a girl who had trusted him. Whispering to her that it was okay, she was safe. Seeing her fear when she realized she wasn't.*

Suddenly, Matt was back in the present—startled by a whisper: "I've been looking all over for you." It was his assistant, Danielle, the girl with the piercing green eyes. The elf with the rosebud lips.

Before he understood what was happening, she was stretched out beside him—settling into the lounge chair as lightly as a perfumed feather. "I know why you come out here all the time," she told him. "You're afraid. We all are."

Matt started to sit up. She put her hand on his chest and murmured, "Don't worry. I just want to be with you. I want to take care of you."

He had too much trouble already, with too many women. There wasn't room for one more. Matt pushed her away. "I'm married."

"I know you're married." She gave a wry shrug. "I overheard what you said to Aidan a while ago...about your wife and some mistake you made. And how she wanted you to pay for it for the rest of your life."

"I don't care what you heard. My wife and I are fine." Matt lifted Danielle out of the chair and stood her on the floor beside it. She weighed no more than a doll might have. But she left a fragrance in the air that was dense—and heady—like flowers in a jungle.

"You won't be fine. Not for a while." Danielle looked around the darkened soundstage. "We're all hoping for a miracle, but it's not gonna come. Next week, when this ends, you'll be shredded. So will I." She put her hands on either side of Matt's face and held them there; they were cool, incredibly soft. "I don't want to be alone when the whole thing implodes. Do you?"

Matt was in an alternate sliver of reality, one that hadn't happened yet—the reality of telling Ali he'd lost his job and didn't know how they would survive.

Would that be the moment for Ali when he'd let her down one too many times? Would it be when she would leave, and stay gone forever?

Something inside Matt snapped—plunging him toward oblivion.

What stopped his fall was Danielle. She put her rosebud lips on his and kissed him.

After the kiss, she said, "When it's over, when we've both come out of this all right and we have our lives back, when you don't need me anymore, I'll go. I promise."

～

Seth Kates's attorneys announced their client was permanently leaving his role on *Darling* to pursue a film career. The fallout was instantaneous. Within minutes, an email arrived from the network: "*Darling* has been canceled and will not resume production."

Matt no longer had a paycheck.

His reaction was a grunt and a glassy-eyed stare. For weeks, he'd been frozen with fear. Waiting for the oncoming train to hit him. Now he'd been hit. And to his surprise, the impact had brought a sense of relief.

The email from the network was still on Matt's computer screen when Danielle walked in, telling him, "They'll probably start packing our offices by the end of the day."

He looked at her in disbelief. "That fast?"

"That fast. I come from show business people. I know how it works. They like to get rid of the bodies while they're still warm." She checked the room, taking inventory. "This is good. Looks like the only things here that belong to you are the books. They'll get boxed and sent to your house." She reached across the desk, picking up the photo of Ali. "But you better take this with you now. Otherwise, the packing morons will break the glass."

Danielle tucked Ali's picture under her arm. "Come on. We're going to my place."

Matt wasn't in the mood for a tumble and some easy sex. "The only place I'm going is home to my wife."

"That's exactly where you should go." Danielle came in close. "It's where you should go...later. After you take a couple of hours to let your emotional dust settle."

The expression in her eyes shocked him. It was fiercely personal, yet seemed completely unemotional.

"I don't want to wreck your home," she said. "I'm just offering you breathing space. For a little while."

With her lips touching his ear, Danielle whispered, "Sometimes it helps to find strength before you try to be strong."

And Matt gave in to his weakness.

Part Three

A WHOLE NEW WORLD

Morgan

GOD, THAT WAS GOOD." MORGAN SIGHED AND PUSHED HER dessert plate away.

"When I saw it on the menu, 'Death by Chocolate,' I knew we had to order it." Morgan's coworker from the museum spooned up a last bite of cake and a mouthful of whipped cream. Her name was Erin. She was the person who had introduced Morgan to sweet, thoughtful Ben Tennoff.

Most of Erin's conversation during lunch had been about Ben and how much he hoped that Morgan was interested in him. Erin moved her dessert plate aside and told Morgan, "I don't get it. He's such a great guy, and for some reason you seem to be hanging back. Why?"

Morgan squirmed a little. "What do you mean, hanging back?"

"I don't know. It's like you're weirdly shy about the whole thing. Most women, when they find the right guy, they're talking about it nonstop, telling anybody who'll listen."

Morgan's smile was uncertain. She was thinking about the last time she'd been with Ben.

~

It was their fifth date. Ben had taken her to a restaurant in San Marino, the tiny town that bordered South Pasadena. The restaurant was a little jewel box of a place that looked as if it belonged on a cobblestoned street in France. It was owned by a stunningly attractive silver-haired woman named Julie, who knew Ben and welcomed him with open arms.

When Ben told Julie, "This is my friend Morgan," Julie's smile got even brighter.

"I'm glad you're here, Morgan. Welcome to our opera salon. We do it once a month. It's so much fun."

Julie moved away to talk to someone else, and Morgan whispered to Ben, "This is like a scene out of a movie." The tables on the flagstone patio were filled with people, all of them laughing and chatting. The patio, which ran along the front of restaurant, had walls on three sides and a series of archways opening onto the sidewalk. The entire area was lit with flickering candles. And within minutes of their arrival, Morgan and Ben were at a table of their own, being served grilled filet mignon, thinly sliced, on a bed of fresh watercress—and a red wine that was exceptionally good.

Afterward, when the plates were being cleared away, Ben held Morgan's hand and told her, "Now comes my favorite part. The music."

A featured singer from the Los Angeles Opera was in the center of the covered patio, in the candlelight, singing the Queen of the Night aria from *The Magic Flute*—her voice clear and glorious.

Morgan had never heard anything so lovely.

When the music and the evening ended, slightly overweight, slightly geeky Ben Tennoff said, "I wanted tonight to be special. I really hope you liked it, Morgan."

And she told him, "I loved it."

Yet there was still a microscopic part of her that was hesitant about Ben. Because he wasn't as smooth and cool as Ali's boyfriends had been. Morgan had spent her entire life measuring herself against her sister, convinced that whatever Ali had was the benchmark and that anything less, anything different, wasn't quite good enough.

"Ben adores you," Erin was saying. "And isn't that what we all dream of? A man with a good heart who actually sees who we are and *loves* us for it, unconditionally?"

Morgan nodded and scooped up some of the whipped cream from her dessert plate. Her hand was shaking, spilling the cream onto her shirt.

"You better go to the ladies' room and take care of that," Erin told her. "I'll dash across the street to the shoe sale and meet you back at the car."

A few minutes later, Morgan had managed to get her shirt clean and was coming out of the restaurant. Two women were on their way in. Thinking about a report she needed to finish at work, Morgan absentmindedly held the door open. The taller woman, a blond, was pushing twins in a double stroller. The stroller pushed by the other woman contained a beautiful little girl who looked to be about eighteen months old.

The woman with the little girl told Morgan, "Thank you…for holding the door."

At the sound of the woman's voice, Morgan gasped and looked up, realizing it was Ali.

The rush of emotion in Morgan was overwhelming, complicated.

Relief that her exile was over.

Gladness that Ali was within reach again.

Hurt and bitter resentment that in all the months they'd been apart, Ali had never come looking for her.

Then there was confusion—Morgan's eyes darting from Ali's face to the child in the stroller.

And, above all, there was elation. Morgan was with her sister again. The first words out of her mouth were, "I've missed you so much!"

Ali was holding her tight. "Oh, Morgan. I started to call you a million times…"

"Me, too. Me, too." Morgan's grip on Ali was as fierce as if she had been lost at sea and Ali had just rescued her.

When Morgan stepped away, Ali gave her a look that said she noticed a difference, something she couldn't put her finger on. And Morgan thought, *I have so much to tell you. I've changed… I'm changing. And I want you to know all the reasons why.*

"Stay," Ali said. "Stay and have lunch with us. With Jess and me."

Morgan realized then that the blond with the twins was Jessica. She stared at Jessica and then at Ali, unable to process what she was seeing. It didn't make sense that all of this could have happened in the time she'd been away from Ali. "You have babies? You both have children?"

"You would have known if you'd talked to Mom," Ali said. "She's been worried about you. I guess I understand why you stopped talking to me, but why did you stop talking to Mom, too?"

"I've been going through a lot… I wasn't ready to deal with Mom." Morgan's attention was on the child in Ali's arms and the twins in the stroller. "How old are they?" she asked.

"My guys are five and a half months old today," Jessica said. "I can't believe I had twins. Maybe it rubbed off from hanging around with you and Ali." She reached down and tousled her boys' sandy-brown hair. "Ed and Joe." She laughed. "We decided to go retro on the names."

Ali lifted the little girl out of her stroller. "You two have met before. Say hello to your Aunt Morgan, Sofie."

Morgan was baffled. "Sofie? *Ava's* Sofie?"

Tears immediately appeared in Ali's eyes. "Ava died. Months ago. Right after Christmas." Ali looked as if she was trying to anticipate Morgan's next question.

Morgan didn't have any questions. She could see how Sofie was fitted against Ali's side, and the loving, protective way Ali was cradling her. *Sofie is Ali's little girl now*, Morgan thought, *and that makes her family.*

Morgan held her arms out to Sofie. Sofie came into them willingly. Instantaneous warmth flowed through Morgan—she was gazing at Sofie in amazement.

Suddenly, Morgan understood the full meaning of this miracle, and she waved to a group of strangers on their way out of the restaurant. "This is Sofie," she told them. "She's my niece!"

The first thing Morgan did after she was in her car on her way back to work was call Sam, to give him the news. "It's a miracle. I have a child in my life. Somebody who doesn't have any preconceived ideas about me. Sofie is my new beginning, Sam. I want to be fun and interesting…the perfect aunt. I want Sofie to see me as spectacular!"

"Then *be* spectacular," Sam told Morgan. "Live with your arms wide open to the world."

Matt

A STRANGE CONNECTION HAD TAKEN ROOT BETWEEN MATT AND Danielle. Matt suspected he should put a stop to it, but he couldn't. He wasn't ready. Not yet.

On the afternoon when Matt had lost his job and had agreed to meet Danielle at her apartment, he'd assumed he was on his way to something weak, and seedy, and completely wrong.

As it turned out, there was weakness in it. But Matt still couldn't decide how much of it was wrong. The one thing he was sure of was that it wasn't seedy. It was astonishing.

On Matt's first visit—when he discovered that Danielle lived in the French Normandy gatehouse of an old limestone mansion in the Hollywood Hills—she had been in the gatehouse's arched entryway, waiting for him. Wearing a floor-length kimono of aquamarine silk. Silk so thin and fine it was transparent.

Danielle's feet had been bare. As Matt came closer, he noticed how perfectly shaped they were—beautifully pedicured, each toenail polished in a sensuous cocoa brown.

After he'd come to a stop in front of her, Danielle bent down and removed his shoes and socks without saying a word. Then she took his cell phone and shut it off.

When she led Matt inside and closed the heavy wooden door, he had the sensation of being abruptly and completely removed from the world, as if he'd stepped into a cloister or a castle in a dream, where the air was still. The sound muffled. And the light was perpetual twilight.

The plaster walls were at least eighteen inches thick. All of the wood floors were dark, almost black. The same dark wood was in the massive exposed beams of the ceiling. The windows were narrow and arched, all of them crosshatched, lead paned. The thick glass in each pane was dull and watery. The furniture seemed made for the room, weighty, opulent. Looking as if it had been undisturbed for a hundred years.

"I've got weed and wine," Danielle said to Matt. "I think you should go with the wine."

Her voice was low, and he felt like this dreamlike place already had him drifting into a trance.

There were stemmed glasses and an open wine bottle on a table near the sofa, where Matt was. Danielle filled one of the glasses and handed it to him. The wine was ruby red. The same color as the satin pillows lining the back of the sofa, the same color as the thick Turkish towels and large pebble-glass bowl that were on the floor in front of it.

Danielle eased Matt back against the satin pillows. When she was satisfied he was comfortable, she sat cross-legged in front of him on the floor. She reached out and neatly rolled the cuffs of his pants up to his knees. Then she took one of the Turkish towels and laid it across her lap. After that, she picked up the glass bowl, which was filled with water, and nested it in the towel. Danielle lifted Matt's feet and lowered them into the bowl. The water was warm. The pleasure of it made Matt slowly inhale and discover that the warmth was scented with sandalwood.

Danielle bent her head over her work, carefully washing Matt's left foot, then his right. The waves and curls of her hair parted to reveal the back of her neck, which was indescribably lovely.

Matt lifted his hand ever so slightly, then dropped it, letting it stay where it was. He was weak. With pleasure? With desire? He wasn't sure.

After Danielle dried his feet and rubbed them with a lightly perfumed oil, she put away the bowl and the towels and climbed in beside Matt. She slid around behind him, cradling him against her chest.

"Where are we going with this?" Something was stirring in Matt, something hot and carnal.

"We're going someplace good," she said. "Someplace safe."

"Someplace safe?" His chuckle was bitter. "Where would that be?"

"Shhh," Danielle whispered. "No talking. No thinking. Just be still." She slowly slipped her fingers through his hair.

There was honesty in her touch. Danielle was making it clear that in this moment, she had no expectation of sex—no expectation that he would dishonor Ali. It flooded Matt with relief. Even in the midst of his weakness, the part of him that was still strong wanted to stay true to Ali.

The brush of Danielle's lips across the back of his neck brought Matt a sense of being able to let go, relax.

He was in a place he'd never been before—in the arms of a woman who was demanding nothing from him. A woman who wasn't trying to know his secrets or peer into his soul. A woman whose only expectation was that he would close his eyes and sleep.

∿

Matt's relationship with Danielle lasted the entire time he was unemployed.

After his final day in the television industry, Matt never said a word to Ali about having lost his job. He continued to leave home every morning as if he were going work, and went to Danielle instead.

It was a futile attempt to shelter Ali from how bleak things were. But even before he lost his job, they'd been living paycheck to paycheck, and the paychecks had stopped two months ago. Matt was barely keeping up with the minimum payments on the credit cards. Soon he wouldn't able to cover the mortgage. He and Ali were in trouble.

And now here he was, coming downstairs at two in the morning, discovering Ali at the kitchen table. Surrounded by printouts of every overdue bill, every red-lined bank statement—heartbroken tears streaming down her face.

It brought Matt to his knees.

"Where did our money go? Why haven't you been paying the bills?" Ali's voice was flat and dead as if, without even hearing the answer to her question, she was already destroyed.

"The show was canceled. I lost my job." Still on his knees, Matt didn't look up; he couldn't face her.

"How long have you been out of work?"

"Eight weeks, almost nine."

"And you never said a word to me."

The sense of betrayal in Ali's voice was crushing Matt.

"I'm sorry," he said.

Ali slapped him so hard he saw stars.

And he stayed kneeling beside her chair—expecting her to slap him again.

The look on Ali's face was awful. Fury. Fear. And a kind of glassy-eyed craziness.

She suddenly turned away from Matt, grabbing a calculator, frantically entering a flow of numbers. Matt reached out to slow the rapid movement of her hand—the same way he'd reached out to slow the movement of her pencil when they'd been at BerryBlue Farm. When she was sketching the plans for her restaurant. When he'd told her he wanted to make all her dreams come true.

I'm sorry for the danger I landed you in, he was thinking, *the danger every woman is in when she puts her trust in me.*

Ali's fingers continued to fly, adding up the debts, exposing the bottomless hole Matt had dragged them into.

"I've got résumés out. All over the place." He was clammy with shame. "I'll take the first thing I find. Writing, teaching, whatever. Whatever makes sense."

Ali moved her attention from the calculator to Matt. Her focus seemed uncannily clear, as if she were seeing all his secrets. His odd, intimately sexless relationship with Danielle. And the awful things he had done when he'd vanished from Rhode Island for those three days. And trespasses he'd committed long before that.

"I don't know how much more I can take," she said.

Matt held his breath, waiting to find out if his secrets were safe, and realizing they were. Ali was talking about herself, not about him.

"My life is in pieces," she was saying. "I was attacked, and whoever did it is still out there. Ava is dead. And my sister's morphed into someone new that I don't quite recognize. My whole world is upside down."

Ali rummaged through the piles of papers on the tabletop, her voice suddenly thin and frightened. "What's going to happen to us? We're completely out of money."

"That's not true." Matt reached to clear away the bills.

Ali snatched them back while he told her, "I bought us a few more months."

She wasn't paying attention. She was busily rearranging the bills, fastening them with rubber bands. As if by shoving them into tight, banded stacks she could corral the threat they represented.

Matt had never been more worried about her—had never seen her this close to the edge. "Ali, did you hear what I said? I got us some breathing room."

"How?" She continued to arrange and rearrange the unpaid bills.

The taste in Matt's mouth was acid, like biting down on metal. "I borrowed money."

"From who?"

"Aidan."

"Aidan?" There was a startled, haunted look in Ali's eyes. "I wish you hadn't done that…borrowing money…from him."

"I didn't know what else to do."

Ali put her hands over her face and moaned.

Matt had made them beggars. He understood why Ali couldn't stand the sight of him.

There was bitter irony in Ali's voice as she said, "One of my waitresses quit. She got a better job…where she's going to make a lot more money."

It was deathly quiet in the room. Matt could hear intermittent pulses of water moving through the ice maker inside the refrigerator.

It was killing him as he asked, "Have you hired anybody to take her place?"

"I've interviewed a couple of people but—"

"I'll do it. I'll wait tables. It'll give you one less check to write every month."

And he thought, *I'm a man with a PhD, and I'll put on an apron every day and ask, "Do you want fries with that?" I'll clean away other people's dirty dishes and scoop up tips, and still not make enough money to keep a roof over my wife's head, or my child's. This is my punishment for all the wrong I've done.*

Matt was helplessly watching what he loved most—his marriage, and Ali—slip away.

Ali

I DON'T KNOW. I HAVE NO IDEA HOW TO DESCRIBE WHAT'S GOING on with my life right now." Ali stopped to shake water droplets out of her hair. A few feet away, Sofie was running through the sprinklers, splashing Ali with each pass and giggling uncontrollably.

Ali scooted closer to the trunk of an old oak tree, to keep her phone dry, while she told Jessica, "I'm glad you called. I've missed you."

"What are you doing at home, playing in the yard? It's the middle of the day. How come you're not at the restaurant?"

Ali smiled, enjoying the calm of the backyard. The sun-dappled grass. The tree branches moving lazily on the breeze. Sophie waltzing away from the sprinklers to dance among the flowers. "I just needed a break," Ali said. "I'm a little overwhelmed."

"Why? Has something happened?"

"Jess, remember when we ran into Morgan at that Italian restaurant the other day? Did she seem different to you?"

"I guess. A little. Wait, now that I think about it, she looked different. She actually looked kind of pretty. And she didn't seem as lame and clueless as she usually is."

"The Sensitivity Awards called. I forgot to give you the message. You didn't win."

Jessica laughed. "Well, there's always next year."

Ali leaned back against the tree, trying to sort out what she was thinking. "It's weird, Jess. I mean it's great having my sister back... and from the minute she laid eyes on Sofie, she fell in love with her, which is wonderful. I'm really looking forward to having Morgan around again, but…"

"What's the problem?"

"There's something different about her. And it's not just the way she looks. It's something about the way she is. Morgan's still my twin. I can still feel her. There's something in her that's confused, unresolved."

"Relax. Morgan's made a career of being the confused kitten. That's not going to change. It's what works for her. Speaking of work, has Matt had any luck getting a job?"

"No. He's still waiting tables at the restaurant. Jess, it's awful. He hates being there. And I hate that he doesn't have anywhere else to go." Ali waited until she was sure she wouldn't cry. "Every morning, when I see him putting on that waiter's apron instead of going to a job with a serious paycheck, it's like this gut-kick reminder. We're another day closer to the end."

Ali looked across the yard toward the home she loved, her eyes swimming with tears. "Matt had us living on the edge, and now there isn't even an edge. We're about to lose everything…the house…the restaurant. Everything."

"You're not making a profit with the restaurant yet?"

"Nope. It's barely breaking even."

"Is Matt looking? Is he really trying to find work?"

Ali sighed. "He's doing everything he can. I know he'll find something eventually. It just doesn't look like he's going to find it in time."

"Where are you with him right now? Do you love him? Hate him?"

"I don't have a clue." Uneasiness was rolling through Ali in waves. "I've got this suspicion that I still don't know everything…that he's keeping some huge secret…and till I know what it is, I won't be able to make up my mind how I feel about him."

Ali didn't want to talk anymore. She just wanted to be in the garden with Sofie, quiet and alone. "I've got to go, Jess. Love you."

Ali ended the call as Sofie skipped past with a fistful of flowers in her hand and a halo of sunlight on her hair. Ali waved her phone, snapping a picture.

But Sofie was moving too fast and Ali's aim had been off.

The image on the screen was eerie, almost sinister—an area at the corner of the house, deep in shadow. And low to the ground, staring out from the heart of the darkness, was a pair of eyes. Close-set and glittering.

Ali lowered the phone, looked toward the shadow. A black cat was there, crouched beside the house, its eyes slitted and unblinking.

It shot a chill through Ali.

She quickly turned back toward the garden, and the sunlight.

Matt

MATT WAS A FLEDGLING WAITER—THERE HAD BEEN COMPLAINTS about his inefficiency. But now, to his surprise, one of his customers had complimented him.

He'd just delivered a plate of eggs to Mr. Wallace, the man who had hair the color of dried orange peels and always sat at the same small table in the dining area. "You're getting much better at this," Mr. Wallace said.

Matt was embarrassed. Grateful for the kindness. Ashamed of being stuck as a second-rate employee in Ali's restaurant.

"When I said you were getting better, I meant you're improving as a server." There was empathy in the look he was giving Matt. "But in the larger sense…things haven't gotten any better, have they?"

"Not yet." Matt had been relentlessly looking for other work for five months. And still nothing on the horizon. Nothing between him and the financial sinkhole that was swallowing more of his life every day. He didn't know how much longer he could last.

"Don't lose heart," Mr. Wallace told him. "No tide stays out forever."

"Maybe…but if it takes too long to show up, you still go down."

Several times lately, Matt had thought about suicide. The way he saw it, he was a zero as a man. Completely inadequate.

Danielle was the fiber-thin safety line keeping him from taking his own life. She was the only place where he didn't feel defective and laughable.

He and Danielle had continued to have emotional intimacy, but no sex. Matt had made it clear he loved Ali desperately and didn't want to cross that line. Instead, he shared a surprising openness with Danielle. He talked to her about everything that had damaged him, everything that was important to him. He told her some of the details he'd told Ali, and a lot of the ones he hadn't.

Early in their relationship, one afternoon when Matt arrived at the gatehouse to spend time with her, Danielle had called out to him from the bathroom. He found her in a long, copper tub that was curved at both ends and was unusually deep and wide.

While she lounged in her bath—after telling Matt how to make espresso in the coffeemaker in the kitchen—she chatted to him through the open bathroom door, saying, "You wouldn't believe how far back my family goes in the movie business. They've owned that crumbly old mansion up on the hill for like a million years. Now they rent it out to B-list rock bands or wannabe starlets and their B-list managers. Back in the day, Charlie Chaplin and Rudolph Valentino used to hang out up there. That's why I get to live in this supremely cool space. My parents cut me a deal on the rent."

Matt had returned with the coffee. But now Danielle was telling him, "Never mind. Put it over there. I don't think coffee's what I want."

"What do you want?" he asked.

She thought for a minute. "I want you to tell me your story."

Matt groaned and leaned against the wall. "You know my story. I'm a former college professor, now unemployed television writer, who's so messed up he's cheating on his wife with a woman he isn't even sleeping with."

"Then can you really call it cheating?" Danielle splashed down under the water and came up sleek and shining.

In the light from the arched window and in the gleam of the copper bathtub, Danielle looked as if she belonged to the realm of the spirit more than to the world of the flesh. Somehow, Matt felt completely free to tell her the truth about everything. And he started with what he'd done in those three missing days, just before he'd married Ali.

His story was long and complicated. There was tremendous violence in it, and shame. And he told Danielle all of it.

When he finished, he waited for her reaction, stone-faced and shaking, like a death-row inmate waiting for the needle prick that will kill him.

After a while, Danielle said, "Could you put my robe on me, please?" She came out of the tub, and Matt wrapped her bathrobe around her. "You've never shed even one tear about any of the things that happened?"

"What would be the point?" Matt said. "It's finished. Nothing I can do will change a single minute of it."

There wasn't a shred of judgment in the way she was looking at him. "Come. Lie down with me." Danielle was continuing to abide by the terms they'd agreed to in the beginning. No demands. No strings. No sex.

He was remembering the afternoon in his office when he'd made it clear he didn't want to dishonor Ali—and Danielle had said, "I don't want to wreck your home. I'm just offering you breathing space. For a little while."

That calm, undemanding attitude was what made being with her so easy, so seductive.

When Matt followed Danielle into her bedroom and got into her bed, he was scraped raw by the confessions he'd made. He held on to

Danielle as if he were afraid of dying. She said that being surrounded by evil wasn't the same as *being evil*. And he cried. Uncontrollably.

After saying it aloud, detailing what he had done, Matt couldn't imagine ever feeling clean, or light, again.

But that was only because he hadn't fully grasped the concept of catharsis. The powerful release that would come, now that he'd finally acknowledged the darkest parts of who he was.

Ali

A LI ADJUSTED THE FLAME UNDER A SKILLET ON THE STOVE. "ALL I said was…the produce guy delivered a bunch of rock-hard tomatoes this morning and—"

Morgan cut her off. "No. That's not all you said. You also said you have a food writer coming to review your lunch menu today." She slapped a container of butter onto the counter.

"And suddenly you're mad because it didn't occur to me I needed to take revenge for a bunch of unripe tomatoes?" Ali dropped a dollop of the butter into the skillet. "Why does it bother you?"

"Because I don't believe you. Everybody wants revenge when they get screwed."

Ali and Morgan were in the restaurant kitchen. Breakfast service was over, and there was still a while before the lunch rush. Ali was fixing a grilled cheese sandwich for Sofie, who was at the other end of the room, playing in the nursery Ava had made.

Morgan was on her way to a meeting at a museum in Los Angeles and had dropped by the restaurant for a quick visit—a visit that for some reason had escalated into an argument.

Ali was catching a glimpse of what she'd recently mentioned to Jessica—confusion in Morgan, something unresolved.

"Morgan, is there someone you want to take revenge on? Somebody you want to hurt?"

Morgan bit her lip. "Not really. It's just that every now and then,

I want what's fair. I want to even the score. Sometimes I want it so much it scares me."

"And if you did something like that, a big act of revenge, what would you get out of it?"

"I don't know. Maybe it would be like putting the period at the end of the last sentence in an old, boring story you're tired of. Maybe with that period there, you could finally end the story and start a new one."

"Or maybe you could just decide to toss the boring story and—" The butter in the skillet started to smoke. Without thinking, Ali grabbed the skillet's handle. The pan was one of her favorites, but it was ancient and the handle wasn't insulated. The burn across her palm was instant.

She dashed for the sink to hold her hand under the faucet. As she passed Morgan, she could have sworn that—just for a millisecond— Morgan had seen the burn and looked smug.

But then Morgan was suddenly at Ali's side. Filling a bowl with water and ice. Sliding Ali's hand into the healing coolness, murmuring, "I'm sorry. I didn't mean it. Don't worry. Everything's fine."

Morgan's visit had left Ali puzzled.

She still had a little frown of worry a few minutes later when the lunch rush started and she was in the restaurant kitchen answering her phone.

The frown disappeared the moment she heard Matt's voice. After eight and a half months of unemployment, they'd been handed a miracle, and he was telling her, "I'm here. I'm all settled in."

Recently, something in Matt had changed. He was calmer, less haunted, like he'd found peace. And Ali had begun very cautiously to let her guard down, to look past his failures and see how hard he was trying to be strong. For her—and for Sofie.

For the first time in a long time, she wasn't closed off and guarded as she spoke to Matt. "And where, precisely, are you?" she asked.

"In my new office."

"Is your name on the door?"

"Yes. It's also on a signed contract. I just finished hanging my PhD on the wall."

The backbreaking weight that had come so close to crushing her was finally lifting. "Oh my God. Even though we've been talking about it for weeks...up until this very minute, I've been afraid to believe it was real."

"Believe it, Al. It's real. I have a job."

Ali dropped the phone onto the kitchen's long wooden table, let out a shout, and did a silly little dance. The cooks and a passing waiter smiled, not understanding the reason for her happiness but pleased to see it.

Ali grabbed the phone and told Matt, "Let's go out to dinner tonight...to celebrate being saved!"

"Ali, it's an entry-level professorship in a screenwriting program in a brand-new film department at a very small, unfamous college. If we're going to make it, we'll still need to do what we talked about."

Ali moved out of the kitchen into the privacy of the walled garden, her excitement fading a little. "I know. We can't afford to keep the house. We have to sell it. I understand that." She brushed away a few scattered rose petals and sat on a stone bench at the edge of the garden. "For now, I just want to be happy about you having a job."

Matt's sigh was deep and contented. "The great thing is...it's not just any job. I'm in a classroom again. It's like you being in the restaurant. I'm home. I'm where I belong."

Ali looked across the garden toward the kitchen's open door. She could see the staff, busy with lunch orders. She left the bench, needing to get back to work, as Matt was telling her, "Kiss Sofie for me."

"I will, as soon as she wakes up. Lately she's been napping a lot."

"Banking her beauty sleep." Matt chuckled.

"I'll give her your kiss as soon as she's awake. And don't forget about us going out to dinner to celebrate. How about Smitty's? Want to see if they can take us around seven?"

There was an awkward silence. Then Matt said, "Ah…that might be a little early. I…uh… There's an errand I have to run, somebody I need to see."

Before Ali could ask who he needed to see, Matt told her, "Thank you for sticking by me." Then he added, "I love you, Al."

She didn't reply right away. She hesitated, just for a second. And in that click of time, Matt ended the call.

Ali thought about the odd pause before Matt mentioned the errand he needed to run, and she wondered, *Will it ever be easy again to tell him I love him?*

But she didn't have time to dwell on that question. There was something important she needed to do. Something that couldn't wait.

~

Ali crossed the dining area on a mission. Her destination was a small corner table where the bill had just been delivered to Mr. Wallace, the man with hair the color of dried orange peels. He was finishing his usual late breakfast.

"It's over," Ali told him, snatching the bill from the table. "This will never happen in my restaurant again, Mr. Wallace."

He laughed quietly. "You gave me eggs, Ali. Now I owe you money."

"Because of you, my husband has a job. You'll never buy a breakfast in this place again. That's nonnegotiable."

Mr. Wallace chuckled, obviously pleased. "You'll stay for a minute and have a cup of coffee with me…also nonnegotiable."

"Okay, but only if I can tell you what a hero you are." Ali signaled for a waitress, then slipped into a chair. "Mr. Wallace, I need you to know how much—"

The waitress arrived with the coffee, and Mr. Wallace used the interruption to say, "It must be good for Matt to be back in the saddle. He went a long time without employment. That's a tough thing for a man, not being able to find work. I know." Mr. Wallace waited until the catch in his voice was gone. "When this restaurant first opened, if you hadn't let me sit here for hours on end, while I made phone calls and sent out my tattered résumés, I would've never gotten on my feet again."

Ali started to speak—Mr. Wallace stopped her. "When my son told me about the new film program he was starting, and about the job opening for an instructor in screenwriting, it was not only my pleasure to give him Matt's name, it was my obligation."

"Most people wouldn't have thought of it. That's what makes you amazing," Ali said. "Matt told me he only mentioned his background to you once, in passing, months ago. You didn't even know him then. It was the first time he'd ever waited on you."

Mr. Wallace laughed. "It was the second time, actually. He was cleaning up the plate of eggs he'd just spilled, apologizing for his shortcomings as a waiter, explaining that his background was in teaching and writing for television." Mr. Wallace's tone was deeply emotional. "Matt never mentioned he was desperate to find work. He didn't need to; it was in his eyes. The same look that was in mine every morning for quite a while, whenever I had to face the mirror and shave."

"You're an angel, Mr. Wallace."

"As are you, dear Ali. We're all meant to be each other's angels."

Mr. Wallace opened his wallet and laid out a generous tip for the waitress. "It's not enough to sit back and rejoice when we receive our miracles. We need to look for opportunities to pass the bounty along. It's the only decent way to live."

~

When they'd finished their coffee, Mr. Wallace went off to work and Ali went back into the busy rush of the restaurant's kitchen. Eventually, Sofie woke up from her nap. And the day passed.

In the days that followed, Ali assumed she and Matt had only each other—and Mr. Wallace—to thank for their success in emerging from their darkness, whole and safe.

Ali didn't know about Danielle, or about the trips Matt made to the gatehouse *after* he'd found his teaching job.

Matt

WHEN MATT ANSWERED THE PHONE, AIDAN IMMEDIATELY asked, "Where are you?"

"In the car," Matt told him.

"Have a minute?"

"Yeah. It'll take me a while to get where I'm going. What do you want to talk about?"

"What happened to you with *Darling* was crap," Aidan said. "And since I was the one who talked you into taking the job, I feel guilty as shit."

"It wasn't your fault. No need for guilt on my account."

"I was raised a bloody Catholic. I've got the whole fucking world to feel guilty about."

Matt grinned. "It's good to hear from you. I've missed you."

"Then this should make you very happy. I'm putting together a major deal on a film. Set in the Australian outback. I want you to be part of it. It'll mean a tough eight or nine months, but it'll be an ass-kicking adventure and the money's huge. Say yes so I can get you, and what happened to you on that fucking television show, off my conscience."

Matt said nothing.

And Aidan asked, "Did I mention the money was huge? Massive amounts of zeroes with a plentiful supply of commas separating them?"

Matt still didn't respond, and Aidan insisted, "Like it or not, mate, you're a damn fine scriptwriter, and I want you making movies for me."

Matt hadn't been keeping up his end of the conversation. He was remembering the night of Ali's rape and how, if he hadn't been so engrossed in his work, things might have gone differently. He was remembering what an all-consuming business show business was.

"Well?" Aidan asked. "What do you say?"

"Thanks, but no thanks. I've accepted a teaching job. The classroom's where I'm meant to be. I'm happy there, and it gives me time at home, time with Ali. I don't think there's any amount of money I'd be willing to trade for that."

Aidan told him to think it over. Matt said he didn't need to.

He didn't have a single regret about declining Aidan's offer. He loathed show business, never wanted to go near it again.

Just as he ended the call, Matt turned into the driveway of the old limestone mansion, heading toward the gatehouse and Danielle.

Danielle wasn't there when Matt arrived at the gatehouse. He had to wander the sprawling property, looking for her.

He found her in the garden with a trash barrel nearby, cleaning debris from the basin of a large stone fountain near the entrance to the mansion. She was wearing an elegantly long, black skirt and a fitted cashmere T-shirt with sequined cap sleeves. For any woman other than Danielle, that outfit, paired with what she was doing, would have been absurd—but on her, it seemed perfectly appropriate.

She held up an empty vodka bottle and a waterlogged basketball shoe. "Can you guess what went on at the big house last night?"

"I'm thinking the tenants had a party." Matt reached over her shoulder, scooping a green nylon wig from the fountain and tossing it into the trash barrel. "Do your parents give you a break on the rent in return for your services as a groundskeeper?" he asked.

"Uh-uh. They have a guy…but when I saw the mess, I figured they could use some help."

"Will you tell your folks you're the one who did the cleanup?"

She thought about it for a moment. "Probably not."

Matt laughed. "That's you all over, isn't it?"

Danielle rinsed her hands in the water flowing from the center of the fountain. Her tone was matter-of-fact. "I didn't expect you today. I'm going out in a little while."

Matt's smile wavered. He picked up a small stone, briefly held it in his hand, and then skipped it hard across the surface of the water in the fountain's basin. "If I said I needed you right now, Danielle… would you still go?"

Danielle was drying her hands on the hem of her skirt. "Back when this started, I told you exactly when I'd go. After we both came out all right and had our lives on track again."

There was a feeling of dread in Matt—the fear that he was losing something he wasn't ready to let go of.

"After we were both all right. That's what you said." Matt touched his fingertips to Danielle's; hers were uncharacteristically cold. "But what you actually meant was that you'd leave after I had *my* life on track." He was quiet for a second. "I have the feeling yours always was. Wasn't it?"

She shrugged and pulled away. "Pretty much."

Matt watched her perch at the edge of the fountain, elf-like and beautiful—the mist from the fountain's spray settling on her hair and glittering like a crown on a fairy queen.

He knew she was finished with him. That she could be so calm about it drove him crazy.

"Why did you do it?" he asked.

"What?"

"Why did you give so much, accept so much, and never say what you wanted in return? What did you get out of it?"

Danielle scooped a handful of water, letting it drip through her fingers. "A long time ago, I figured out the truth about me. I don't have the face, or the tits. I'm cute, but I'm not dream-girl material. I'm way too short, and way too freaky in the way my mind works. Definitely too freaky for most guys." When she spoke again, it was with absolute tranquility. "But I always knew I had bigger things to do than be a hot chick." She glanced at Matt. "Do you have any idea what I'm talking about?"

He skipped another stone across the water, annoyed. "Why don't you tell me?"

"I'm pretty satisfied with who I am," Danielle said. "I'm happy almost all the way through, so it's easy to offer myself without any strings attached. I like doing it. I like seeing what it does. I like watching how good I can make people feel."

"That's what you're all about? Giving to the other person and wanting nothing of them in return?" Matt's question was filled with bitterness. "You enjoy sitting back, uninvolved and clinical, like what you're doing isn't anything more than a lab experiment?"

"It worked for you, didn't it? You said it was what you wanted. You seemed to like it." Danielle's reply was mild. But buried in the mildness there was something combative.

Her tone irritated Matt. "I liked it. I liked everything you did for me. But for Christ's sake, Danielle, I liked you, too."

"Just so you know…I meant what I said about wanting to give you comfort and understanding, and not wanting to break up your marriage. But I guess I had you figured wrong."

"How?"

"I figured you were like most guys. And eventually we'd get around to fucking."

She'd said fucking—not being intimate, not making love—just generic, garden-variety fucking. Matt suddenly understood every-thing. He ached like he'd been sucker punched.

"While we were together…you were seeing other people."

Danielle seemed amused. "Weren't you crawling into bed with your wife every night?"

Her focus had gone back to the fountain. She was flicking leaves from the surface of the water. "In the interest of full disclosure, I'm ready to be with somebody, head over heels in love. I'm ready right this minute."

There was the slightest stutter in Matt's heartbeat. Some irrational part of him hoped to hear her say he was the man she wanted. But the fantasy evaporated before it had taken shape. Matt belonged to Ali. Completely. Emotionally and physically. He would never, for any reason, hurt her, or leave her. His relationship with Danielle hadn't been about unhappiness with Ali; it had always been about Matt's unhappiness with himself.

The person he needed to leave was Danielle. Matt understood it was over between them. Yet he couldn't move. He was immobilized by a sad-sweet feeling of commencement. The ending that marks the beginning. The moment of letting go where there's both anticipation and mourning.

Danielle slipped her arm through his and walked him toward his car. "I'm definitely ready to fall in love," she said. "With somebody who doesn't care about strings…a guy who can share himself with me, and other people, just for the happiness of it."

"It sounds like you're waiting for a saint."

"I'm waiting for what everybody's waiting for," Danielle said. "I'm waiting for my soul mate."

~

When he thought about it later, Matt couldn't honestly say how much, if any, of what Danielle had told him was the truth. Her version of love was probably just as passionate and clinging and messy as everyone else's.

But the bottom line was that they were done.

Danielle had cut him free.

And Matt was back in a familiar place. Alone with his secrets.

Morgan

"M Y GOODNESS, MORGAN, YOU'RE ABSOLUTELY BEAUTIFUL." HER mother stared at her in wide-eyed surprise.

Morgan loved the compliment, hated the surprise.

"I can't believe how good you look…the muscle tone in your legs." Her mother was taking in every detail. "You have highlights in your hair. And that outfit…it's fabulous. I've never seen you in anything like it. And, honey, your skin…it's—"

"Stop it," Morgan snapped. "All that happened is I've been spending time outdoors, with Ralph."

"Ralph?"

"Ralph's my dog. On the weekends, we go running. And because of that, I'm in better shape. And being out…running…I made some new friends. One of them's a stylist. She goes shopping with me, gives me advice on clothes."

"Simply having a dog brought about all these wonderful changes? It's like you're a completely different person, inside and out."

For a fleeting second, Morgan was about to say, *Ali changed me. Without even knowing she did it, she showed me how much better I needed to be.* But it seemed too personal. Sharing her innermost thoughts with her mother wasn't something Morgan was comfortable with.

Her mother gazed at Morgan, fascinated. "Honey, you look incredibly lovely."

"Do you really have to act so surprised?" Morgan bit her lip to keep from crying. "Didn't it ever occur to you that I could look good?"

"Oh, honey, no. I just meant—"

"Mom. I made a couple of friends, bought some new clothes, and started exercising. It's no big deal." Morgan quickly turned away and began brushing the curls back into Sofie's sleep-flattened hair. Sofie had just woken up from a nap. And the three of them—Sofie, Morgan, and Morgan's mother—were in an upstairs bedroom in Jessica's magnificent hilltop house. Downstairs, there was a party going on.

Morgan hadn't expected to find her mother in the room when she came to look in on Sofie. The tension had been immediate—and in the fifteen minutes they'd been alone together, it had steadily escalated.

"You know, Morgan, I loved my job in retail," her mother was saying. "I loved the clothes and the customers, but I was counting the days till I could retire, just so I could come to California and have a nice, long visit."

Morgan put down the hairbrush and let Sofie scamper away.

The fight was on. And, unable to stop herself, Morgan threw the first punch. "About that nice, long visit…who did you really come out here to see, Mom?"

"Well, I—"

"You didn't come to see me. You were here for almost a week before you—"

"Morgan, you had stopped speaking to me for the better part of a year. I didn't know what to do…didn't know whether you wanted me to contact you or leave you alone."

"Face it, Mom. The reason you came to California was because you wanted to see Ali. And you wanted to meet Sofie."

"Of course I wanted to be with Ali and Sofie, but…"

Morgan's expression was hard as stone. But she sounded fragile, vulnerable—like a little girl. "Would you have come if it was just me?"

"Honey, of course I would."

Her mother reached for her, and Morgan pushed her away. "Go downstairs, Mom. Go help everybody celebrate the end of summer."

"I will. In a minute. First, I want to catch up. I want to know what's happening with you." Her mother sat on the arm of Morgan's chair. "Are you dating anyone? Anybody special?"

Morgan shook her head no. She didn't want to talk about Ben Tennoff. He might not seem big and bright enough. Ben hadn't ever been in the Hollywood fast lane, the cocreator of a hit television show like Matt. And he wasn't a big-time businessman like Jessica's husband, Logan, driving a Porsche and playing country club golf. Ben taught high-school history and loved opera.

Ben was a great guy. Morgan truly liked him, but she was still ambivalent about his appearance and his lack of a high-powered job. Handsome and high-powered had always been the first things Morgan looked for. That was the kind of man who was attracted to Ali. And Morgan hadn't wanted to settle for second best. But now Ben Tennoff was making her wonder about all of that. It wasn't something she was ready to discuss. Especially not with her mother.

"I worry about you," her mother said. "I worry that you'll waste too much time looking for the wrong man and end up spending the rest of your life in an extra chair at somebody else's dinner table."

Her mother had touched a nerve. "If I do end up alone, it'll be because of you."

Her mother took a step back, didn't say anything—but Morgan knew she'd hurt her.

"Mom, you never showed me how to have a decent relationship. You couldn't even hold it together with Dad long enough for me to get out of elementary school."

"Oh, that's not fair, Morgan. You had examples of strong, loving relationships. You had my parents, and you had—"

"I didn't have what I *needed*!" Morgan was caught in the

emotional firestorm that had been going on since childhood. She was still grieving over her parent's divorce and her father being gone, married to somebody else. She was still envious of, and intimidated by, her mother's green-eyed beauty. And she was still furious that her mother was never able to understand what it was like to live in Morgan's skin.

And in the midst of all of this, she was longing for her mother's touch.

The longing was so intense, it made Morgan say something she didn't really mean: "I've never been loved the way you love Ali. And I hate you for that."

Before Morgan could take back what she'd just said, her mother was in tears.

Seeing her mother's pain broke Morgan's heart. "Mom, I—"

"Go away, Morgan," Her mother's tone was flat. "For a little while, please, just leave me alone."

Still feeling the sting of the hurt she'd caused, Morgan went downstairs. Desperately wishing she knew how to turn around and ask her mother for a hug.

⌢

Morgan had finished crying but was still hiding. On Jessica's terrace. Sitting on a plush patio lounge, behind a wall of ferns. For several minutes, she'd been there in total silence. Then the wind shifted, and she heard Matt's voice, and Logan's.

Morgan immediately ducked down. It was silly, but she didn't want Logan to see her with her eyes puffy from crying. Ever since their brief encounter on his wedding night, she'd been fascinated by his magazine-cover looks, and by the idea that he had been briefly attracted to her. Keeping low to the ground, she scooted closer, peering through the ferns. Logan was only a few feet away with Matt—drinking margaritas and firing up the barbecue.

Logan nodded in the direction of the pool, where Ali and Jessica were playing with Logan and Jessica's twin boys. "So how do you like suddenly having a kid?" he asked.

"Still getting used to it," Matt said.

"Let me tell you, buddy, having kids changes things." Logan took the plastic wrap off a platter of steaks. "Before the twins, my wife was moderately good at giving me orders and occasionally mentioning my failings as a husband. But now? It's nonstop orders and constant harping. Mostly about how supremely shitty I am at being a dad. Apparently fatherhood's opened up a whole new category for me to fuck up in." Logan's laugh had an undercurrent of real hostility.

Morgan was startled by it.

Yet Logan appeared to be completely calm, laying out a line of steaks on the grill and telling Matt, "The company has offices everywhere from Palm Springs to the Sierras. It's good that my work keeps me on the road. All I can take is maybe twenty minutes of Jess yakking about earth-friendly diapers and stuffy noses before she has me ready to put my fist through a wall."

Matt gazed across the lawn toward the pool, toward Ali. "At least your wife still talks to you. All those months I was out of work, Ali hardly said a word to me. I've never been so alone."

"Men and women are wired completely differently," Logan said. "If it wasn't for sex, I don't think we'd have any interaction with them at all."

"You're wrong." Matt seemed thoughtful. "During the time I'm talking about, there was a woman…somebody I never slept with. I couldn't have survived without the connection we had. In a way, I think she saved my life."

"And you never fucked her?"

"No. It wasn't like that. It never got to the point where it was about sex. It was…it was something different. When we were together, it was always at her place, and only for a few hours. Mostly we talked. Sometimes we listened to music…or cooked a meal. She lived in the gatehouse of an old mansion. We'd take long walks through overgrown gardens that were like jungles, and…" Matt shook his head, as if bewildered by what he was about to say. "With her, there was never any judgment. No criticism. I felt totally free… had this amazing openness. I've never experienced anything like it."

Morgan couldn't believe what she had just heard. Matt, Ali's perfect husband, had been cheating on her.

For the first time in her life, Morgan felt lucky not to be her sister.

Not wanting Matt to catch sight of her, Morgan carefully sidestepped out of her hiding place and headed toward the pool.

Ali was at the shallow end, guiding one of Jessica's little boys through the water, telling Jessica, "It felt like Matt was having an affair. I was sure of it. There were lots of times I'd call his cell, and it went straight to voice mail. He'd never done that before. He'd always pick up, even if it was just to say he was busy and couldn't talk."

"Was he?" Jessica asked. "Having an affair, I mean."

Ali shook her head. "He was trying to hide that he was out of work. After his show was canceled, he didn't tell me for weeks."

"Okay, but what does that prove? He could've been out of work *and* having an affair."

"No. That would've been too much."

Morgan was now close enough to the pool to hear how frightened Ali sounded. Jessica had obviously touched pain in Ali that was very personal. It was clear to Morgan that her sister was wrestling with something bigger, and far worse, than Matt being unfaithful. Morgan couldn't figure out what it was. But from the look in Ali's eyes, it was devastating.

Jessica lowered her voice and asked, "How could you not know Matt didn't have a job? You never called his office number...only his cell?"

"The truth is, around that time, I was hardly calling him at all. We didn't have a lot to say to each other after the..." Ali faltered. "After a problem I'd had."

What problem? Morgan wondered. *What could've happened that was dreadful enough to leave such a haunted look in Ali's eyes?*

Jessica seemed not to notice Ali's distress. "Wow...so the issue was you and Matt. For a while there, right after your housewarming, I thought you were pissed at me for some reason. You wouldn't answer my calls, my emails. Then you had Matt blow me off about the Perfect Ten...in a text. It pretty much killed me."

"There was no way I could've gone on a ski trip right then, Jess. Everything was just too weird."

Ali had put a shiver into Morgan. Even though they weren't as close as they used to be, Ali was still Morgan's twin. And Morgan suspected that whatever her sister was covering up wasn't over. An aspect of it was still a threat to Ali.

"So that's it? That's all you're gonna give me...that around Christmas, something weird happened?" Jessica said. "No details?"

"No details." Ali's smile was tense, as if she was trying not to cry.

"But everything's okay with you now? Right?"

Ali gathered her hair onto the top of her head and let it fall free again, giving herself time to regain her composure. "Yeah. Things are looking up, but..." Her voice trailed away. Then she said, "Money's a problem. Matt has been getting his office ready, but classes at the college don't start until next week. We're still a month away from his first paycheck."

One of Jessica's sons splashed past, and Ali wiped pool water from her eyes. "We're selling the house. Even with what Matt will make as a teacher and what I'm bringing in from the restaurant...there's no way we can afford to stay."

Morgan dropped down onto one of the lawn chairs, shocked. She'd had no idea Ali and Matt were about to lose their house.

"Oh God," Jessica said. "I know how much you love that place."

"It's my dream house, Jess. I can picture myself getting old there. And it's where I wanted Sofie to grow up. I was looking at the staircase the other night...imagining Sofie walking down it in her wedding dress."

Jessica's boys had collided, briefly dunking themselves under the water. Jessica scooped them up and waded toward the side of the pool, telling Ali, "You know how much I love you, and that I want to help, but—"

"Jess, no. Please, that isn't what I meant. I wasn't asking for help."

With her children settled onto the pool deck, Jessica made an unnecessary adjustment to her bathing suit. Morgan noticed that Jessica wasn't meeting Ali's eyes as she said, "You know I'd do anything I could." Jessica abruptly faced away from the barbecue area where Logan and Matt were. "Ali, this is so off the record that if you tell anybody, I swear, I'll murder you. The reason I can't help you out is..."

Morgan leaned forward in her chair, straining to hear.

"My connection to cash isn't what it used to be," Jessica said. "Daddy had his money invested with some A-list scammer, and the family fortune's gone up in smoke, thanks to a good, old-fashioned Ponzi scheme." She gave one of her tough-girl laughs. "You're lucky you don't want my help. Al, I couldn't lend you a dime. I—"

A shout had come from the barbecue area. Logan saying, "Two-minute warning on the gabfest. Steaks are ready."

"I just hope you didn't overcook them like you always do!" Jessica shouted back. Then she confided to Ali, "I can still talk to him like that because he doesn't know he isn't married to money anymore." She began gathering up pool toys. "I haven't told him yet, so don't say anything, okay?"

"Not a word. I promise."

"And don't worry about me. Even in my newly impoverished state, I'm okay. It's only the extras that'll have to go. Things like Logan's boat and some other stuff. But our basic monthly expenses are covered. He's doing fine money-wise. We're not going to lose the house or anything."

Morgan saw the stab of envy her sister was experiencing. It broke Morgan's heart.

"You know that old saying?" Jessica murmured. "'He who has the gold makes the rules'? Well, it's always been 'my gold, my rules.'" She looked in Logan's direction. "I wonder how I'll keep him in line when he finds out he's the only one around here with cash."

Morgan watched Jessica's mood turn on a dime as Jessica leaned in close to her twins, sniffing the air with a wry grin. "Tell me again why fourteen months is too soon to start potty-training these people?"

~

Afternoon had faded into early evening. The steaks had been served, and the meal was finished.

Everyone was lingering at the table, chatting and watching the children play on the lawn. Jessica and Logan's sons were busy with toy trucks. Sofie was romping with a huge orange-colored helium balloon that was attached to her wrist by a long, thin length of Mylar.

Morgan wasn't focusing on any of it. She couldn't get her mind off what Ali had told Jessica about having to sell the house, and about that other "problem." The one Ali wouldn't name. *What was it?* Morgan wondered. There had been so much pain in her sister's eyes.

She was worried, wanted to help, needed to figure out where to begin. But Jessica was tapping her on the shoulder, saying, "Would you be a love and run up to the house...tell the housekeeper to bring dessert?"

Morgan walked away with the feeling that Jessica's gaze was following her. A split second later, she heard Jessica whisper to Ali, "Am I crazy, or has our little caterpillar turned into a butterfly?"

~

Jessica's kitchen was empty. The pantry door, which had a center panel of textured glass, was slightly ajar. Morgan noticed someone moving around on the other side of it and assumed it was the maid.

When Morgan pushed the door open, she discovered the pantry was surprisingly large. Chrome shelves lined all four walls, and in the middle of the room, there was a waist-high storage island with a black-granite top. Logan was at the far end of the island—an open bottle of vodka in one hand and a half-empty glass in the other.

Morgan was surprised to see him there. "Oh. It's you. I was looking for the maid."

Logan lifted his glass. "This is my way of having another drink without listening to my wife bitching that I don't need one." He drained the vodka in a series of slow gulps. When the glass was empty, he put it down and looked at Morgan. He held the look for a long beat, as if he was evaluating her, as if she were a car he was thinking about buying.

When he finally said "Shut the door," Morgan was reminded of that night in Newport, on the terrace of her guest room, when Logan had offered her what sounded like a playful dare.

"Jessica wants the dessert brought out." Morgan could tell that Logan was slightly drunk. It made her a little uncomfortable.

He seemed amused and slowly repeated what he'd just said: "Shut. The. Door."

She closed the door carefully. Thinking about Ben, what a nice guy he was, but she was curious to see how these next few minutes would play out. Earlier, in the upstairs bedroom, her mother had told her "You're absolutely beautiful." And Morgan wanted, just for a little while, to flirt. To enjoy the power of being pretty.

She was close enough to Logan to inhale the scent of his cologne, along with the salty smell of sweat and barbecue smoke.

He was grinning at her.

She smiled back, enjoying their little game of cat and mouse.

Logan reached out and touched Morgan's silky, summer dress; it was knee length, fitted loosely at her hips. Before she could move away, he lifted her skirt, letting his gaze quickly travel the length of her thigh.

Watching her skirt float back into place, he murmured, "Sweet. Even better than I remembered."

Morgan stepped away, smoothed her skirt. "While my sister and I weren't talking to each other, I got a dog. I'm outside a lot. I'm in better shape than I used to be."

The atmosphere shifted, the playfulness gone. There was unmistakable sexual tension now. Logan's look told Morgan exactly where he planned to go next. She knew she should leave.

But his fingertips were already on her skin—tracing the scar at her hairline, the tiny healed-over wound that vaguely resembled a question mark.

For a split second, she felt a rush of excitement and was tempted. The same way she'd been tempted in Newport on Logan's wedding night. But things were different now. She was different—not so lost and desperate.

Morgan opened her mouth to tell Logan she was leaving but didn't have the chance to say it. She was drowned out by a series of terrified screams.

They were coming from outside the house. From the backyard.

~

Ali was screaming when Morgan raced onto the lawn. Matt was running toward Sofie.

Sofie was on the patio, unconscious. A few feet away from an overturned barstool. One of her arms was twisted underneath her like a pretzel, tangled in the Mylar string attached to the helium balloon she'd been playing with.

The balloon floated above Sofie's body. In the light of the setting sun, it looked like a ball of orange fire.

Ali

T HE HOSPITAL ROOM WAS SPOTLESSLY CLEAN, RIGHT DOWN TO the floors. At the slightest touch of a shoe, they squeaked. The bed had chrome rails, and the sheets were blizzard white. Although the bed was tiny, it looked enormous to Ali, because it was empty.

Her mother was insisting, "We need to pray. All of us together," while Morgan kept asking, "Where's the doctor? Where the hell is the doctor?"

"Shut up!" The words came out of Ali in a frightened shout. "Both of you! Shut up!"

Matt looked anguished, and said absolutely nothing.

Ali couldn't stop thinking that she was to blame for what had happened to Sofie. At Jessica's party, Ali had turned away, just for a minute. When she turned back, Sofie was up on that ridiculously tall barstool. Before Ali could get to her, Sofie toppled and hit the cement.

"They've finished all the tests and the imaging." There'd been the squeak of a shoe in the doorway—a doctor was in the room. A man with a haggard, soulful face. "We've sent her upstairs. She's being prepped for surgery."

Ali reached for Matt, holding on to him for support. "How serious is it?"

"We were lucky," the doctor told her. "The EMTs did a great job stabilizing her arm. As far as the surgery goes, she has an outstanding team around her. The surgeon who's doing your daughter's procedure is the best."

"And once the surgery's finished, then what? She'll be fine?" Ali was torn between hope and fear.

"Your child managed to fall from a high perch onto a hard surface. She shattered her arm in a way that will make it a challenge to repair. The injury is significant. We can put things back together for now. But there's a strong possibility that as she gets older, she'll need additional surgeries."

Ali dropped into a chair. Worried. And relieved. She looked up at Matt, wanting to say, *Thank God. Sofie's going to be okay*, but the odd mix of emotions on Matt's face shocked her into silence.

The first thing Ali noticed was Matt's look of resentment, as if something he cherished was being unfairly taken away from him. Then, almost immediately, the resentment was swallowed by anguish and a kind of cold-eyed determination—as if he was voluntarily killing off some vital part of himself.

It was frightening to watch. Ali wanted to ask Matt what was going on. Before she could, the doctor was telling her, "Don't blame yourself. Kids move like lightning bugs, and they have accidents. No parent can keep them safe every minute of the day."

The doctor put his hand on her shoulder for a moment. "I need to go upstairs now. I'll make sure they take good care of your little girl. The surgeon will be here in a minute to talk to you."

As soon as the doctor left, Morgan leaned against Ali and asked, "Why does life have to be like this? Why is something terrible always waiting to happen?"

Their mother tried to speak, cleared her throat, and tried again. "I don't know if you girls remember, but your father used to say that our life on earth is the cosmic version of fourth grade. It's a test...and we're not here primarily to be happy. The big reason we're here is that we're supposed to be learning something."

"Like what?" Morgan's question was pure bewilderment.

"I think it's different for everyone. I think we each have our own individual lessons to learn. And life keeps testing us on the same things till we figure out how to get them right...or at least come closer to getting them right."

Ali's mother glanced toward the window, seemed to be looking into the past. "Maybe happiness isn't about never having problems. Maybe it's about learning from them. And doing better every time the test shows up."

When her mother uttered that phrase—*doing better every time the test shows up*—Ali watched Matt tremble and noticed an angry flush spread across his face.

In that same moment, another squeak came from the doorway. A new doctor was in the room. The man who would perform Sofie's surgery.

Ali couldn't believe what she was seeing.

His hair was longer now, slightly messy, as if he was in the habit of running his hands through it. His body was leaner, not as chiseled and rock hard. His face was thinner. His eyes weren't as open and bright as they'd been. But there was no doubt about who he was— Ali's former neighbor from the apartment complex.

"Peter!" she said. "Peter Sebelius."

Morgan

WOW. IT'S INSANE HOW FAST KIDS HEAL. IT'S ONLY BEEN A FEW weeks, and Sofie's doing so well." Morgan was on a step stool, looking down at Ali.

Ali smiled up at her. "It was like an answer to a prayer, having Peter Sebelius handle her surgery. He's an incredibly good doctor."

Ali and Morgan were in the closet in Ali's bedroom. Ali was searching the floor while Morgan, on the step stool, searched the overhead shelf. They were hunting for a pair of sandals Morgan wanted to wear to a garden party fund-raiser at the museum. She and Ali had spent the day together, talking and laughing. It had been good but not exactly the way it used to be. Something between them was different, something fundamental.

All afternoon, Morgan had been trying to determine what had changed, and she finally had the answer. She had changed. *Up until now, it was always like Ali was on a pedestal, in a spotlight, and I was in a dingy hole. I thought it was her fault that I was stuck in that hole. And I wanted to punish her for putting me there.*

"But I'm not in the hole anymore." Without intending to, Morgan had spoken her thought aloud—and Ali asked, "What hole?"

And Morgan immediately remembered a horrible thing she'd done while she'd been in that jealousy-filled hole. It took every ounce of courage she could find to ask Ali, "Do you remember that guy Zev Tilden, the big-time chef you were supposed to do the internship with?"

"Yeah. I still think about that… I never did understand what happened. One day he was saying I was a gift to the world of food, then the next thing I knew, he'd handed my spot to somebody else. And he claimed I told him to do it."

"I saw something on TV yesterday." There was a flutter in Morgan's chest—remorse and a desperate hope that this would make everything okay. "Zev Tilden's been arrested. Apparently great food isn't the only thing he likes. He also likes taking videos of himself having sex with thirteen-year-old girls."

"Oh my God. That's completely disgusting."

Morgan was nervous. This was the make-or-break. "So it probably turned out to be a good thing…you not getting the apprenticeship. You wouldn't have wanted to work with a guy who's a total pig, right?"

"No. Of course not."

Morgan was flooded with relief.

"You look happy," Ali said.

"I am." Morgan went back to searching for the sandals.

"That nice guy you're seeing. Ben. When do I get to meet him?"

"Not for a while. He's going out of town. He'll be in Washington, DC, on a big field trip with his students."

Even before Ben told her about his trip, Morgan was having trouble scheduling time to see him. Her new job kept her incredibly busy. And the truth was, she'd been grateful for the built-in buffer. Her dates with Ben were low-key and wonderful. Their relationship was moving toward the next level—something Morgan wasn't quite ready to do.

Her feelings for Ben were tender, and it was the reason she'd asked him to be patient about having sex. Sleeping with sweet, gentle Ben Tennoff would make her want to stay with him. She'd been out in the world for only a handful of months. Discovering who she was, spreading her wings. Morgan needed time to be sure that Ben—the quiet, serious history teacher—was the man she wanted to stay with.

"And what about work?" Ali asked. "Are you still liking your job? Your boss?"

"Mr. Dupuis? He's the best. He's seriously old school and formal... intimidates me like crazy...but what I'm learning from being around him is amazing."

"It's great to see you this upbeat."

"I have a terrific job and a pretty place to live. A little niece I adore. And a sister I love. How could I not be happy?" Morgan looked up at the shelf full of shoe boxes and whistled, as if calling a pet. "Come on, you fabulously cute sandals, come to Morgan!"

Ali answered with a playful singsong, "Come out, come out, wherever you are!"

Morgan laughed—like she used to laugh when she and Ali were little, in the summers on BerryBlue Farm.

"It's nice, us being together and having fun." Ali had abandoned the search for the sandals and was gathering up some of Sofie's toys that were scattered on the bedroom floor.

Morgan was slightly embarrassed as she said, "I won't miss her. Will you?"

"Who won't you miss?"

"That idiot. 'Poor Morgan.'" Morgan was thinking about all the pain she had caused her sister.

She remembered when they were seniors in high school. Ali was devastated because her three best friends had left on a graduation trip to Myrtle Beach, without her. Ali had been looking forward to the trip for months. And the reason she didn't get to go was Morgan. Morgan had been jealous that Ali hadn't invited her to come along. It didn't matter that the other girls who were going to Myrtle Beach were Ali's friends, not Morgan's—and they were the ones who'd organized the event. All Morgan cared about was making Ali include her. When it became clear Morgan was staying home, she found a way to be sure Ali stayed home, too.

A week before Ali was scheduled to leave, she and Morgan were running errands in their mother's car—Ali driving, Morgan in the passenger seat. Ali had been pulled over by a state trooper. Never moving from the passenger seat, Morgan slipped their mother's camera out of the glove compartment and took a photograph of the trooper handing Ali a speeding ticket. Worried that the ticket would ruin her chances to go to Myrtle Beach, Ali begged Morgan not to tell. Morgan swore she wouldn't say a word. Then she left the photograph where she was sure their mother would see it.

Ali was grounded. Heartbroken about missing the trip. And furious with Morgan for taking the picture. Yet, later that night, when Morgan was frightened by a nightmare, Ali had let her climb into bed with her, drowsily draping a protective arm around Morgan's shoulders. Morgan had drifted off to sleep with her head on Ali's pillow, breathing in Ali's scent. A cool, sweet smell that had always reminded Morgan of spring flowers.

Now, as Morgan was watching Ali gathering Sofie's toys, she realized that all along the way, life had been inflicting hurt on Ali.

Only a short time ago, at Jessica's party, Morgan had heard the sorrow in Ali when she said, *"We have to sell the house. There's no way we can afford to stay."* And then there was the grief in Ali's eyes when she mentioned a problem she'd had, something that happened to her just before Christmas. Something Morgan still hadn't figured out. And there was what Morgan had seen on the day after Ali's December housewarming—Ali in a gray nightgown, deathly pale, with a ravaged, haunted look on her face.

For the first time, Morgan was seeing the amount of pain Ali had been given, and the grace with which Ali endured it.

Morgan was ashamed of how she'd gobbled up so much of Ali's happiness, assuming happiness was all Ali ever experienced. She was ashamed of the decades she'd spent laying siege to Ali's life, dragging behind her sister like a boat anchor. But most of all, Morgan was ashamed of having been too selfish to see it had been her job to take care of Ali, just as much as it was Ali's job to take care of her.

Tears were pooling, and Morgan fought them. She didn't want to think about what used to be. She wanted to stay right here, right now. Where she was a new person—and she and Ali were so good together.

Ali had picked up a storybook and a doll from the bedside table, Morgan's latest gifts to Sofie. The book's cover was a magnificent drawing of a doe-eyed Navajo girl, and the doll was a costumed replica of the girl. "I've never seen anything this beautiful. Morgan, where did you find these?"

"I don't know. It's sort of like they found me." Morgan hastily wiped away a tear. "I had a copy of that book when you and I were little, and I hated it, because the Navajo girl got lost from her magic twin. I hated it so much I tore the pages out and burned them in the fireplace."

"You hated this book, and now you've bought it for Sofie?"

"I should've finished it before I decided to tear it up. It turns out the girl has this awesome adventure while she's searching for her twin. In the end, she finds her sister and rescues her, and discovers she has magic of her own." Morgan's smile was sheepish.

Ali was admiring the doll's intricate costume. "This must have cost a fortune. You're spoiling Sofie like crazy. You know that, don't you?"

"Don't worry, this stuff isn't for now. It's for when she's older." Morgan took the doll from Ali and put it next to the book. This was a new experience for Morgan, being the giver, spontaneously delivering a present to someone she loved, doing it just for the joy of doing it. She thought about the phone call with Sam when she'd said, "I want Sofie to see me as wonderful!" and Sam had told her, "Then *be* wonderful. Live with your arms wide open to the world."

Suddenly, Morgan understood what Sam was trying to tell her. Love can't be demanded. The only way it can exist is as a gift. Given from an unlocked heart.

Morgan was smiling as she headed back toward the closet, telling Ali, "It doesn't matter how much the doll and the book cost. It's my job to spoil Sofie. That's what fabulously wonderful aunts do. And this fabulous aunt still needs a pair of sandals to wear to a very cool garden party."

Morgan happily climbed onto the step stool and went back to her search. Ali was contentedly putting away the last of Sofie's toys.

And then, out of nowhere, Ali's mood changed. She seemed uncomfortable, worried.

Under a stack of shoe boxes, Morgan had found a file folder full of clippings and scribbled notes and printouts from the Internet.

As quickly as she could, Ali jerked the folder away from Morgan and whipped it closed. But not before Morgan had looked at several of the articles. She'd also seen that a note was paper-clipped to the folder's inside cover. A sheet of expensive stationery with a handwritten message: *Like I told you, the guy's trademark was the name he called his victims, the name of a summer wildflower...and he always took their underwear. Here's the info you asked for—the news stories on the rapes. Love, Jessica.*

Morgan almost fell off the step stool.

She knew. She just knew. This had something to do with the ravaged look she'd seen on Ali's face the day after the housewarming.

Morgan was shaking when she asked her sister, "Why are you keeping articles about rapes in your closet?"

Ali

"WHY ARE YOU KEEPING ARTICLES ABOUT RAPES IN YOUR CLOSET?" The question hung in the air like a bomb waiting to explode.

Clutching the file folder Morgan had just found, Ali ducked her head—buying time to think.

When she'd asked Jessica for this folder, and Jessica had asked why she was borrowing it, Ali hadn't told her the truth. Now that Morgan had unearthed the folder after all these months, Ali still wasn't prepared to tell the truth. She was still too frightened to talk about her rape.

Her attacker hadn't been caught. It was like he was always lurking, just out of sight. Stalking Ali with fear. Every day. Every night.

She'd wanted him found and punished. She'd borrowed the folder believing she had the strength to search for him herself. But when she got the folder home, what was inside it—the catalog of violence and perversion—was more than she could deal with. Ali had shoved the folder onto her closet shelf. And never looked at it again.

"Did you hear what I said?" Morgan asked. "What's the deal with this thing?"

Ali recognized the unspoken statement buried in Morgan's question: *I'm your twin. I already know it's something big. The only thing I don't know is what the "something" is.* Ali was tempted to confess and lighten her burden by sharing it with her sister. But it wasn't the right time. Not now, when she and Morgan were in such a good place, and Sofie was home from the hospital, and Peter Sebelius and his wife were coming for dinner. And *life* was coming back into Ali's life.

She reached up and slipped the file folder back onto the closet shelf, deciding to give Morgan the same story she'd given Jessica. "I borrowed it for Matt. He was doing research for one of his scripts."

Morgan seemed surprised. "Matt's still writing scripts?"

"It's…it was from a while ago. When he was working with Aidan." Ali needed a way out of this conversation before she was tripped up by any more lies.

To Ali's relief, Morgan appeared to accept her explanation. She'd gone back to looking for the sandals, excitedly announcing, "Here they are! I found them!"

Downstairs, the oven timer was buzzing in the kitchen. Ali hurried toward the door, calling over her shoulder, "Stay for dinner, okay?"

"I can't," Morgan said. "A friend, the stylist who's been helping me with my clothes…the woman I met at the dog park where Ralph and I go. I asked her to come over."

Ali looked at her sister in disbelief. Morgan had never, ever, cooked for anyone.

"It won't be gourmet like yours. Just a takeout pizza, and I'm making a salad." Morgan's shrug was shy, uncertain. "But I am going to be the host. I've never been a host before. I've only been a guest. I'm excited."

Ali was experiencing two very different emotions. Genuine happiness for her sister's newfound independence. And a sense of betrayal, as if Morgan had abandoned her by pursuing a life of her own.

Ali suddenly wondered, *How will I stay balanced without Morgan always being there, leaning on me?*

Although dinner with Peter Sebelius and his wife was supposed to be a casual midweek get-together, Ali had wanted to make it a celebration.

And now she was putting the finishing touches on a menu that included burgundy-braised short ribs on creamy polenta, sautéed French beans sprinkled with lemon zest, and a flourless chocolate cake, which Ali would later top with whipped cream and homemade caramel sauce.

One of Seal's old albums was on the sound system. A few minutes earlier, Ali had been drifting to the soulful lyrics of Sam Cooke: "It's been a long, long time comin', but I know a change is gonna come…" Now she was dancing to the upbeat Curtis Mayfield: "…have a good time, 'cause it's all right."

Being in her kitchen, with good food and good music, always made Ali feel content.

When she heard Matt's car pull into the garage, she wasn't thinking about the bittersweet changes in Morgan, or Morgan's discovery of the file folder in the closet. Ali was lost in the food and the music.

The garage and the house were connected, and Ali assumed Matt would be coming in almost immediately. It was only a few steps from where he parked his car to the back door. Yet several long minutes passed between what sounded like the opening and closing of the car door, the opening and closing of the car's trunk, and Matt's eventual arrival in the kitchen.

Ali was curious. "What took you so long? What were you doing?"

"Nothing. Shuffling some papers." Matt gave her a quick peck on the cheek. "How's Sofie?"

"Great. I put her to bed about half an hour ago. She had a terrific day." Ali went back to the dinner preparations.

"I want to run up and kiss her good night," Matt said. Then, just as he was asking, "How long before Peter and his wife get here?" the doorbell rang.

"About *that* long," Ali told him. "Seems like the evening is underway."

"Yeah, I guess it is." Matt's expression was hard to read. "It'll be a night I'll never forget."

Ali wasn't sure if Matt was talking to her or to himself.

It was a fabulous night. The conversation and the laughter were absolutely effortless. In spite of the fact it had been over two years since Peter was a neighbor, the only thing about him that seemed different was that he was a little less boisterous, and he didn't drink anymore. It was easy for Ali and Matt to slip back into their friendship with him. And his wife, Quinn, only added to the enjoyment. She was a plump, pretty brunette with luminous, smoke-gray eyes, unassuming and fun to be with. Ali had liked her the minute they met.

As the evening was winding down, Quinn said, "I'll need to improve my cooking skills before I have the courage to invite you guys to our house. I never tasted anything as good as this caramel sauce. Ali, you've got to tell me what you did to it."

"I added a pinch of fleur de sel."

Peter laughed. "Fleur de *who*? Help me out here, Matt. Does that or does that not sound like the name of a French hooker?"

"It's a type of sea salt." Quinn rolled her eyes. "My husband may win awards for his surgery, but he's never going to take any prizes in the kitchen."

"You've won awards?" Ali said. "I'm impressed."

Peter waved her comment away. "Y'know what? It's not that big a deal. It wasn't an award. It was an article in a medical journal."

"It was the lead article. In a very important journal." Quinn winked at Peter. "And that's all I'll say, I swear. 'Cause I know I'm embarrassing you."

"I'll tell you what I do deserve a prize for." Peter lifted Quinn's fingers to his lips and kissed them. "I was smart enough to talk the most amazing woman on earth into marrying me."

"Did he have to do a lot of talking?" Ali asked.

Quinn's shrug suggested she was trying to be diplomatic. "The truth is, in the beginning, I didn't like him very much."

Peter leaned back in his chair and chuckled. "That's an understatement. Want to hear her first words to me? I can give you the exact quote." He sat up a little straighter, breaking into a girlish falsetto and announcing, "'It's because of idiotic, egotistical doctors like you that surgeons are perceived as arrogant jerks. I assure you, Dr. Sebelius, I'm speaking for every nurse in this hospital.'"

Ali and Matt burst out laughing as Peter added, "Hey, she was telling the truth."

"He was drinking and partying way too much," Quinn explained. "It really scared me."

Peter cleared his throat. "Just for the record, let's make it clear: I wasn't a full-time drunk. I had a short-lived career as an asshole medical resident who was binge drinking and blacking out when I wasn't on call. It lasted maybe eight or nine months." Peter paused. "Then I got together with Quinn, and she saved me. She absolutely saved me."

There was such love and gratitude in Peter's voice that, for a moment, everyone was quiet.

Then Ali said, "Well, I always thought you were a great guy, and it sounds like in the last few years, you've gotten even more great." Every word was heartfelt as she told him, "Peter Sebelius, you held our little girl's shattered arm in your hands and made it whole. I'll never stop honoring you for that." Ali raised her wineglass. "What you are is a hero."

And Peter said, "Ali, you have no idea how far that is from the truth."

The toast to Peter Sebelius had been the perfect grace note, a natural place for the evening to end. Within minutes, Peter and Quinn said their good-byes and Matt went upstairs to check on Sofie.

Ali was in the kitchen, rinsing one of the dinner plates. It knocked against the edge of the sink. She quickly checked for damage. On the surface, where the pattern was, everything looked fine. It wasn't until she turned the plate over that she saw the crack, no wider than a hair, running from edge to edge.

And at the sight of that fatal, hair-thin crack, Ali was grief-stricken.

The plate was the same pattern her Grandma MaryJoy had used—Blue Danube. Ali had bought the set of china right after she and Matt moved in. She'd pictured it always being here, in this house—part of every anniversary, every birthday, every graduation. It represented consistency, stability.

The crack in the dinner plate, the shattering waiting to happen, was a reminder. Ali's house—where she dreamed of raising her child and growing old with Matt—was for sale. It would soon be gone.

Losing her home—and the heartache that brought—buckled Ali's knees and crumpled her onto the kitchen floor.

A little bit later, when Ali pulled herself together and went into the garage looking for a new box of trash bags, she experienced a moment of panic. The same panic that grabbed her every time she entered a darkened room, her ongoing terror of her rapist.

Fighting the urge to turn and run, she slapped at the wall switch. The overhead fluorescents came on, flooding the garage with light.

Ali hurried down the concrete steps, near the place where Matt's car was parked. And she suddenly understood what had caused the odd delay earlier in the evening when he came home from work.

She was looking at clear evidence of *what* Matt had done. The only thing that was unclear was *why* he'd done it.

A cardboard box had been placed on top of a large metal sign. The sign was lying flat on the garage floor. Matt had obviously taken the time to remove these two items from his car and put them on the ground near the back door before entering the house.

Ali quickly searched the box and found an assortment of things that included books, the photo of her that Matt always kept on his desk, a framed copy of his PhD, and a plastic nameplate with Matt's name on it—the kind that would slide into a metal sleeve on an office door.

Her pulse pounding, she reached down, scooted the box aside, and picked up the sign it was sitting on. She recognized it instantly— the For Sale sign that had been hanging in the front yard. After uprooting it, Matt must have tossed it into the trunk and driven it into the garage.

Ali could hear him in the kitchen, walking around. She started to call out but didn't know what to say. She was too bewildered by what she was looking at.

And now Matt was coming into the garage. His tone was deliberate and controlled. "I planned to tell you about this. Later tonight. After we were in bed."

Ali lost her grip on the For Sale sign. While it clattered to the floor, she was saying a silent prayer. *Whatever this is that's about to happen… please don't let it kill me.*

Matt

M ATT CHOSE HIS WORDS CAREFULLY—EACH ONE ECHOING OFF the metal and concrete of the garage. "I took the For Sale sign down because we won't need it," he told Ali. "And I brought the stuff home from the college because I don't work there anymore." There was a sense of apprehension in Matt, and triumph, and something that felt like death.

"I resigned," he said. "We were only a few weeks into the fall term. There's a line of qualified people who want my position."

Ali had her hands over her mouth, staring at him in shock. "What've you done? You needed that job. You loved it. You were teaching again."

He was determined not to let her know how much this was destroying him. "It doesn't matter. My responsibility is to take care of you and Sofie. And that's what's happening. I'm going to Australia to do a film with Aidan—"

"When?"

"Right away. Production has started... Aidan offered me this thing a while ago. I'm already late getting on board."

"But, Matt, what about—"

"After I get back, I'll keep working for him. I signed on as one of the partners in his production company...movies, not television. I'll have a job with him doing movies for as long as he's around. He's produced a lot of hits. He'll be around for a long time."

Ali sounded utterly confused. "But you said you hated working in show business."

Matt wanted to get this done before he fell apart. "I'm focusing on the mountain of money I'm going to earn. Money that'll keep you in this house. Where you need to be. Where you deserve to be. I'm focusing on taking care of you."

A tremor shot through Matt, the same tremor that had shot through him in Sofie's hospital room—when Ali's mother said that everybody has a test life keeps giving them till they get it right. "I know it seems bizarre to walk away from teaching, a life I love, and lock into a career I can't stand. But it's part of my test, Al…the one that, up until this point, I've always failed."

Matt was dying—and at the same time he was proud. He was finally the protector he'd never been. "In addition to the money, the job with Aidan comes with amazing health insurance. I've never seen anything like it. Sofie's going to need that coverage, somewhere down the line. Her adoption will be final soon. Sofie's our daughter, and I have to make sure she's safe. That's my real job. The rest of it's only a way to earn a living."

Ali didn't appear to understand what he was telling her. Matt was worried he'd taken too long to step up and make things right—afraid Ali didn't love him anymore. Worried that in addition to the other women he'd lost, now he'd lost Ali, too.

It seemed like her response took forever.

But when, at last, Ali came into Matt's arms, it was with relief and joy.

After he took Ali upstairs and she was sleeping the first untroubled sleep she'd had in weeks, Matt returned to the garage.

The first thing he did was pick up the For Sale sign and place it flat against the garage's back wall. Then he pulled his PhD out of the cardboard box and held on to it for what felt like an eternity. It wasn't easy, saying good-bye to a dream he knew he'd never return to.

Matt put his diploma facedown on a dusty ledge above an overflowing trash bin.

His final act was to move the cardboard box containing his books and the nameplate that documented the existence of Professor Matthew Easton—the only man Matt had ever wanted to be. The man he had executed tonight.

Matt pushed the box into a corner dark with shadows—and he kept pushing it deeper and deeper into the shadows until the box was completely out of sight.

Then he went into the house and locked the door.

In the morning, Matt would be gone.

Ali

"HOW HAVE YOU BEEN COPING SINCE MATT LEFT?" QUINN asked.

"I guess I'm trying to deal with it by focusing on being a good mother to Sofie…and on making a success of the restaurant," Ali said.

Quinn gave Ali a sympathetic smile. "I don't know what I'd do if Peter ever left me."

It was midmorning on Monday, Ali's day off from the restaurant, and Ali and Quinn were in Ali's living room, sitting side by side, sharing a plate of homemade peanut butter cookies. "It's been tough, being on my own for the last six months," Ali said. "But it's not like Matt's left me in the 'I'm out of here and I'll never see you again' way. He'll be back…as soon as they finish shooting the movie in Australia."

"Still, you must miss him like crazy." Quinn reached for another cookie, and Ali let the distraction cover the fact she hadn't automatically agreed with Quinn's comment.

Since the day Matt left, Ali had been in constant contact with him—Skyping and emailing. Strangely, although they were thousands of miles apart, Ali felt closer to Matt than she'd been in years, as if their love was being reborn. Yet Ali was thinking, *I don't even know if it's real. What if when he comes home, everything changes, and we end up where we were before, when I wasn't sure he was there for me in that protective, take-no-prisoners way you want your husband to be? What if it goes back to how it was…my feelings about him flickering on and off, ready to burn out?*

"Oh my God. Look what time it is. Almost eleven. Time to run."

Quinn grabbed her purse, rummaging through it. "Did I get everything I need?" She was planning a surprise thirty-fifth birthday party for Peter and was putting together a tribute video. She'd stopped by to borrow photos—pictures from when Ali, Matt, and Peter lived in the apartment complex.

"I have a few more you might want." Ali had already given Quinn six or seven photographs, which Quinn had put in her purse. Now Ali was sliding two additional photos across the coffee table. They'd been taken at a poolside barbecue, and Quinn asked, "Who's the pretty blond?"

"My friend Jessica. The guy next to her is her husband."

"I know him! Well, I don't really *know* him. I've run into him a few times. His company does consulting work for the hospital. He—" Quinn stopped. "Hey, what's going on?" She'd caught Ali tucking a photograph into her pocket, trying to hide it.

Ali blushed. "I just thought you might not want to see this one. It's of Peter and Liz...the girl he was dating back when Matt and I first met him."

"Oh, I know all about Liz. She was on the nursing staff for a while. I was her boss. Talk about somebody with anger issues. The fights she had with Peter were epic." Quinn leaned in, peering at the photograph. "This is the first time I've seen her in a bathing suit though. Very dynamic." Quinn dropped the picture into her purse.

"You're actually going to show that at Peter's party? Doesn't it make you even the least bit jealous?"

"It definitely would have when Peter and I first got together. But now? No. We're married. We're solid." Quinn flashed a self-confident grin. "So what? She's hot in a bikini. That means whatever I have must be even hotter. After all, I'm the one he decided to marry." Her laugh was light, relaxed. "It's me he calls three times a day just to say 'I love you.'"

Quinn's expression turned serious as she said, "I trust my husband with all my heart. After seeing the way Matt is with you, and with Sofie, I have to believe you feel the same way." She looked into Ali's eyes, searching for something. "Can you tell that I want the whole world to be just like Peter and me…happy, happy, happy?"

Almost before Quinn finished her thought, a delighted little voice called out, "Happy! Happy!"

Sofie ran into the room ahead of Ali's mother, making a beeline for Ali, climbing into her lap, announcing, "Happy is birthday and kitties!"

While Matt was away, Ali's mother was staying with Ali, helping with Sofie. Ali was grateful. She loved being with her mother. It was also good not to be alone at night, when every creak in the dark was a reason to panic because her attacker was still on the loose.

Ali pushed away the dark thoughts, tickled Sofie's tummy, and told Quinn, "Miss Sofie went to a birthday party last weekend. She still hasn't gotten over it. When you're two and a half, birthday parties are major excitement."

"You should've seen what a production it was," Ali's mother said. "The birthday girl's parents hired a petting zoo. Puppies and kittens and lambs. That's not counting the clown and the pony."

Quinn laughed. "I can't wait till Peter and I are into babies and birthday parties and all that stuff."

"The babies are wonderful," Ali's mother agreed. "But their parties are outrageous." She took the empty cookie plate from the coffee table and headed toward the kitchen. "Some people spend more on a toddler's birthday than I did on my wedding. It's unbelievable, Quinn." Ali's mother stopped and turned to Ali. "That reminds me. Luci Quindley called. I forgot to tell you."

"Luci? From high school? Luci from across the street who was always peeking out her front window at people? Creepy Luci?"

"Oh, she wasn't *that* creepy, Ali. She was a little different."

Ali looked at Quinn. "This girl was unbelievably weird. She could've been voted most likely to become a stalker."

"Don't be silly." Ali's mother was trying not to smile. "She's a hairdresser living in San Diego now, and she'd like you to call her. She's excited about you being married to a film writer and having your own restaurant, and—"

"How does she know all of that? How did she even get my number after all these years?"

"Aren't you on that Facebook thing?"

"Not lately." Since her attack, Ali had no desire to be on social media.

"Well," her mother was saying, "apparently Morgan's been posting lots of news on Facebook. She talks about you and Matt and—"

"Well, tell her to stop," Ali said. "Morgan's got a life now. Let her go out and make her own news."

Even as the words were coming out of her mouth, Ali wasn't completely sure that Morgan was ready to be out in the world on her own.

Morgan

I T WAS A SUNLIT SATURDAY AFTERNOON, AND MORGAN WAS ON black silk sheets. With a cool breeze wafting through an open porthole above her head, sending a delicious chill across her breasts, raising goose bumps along the top of her thighs.

The boat was elegant. Gently rolling from side to side, thumping against the edges of the slip. While the riggings made swaying, tinkling music.

"I feel like I'm in heaven," Morgan murmured.

"Lucky thing we ran into each other today." He was entering Morgan with force and speed, leaving her barely enough breath to whisper his name—"Logan."

Morgan's sexual history included only a few brief encounters with a couple of guys back in Rhode Island. She'd never experienced anything like this. It was as if every soft, hidden place in her was being discovered, and awakened.

She wasn't noticing the way Logan had grabbed her wrists and pinned them against the silk sheets—almost hard enough to leave bruises.

Morgan was drifting between this moment and the blur that brought her here. A few hours ago, she'd been in Santa Monica, at Pacifica, an exclusive private club where members enjoyed beach-front tennis courts, a state-of-the-art gym, and a world-class spa.

Morgan was there to pick up a gift certificate—Pacifica's generous donation to the museum's upcoming fund-raiser. When she entered the lobby, she bumped into Logan. And experienced the little gut jump, the jolt of attraction Logan always triggered in her.

He explained he had a membership at Pacifica because he spent time in the area; he kept a boat in Marina del Rey.

"Want to have lunch?" Logan was looking at her from head to toe, smiling.

This was still new to Morgan, and it felt good to be looked at by a man who looked as good as Logan. There was a brief thought of Ben, and Jessica. But Morgan realized there wasn't anything to worry about. She wasn't planning to do anything wrong. She was simply accepting an invitation to spend a little time being admired.

"Just lunch," she told him. "That's all."

Logan laughed. "If you say so."

A top-down ride in his Porsche whisked them to a seafood grill with a panoramic view of the ocean and a free-flowing martini bar. Morgan and Logan chatted their way through two enormous lobsters and enough martinis to make Morgan giddy.

Another Porsche ride had brought them here, to Logan's boat. Mellow jazz on the sound system and Logan's guiding hand on Morgan's unsteady back had brought them onto the black silk sheets.

And now she'd had sex with someone else's husband.

Morgan felt sick.

~

Ten minutes later, Logan was dressed and on the deck of his boat, checking his phone.

Morgan was still down in the cabin, putting on lipstick, stepping into her shoes—and hearing Logan's impatient shout: "Hurry up. I need to take you back to your car. I have someplace to be."

The boat rocked a little. She lost her balance and grabbed the handle of one of the highly polished wooden drawers built into the cabin wall.

The drawer immediately slid open—showing Morgan that she wasn't the only extra woman in Logan's world. Neatly tucked in among Logan's T-shirts was a pair of panties. Zebra-striped, with a heart-shaped charm on the waistband. The panties were too small to be Jessica's.

And they weren't the only ones in the drawer. But before Morgan could take a closer look, Logan was calling to her again, shouting that he had to hit the road.

~

Seconds later, Morgan was in the marina parking lot, heading toward Logan's black Porsche.

With the image of the zebra-striped panties fresh in her mind, Morgan's question was, "Do you ever think about leaving Jessica?"

Logan pressed his key remote, unlocking his car.

"Would I leave Jessica?" He thought for a moment, then shrugged. "Not unless I met somebody who gave me a reason to. So far, nobody has."

Logan was a narcissist and an asshole—the exact opposite of decent, caring Ben Tennoff.

Logan was a man who wore a wedding ring. And screwed around. And kept panties that he had tucked away in a drawer, like trophies.

And Morgan had just taken a martini-drunk sheet dive with him.

She was trying not to vomit.

Ali

I T WAS A LITTLE AFTER TWELVE O'CLOCK. QUINN HAD GONE HOME an hour ago to work on her video tribute. Ali and Sofie were on the grass in the backyard, under a tree. They'd just finished a picnic lunch—turkey sandwiches, apples, and a shared chocolate-chip cookie.

Snug in Ali's lap, Sofie was drowsily watching a butterfly dance in the clear afternoon light. The feel of Sofie's sleepy weight filled Ali with contentment. She leaned back against the tree and closed her eyes.

At first, the only sounds were the quiet rustle of the tree branches and, from down the block, the music of a piano being played in dreamy intervals.

And then, gradually, Ali became aware of a new sound—one so muted it was almost lost in the rustle of the trees and the melody of the faraway music.

She opened her eyes. Waited. Listened.

Nothing.

But after a second or two, there it was again, elusive and quiet. Cautious footsteps moving across freshly tilled earth.

Ali and Sofie were alone in the yard. Someone was coming toward them—from around the side of the house. Where Ali had dug a new garden bed but hadn't planted the flowers yet.

It's him...the man who hurt me.

Terrified, determined to protect Sofie, Ali scrambled to her feet, holding Sofie tight, planning to make a dash for the safety of the house.

There wasn't time.

The side gate had already swung open. A man was in the yard, a shadow cast by the house obscuring his face.

Ali let out a scream.

And Sofie wailed, "Mommy! Scared!"

He was huge. His body didn't have an ounce of fat—looked like it was chiseled out of stone. "Don't run," he told Ali. "It's me."

Still clutching Sofie, Ali collapsed onto the grass. Confused and relieved.

"Levi. What are you doing here?"

"I've been wanting to see you. For a long time." Levi stepped out of the shadows, the sunlight glinting off his ginger-colored hair. "I… um…I've been parked across the street all morning. Sometimes when I'm in town, I come by…and watch your house. Today, I couldn't take it anymore. I had to see you, hear your voice. So a little while ago, after your mother and your visitor left, I rang the doorbell. But you didn't answer." He made a helpless gesture, indicating he'd run out of words.

Ali was whispering to Sofie, soothing her and kissing her. "It's okay, baby. Everything's okay."

After she was sure Sofie was calm, Ali looked up at Levi. Her reaction was the same attraction that existed all those years ago, when she'd loved Levi and swore she'd never leave him—the same attraction that had lured her into the texting fling. The flirtation they'd shared. After Ali had moved to California, and Matt had disappeared into his work and made her feel abandoned.

Levi was slowly moving his gaze away from Ali, shifting it to Sofie with a look that was wildly unsettled.

What was that look? Anger? Jealousy? Ali instinctively held Sofie a little closer.

Levi's attention returned to Ali. She could hear disappointment and frustration when he said, "After you and I started texting last year, I kinda got my hopes up. Then right before Christmas, you wanted to stop. I didn't understand why you cut me off like that. Some of the things we said in the texts... I thought, even after all the time that had gone by, you'd started to want me again."

He wavered, seemed embarrassed. "That's why, when I'm in LA, I come here, and watch your house, and wait. I'm waiting for you."

Ali glanced at Sofie—she was fast asleep. Yet Ali kept her voice low. It was crushing, having to make these confessions with her daughter in her lap. "Levi, what I did was wrong. I'm sorry about the texting, the things I said, the things I let you say. Matt was working way too much, and I was lonely." She was cringing. "I'm so ashamed of what we did."

"I don't like hearing you say that, Ali." Levi crouched in the grass beside her, very close, as if he wanted to kiss her. There was a disturbing intensity in his whisper. "I haven't ever stopped loving you. I've never stopped believing you belong to me."

He took her hand. Ali quickly pulled away. That's when she caught sight of the jagged scars on his knuckles.

Suddenly she remembered the high-school parking lot, the night of the senior dance. The fury of Levi's attack on the school counselor's son. The noise of the boy's glasses shattering, the sound of bones in his face breaking under Levi's iron-fisted blows. The boy had suspected Ali might be pregnant, and he'd called her a whore. Ali remembered the beating that Levi gave him, how savage and bloody it was.

And she remembered something else, too. While Levi's influential father settled things with the police, Levi took Ali into a field of flowers. He'd opened a pack of gum and used the wrappers to weave a pair of delicate bands—putting one of them on Ali's ring finger, and the other on his own—telling her, "The two of you will belong to me forever. You. And our baby."

But their baby had ended where it began, as a secret. It ended in a miscarriage.

And Ali had continued on as the golden girl, while rumors ran wild about Levi's taste for violence.

Ali eventually left Levi. All the blood—the blood spilled in the parking lot, and in the miscarriage—had been too much.

Now the memory of that blood was frightening her, and she said, "You need to go. I'll always care about you, always…but don't come back."

The look on Levi's face was a mask of resentment and stubbornness, a violent refusal to let go.

Finally, he said, "I'll try to stay away. I'll do my best." The blank way he said it made it sound like a threat.

Ali held Sofie tight and stared him down. After a while, Levi walked away and disappeared around the side of the house.

Ali was thinking that she was afraid of him, that she hoped he would stay gone—and that she should change the locks.

In that same fleeting splinter of time, she was thinking about the blood in the high-school parking lot. And the gum-wrapper ring on her finger. And the baby that never was.

∿

The anxiety caused by Levi's visit was still with Ali later that afternoon. When Jessica stopped by to pick up some toys and baby clothes that Sofie had outgrown—Ali's donations to the community center where Jessica was a volunteer.

As Ali, Sofie, and Jessica climbed the stairs leading to Ali's attic, Jessica was saying, "I feel like a total fraud when I counsel the women at the center about parenting. I'm a shitty mother. Where do I come off telling anybody how to raise their kids?"

"What makes you think you're a bad mother?" Ali was a few steps ahead of Jessica, giving Sofie a boost up the stairs.

"For a lot of women, motherhood is the most fabulous thing that ever happened to them. They swim in it, like champagne." Jessica shot Ali an unhappy glance. "All I feel is scared. My guys are so little. They're looking at me for everything. What if years from now, all the stuff I'm doing...the food, the vaccinations, the discipline...turns out to be wrong? Hell, what about the fact I'm staying home instead of providing them with a mother who has a career, who's got more going on than stroller rides in the park and kissing their boo-boos? What if it *all* turns out to be wrong? I'm scared shitless."

Jessica made a frustrated, snorting sound. "I get flashes when all I want is to slap on a really short skirt and go out and have a good time. There're days I'd give a kidney not to have to listen to crying while I'm walking around with cereal in my hair."

Ali stopped halfway up the stairs, looking back at Jessica. "So. You don't like Ed. Or Joe. Even a little bit?"

"That's the nutty thing. I'd kill for those two. My hand to God. I would."

"I'm no expert, Jess. But I think that's pretty much the definition of a good mother."

Jessica grinned. "Have I told you lately that I love you?"

"I love you, too."

Then Ali continued up the stairs and went into the attic.

The last time the attic had been cleaned was when Ali and Matt moved into the house. The floor was covered in dust, littered with fallen flies and dead moths. The small, round windows at either end of the room were shrouded with cobwebs.

Ali was anxious to get this job done and get out. She'd never liked being in attics; the mustiness and the shadows made her uncomfortable.

Sofie, on the other hand, was charmed. Happily running through mazes of empty moving boxes.

The baby things were in heavy-duty plastic bags that were scattered everywhere. Ali quickly began moving the bags to a spot near the doorway. "I hope we find all of it. Matt's really the one who knows where stuff is. He's the only person who's ever brought anything up here."

"You've got to be kidding." Jessica was wiping cobwebs away from one of the windows. "I refuse to set foot on Logan's boat because it makes me seasick, and I hate that fucking marina smell. But not going into your own attic? What's that about?"

"I just never wanted to come in here. Attics give me the creeps."

Sofie was busy climbing onto a wobbling stack of moving boxes. Ali quickly lifted her down, and then grabbed a dust-covered plastic bag. "Jackpot, Jess. This one looks like it has tons of cool baby things in it." But as she lifted the bag, it broke, scattering toys all over the floor—and Ali muttered, "I'll go downstairs and find something else to put this stuff in."

"Wait." Jessica pointed out an empty basket wedged between two stacks of moving boxes "Maybe you could use that."

While Jessica was talking, a giggling Sofie scampered past, heading for the open door. And Jessica dashed out of the attic, instinctively chasing after her.

Knowing that Sofie was in good hands, Ali ducked between the stacked moving boxes and reached for the basket. As soon as she moved the basket, she saw there was something behind it, wedged against the wall.

Ali was surprised. When she lifted the thing off the dusty floor, it left an immaculate outline of itself. It had obviously been put in place when Ali and Matt first moved into the house, when the attic floor was clean.

Ali instantly had a flash of memory: *The cab, gaining speed...carrying her toward the airport, toward California. The little brown suitcase at her feet. The sensation of stepping off the edge of a cliff.*

What Ali had just found was that brown suitcase. The wedding present from her stepmother. The ugly item Ali had tossed onto a pile of Salvation Army discards a long time ago.

The thing had been thrown away before she and Matt left the apartment. How could it possibly be here now?

Bewildered, Ali pulled the suitcase closer—and opened it.

What she saw knocked the breath out of her.

She was looking at a pair of jeans, and a satin cowboy shirt with black edges around its pocket and cuffs. Beneath the jeans and shirt, she found a wide leather belt with a heavy buckle shaped like a horseshoe. Under the belt, a pair of ostrich-skin cowboy boots, dark purple, the color of an eggplant.

Someone had packed her rapist's clothes in this suitcase and deliberately hidden it here, right above her bedroom, right above her bed.

As fast as she could, Ali shut the suitcase.

It wasn't until she reached the bottom of the stairs and caught her breath that she started to scream.

⁓

After a scalding shower, where she scrubbed herself raw, Ali was in her bedroom, as dazed as if she'd just taken a beating.

The chaos that happened after she opened the suitcase was coming at her in jagged bits and pieces. Ali saw herself running out of the attic. Reaching the bottom of the stairs, and screaming. Then there was Jessica, with Sofie in her arms, asking, "What happened? What's wrong?" And Ali, frantically grabbing Sofie and begging Jessica, "Go up there and lock the door. Lock it. *Please!*"

Then somehow Ali was in a chair in the family room, rocking back and forth and moaning, holding Sofie. The next thing Ali knew, she was struggling to answer Jessica's questions, too terrified to talk about finding the suitcase, only able to say, "The night before Matt and I moved into this house…I was attacked."

Now Ali was overhearing the sounds coming from downstairs. The front door opening and a rush of footsteps—the clatter of her mother coming back into the house and Jessica running to meet her, saying, "Oh my God, I had no idea Ali'd been raped."

Instantly there was noise, things breaking, as if her mother had lost her grip on a bag of groceries—eggs and cartons of milk and jugs of orange juice smashing onto the floor.

Listening to the mayhem, Ali was thinking how surprised she always was by the clarity of the sounds that traveled up the stairwell.

Downstairs, her mother was frantically asking, "Where's Ali?"

And Jessica was saying, "She's in her room, lying down. She's—"

Ali could hear her mother rapidly climbing the stairs. "Is Sofie all right?"

"Sofie's fine," Jessica said. "We've been in the family room all afternoon, watching cartoons."

There was an abrupt silence. Ali's mother had stopped in midstride. "Ali was raped? And you're watching cartoons?"

"Oh, no. That isn't what happened." Jessica sounded panicked. "We were in the attic… Ali said she hated being there. It gave her the creeps. I left her alone up there for a minute. It must have frightened her. And all of a sudden she was running down the attic stairs and screaming. Then when she calmed down a little, she told me she'd been attacked…a while ago. You know, right before she and Matt moved into this house. I guess she must still have flashbacks…"

Ali could only imagine the look of horror on her mother's face.

"Oh my God," Jessica whispered. "You didn't know about it?"

"No," Ali's mother said. "I didn't."

It was several minutes before Ali heard her mother start back up the stairs.

"How about if I take Sofie home with me and bring her back tomorrow?" Jessica asked.

And Ali's mother replied, "That would be nice. I need some time with my little girl."

~

The bedroom was in semidarkness, the curtains closed, when her mother came in. Ali was curled in the center of the bed. What she saw in her mother's eyes was the love-filled bond between parent and child.

Their conversation was short.

"You were raped?"

"Yes, Mom, I was raped."

"Honey, why didn't you tell me?"

There was a silence. Then Ali said, "Because I was ashamed."

"Do you want to talk to me about it?"

"Mom. I can't. The one time I talked about the details was the night it happened. I told everything to a female detective who wrote it down in a notepad. The only reason Matt knows exactly what happened is because he was in the room when I talked to the detective. To lay it all out again would mean having people poking at me, probing…asking questions. I don't have any answers. And I'm in too much pain to be poked and probed."

Her mother had come only a step or two into the room. She seemed to be letting Ali decide where she should go next.

Ali sat up in bed, began to cry, and reached for her mother.

Her mother held her. Cradling Ali and telling her she was loved and safe.

Hours later, when her mother asked, "What do you need now, my darling?"

Ali said, "Morgan."

Morgan

ORGAN CAME THROUGH THE FRONT DOOR OF ALI'S HOUSE TO find her mother crouched on the floor, cleaning up spilled milk and shattered eggs. She looked old and broken; Morgan almost didn't recognize her.

Apprehensive, Morgan said, "I got here as soon as I could. What's wrong?"

After a long beat, her mother told her, "Ali was raped."

Morgan staggered a little.

"It happened some time ago...on Ali and Matt's moving day."

For a split second, it was as if everything had gone black.

Moving day. The day Morgan had stormed into Ali's guest room with that pizza receipt.

Moving day. When something terrible was going on with Ali, and Morgan had screamed, "I hope it's something awful. You deserve it."

Moving day. The day Ali was raped.

The impact sent Morgan sprinting for the stairs.

As soon as Morgan went into Ali's bedroom, she took off her shoes. And got into bed. And lay down beside her sister.

The only thing Morgan said was, "I love you."

"I love you, too" was Ali's answer.

"You don't have to tell me about it," Morgan said. "You never have to say a word."

Morgan didn't need to hear the specifics. Morgan was Ali's twin. The wounds inflicted on Ali—the violation and the fear—were as real to Morgan as if she'd been the one slammed to the floor in that rented apartment.

Morgan was sobbing, grieving for what happened to Ali. Ali. Who had always been Morgan's strength.

Ali. Firmly holding Morgan's hand as they walked toward their first day of kindergarten.

Ali. Her voice steady and sure at their sixth-grade dance recital—her breath sweet and warm as she whispered, "Don't worry, Morgan. If you fall down at the hard part, I'll just fall down, too…and it'll look like that's the way we meant it, like a joke we made up together."

Ali. In high school, when she was the homecoming queen, circling the football field in the back of an antique convertible—her smile at its brightest when she saw Morgan waving to her from the bleachers.

Ali. In the guest room of this house, brutalized and mute, while Morgan screamed at her and called her a bitch.

"I'm sorry for what I said to you that day, the day you moved in here," Morgan murmured. "I let you down. I wasn't paying attention."

Ali slipped her hand into Morgan's and intertwined their fingers.

And Morgan knew she'd been forgiven. For what she'd said on that terrible moving-in day. And for what she had done in all the years when she'd been jealous of Ali's life and blind to Ali's pain.

"I'm glad you're here," Ali said.

"I'll always be here" was Morgan's hushed reply.

Ali

H ER MOTHER SAT ON THE SIDE OF THE BED, GENTLY RUBBING
Ali's back. "You've been in here for almost a week."

"I know. I'm hiding."

"You can't stay in your bedroom, hiding from this thing forever.
You understand that, don't you?"

Ali nodded, letting her mother think it was the trauma of revealing
she'd been attacked that had knocked her into bed and kept her there.
But what Ali was really keeping her distance from was the suitcase
in the attic.

She didn't know how to talk about her rapist's clothes. Or how
they'd gotten into that suitcase. Or who could have hidden the suitcase. She wouldn't know how to talk about any of it, with anyone,
until she found a way to deal with the terror she was experiencing.

"I left today's messages from the restaurant staff on your night-
stand," her mother said. "Let me know if you need me to return
any calls."

"I will." Ali rolled over and closed her eyes. All she wanted to do
was lie safely in her bed—taking comfort in her mother's love, and
Morgan's, and the sense of peace that came from singing Sofie to
sleep every night. She didn't want to think about anything else.

There was worry in her mother's voice. "Matt called this morning…just like he does every day. He asked me to tell you he was glad
you finally told us about what happened to you…the rape. He said he
knew how difficult it must've been, and he understands why it would

make you want to escape from phones and emails for a while. But, honey, it would mean the world to him to hear your voice, even if all you said was hello. Matt's very concerned about you. Don't you think you should call him? At least send him an email?"

Hearing Matt's name made Ali queasy. The house had been empty when they moved in; Matt was the only one who had ever taken anything into the attic. The implications were grotesque. Ali couldn't begin to get her head around it.

She waited for the queasiness to fade. Then she changed the subject, asking, "Who won?"

"Me," Sofie said.

Sofie and Morgan were stretched out at the foot of Ali's bed. Locked in a contest to see who would be the first to finish a page from Sofie's coloring book. Sofie was holding up her page—a jungle scene scribbled in parrot green, canary yellow, and hibiscus red.

"Look at all the brilliant colors," Morgan said.

Sofie crawled in next to Ali, pillowing her head on Ali's shoulder.

"Those colors make me think of Ava," Ali murmured.

As she stroked Sofie's hair, Ali made a silent promise to this little girl she loved so dearly. *I'll protect you. And celebrate you. I will try, always, to lead you toward the light, to places where you'll find strength and beauty.*

"I think I need to teach Sofie about God," Ali said.

"Why?" Morgan asked.

"Because Ava believed in God, and I want Sofie to have the same things in her heart that Ava had."

Morgan's response was fast and frightened. "God let Ava die, and he let you get raped. Maybe he isn't somebody Sofie'll want to meet."

The lights in the room were low. Ali's mother had moved to a chair near the window—and she appeared to be dozing. It caught Ali off guard when her mother said, "Tell Sofie the truth. God isn't Santa

Claus. He isn't an all-powerful granter of human wishes. But he is…
continually and constantly…all loving."

"That makes no sense," Morgan said.

"Yes, it does," her mother insisted. "Remember when the two of
you were little, and you kept going out to the curb with your dolls?"

The memory made Ali smile. "Feeling that whoosh when a car
went by used to get us just stupid happy."

"And every time I found you and brought you back into the yard,
you'd be so upset." Her mother's sigh was good-natured. "You
didn't understand that I knew things you didn't know."

That comment sparked an angry confusion in Ali. "What could
God possibly know that would make what happened to me all right?"

"I have no idea." Her mother's tone was gentle.

Morgan looked baffled. "Ava said her prayers every night, and I'm
betting she never prayed to die young."

Ali's mother took a blanket from the end of the bed and tucked
it around Ali's feet. "Just tell Sofie that no matter how difficult life
gets, God will be there walking beside her, and loving her, as she
goes through it."

"That doesn't seem like much," Ali said.

"Honey, it's the most powerful thing imaginable. Look around
this room…at Morgan, and Sofie, and me. We're not God. We're
just human beings. Think about the strength that comes from simply
having us near. Think what it would be like for you right now if you
had to go through this alone, if you weren't surrounded by love."

What Ali was thinking about was the brown suitcase in the attic,
a place where only Matt had been. She'd known from the beginning
that he was a man with secrets, but she'd never asked herself the
questions she was asking now. Was Matt hiding more than just old
wounds and childhood pain? Was he covering up things that were
perverted and sick?

Ali doubted there was enough love in heaven, or on earth, to help her survive the answer to those questions.

⌒

Since the former guest room was now Sofie's bedroom, Ali's mother had been sleeping on the convertible sofa in Matt's study.

She was reaching to turn off the light just as Ali came in. "Honey, what is it? I thought you'd be asleep by now."

"I want to be...but I keep waking up."

"Would you like me to bring you some tea?"

Ali shook her head. What she wanted was something that didn't exist. She wanted to be in a place where she was a little girl again and her mother had the power to make everything right. "Mom, is it okay if I stay with you for a while?" she asked.

Her mother was already scooting over, making room on the bed—and Ali snuggled in beside her.

"What's keeping you up, honey?"

Her mother slowly circled her fingertips across Ali's back. Ali was seeing the image of the suitcase on the attic floor, remembering all the times she'd watched Matt climb the attic stairs. "There're things I don't know how to begin to understand," she said. "Things that feel like they're going to kill me."

The steady circling of her mother's fingertips continued. "Ali, I can't imagine the agony you're in. I have no way of guessing what the problem is. You still haven't explained what happened in the attic that sent you racing out of there screaming. I want you to understand why I haven't pressed you to do that, and why Jessica hasn't. It's because we can see how fragile you are right now. We don't want to push you beyond where you have the strength to go."

Her mother lifted her hands from Ali's back and nestled in beside her. After a while, she told Ali, "Whatever it is you're afraid of, don't let it scare you enough to make you run. The only way to deal with fear is to stop and face it. See it for what it is and know you have the power to get past it." Her mother waited, and then said, "As long as a woman has a good heart, a clear head, and plenty of determination, there's nothing she can't survive."

Ali's mother adjusted her position so that they were looking directly at each other. "And it's not enough just to survive, Ali. You have to prevail. You have to come out whole, in a way you never were before. Ready to build a life that's much better than the one you had."

Hard-won knowledge, a lifetime's worth of wisdom, was what her mother was offering. "No matter what happens to you, never let it turn you into a victim, honey. Always fight back. Stay strong."

Early the next morning, as soon as her mother left to take Sofie to the park, Ali got out of bed, showered, and put her clothes on. The terror that had hijacked her when she first saw the contents of the suitcase was shrinking further into the background with each passing minute.

Ali was taking her mother's advice. She was fighting back.

The first thing Ali did was call Matt's mobile phone in Australia. It was time to find the truth, no matter how horrendous it might turn out to be.

Matt didn't pick up; Ali's call went to voice mail. Hearing the sound of Matt's voice made her want to cry. "Call me," she said. "I need to talk to you."

After leaving the message for Matt, Ali went into his study. Her plan was to tell the police about the suitcase. Contact information for the detective who had talked to Ali on the night of her attack was in an old email file on Matt's computer.

While Ali was clicking through files, trying to find the right one, she made an unexpected discovery—a travel confirmation sent to Matt just before he left for Australia. The itinerary listed two trips. One was for Matt's Wednesday departure to Sydney. The other was for the day before, for Tuesday morning—a one-day, round-trip flight to Phoenix, Arizona.

Ice-cold dread raced through Ali. She and Matt didn't know anyone in Arizona. And she'd had no idea that on the day before he left for Australia, Matt had been out of town.

It took only a few keystrokes, opening less than a half-dozen stored emails—and she found the one that made her gasp.

The message contained two briefly worded pieces of information. The directions to an address in Phoenix. And a demand for ten thousand dollars.

～

By noon, Ali had been on a plane for an hour and was landing at Sky Harbor Airport. A short time later, she was in a rental car, inching down a nondescript Phoenix street. Checking the front of each house, looking for the address she'd copied from the email.

Even though it was February, it was the desert. Heat was on the surface of the road and the hood of the car, on the dashboard and the windows. Yet Ali was teeth-chatteringly cold. Her bones were aching.

She had just spotted the house she was searching for. And she had no idea what, or who, she was about to find.

Ali was facing a squat, tan, single-storied box with brown trim and a black iron-grate security door. The place looked like it was barely two rooms wide. Ragged patches of cactus dotted the area where a lawn should've been. And in the narrow driveway, a woman was wiping down an old rust-spotted Jeep.

The woman watched coolly as Ali's car came to a stop.

When Ali switched off the ignition, got out of the car, and began the walk up the driveway, her legs turned to jelly. The only thing keeping her upright was the intensity with which she was studying the woman standing at the side of the Jeep. Ali was trying to decode who she could be, what connection she had to Matt.

The woman was in her midtwenties. Lean, pretty. Gracefully tall. Her hair was spectacular. Long and golden brown. Her eyes were cornflower blue. The features of her face were elegant, and underneath the elegance there was a tough wariness. She was in shorts and a pair of cheap flip-flops. The sleeves and midsection of her T-shirt had been cut off; the body of the shirt ended at the top of her rib cage, just below her breasts.

She cocked her head to one side, casually assessing Ali, sounding bored as she said, "Lemme guess. You're a wife, right? You have that look."

Before Ali could answer, the woman told her, "Here's the thing, lady. I'm a stripper, not a hooker. If your husband's cheating on you, it isn't with me."

The woman turned and walked away. That's when Ali saw the scar on her back—a wire-thin crescent, curving from beneath the uneven hem of her T-shirt and disappearing into the waistband of her shorts.

It wasn't until the woman was going into the house and about to close the door that Ali was able to speak. "Matt. Matt Easton," Ali said.

The woman's toughness vanished. "Who're you?"

"His wife." Ali's words were a thready whisper. "Who are you?"

The defenselessness in the woman's voice was heartrending. "I'm Kim. I'm his baby sister."

The living room Kim invited Ali into was tiny and bland—a glass coffee table, a floor lamp, a white imitation-leather sofa, and two matching chairs.

Kim and Ali sat across from each other, Kim on the couch, Ali in one of the chairs. The space was so cramped that neither of them could move without bumping the coffee table, rattling the beer bottle and soda can that were there.

Ali reached to steady the soda can, relieved and baffled as Kim told her, "The ten grand I asked for was for school. I ran out of money."

"But I thought you said you were a stripper—"

"I am…and in two more years, I'll be a pharmacist."

"Has Matt been giving you money for a long time?"

"Not hardly. My bro and I aren't close." Kim's laugh was cynical. "The only reason I tapped him for the cash was 'cause I was desperate. Luckily, he had a new contract for a job writing movies and his agent arranged for him to get a signing bonus." She picked up the beer bottle, rolling it along the side of her neck. "It's hot in here. I'm not in the mood to cough up a lot of answers. So let's just hit the highlights, okay?"

Kim put the beer bottle down and looked at Ali with a smirk. "I bet my brother never told you about me. Or about who our mother was. Or about how I got this nasty-ass scar on my back. I bet he made up some story…lied his ass off to you." She allowed time for what she'd said to sink in. Then she asked, "Want to know what else I can tell you about my brother?"

Ali was tense, hoping to hear the truth, yet deeply afraid of what it might be.

Kim leaned forward, locking eyes with Ali. "After where he's been, he has the right to be one sick fuck." She settled back, picking up the beer bottle, tipping it to her lips.

Ali understood Kim was toying with her, testing her—she kept her face expressionless. "Where, exactly, has Matt been?"

"I guess you could say he's been right through the heart of stinking hell." Kim took her time, kicking off one flip-flop and then the other. "So here's my brother's story. Starting when he was three months old, he was in a ritzy house in Boston, with his grampa and an imported English nanny. Our mother dumped him there because she needed to go on the road. She had a shot at screwing rock stars and jamming cocaine up her nose. And of course she didn't want to miss that."

Kim seemed to be enjoying the look of shock on Ali's face. "Like they say…the truth'll set you free. I'm assuming you want me to tell you the truth, right?"

Ali nodded.

"Well, my brother's truth may not make you free. But I guarantee it'll make you want to puke."

Kim's version of Matt's history was bewildering. "Why was Matt left with his grandfather?" Ali asked. "Where was Matt's father?"

"Out of the picture. Matty's dad came from money, just like our mom did. But she divorced his dad before Matty was born. The guy's respectability probably bored her." Kim put the beer bottle to her lips and drained it. "Anyway, in the middle of her post-divorce rock-and-roll haze, she got knocked up. I was born in Cleveland so I'm guessing my father wasn't anybody super-famous…or if he had been, he wasn't anymore. Anyway, he unloaded my mother before I got here." Kim pointed to the soda can Ali was holding. "Want another one?"

Ali shook her head. "No thanks."

"Want a bathroom break?"

Kim was toying with her again, adding to the tension by putting space between the pieces of the story. But Ali didn't think she was doing it to be malicious. She sensed Kim was playing for time, because it was difficult for her to discuss whatever was coming next.

"Okay, so here's the deal." Suddenly Kim was talking very fast, as if even while she was telling the story, she was trying to get away from it. "Right after my mom had me, she went back to Boston and snatched Matty. He was only four, but maybe she was looking for a babysitter. I don't know." Kim abruptly crossed her legs. She seemed irritated and jittery. "I swear to God, from the minute I was born, all I ever heard my mother say was 'Matty, it's your job to take care of your baby sister. She's your responsibility.' It was like her fucking mantra."

The tension in Kim eased a little as she told Ali, "There was this one time I remember my mom laughing her ass off at Matty. We were out in front of the ratty motel we were living in. I was wearing this crummy dress I used to wear all the time. It had little flower sprigs all over it. And Matty was holding me…y'know…the way parents hold their kids with their hands kind of cupped under the kid's butt? My arms were around his neck, and I had my legs wrapped around his waist. I was way too heavy for him, and he was trying super hard not to fall over.

"He was maybe eight and a half, and I was going on five, but giant big for my age. Matty was staggering all over the place. And Mom was laughing like she was gonna pee herself. Matty must've looked really dopey. But there he was, fighting like hell not to drop me. He's just this little scrawny kid, and he's killing himself trying to keep me from hitting the pavement…" Kim's voice trailed off. She looked down and rubbed at a speck of beer foam on the sofa cushion.

"You were living in motels?" Ali asked. "I thought you said your mother's family had money. Why didn't your grandfather help?"

"My mother was a nutjob junkie. The old man probably didn't

even know where we were." Kim shifted her position, bumped her shin on the coffee table, and winced. "The bottom line is we were always blowing through motels and trailers and crappy apartments... whatever got my mother closer to some new guy she was hot for."

Kim sighed and ran her hand over the place where the speck of beer foam had been. "If it wasn't for Matty, I probably would've never gotten my hair combed or my teeth brushed." She sounded like she was talking to herself as she said, "It's taken a real long time for me to figure out what a good person Matt is."

Tears were welling in Kim's eyes. She sounded exasperated. "Our mother was fucking insane. One time, this guy she was living with was beating the tar out of her, screaming he was gonna kill her and then kill us. Matty crawled into my room, hoisted me through the window, and we ran like maniacs. We hid under a bench in a bus shelter. It was like being jammed into a box of garbage and piss. But he stayed there with me, all night long, shaking like a leaf. Lying in that stink. Telling me I was safe, everything was going to be okay."

Kim blinked away her tears and cleared her throat. "The next morning, my mom had a pair of black eyes from the beating she got from her three-hundred-pound boyfriend. Want to know the first thing she did when we came home from hiding under that bus bench? She smacked the shit out of Matty. Told him he was a coward. For running away, and deserting his mother when she needed him to protect her."

Ali couldn't speak. Her heart was breaking.

"I told you it would make you want to puke." Kim turned around, displaying the scar on her back. "I got this when I was eight, from one of Mom's drug dealers. She owed him money. He came by the trailer where we were living. She was off partying and the guy wanted to send her a message, so he ran a knife down my back. He did it while Matty was fighting him like a madman. The guy had to practically break both of Matty's arms to make Matty stop. And when my mother saw the scar on me, she screamed at Matt that he'd torn her apart...that she'd counted on him to be the man of the house and take care of his baby sister...and he'd fucked it up. She told him he was a lightweight and nobody could ever feel safe with him."

Ali thought about the broken lock on the apartment door and her rape—about how many times she'd told Matt he'd failed her and that she couldn't rely on him.

"That's when Matt left," Kim was saying. "After the thing with the guy and the knife, Matty went back to live with our grandfather. He wanted me to come with him, but I didn't. I was mad at him. I believed my mother's bullshit about him letting us down."

Ali was having trouble understanding all of this. "But Matt always said he had no family..."

"He doesn't. Not really." Kim got up from the couch and sat in the chair across from Ali. "Matt wasn't lying about that. He *is* on his own. He's got nobody. Before I tapped him for the ten grand, I didn't even know if he was alive. I hadn't said word one to him for years, not since that nightmare in New York, right after you guys got engaged."

The soda can dropped out of Ali's hand, thumping to the floor, spilling its contents. Ali didn't care.

She was about to find out what Matt had done back in Rhode Island. During those three mysterious days when he had vanished.

Kim

"Brace yourself," Kim said. "Because I'm gonna tell you exactly what happened, and it's gonna be nasty." Kim cocked her head and looked at Ali for a beat. "You sure you wanna hear it?"

Ali, Matt's wife, was delicate. A girlie girl. Usually Kim didn't like that type, but Ali had a real streak of tough in her, too—which made her okay. Right now, she looked scared shitless, like her mouth was so dry she couldn't swallow.

Kim felt sorry for her. "Okay. So here's what happened. On the day Matty went to that book-signing party in Providence, our mother, who hadn't seen or spoken to him since he was twelve, checked herself out of a treatment facility in upstate New York and into a crappy hotel in Manhattan. She registered as Althea Ann Kenner, her maiden name, the hotshot family name she'd never given up."

Telling this story was hard, harder than Kim thought it would be; her hands were clammy. She wiped them on her shorts. Then she said, "That night, the night of the book signing, I was with my mother in the sleazy Manhattan hotel room. Mom was paranoid, going through these violent mood swings. I had my laptop with me, and I managed to calm her down by getting her to play games and letting her surf the Net. And then—"

Suddenly, Kim didn't want to go on.

"And then what?" Ali's question sounded frantic.

Kim wanted to find a way out, but there wasn't one—she had to finish the story. "Then Mom Googled Matt's name. She found an article about Matt getting his PhD from the college in Rhode Island and about him being an assistant professor there. Then she came across a newspaper photo of him in this fancy wedding at some big mansion in Newport. And she found an announcement about his engagement to you."

Kim grabbed another bottle of beer from the coffee table, chugged it, and said, "Mom started yelling, 'Where does he come off with this shit? Graduating from a fancy college? Partying in Newport? Spending money on diamond engagement rings?'"

Ali was so pale Kim thought she was going to pass out. "You sure you want to hear the rest of this?"

Ali mouthed the word *yes* but didn't make any noise.

Kim couldn't look at her. It was too sad—how scared Ali was. Kim kept her attention on the beer bottle while she said, "Mom got mental-patient violent, screaming that Matty had stolen her inheritance, saying stuff like, 'Where would the little bastard have gotten all that money unless he weaseled it out of my father before my old man died?' By the time she found Matt's info on his college's website, she was convinced he'd cheated her out of millions. That's when she sent him the email."

"What email?" Ali asked. "What did it say?"

"It was just one sentence: 'You're not going to get away with this.' Matty wrote back and asked Mom what she wanted. She said, 'To make you pay.'"

Kim got up and started pacing; she couldn't tell the rest of this sitting still. "A few hours later, Matty was outside our door. He only had the chance to knock once before that door flew open and Mom hit him so hard she knocked one of his teeth loose. He tried to cover his face, but she kept clawing at him with her fingernails, kept digging them into his skin, raking them down his forearms, leaving these bloody trails and…"

Kim clamped her hand over her mouth, stifling a moan. The look in Matt's eyes while he was being brutalized by his mother had been awful. And, for a minute, it wasn't just a memory. Kim was reliving it… *Matt lunging at their mother, Althea. Slamming her against the wall. Her head bouncing off the plaster with a sharp, cracking sound. The rage between Matt and Althea freezing Kim with terror while she watched Matt yank their mother away from the wall. And shove her backward, out the open door. Sending her scuffling, barefoot, across the matted carpet of that dingy hotel corridor.*

"I was ashamed of him," Kim said. "In spite of everything, it seemed totally wrong for a son to treat his mother like that." She thought for a moment, then looked at Ali. "But I was the one that was totally wrong. Instead of being ashamed of Matty, I should've been trying to save him. I was giving a sacredness to Althea Kenner she didn't deserve. She wasn't Matty's mother. Women like her? Their claim to motherhood ends with the push that shoots their slime-covered kid down the birth canal."

Ali cringed and looked away, leaving Kim alone. And Kim had been alone for way too long. She needed somebody to listen—to understand her story, and Matt's.

"After Matty shoved Althea through the open door, he ran out in the hall to help her. Mom was fighting him, hitting him. And while he was getting her back into the room, she was spitting at him and kicking him…screaming, 'You stole my money! You turned my own father against me. You're a thief!'"

"And what were you doing?" There was a hint of accusation in Ali's tone.

"I was pleading with him. 'Matty, don't hurt her. She'll calm down in a minute. She'll calm down.'" Kim was doing her best not to cry. "When he heard me call him Matty, I could see this longing in him. It was like, after so many years of us being apart, he was back with his baby sister again, and he wanted to say he loved me.

"But then something changed, and I could tell he was looking at me and thinking, 'This person isn't the little girl I remember. She's a woman I don't know.' Which I guess is why Matt stayed quiet. After that, the two of us wrestled our mother, kicking and screaming, into a chair and tied her down with a bedsheet."

Kim was remembering every detail… *The violence as she and Matt wrestled their mother into a chair. Althea was almost six feet tall, had just turned fifty…and the fight she gave them was a mash-up of an athlete's muscle and the unbelievable strength some people have when they're batshit crazy. At one point, Althea broke free, roaring out of the chair, screaming at Matt, "I'm the last of the Kenners, not you. My father's money belongs to me!"*

Kim watched their mother grab at Matt's throat, trying to strangle him. Almost immediately, Althea exhausted herself and flopped back into the chair. She left a trail of painful-looking bruises on Matt's neck. He was gasping for breath as he told her, "The only money Grandfather gave me was for my college tuition."

Althea glared at him—but the fight had gone out of her. She was wheezing, groggy, as she mumbled, "Bullshit. He was worth millions."

Matt pulled a tissue from a box on a table beside the bed and slowly wiped the film of sweat from their mother's face and the bubbles of spit from the corners of her mouth. "Grandfather was proud of having made every penny on his own," Matt told her. "When he was dying, he said he wanted me to have the same opportunity, and he was leaving his money to charity…all of it. I didn't have any problem with that."

Althea mumbled "bullshit" again and drifted off into a muttering daze.

Matt sat at the end of the bed, looking at Kim, defeated. "What's wrong with her?"

"She's high," Kim said. "And she's crazy. It's the same thing that's always been wrong with her."

"She should be in a hospital."

"She just ran away from one." Kim was stroking her mother's tangled

hair—still needing her, still loving her—saying, "It's okay, Momma. We're going to take care of you."

Then Kim had fixed her cornflower-blue eyes on Matt's lighter-blue ones and asked, "Isn't that right, Matty?"

That's when Kim saw something sad inside Matt. A little sealed-off corner where he'd never stopped wanting to treasure his mother and was still yearning to be treasured by her.

For three days, Kim stayed in that room while Matt never left Althea's side. He held her down while she raved. He watched over her while she slept. And in the moments when she was rational enough, he talked gently to her about her need for medical care.

Finally, around eight o'clock on the morning of that third day, the worst of Althea's rages stopped—and around noon, she agreed to go back to the hospital she'd run away from. Kim went down to the lobby, out onto the sidewalk, to flag down a cab. Matt stayed upstairs on the fourteenth floor with their mother.

And that's when it happened.

Matt was in the bathroom, getting a glass of water, listening to Althea pacing and muttering outside the door. Then the muttering stopped, and there was the scraping sound of a window being raised. It was followed by an eerie quiet.

In the time it took Matt to rush out of the bathroom, his mother was already crouched and grinning—perched on the sill of the open window.

Althea murmured "Fuck you" as if she were saying it to someone who wasn't quite real, someone only she could see. She did it calmly, the way she might've said "Good morning." Then she threw herself backward.

Matt made it to the window in time to reach out and grab hold of her wrists. But his mother's full weight was already plummeting toward the sidewalk. The momentum of her fall, as she slipped out of his grasp, jackknifed Matt, slamming him forward and down onto the windowsill. Two raised strips of metal that spanned the grimy width of the sill sliced into Matt's abdomen, just above his navel.

The lacerations were painfully deep, laced with grit and filth. But the paramedics and police, who arrived within minutes, were focused on something else. Althea's suicide. Nobody paid attention to the wounds that had been left on Matt.

"I saw how much pain he was in. After the police and paramedics left. When he was arranging for the disposal of our mother's body." Kim's face was hot with shame. "But when it was all over, when Matt tried to say good-bye to me, good-bye to his baby sister, I wouldn't even look at him."

"Why?" Ali sounded appalled.

Kim couldn't raise her voice above a guilty whisper. "I was mad at him...for letting my mom die."

Ali

THE ONLY THING MATTY'S GUILTY OF IS BEING THE SON OF A selfish, crazy-ass druggie." Kim said this while she and Ali stood at the end of the driveway.

As Ali opened the door of her rental car, Kim told her, "My brother has every right to be sick and twisted, but he isn't. He's a good man."

For each question that Kim's story had answered, it had raised a dozen more. "Why didn't you stay in contact with Matt after you were with him in New York?" Ali asked.

Kim bit at her thumbnail, looking embarrassed. "I don't know. I guess it's because part of me still wants my mom." She gave a quick, uncertain shrug. "I guess part of me is mad at Matt 'cause she's gone...'cause he wasn't strong enough to hang on to her when she went out that window. Pretty stupid, huh? Sounds like I'm looking at Matty the same crappy way she did."

Kicking at a pebble, Kim told Ali, "I was there when Mom landed, y'know. I was right outside the hotel, trying to get a cab, so we could take her back to the hospital. I was close enough to see her face coming toward me and hear the god-awful noise she made when she hit the sidewalk."

Ali wondered how anyone could survive such an experience.

Kim calmly told her, "I know it'd be just as easy to be mad at Althea, instead of Matt. She's the one who decided to jump out a window and turn herself into an omelet right in front of her own kids, but…" Kim's eyes were swimming with tears. "But I loved her. She was my mom." Again, Kim bit at her thumbnail. "That sounds crazy, I guess."

"No, it doesn't," Ali said. "I know what you mean." And Ali did know. She understood the confusion of loving someone you were capable of hating. The helplessness of being unable to stop loving them. Because their blood flowed through your veins.

Ali had lived that kind of logic-defying love.

It was her bond with Morgan.

～

Watching the Arizona desert recede beneath the wings of the plane, Ali thought about Matt's mother's suicide and Matt's grim childhood—and she realized Matt had never stopped fighting for something that she, and his mother and sister, had never given him credit for. He'd never stopped fighting to be a hero. And for a moment, Ali loved Matt for that.

But then a man across the aisle pulled a brown briefcase out of the overhead compartment, and Ali's thoughts went to the suitcase in the attic, to the question of who could have put it there.

And her feeling of love for Matt was riddled with uncertainty.

～

During the flight from Phoenix, like everyone else on the plane, Ali had her phone switched off. As she walked into the terminal, switching it on, a call came in.

It was Matt, sounding worried. "Al, I just picked up the message you left me. I could hear in your voice…there's a problem."

Ali left the flood of passengers surging toward the exits and found a chair in an empty boarding area—while Matt told her, "Your message said there's something in the house you want to talk to me about?"

"Yes, I—"

Ali suddenly realized that he was returning a call she made before she'd left for Phoenix, when the only thing she'd wanted to talk about was the suitcase in the attic. Now, there was so much more. Now, she had met his sister and discovered the truth about the three days he'd gone missing, and the appalling things that had happened to him as a child. These weren't things she could handle in a phone call.

"I need you to come home. It's important" was all Ali said.

It was all she needed to say.

In two days, Matt would be back from Australia.

Morgan

T HE SCARY PART IS…MY SISTER'S ATTACKER STILL HASN'T BEEN caught."

It had been too long. Things like her job and Ralph and time reconnecting with Ali had kept Morgan busy twenty-four seven. It was good, finally, to have Sam at the other end of an early-morning phone call. There was so much she needed to talk to him about.

And at this particular moment she was telling him, "The thing that's driving me crazy is that whoever hurt Ali is still *here*, somewhere nearby."

Sam's voice was fainter than usual. But, as always, calm and compassionate. "How do you know he's still in close proximity?"

"I can feel it. I can just feel it."

Morgan pressed the phone to her ear, overwhelmed with guilt. "Sam, how could I have been so completely blind to what my sister was going through? The night she was attacked, why didn't I sense she was in danger? And the day after, when she must have been in agony, I screamed at her. I told her I hoped whatever happened was something awful, because that's what she deserved."

"Why do you think you were so closed off back then?" Sam asked.

"I was angry. It was completely different for me then. I wasn't listening to anything other than what was in my own head. Now. With you, I'm open to everything you tell me, and grateful for it…but back then, when my mom, or Ali, tried to help me see stuff I was missing, all I'd hear was criticism, and it made me furious."

"Why are things different now?"

"Maybe, with us, I was able to hear what you were saying because we started out as strangers. I didn't have a history with you. I got to a place with Mom and Ali where I was so mad at them I couldn't think straight. I was jealous because I thought Ali was always getting life handed to her on a platter. And I was angry with my mother because I thought she loved Ali more than she loved me. Every time Mom tried to come close, I pushed her away. Eventually, I think she was so hurt and frustrated she didn't know how to deal with me anymore."

Morgan took a deep breath. When she let it out, she said, "Sam, up until recently, I spent most of my time feeling cheated...keeping track of what I thought everybody owed me. I treated my mother like she was an enemy. And I treated my sister like she'd committed a crime against me and I had the right to be horrible to her."

Sam's reply was unhurried and kind. "We're all works in progress, my friend. From the moment we're born, we're continually in the process of becoming...learning and growing. As long as you don't stop and give in to who you are, and you keep reaching toward who you could be, then you're on the path to becoming your best self, the person you were created to be."

"What if I've already spent too much time being less than my best? What if I'm fooling myself and it's too late to become a truly good person?"

"It's never too late."

"I don't know where I'd be without you, Sam." Morgan's voice was soft, almost embarrassed. "And yet I'm always wondering who you are."

She didn't want to go too deep, ask too much, change anything between them, but she couldn't help wanting to know more. And before she could stop herself she said, "Tell me about something you just love to do."

At the other end of the call—stillness.

Then Sam's voice, very quiet. "The speed of ski slopes and race cars and parachute jumps. There was a time when what I loved was speed."

"But you stopped loving it?"

"No. Never."

Morgan waited for an explanation. She didn't get one.

Eventually Sam said, "But life is the process of becoming. It starts with your first breath and stays with you until your last. Just think of the power of it…being able to continually reach toward the light. The possibilities are infinite."

Later that morning, around seven, Morgan left home—still thinking about her phone call with Sam. About the idea that every moment was a new opportunity to grow and change—the possibilities infinite.

She arrived at work early, before anyone else. And went straight to her office computer. It had been a while since Morgan had posted on Facebook, and she decided it was time to reconnect. In her post, she talked about her job, and Ralph, and how she was settling into life in California. She also mentioned Ali's attack, without giving any details, saying only that a family member had suffered a terrible tragedy. What Morgan did describe in detail was the pain of the tragedy—and how much she wanted to help ease that pain.

About an hour after Morgan arrived at the museum, her office door opened. Erin, the colleague who introduced Morgan to Ben Tennoff, peeked in. "Did Ralph like the organic dog treats?"

"He's a huge fan. Thanks for telling me about them."

This was one of the things Morgan loved about her new

world—the connection she had with people, the shared interests and small talk, being a part of life, instead of apart from it.

"How's Max?" Morgan asked.

"The vet says it's just allergies. He'll be fine. And in case Ralph's interested, Max would love another playdate. Will you be bringing him to my barbecue? Don't forget. It's two weeks from this Saturday."

"I can't wait. And yes…Ralph's coming, too."

Erin smiled. Raised a questioning eyebrow. "How's my cousin Ben? Is he still in DC?"

Morgan nodded. "Yeah. He'll be back soon though."

"And when he comes home…will you two be getting together?"

"I think so." Morgan ducked her head, blushing a little. She was looking forward to seeing Ben.

"That's great. You guys make a terrific couple."

Somewhere nearby, a door opened and closed. Erin glanced over her shoulder, then back at Morgan. "By the way, Mr. Dupuis wants to see you in his office."

Morgan was instantly on her feet, heading down the hallway.

Mr. Dupuis, Morgan's boss, was French and known for being punctual, polite, and impeccably dressed. His small office was Persian carpeted and oak paneled. A bowl of fresh gardenias was always on the windowsill. The scent in the room was theirs, heady and lush.

Although Morgan sincerely liked Mr. Dupuis, she was also overwhelmed by him. As she perched on the Queen Anne chair at the side of his desk, Morgan was nervous.

Mr. Dupuis gestured toward a table where there was a tray containing chilled bottles of Perrier. Morgan shook her head. "No thanks, I'm fine."

"Well then, my dear, we'll get directly to the matter at hand." Mr. Dupuis's smile was bland.

Morgan felt like she'd just swallowed a swarm of bees.

At her last job, at the museum in Rhode Island, a bland smile and the words "the matter at hand" had been followed by the news that she was being fired. The biggest reason her boss Veronica wanted to get rid of her was personal, the incident with the copier salesman. But there were other issues, too. Morgan had spent a lot of time distracted. She'd been so busy feeling insecure and keeping tabs on Ali's life that her job performance could have been best described as middle of the road.

Morgan was braced for disaster as she waited to hear Mr. Dupuis's version of "the matter at hand."

When he announced, "We're here to discuss your promotion," she was shocked.

"I know this is arriving a bit soon," Mr. Dupuis said. "However, your creativity and dedication are remarkable. You're someone we want to retain. At all costs."

Retain? Where does he think I'm going? Morgan wondered.

Mr. Dupuis smoothed his flawlessly smooth tie, smiled warmly, and told her, "The museum world is a small one. It's come to my attention that another quite prestigious institution here in Southern California is considering stealing you away from us. I'm hoping to prevent that…with this." He slid a thick, white envelope across his desktop. "Here is the information on your new job description and the proposed increase in salary."

Morgan didn't know what to say.

"No need to rush. Review the proposal. Take your time making a decision." Mr. Dupuis came around the desk and walked Morgan to the door. "What's important is that you know how extraordinary you are, how much we value your passion and focus."

Passion and focus—the phrase seemed unbelievable.

Mr. Dupuis had described her as someone with passion and focus.

She was being offered a promotion. People in prestigious places wanted her to come work for them because they thought she was extraordinary. How had this happened?

The answer came to Morgan in an echo—the sound of Sam's voice saying, *"...the process of becoming. Just think of the power of it...being able to continually reach toward the light. The possibilities are infinite."*

Morgan realized that she had become a new person. She was working hard, paying attention, spending more time loving than demanding to be loved. She was smarter, more courageous, more alive. And she was incredibly excited by that.

Morgan's excitement about her conversation with Mr. Dupuis and about the new person she'd become were still with her at the end of the day. As she crossed the museum parking lot. With the envelope containing her new job offer in one hand, and her purse in the other.

Just as she was getting into her car, her phone rang. It was Logan. She could hear traffic noise in the background. He had the top down on his Porsche. The call was being put through the car's sound system. "I'm on the road, driving down from the corporate office in Santa Barbara," he said. "I'll be at the boat in an hour. Want to see me?"

Morgan didn't even have to think about it. "Yes. I definitely want to see you." She smiled. "There's something I can't wait to tell you."

"What?"

"Not on the phone. It's too important. I need to be looking at you."

What she wanted to say to Logan had Morgan shooting out of the museum parking lot and flying toward the marina.

Morgan's visit to Logan's boat didn't take long.

When she got there, Logan was sprawled on the black silk sheets, naked. An open champagne bottle on the shelf beside the bed. His clothes scattered across the floor—a faint trace of lipstick on his shirt collar, and his underwear lying in front of the drawers built into the cabin wall.

An image flashed through Morgan's mind, something she'd forgotten about—the zebra-striped panties tucked into one of those drawers.

"Hey, get your clothes off." Logan scratched his belly absentmindedly. "We gotta do this fast. I'm expected home for dinner and you know what a ballbuster Jessica can be."

He took a pull from the champagne bottle. "I fucked up. I shouldn't have let Jess know I was driving from Santa Barbara. It works better when she thinks I've taken a plane...then there's always, 'Hey, there was a mix-up with the flight.'" His grin was smug. "Very easy to open up an evening that way."

"It can't be that easy," Morgan said. "How many times can you keep using the same excuse?"

"I don't know. But so far, so good." He tossed a pillow toward the end of the bed and put his feet up. "Now take your damn clothes off."

Morgan nailed him with a cool, confident smile. "Remember me saying there was something I needed to tell you face-to-face? Well, here it is. I'm finished chasing things that aren't worthy of me. There's no way I would ever again come anywhere near a pig like you. Ever."

Logan lunged at her, grabbing her arm, knocking her purse out of her hand. "What the fuck did you just say?"

Morgan jerked free of him, grabbed her purse—and looked around the cabin. At his wedding ring. And the rumpled sheets. And his clothes on the floor. And the lipstick on his shirt collar. Then she looked at him.

"This is…" She couldn't think how to express what she was feeling.

"It's what?" Logan's tone was warning her to be careful.

The word that came to Morgan's mind was one her grandmother MaryJoy always used when disgust flashed in her violet eyes. "This is seedy," Morgan said.

"You might want to think that over and take it back while you can." Logan's delivery was vicious. "I don't give second chances."

Morgan shrugged.

And when she walked away, she was walking tall. Thinking about Mr. Dupuis calling her capable and extraordinary. Remembering the weight of that fat, white envelope he'd handed her, and the delicious promises it contained. And deciding that sweet, caring Ben Tennoff was somebody she definitely wanted to spend more time with.

～

The drive to South Pasadena went swiftly, took about forty-five minutes. It wasn't until she was in the supermarket down the street from her duplex that Morgan felt the jolt. She was in the checkout line, buying dinner for herself and more dog food for Ralph—and she discovered that the white envelope containing her new museum contract wasn't in her purse.

The minute her groceries were bagged and she got them to her car, she called Logan. He answered on the second ring. "When I was on your boat, I think something fell out of my purse," Morgan told him. "I need you to look around the floor and—"

"Are you fucking nuts?" He sounded angry enough to kill her. "This thing's on speaker, and I just pulled into my garage." Morgan could hear him switching from the hands-free system. Now he had the phone so close to his mouth Morgan could almost feel the heat of his breath. "Back off. This is my goddamned home. Where my fucking wife is!"

Morgan was annoyed, sick of him. "You mean Jessica the ballbuster?"

"What do you want? I told you, you don't get a second chance."

"That's not why I'm calling. There's something of mine that's important... It's on your boat, and I need you to do me a favor."

Logan's laugh was fast and harsh. "Do you a favor? What alternate universe are you from? Wake up, buttercup."

Then there was nothing but dead air. The call had ended.

Morgan took the phone away from her ear and dropped it into the car's cup holder. That's when she saw the white envelope—on the floor mat in front of the passenger seat. It must have fallen out of her purse without her noticing.

For some reason, when Morgan reached for the envelope, the zebra-striped panties tucked away on Logan's boat flashed through her mind—and she thought about Logan saying *Wake up, buttercup.*

The memory of the panties was disgusting. But what Morgan didn't understand was why *buttercup* was sending a cold shiver through her.

Ali

ALI WAS IN THE FAMILY ROOM, COZY, WEARING PERSIMMON-colored pajamas and a pair of Matt's white tennis socks. She was on the phone with Jessica, thinking how tired Jessica seemed, how raw her throat sounded.

"After we have fights like this, I just hate him," Jessica said. "Logan can be such a bastard. He waltzes in here two hours late, with lipstick on his shirt, and when I get upset, he tells me *I'm* paranoid. I'm a ballbuster."

"Where did he say the lipstick came from?" Ali asked.

"He was up at the corporate office in Santa Barbara. He's always at one of those fucking outposts. Last week he was at the La Jolla office. The week before, it was the one in fucking Sacramento."

"Jess. What did he say about the lipstick on his shirt?"

"He said he must've hugged one of his coworkers when he was leaving." Jessica's sigh was weary. "I don't know. Maybe. Maybe not."

"And being two hours late...what did he say about that?"

"The old standby. Traffic." Jessica gave a sarcastic grunt. "It's shit like this...it makes me so ready to fucking divorce him."

"Are you serious? You're thinking about leaving?"

"Yeah, I think about it. Then I think about the boys. They adore their dad. And I think about the fact that I don't have money anymore, and Logan is what's keeping this show on the road right now." Jessica paused. There was the sound of ice being dropped into a glass and the splashing noise of a drink being poured, probably tequila.

"Shit, Ali. I still haven't told him about Daddy and the Ponzi scheme and all the money being gone. Shit. Shit. Shit. If Logan's cheating on me now, what will it be like when he knows he's not married to a big, fat trust fund anymore?" There was another pause and the sound of another shot being poured. "Oh, fuck it. The truth is, I don't even know for sure that he *is* cheating. Maybe I'm making a big deal over nothing. Maybe he's just a guy who doesn't like a lot of rules, y'know?"

"Jess, you need to talk to him."

"I know. You're right. But if I rock the boat...what about the kids? Before you know it, my boys'll be in school and have friends. They won't have the right ones...school or friends...without good clothes and an address that means something."

"Jess. You need to talk to Logan. Right away. You have to know what's going on."

Jessica's tone was flippant, irritated. "I need to talk to him, but I won't be able to. The fucker's leaving on a ski trip in the morning."

"Can't you ask him to postpone?"

"Not a chance. Remember the Perfect Ten trip to Deer Valley? The one I wanted you to come with me on, and you never did? Well, this year, it's the husbands jumping in the private jet and heading for the slopes. There's no way Logan's going to give that up to stay home and haggle about our stupid marriage." Jessica laughed her tough-girl laugh. "I know I wouldn't."

"That is so you." Ali chuckled.

"Y'know what? Let me sleep on this. I'll call you tomorrow."

"Love you, Jess. Take care. Talk to you tomorrow."

As the call ended, Ali glanced at the clock—almost midnight. *By this time tomorrow, Matt will be home. I'll have shown him the suitcase, my attacker's clothes...and I'll already have asked Matt why he put them there.*

Ali shuddered.

What could Matt's answer possibly be?

Sofie was asleep when Ali went upstairs to check on her, the room lit by the soft glow of a night-light.

Ali's mother was dozing in a rocking chair with a piece of half-finished knitting in her lap.

"Mom, I thought you went to bed hours ago," Ali whispered. "What are you doing in here in the dark?"

"It'll be a while before I see Sofie again. I wanted to spend a little more time with her."

"You'll see her in the morning, won't you?"

"I don't think so. The airport shuttle bus is coming at five."

Sofie stirred under her blankets. A stuffed elephant slipped off her bed. Ali picked it up, then said, "Mom, you know you don't have to do this."

"Honey, our deal was that I'd come and help you with Sofie while Matt was in Australia. Now he's on his way home."

"Okay, but that doesn't mean you need to go running back to Rhode Island right this minute. You can stay as long as you want."

"Ali, it's February. I have a house and friends I haven't seen since last fall. And besides, I miss your father."

Ali did a startled double take. There was something in how her mother had said *"I miss your father"* that seemed to suggest he was being missed in a very intimate way.

Even in the dim glow of the night-light, Ali could see her mother was flustered.

"Your father and I get together once a week." Her mother carefully folded her knitting. "I make him dinner. Those chicken pot pies he likes." Her expression was bashful. "It's a nice time. For both of us."

Ali stared at her mother, speechless. What she'd just heard was insane. "A nice time? After what Dad did to you? After he ran off and left you and me and Morgan for Petra, that prune-faced moron?"

"It's not that simple. Your father knew he'd made a mistake the minute he married Petra, and he told me so. He begged me to let him come home. But I said no." Her mother shifted in her chair, uncomfortable. "I wouldn't let him come back because I wanted to hurt him. Wanted to hurt him as much as he'd hurt me." There was the sound of loss in her mother's voice as she told Ali, "Your father is the only man I ever loved. That has never changed."

"So you just let him get away with what he did? Let him come over once a week for a pot pie and a hug?" Ali couldn't believe what her mother was saying.

Her mother's sigh had tenderness, and regret. "Your father made a mistake, and he owned up to it. It isn't his fault that I wouldn't let him make it right, couldn't forgive him."

"There are some things that can never be forgiven." Ali was picturing that night in the apartment when she'd been torn apart. And she was remembering being a little girl in Sunday school, listening to the story of the prodigal son.

"You have the strangest look on your face, honey. What are you thinking about?"

"The prodigal son," Ali said. "His brother was completely innocent, a good guy who did everything right, while the prodigal son was a horrible sinner. A runaway. A selfish, whoring jerk. Then when he decides for whatever reason to roll back into town, his father gives him a feast and a do-over. Just forgives him. How is that right? Why didn't he deserve to be punished?"

Her mother thought for a moment. "Maybe he'd already been punished. Who knows what he went through, what terrible dues he had to pay, before he smartened up and came home? Maybe he had his punishment long before he had his feast."

"And what punishment did Dad get that entitles him to his pot pies?" Ali's question was sarcastic and cold.

"Your father's punishment is ongoing. He's married to Petra."

Her mother gave Ali a knowing look. "I don't think all this frustration is just about your father. There's something wrong between you and Matt, isn't there? What has he done that you can't quite forgive him for?"

Ali's knees were suddenly weak. She sat on the floor beside her mother's chair, her face in her hands. "Mom, it's something awful."

Her mother put her hand on Ali's bowed head. "Talk to me, honey."

Ali was struggling to deal with the mind-bending implications of finding her attacker's clothes hidden in the attic, and Matt being the only person who could have put them there. "Mom, the man who… who raped me…he…" Ali couldn't finish the sentence.

"What are you trying to say, honey?"

"He got into the apartment through a door that had a broken lock. A lock Matt never fixed." Ali knew she'd swerved away from the truth—talking about the lock instead of the clothes in the attic. There was something so ghastly about their existence she couldn't bear to tell her mother about them. All she could manage to admit was "I feel like Matt had something to do with my rape."

Her mother's voice was full of compassion. "I can see how you feel that Matt let you down…but, honey, all it would've taken to fix that door was a call to a locksmith. You could've picked up the phone and fixed it yourself." She waited a moment. Then added, "People who do pure evil, they probably shouldn't get a second chance. But when somebody who loves us makes a mistake, the way we all do… even if it's a big mistake…don't you think we should forgive them, like we'd want them to forgive us?"

Ali didn't answer. She didn't know how.

Morgan

MORGAN HAD BEEN DREAMING A DREAM WHERE THERE WAS nothing but darkness, and the only sound was an eerie whisper: "*Buttercup.*"

Like a bolt out of the blue, she was wide awake. Sitting up in bed, in her duplex, in South Pasadena. "Oh God, I think I know what *buttercup* means."

Ralph jumped onto the bed, burrowing close, doing his best to comfort Morgan. She was trembling—horrified by what she'd just figured out.

If I'm right about buttercup, *it's hideous. And the proof is in Ali's house. Oh my God. I have back-to-back meetings that will keep me trapped at the museum all day. The earliest I could get away would be six, six thirty.*

It would be at least twelve hours before Morgan could be sure about *buttercup.*

Realizing the awfulness that could happen in that time was scaring the life out of her.

One hundred five miles from South Pasadena,
   early morning.
Merciless cruelty.
   Hot sand.
   The flicking tail of a lizard against a bare ankle.
   And a curl of lace the color of a blueberry.

Ali

IN THE EARLY MORNING OF THE DAY MATT WAS SCHEDULED TO come home, Ali was in the bookstore across the alley from the restaurant, trying not to let anyone see how on edge she was.

Ali was near the door, with a group of young mothers. She was waving to Sofie, who was in the center of the room, in a circle of children gathered for the weekly story hour. All of them cross-legged on a braided rug. Their eyes shining as the elderly bookseller, in his Burberry-plaid bow tie, told the tale of *The Cat in the Hat*.

One of the mothers in the group whispered to Ali, "You look super-stressed. Go back to the restaurant. I can see how busy it is over there. I'll watch Sofie and call you as soon as story time is over."

Ali mouthed the words *thank you* and hurried out of the bookstore. While she was crossing the alley, she took deep breaths, doing her best to keep her anxiety under control. What was waiting for her— Matt coming home tonight, and the confrontation about the clothes in the attic—was overwhelming.

When Ali entered the restaurant, the dining area was packed to capacity. Most of the customers were headed to work, stopping for a muffin and a fast cup of coffee. There were only a few tables occupied by people having a leisurely breakfast. As Ali made her way toward the kitchen, she saw that two of those people were Peter Sebelius and his wife, Quinn.

Peter had a bowl of oatmeal in front of him and was offering a spoonful to Quinn, telling her, "You've got to taste this. It's incredible."

Still worrying about Matt and the suitcase, Ali hoped to slip past unnoticed—but she'd been spotted. Quinn was calling to her.

Ali forced a cheery grin and went over to the table. "I'm glad you're enjoying the oatmeal. It's Sofie's favorite. We only use steel-cut Irish oats, and before we cook them, we sauté them in a little butter to bring out a nice nutty flavor."

Quinn was smiling up at Ali. "I'm crazy about the way you top it off with roasted pecans and these amazing bananas."

"They're plantains, with a butter-and-brown-sugar glaze that has cinnamon and a touch of vanilla in it." There was wistfulness in Ali's voice, as she added, "I got the idea from my friend Ava. She grew up in Belize."

"No wonder people rave about the food in this place. Everything's laced with butter," Quinn told Peter.

"As a doctor, I disapprove. As a guy who likes to eat, I'm loving it."

Ali put her hand on Peter's shoulder. "I just realized this is the first time you've been in here. What took you so long?"

"He's a workaholic," Quinn said. "He's always at the hospital, always—"

Ali's phone signaled the arrival of a text. She saw the message and told Quinn, "I'm sorry. I have to deal with this." She moved away, pressing a number on her speed dial.

Morgan picked up immediately, sounding hysterical. "Where's the spare key to your house? I'm looking in the planter at the side of the garage. It isn't here. Why isn't it where it's supposed to be?"

"Morgan, you texted me there was an emergency. Why are you at my house? Why aren't you at work?"

"A meeting with my boss was canceled, and I ducked out." Morgan's words were coming in a rush, as if she were being chased. "I only have a little while before I need to be back. Where's the key?"

"I gave Mom the spare key to use while she was visiting. She probably forgot it was in her purse when she left."

"Is there another one somewhere?" Morgan's tone was insistent.

This conversation seemed ridiculous to Ali, as if Morgan had somehow flipped back into being her old self—irrational and demanding. It made no sense.

Morgan's voice was edging into panic. "I need to come and get your key. I'll bring it right back. I promise."

All Ali said before she put her phone back into her pocket was "I can't talk. I'm busy." She was under too much stress to deal with Morgan's sudden return to craziness.

"Now that I've discovered JOY, I'll be here every chance I get." Peter Sebelius was calling Ali back to the table—and Quinn was saying, "Well, since we're going to be regulars, I better get to know the layout. Ali, can you show me where the ladies' room is?"

The request was so chirpy and self-conscious that Peter shot Quinn a puzzled look. "Finish your oatmeal," she told him.

As Ali and Quinn walked away, Quinn glanced over her shoulder, making certain Peter was out of earshot. "Is everything set for his surprise party?"

"Yup. We're good. The food. The equipment for the video tribute. All of it. I even hired a team to handle the decorations. They do great work."

Quinn squeezed Ali's hand. "I can't wait! I wish it wasn't happening the day after tomorrow. I wish it was happening right now."

"This is the first private party we've ever had here. I intend to make it an evening to remember."

Ali and Quinn exchanged a quick hug.

Then Ali went back to worrying about what would happen tonight when Matt got home—and she hurried through the kitchen's swinging doors, barely avoiding a collision with a waiter. When he moved past, Ali saw that in addition to the restaurant staff, there was a stranger in the kitchen.

A man had just walked in through the back door that led to the walled garden. It took Ali a moment to realize who the man was.

"I caught an earlier flight," Matt told her. "I couldn't wait to see you."

He had left for the movie job in the Australian outback only seven months ago. Ali was startled by how much he had changed. He was muscular and tanned. As if he'd been living outdoors, herding cattle or working at some sort of manual labor. His hair was longer, tousled and casual. And he had a close-trimmed beard—a shade or two darker than his blond hair, a golden-honey color. She'd never seen Matt with a beard before.

Everything about him was different. Rugged, and sexy, and new. For the space of a heartbeat, Ali felt an intense physical attraction to him. And in the next heartbeat, there was an overwhelming sense of danger. Her beguiling husband was a potential monster. He had covered up horrible secrets about his past. He'd put out a welcome mat for her attacker by leaving that lock unrepaired. And he was the only person who'd had access to the attic, the hiding place for her attacker's clothes.

"Aren't you going to say hello?" Matt asked.

Ali was so afraid, so confused. "You look completely different."

Matt gave her an easy grin. "Aidan's into horses. He taught me how to ride. And we played soccer like it was a religion." Then he said, "I'm a little more buff, but I'm still me."

And I have no idea who that is, Ali thought.

He brushed his lips along the curve of her neck. "Why did you need me to come home, Al?"

All Ali could feel was dread. She pulled away and wiped at the place on her neck where his lips had been.

"We have to go, Matt. There's something at home that you need to explain."

Before she left the restaurant kitchen, Ali had texted Jessica, asking her to pick up Sofie from the story group and babysit for a few hours. Now Ali was alone in the attic, with Matt.

The brown suitcase was open on the floor. Matt was staring at the satin shirt and the jeans. The horseshoe-buckled belt and the ostrich-skin boots.

All the color was gone from his face. "Who else knows about this?"

"Nobody."

"Not even Morgan or your mother?"

"It was hard enough just telling them about the attack. I didn't have the strength to talk about this... It scared me too much."

Matt sounded like he was having trouble breathing. "How did it get here?"

Ali had to hold on to the wall for support. "You're the only one who ever brought stuff into the attic."

"But how could I have brought *this*?" Matt circled the suitcase, looking confused. "We gave this suitcase away. I remember. You put it on the Salvation Army pile at the apartment. Before we ever moved here."

Ali's voice was thready and scared. "Tell me why I found my attacker's clothes hidden in our house, Matt."

Matt kept his attention on the contents of the suitcase.

Ali backed away until she was safely on the other side of the room. "I asked you a question. How did that stuff get in here?"

"I have no idea," Matt told her.

Ali looked from the suitcase to Matt—and was suddenly furious. "What is your connection to those clothes?"

Matt just stared at her, blankly. Then a realization seemed to dawn. "Holy Jesus. You're still blaming me for that night?" He let out a groan. "Ali, I'd give anything to go back and make it so it never happened. I swear. I'd fix the lock. I'd sit outside our fucking bedroom with a hatchet and bury it in anybody who even thought of coming near you."

"But that wasn't what you did, was it?" Ali crossed the attic and stopped a few feet away from her attacker's clothes. Without planning to, she punched Matt—as hard as she could.

And kept the punches coming. She wanted to kill him.

Matt made no attempt to defend himself. It wasn't until Ali's fists slowed and she said "I hate you for not taking care of me" that Matt gently pushed her away.

"Ali, I didn't fix the lock. I let you down…but I didn't let you go home to be raped." His mystified gaze went back the suitcase and the clothes. "I swear to God, I don't know how this stuff got into our house." Matt sounded shattered. "I can't believe you thought I was the one who brought these things in here."

She had to look away. The depth of his hurt was too gut-wrenching, too real. Ali instinctively knew he was telling the truth.

She wanted to let go, forgive Matt. Wanted to say she was sorry and that she loved him. She wanted to lean on him and have him hold her up.

But some self-protective part of Ali was warning her to be careful, to take this very slowly.

Looking like he was fighting to keep his composure, Matt was again circling the suitcase. "We have to deal with this. Then we have to decide what to do about the rest of our life together."

"The rest of our life together?" Ali's mood of love and forgiveness was suddenly gone. "How am I supposed to figure out how to have a life with you when all you are is a wall of secrets?"

"What secrets?"

"Your sister. And your mother."

Matt froze.

"I went to Phoenix," Ali told him. "I met Kim."

His eyes were wide, like he was caught in a hunter's crosshairs. "Ali, I—"

She cut him off. "If you can cover up things as huge as what I discovered in Phoenix, how am I supposed to trust you...about anything?"

Matt's mood instantly changed. He came across the room fast— grabbing Ali and telling her, "We're both guilty of covering up the truth. And we did it for the exact same reason." The way he said it was quiet, a warning.

They were at the edge of a cliff, and Ali wasn't sure if Matt was trying to push her over it, or away from it. She had no idea what he was talking about.

"Your rape," Matt said. "After it happened, why did you hide in the house and pretend to have the flu? Why didn't you just come out and tell everybody the truth? Why did you cover it up?" His tone was harsh, yet what Ali saw in Matt's eyes was empathy.

She suddenly understood what he was asking her, and what he was explaining to her. Matt was throwing out a lifeline they could pull themselves to safety with. And Ali said, "I didn't tell anybody I'd been attacked because it was too awful. I didn't know how to talk about it. I lied because I didn't know what else to do."

"Me, too." Matt swallowed hard, and then said, "That's why I didn't talk about my mother and my sister, why I lied about the way I grew up. It was so awful I didn't know what else to do."

Matt wrapped his arms around Ali. "Neither one of us is a saint, or an unforgivable sinner," he whispered. "The only way we'll survive is if we can accept that and just keep on loving each other anyway."

He made it sound so easy—but Ali had the feeling it might be hard to do.

Matt moved away and crouched beside the brown suitcase. "Al, all I can give you on this is the same promise I gave you back in Rhode Island, when I asked you not to call off the wedding." He stared at the suitcase's contents. "I swear I haven't done and will never do anything to deliberately dishonor our love." He stood up and waited until her eyes met his. "I have no idea how these clothes got in here."

Ali let Matt take her hand. As they walked toward the attic stairs, she asked, "Where are we going?"

"To call the police," was Matt's answer.

Morgan

MORGAN WAS AS JUMPY AS IF THE POLICE WERE AFTER HER. Her dash to Ali's house this morning, hoping to find proof of the meaning of *buttercup*, had been a disaster. After not getting into the house because the spare key was gone, Morgan had gotten caught in traffic on her way back to the museum and missed an important meeting.

She returned to work and discovered that her next meeting was scheduled to begin in minutes. Racing the clock, Morgan ducked into her office—heading straight to her computer.

With *buttercup* still buzzing in her mind, she swiftly navigated a corporate website, jotting down the locations of the company's impressive number of regional offices. The information sent a spidery, creeping sensation down the back of her neck. Earlier in the day, she had scanned several other websites, looking for information on unsolved crimes. What she'd found had rattled her.

She could hear someone coming into her office. She closed her computer and quickly turned away from it. Her boss, Mr. Dupuis, was watching her through narrowed eyes. "Is there a problem, Morgan? They're waiting for you in the staff meeting."

"No. No problem. I was just...um...I was just on my way." Morgan made a show of efficiently gathering up her files and her museum-issued iPad. But all she could think about were the notes she'd jotted down from the website she'd just visited. Addresses that spanned the state of California, from mountaintops to desert valleys.

Those addresses terrified Morgan. But she was determined to do what was needed. Walk into the mouth of hell. Risk her life, if she had to.

Morgan intended to do whatever it took to make Ali safe.

Ali

ALI WAS, AGAIN, IN THE ATTIC. MATT WAS WITH HER.

Ali's attention was focused on the two strangers on the other side of the room. A wide-shouldered black man. And a ferrety, sallow-skinned woman. The woman was meticulously photographing every inch of the attic.

From the moment he arrived, the man had maintained an impersonal, businesslike attitude—but he seemed genuinely sympathetic as he told Ali, "I'm gonna help you all I can, ma'am. You have my word on that. The original detective on your case has left the department, and now that I've inherited your file, I'll make sure nothing falls through the cracks. However, like I told you, this is real life, not TV. In real life, sometimes there are crimes that don't get solved."

Ali understood he was pointing out the truth—and she stubbornly refused to accept it. Until her attacker was behind bars, she couldn't feel safe. Which is why she was insisting, "But now you'll know who he is, you can arrest him. The clothes in that suitcase must have his DNA and fingerprints."

The detective stepped aside to allow his companion to photograph the items in the suitcase. "Ma'am, if these really are your rapist's clothes, and not somebody's idea of a sick joke, the DNA evidence we get will be the same as the samples collected from the rape kit they did on you in the hospital the night you were attacked. Samples we haven't been able to match to anybody in our database. We still won't have the guy's name."

Ali's response came through gritted teeth. "This isn't fair."

"I understand your frustration," the detective told her. "But if you think about it, we don't even know for sure this is your old suitcase. Most suitcases look pretty much alike. And even if it is the one you used to own, any of a hundred people could've brought it up here."

"No. That's impossible."

"Ma'am, you were attacked the night before you moved into this house. By seven o'clock the next morning, the doors were wide open and the place was crawling with people. The movers. The people delivering your new furniture. People installing the alarm system, cable TV, and computers. It probably stayed that way most of the day. In all that confusion, it would've been easy for somebody to walk in and slip a suitcase into your attic. Nobody would've noticed, certainly not your husband, or you. You were both in shock. You'd just been raped. Chances are that neither one of you was paying attention to every single individual carrying a box or wearing a uniform."

For a minute Ali was speechless. "I never thought about that. You're right. There were all kinds of people fixing things and delivering things on the day we moved in."

"And as far as potential suspects go, it's only the tip of the iceberg. Who knows how many others we could be talking about? Think about all the people who knew when you were moving, where you were moving from, and where you were moving to. At your restaurant alone there would've been kitchen staff, waiters, vendors, cleaning crews, window washers, gardeners, and, more than likely, a lot of customers. You probably talked about your move for weeks before it happened. You would've made phone calls, scribbled down notes, had papers all over the place that showed your new address—"

"Oh God." Ali couldn't believe what she'd done.

"What is it?" Matt asked.

"I did talk about the move." She felt sick. "And I talked about the broken lock, too. I must've mentioned it to Ava a million times. I was so mad that you never fixed it."

Ali turned to the detective. "People were always around when I was talking about the lock…and about the move. Dozens of people. Coming in and out of the kitchen all day long…people who knew I was moving, and that the patio door to the apartment was unlocked."

"We're looking for a needle in a haystack." The detective sounded sorry to have to tell Ali, "It would've been the simplest thing in the world for your rapist to take the suitcase out of your apartment garage on the night of the rape, pack his clothes in it, and then bring it up here to your attic, unnoticed, on the day you moved in."

And there were other people, too, Ali thought. *People the detective hasn't even mentioned. Everybody who was in this house the night of the attack, the people who were here for the housewarming…like Aidan. I remember that odd tone in his voice, in the garage…when he put his mouth on my ear and said,* "A girl from Rhode Island, who wants babies and loves to cook, is married to the producer of a hit television show and can't figure out why she's a work widow. I'd call that Hello Kitty in the Land of the Barbies." *And then later, his weirdly hostile kiss on my cheek when he told me,* "I'm leaving. But I'm sure I'll see you again. Soon." *And what about Levi, and the text he sent me that night? The text that said,* "Don't make me crash your housewarming and cause a scene. Don't forget. Am on my way into LA…"

Ali was scared to the point of being dizzy. "Why did the person who hurt me hide that suitcase in my attic?"

"My guess? A power play," the detective said. "He knew it would be found eventually, and when it was, without even lifting a finger, he'd be terrorizing you all over again."

"Then he got what he wanted," Ali murmured.

Matt looked at the open suitcase. "You'll never catch the guy, will you?"

"We plan to turn over every rock we can." The detective briskly put on a pair of latex gloves. The soothing tone was gone from his voice. "There was some sloppy police work on your wife's case. The original investigating officers didn't take a DNA sample from you on the night of the rape, Mr. Easton." The detective ejected a cheek swab from a plastic case. "Mind if I ask for one now?"

Suddenly Ali felt a tickle of doubt about Matt. "How could my husband have had anything to do with what happened to me?"

"That's what we're about to find out," the detective told her.

Morgan

WHEN MATT OPENED THE DOOR, MORGAN WAS SURPRISED. She'd been expecting Ali. "What are you doing here? I thought your flight wasn't coming in until late tonight."

"I caught an earlier flight." Matt seemed tense.

And it made Morgan wary. She was watching him carefully as she told him, "I almost didn't recognize you. You look like a completely different person."

"It's the beard," he said.

Morgan took a step toward him, hoping Matt would open the door a little wider and let her into the house. He didn't. "This isn't a good time for a visit, Morgan. Ali isn't here…and she won't be back for a while."

Morgan was sick-to-her-stomach frightened. The missing spare key had kept her from getting into Ali's house this morning, and now it was after seven. The whole day had gone by. She needed to get this done before any more violence happened. She had to get upstairs and confirm her suspicions about *buttercup*.

Morgan blurted out the first cover story that came into her head. "I want to run up and say hi to Sofie. Just for a minute."

Matt was already closing the door. "Sofie is at Jessica's. That's where Ali is…picking her up."

Determined to get into the house, Morgan shoved herself through the narrow space between Matt's body and the doorframe. He made a grab for her, but she broke free and ran, telling him, "I won't stay long. I bought a little present for Sofie. I'll just dash in and leave it on her bed."

Worried that Matt might follow her up the stairs, Morgan yanked her keys from her coat pocket and tossed them in his direction. He instinctively dove to catch them. "I left my purse on the front seat," Morgan said. "I'm not sure I locked the car."

She knew Matt was losing patience. From the way he was holding the keys, it was obvious he wanted to throw them at her.

"Please. My purse is wide open, and my wallet's in there…all my credit cards, everything." Morgan glanced toward the stairway. "I'll just be a minute, and I'll be out of your hair."

Matt hesitated for a second, then went toward the door. As soon as he was outside, Morgan bolted up the stairs, taking them two at a time.

She went directly to Ali's bedroom and headed for the closet, grabbing a chair to stand on and swiftly sliding her hand under the shoe boxes on the overhead shelf—finding nothing but a feathering of dust. Morgan stifled a scream.

But suddenly, at the back of the shelf, there it was. The item Morgan had stumbled across that afternoon when she and Ali were rummaging through the closet—the file folder Ali had borrowed from Jessica. Information about rapes that had occurred all over California.

Morgan took the folder and ran to the bedroom window—Matt was walking up the front path toward the house. Morgan quickly ducked into the bathroom, closed the door, sat with her back against it, and flipped through the folder's contents.

Other than the handwritten note from Jessica clipped to the inside cover, most of the stuff in the folder had nothing to do with the evidence Morgan was searching for. But tucked in, at random intervals, were some of the articles she remembered looking at earlier. News stories that gave a gruesome significance to the word *buttercup*.

They were printouts from the websites of different newspapers—each paper published in a different California town, documenting rapes that had occurred in different months and different years. At first glance, the crimes seemed to be unconnected. But when Morgan laid them out on the bathroom floor, side by side, they formed a pattern.

The article with the earliest date was from a Pasadena newspaper and described an attack that happened in an upscale neighborhood. The other articles came from all over California, and every one of them had a connection to the corporation Morgan had researched that morning, before Mr. Dupuis called her into the staff meeting.

Each rape was within a few miles of one of the corporation's regional offices.

The Pasadena attack and the other rapes shared a pair of identical details. Details that had Morgan shaking. She'd been right about the meaning of *buttercup*. And she now realized the awful significance of what she'd seen in the drawer on the boat—the panties.

In the articles she was reading, the victims all reported that as the assault began, the attacker said *Time to pay up, buttercup.* And in each case, the attacker had also taken the victim's underwear.

Morgan rapidly gathered the scattered contents of the folder, and then put her ear against the bathroom door to hear if Matt was coming upstairs. When all she heard was silence, she pulled her phone out of her pocket. Morgan's focus was the note from Jessica, clipped to the inside of the file folder: *The guy's trademark was the name he called his victims, the name of a summer wildflower…and he always took their underwear.*

The instant Morgan's mother answered her call, Morgan said, "Mom…those yellow flowers on Grandma MaryJoy's farm, the ones that used to grow wild in the summer…they were buttercups, right?"

"Yes, honey, but—"

"And the person who hurt Ali…when he was attacking her, did he call her *buttercup?*"

"I'm not sure. I don't know. Ali never gave me the details. But what's going on with you? What do flowers on Grandma's farm have to do with any of this?"

"It's not the flowers. It's their name…*buttercup*. I think I've found Ali's rapist." Morgan checked the file folder again. "I was just hoping you knew if he took Ali's underwear."

But the truth was that not having absolute proof Ali had been called *buttercup*, or that her underwear was taken as a trophy, didn't change anything. Morgan's gut instinct had already told her everything. She knew, without a doubt, who Ali's attacker was.

And Morgan intended to punish him—to do it up close and personal, looking straight into his eyes.

Without saying good-bye to her mother, Morgan switched off her phone and dropped it into her pocket, her heart racing. She could hear Matt coming up the stairs, and that Ali was with him.

By the time Morgan scooped up the file folder and walked out of the bathroom, Ali and Matt were on the other side of the doorway, in the bedroom. Matt shot Morgan an exasperated look.

Holding the folder behind her, she slipped it out of sight between the bedroom wall and the dresser she was passing.

Cradling Sofie in her arms, Ali had her attention on Matt. "I'm glad Jess could take Sofie this afternoon. I wouldn't have wanted her here when we were dealing with the awfulness of that suitcase—" Ali stopped.

Startled to see Morgan in the room, Ali looked horrified.

"What suitcase?" Morgan asked.

Ali nervously transferred Sofie to Matt. "She's been asking for her teddy bear. Can you help her find it? I think it's downstairs in the kitchen."

Matt didn't seem to want to leave. Ali gave him a look that said *Go. Please.*

Ali waited until Matt and Sofie were out of the room before she said, "How much do you know, Morgan?"

"I know that right now I'm feeling what you're feeling. It's horrible. I'm guessing it has something to do with the suitcase you just mentioned. And I want to help."

Ali was adamant. "There's nothing you can do. And I don't want to talk about it. I can't. Not yet."

Ali looked so fragile and unprotected.

Morgan wrapped her arms around her sister, wanting never to let go. "It's my turn to be the strong one. Let me take care of you...the way you've always taken care of me."

∽

Morgan held Ali until she sensed that Ali understood. Morgan was no longer a burden. She was a source of strength.

As soon as Ali went downstairs to start dinner, Morgan closed Ali's bedroom door. After she made sure the door was locked, Morgan reached behind the dresser, pulled out the file folder, and slipped it back onto the closet shelf. She wasn't ready to tell Ali, or the Pasadena police, about what she'd found.

What she wanted to do first was deliver a very specific kind of vengeance.

Six hundred ninety-three miles from Pasadena,
in a winter twilight.
Retribution.
Intense cold. Gusts of icy, fast-falling snow.
Halfway up a steep mountainside. A schussing
sound—growing louder.
A man on skis. Moving down the face of the mountain
like a bullet.
Suddenly. A small, brown rabbit darting out of the
shadows.
The man swerving. The tip of his ski snagging a snow-
dusted tree root.
For a fleeting moment, the man is airborne, in silent
flight.
Then he is falling to earth.

Ali

THE RAIN STARTED SHORTLY AFTER MORGAN CAME DOWNSTAIRS and kissed Ali good-bye.

There was an aspect of the kiss that was strange. Ali couldn't shake the feeling something had been left unfinished between herself and Morgan. And thinking about things that were unfinished took Ali to what the detective had told her earlier in the day when Ali and Matt were with him in the attic—that the man who attacked her might never be caught or punished.

While she was feeding Sofie the last few bites of dinner, Ali was anxious. Glancing at the back door, checking to see that it was locked. The conversation with the detective had her worried.

She took another look around the room. Something wasn't right—the knife block was at a crazy angle. The boning knife was missing.

Ali started to call out to Matt and tell him about the missing knife, ask him if he knew where it had gone. Then she remembered how a little while ago, when she needed to talk to Morgan and asked Matt to watch Sofie, he'd immediately put Sofie down for a nap—disappearing into his study to make a series of muffled phone calls.

Now she was hearing his footsteps in the entryway, followed by the slam of the front door.

Seconds later, she heard the sound of Matt's car, tires squealing on the rain-slicked street, racing away from the house.

It wasn't until Ali was upstairs and Sofie was asleep for the night that Ali realized Matt had come back into the house. He was standing just outside Sofie's room, looking in. The collar and cuffs of his shirt damp with rain.

Ali kept her voice low, not wanting to wake Sofie. "Matt, what're you doing?"

"Thinking how much I love you."

There was something in the way he was gazing at her that wouldn't let Ali look away. "What's happening?" she asked.

"You'll see. Right now, I just need you to come here."

Ali stepped out into the hall, not sure what Matt wanted—not entirely sure about Matt.

He carefully shut Sofie's door. Then he kissed Ali and said, "Your lips are cold."

"I'm a little shivery."

"A lot of shivery things happened today."

Ali hoped that whatever this was, it wouldn't be another hurt, another shock.

"I've been thinking about what the detective told us," Matt said. "I'm wondering if he was right about your attack being one of those crimes that'll never get solved."

"Where are you going with this?"

"Al, I don't want you to spend the rest of your life afraid, waiting for the guy to come back. I don't want him to win."

Matt moved close to Ali. She could see her eyes reflected in his. The same as when they were on the staircase at the wedding in Newport. When she'd caught the bridal bouquet. And Ali was seeing exactly what she'd seen then. The sweetness in Matt, and how much he truly loved her.

"That bastard who hurt you won't win, Al. We won't let him."

Matt took Ali into his arms reverently. Like a bridegroom lifting his bride at their threshold. Their beginning.

And then Matt carried Ali into their bedroom.

The room where Morgan had so recently unearthed the terrible truth about *buttercup*, and about the identity of Ali's attacker.

Matt

W HEN MATT CARRIED ALI INTO THE BEDROOM, WHAT HE HAD waiting for her were forests of white candles flickering in jewel-like glass containers and dozens of mahogany-brown baskets filled to the brim with red and white roses. The roses were in full bloom. The edges of the baskets and the petals of the flowers were dusted with raindrops. The way a cloudless night sky is dusted with a glitter of stars.

Matt could see Ali was dazzled, and puzzled.

"Happy Valentine's Day," he told her.

She was so innocent, so sweet. "Valentine's Day. Oh, Matt. I'd forgotten!"

"I had, too…for a while."

Ali looked at the baskets of flowers, delighted. "How did you manage to find a florist that was still open, much less one that had all these incredible roses?"

"It was a miracle. We were overdue for one."

Matt moved toward the bed, wanting Ali to notice that he'd turned down the sheets—and that there was a single red rose on her pillow.

It had been a very long time. He waited. Letting Ali decide.

As she made her decision, Matt saw a look in Ali that he'd only seen on one other occasion—when they'd had sex on that bluff in Newport, just before a gust of wind had blown them apart.

Morgan

THE NIGHT RAIN TAPPED LIGHTLY ON MORGAN'S LIVING ROOM window. She was in her favorite chair, safe and snug, with Ralph sleeping at her feet.

There was soft music on the sound system, the songs of Billie Holiday. But what Morgan was hearing was the snippet of conversation she had with her mother earlier in the day, while she'd been crouched in Ali's bathroom holding the file folder.

"Mom. The person who hurt Ali...when he was attacking her, did he call her buttercup?"

"I'm not sure. I don't know. Ali never gave me the details. But what's going on with you?"

The tender tone that had been in her mother's voice was filling Morgan with yearning. Yet as she reached for the phone, she was immediately pulling back.

Morgan had spent her life pushing her mother away. She was afraid to find out just how much of a toll it had taken on her mother's love for her.

Switching screens on her phone, Morgan checked her voice mail. There was a new message—Ben Tennoff, gentle and concerned. "I know I've been gone and you've been busy, and we haven't seen each other for a while. But I just got home and read your Facebook post...that there was a tragedy in your family. I want you to know I'm here. If you need me." He paused. "Or if you just want a friend to rent you a movie and bring you some popcorn." There was another pause. "Oh. And, Morgan? Happy Valentine's Day."

Being with Ben was something Morgan very much wanted to do. But she was thinking about the martini-drunk afternoon she'd spent on Logan's black silk sheets. For a minute she wasn't sure she deserved kind, openhearted Ben Tennoff.

But there was that thought that Sam had shared: *"Life is the process of becoming. It starts with your first breath and stays with you until your last. Just think of the power of it…being able to continually reach toward the light. The possibilities are infinite."*

Morgan quickly typed a text: **So glad you're home, Ben! xo**

After the text was sent, Morgan leaned back in her chair, her feet propped on the coffee table, her thoughts going back to *buttercup*—to the rapist, the man who'd harmed Ali.

The white envelope, the one from Mr. Dupuis, was in the center of the coffee table. Beneath it was a second, slightly larger envelope. The issue of the rapist and the punishment Morgan planned to inflict were momentarily pushed aside.

Morgan let out a sigh. Happiness, with a touch of anxiety. She picked up the larger envelope and held it between her hands. She didn't have to open it. She'd read its contents a dozen times.

After a few minutes of deliberation, Morgan made her decision. She put the larger envelope squarely on top of the slightly smaller one. And she was at peace. Lulled by the crackle of the fire, and the whisper of rain on the window.

Billie Holiday was singing about love and desire, her voice as warm as the taste of whiskey: *In my solitude…you haunt me.* The lyrics turned Morgan's thoughts back to the monster she'd found, and all the women he violated.

And Morgan was thinking about how much she'd changed since she'd first laid eyes on him. Back then she'd been so completely lost.

Out of habit, she crossed her arms. Ready to dig her fingernails into the crooks of her elbows, about to break down and cry.

But crossing her arms was as far as Morgan got.

She realized she didn't need to feel sorry for herself, or cry. She wasn't broken anymore. She was fine. Strong. Resolved. And she suddenly had the urge to call Sam—just to say hello, just to tell Sam that everything was good.

She pressed Sam's number and heard a voice she'd never heard before. It was high and clear. A woman's voice.

Morgan was confused. "Is Sam there?"

"Sam?" The woman sounded just as confused as Morgan. Then she said, "Are you the special friend? The phone friend?"

"Yes." Morgan still wasn't sure what was going on.

The woman's voice went low, sorrow-filled. "I don't know how to tell you this, other than to just say it. My brother passed away. He'd been ill for a long time."

Morgan's pain was as real as if she'd been hit by a gunshot. She was grief-stricken.

"My brother said finding you was one of the loveliest miracles he'd ever been given."

Morgan tried to organize her thoughts, her emotions—she couldn't. Grief was battling with confusion. She was refusing to accept that Sam was dead, and she wanted to know how he had come into her life. "How did your brother find me, really?"

"He was trying to text his new caregiver. When he entered the number in his phone, he mixed up the last two digits."

"He had a caregiver?" Morgan was overcome with sadness. "I never thought of him as being old."

"My brother was forty-three." The woman was crying now. "He had very aggressive bone cancer. He hadn't been able to leave the house in a long time."

Morgan wiped away tears. "I don't understand. When we first started talking, he told me how much he always looked forward to his afternoon swim."

The woman chuckled, as if she was comforted by the memory. "My brother loved the ocean. Our family home is at the water's edge. And I went swimming. For him. Every afternoon. While he watched from the window."

Morgan wanted to stop, take time to grieve, but there were too many unanswered questions. "He told me he liked speed...race cars and parachute jumping. When did he do all that?"

"He spent most of his life doing it." The woman was quiet for a second. "My brother was a Wall Street shark. He made enormous amounts of money, and in his free time he was a thrill chaser. He was also self-involved and shallow."

"When did he change?" Morgan asked.

"After he got sick. That's when he became a beautiful soul trapped in a broken body. He spent a lot of time reading...and learning. Thinking about who he was and who he wanted to be in the time he had left. He said that, at some point, he started to pray, and his prayer was 'Use me.' He wanted to be of service. He believed that, right up until the end, people can grow and change...can keep on giving to each other, no matter what life throws at them. He said his relationship with you was the proof of that."

"But he did all the giving. I didn't give him anything in return." Morgan's face was wet with tears.

"You gave him the best gift in the world," the woman said. "You gave him someone to take care of, and love."

The tears were crowding in, making it difficult for Morgan to speak.

"What was his name?"

"It was—"

"Wait."

Too much had changed, too fast.

"Don't tell me. I need him to stay the way he was. I need him to stay Sam."

Before the woman could reply, Morgan ended the call.

She gathered Ralph into her arms, rested her head on his warm fur, and cried like she'd never be able to stop. The dearest friend she'd ever had was dead.

It took a very long time for Morgan to wipe away her tears—and tell Ralph, "I don't have to cry. Sam isn't gone."

Morgan had realized that as long as she lived, wherever she went, Sam's quiet voice would be there. Guiding her toward what was strong and good.

And the possibilities were infinite.

Morgan smiled as she dimmed the lights and enjoyed the comfort of her favorite chair. Ralph climbed in and snuggled next to her, his heart beating in rhythm with the rain on the windows.

Drifting off to sleep, Morgan saw the image of the boning knife she'd taken out of Ali's kitchen earlier in the evening, just before she kissed Ali good-bye. She knew exactly how she would get justice for Ali. The only thing still to be decided was when.

As sleep finally overtook her, Morgan was utterly relaxed—her hands loosely folded on her belly.

Ali

I HAVE A QUESTION." THE YOUNG WAITRESS WAS WEAVING THROUGH the crowd, making her way toward Ali. "When do you want the appetizers served?"

"You can go ahead and start." Ali's response was subdued.

Most of the people Ali loved were gathered in her restaurant. Peter Sebelius's surprise birthday party had started, and Ali was having trouble getting into the spirit of the evening. She was still unsettled by the bizarre discovery of the brown suitcase—and by the strange quality of Morgan's good-bye kiss last night. Ali had the feeling Morgan was hiding something from her.

But now, as Ali watched Morgan move through the glitter and sparkle of the party, she wondered if she'd simply imagined that Morgan was keeping secrets. Morgan seemed relaxed and self-confident. Getting compliments and congratulations from almost everyone she passed.

The transformation of the restaurant's dining area into the setting for Peter's celebration had been spectacular, and it was Morgan who had accomplished it.

That morning, Ali had been frantic when she was on the phone with Morgan. "The team I hired to do the decorations for Peter Sebelius's party just called. They're stranded at the Denver airport. The party starts in less than eight hours, and there's no time to book another decorating company."

Ali was expecting something like "Wow. That's awful. What're you going to do?"

Instead, she heard Morgan say, "Don't worry. Everything will be fine. I'll take care of it. Today's Saturday. I don't have to be at work. That gives me the whole day to handle what needs to get done."

Bursting with inspiration and enthusiasm, Morgan had swept into JOY and created a setting more incredible than Ali could have ever imagined.

With Ali as her assistant, Morgan worked for seven straight hours. She filled the restaurant's high, curved ceiling with a sea of matte-black balloons, all of them trailing constellations of shimmering streamers. The effect was breathtaking. Then Morgan covered the tables with snow-white tablecloths and graced each one with a golden bowl containing a single cream-colored camellia. Beside each bowl was a crystal candlestick holding a slim, gold-hued candle. Simple and elegantly beautiful. After that, she laid out the place settings—all of them similar, none of them identical—imaginative combinations of shiny black dinner plates, gleaming silver flatware, and oversize linen napkins patterned in swirls of black and cream.

Now Morgan had her arm around Ali's waist; the two of them taking in the beauty of Morgan's work. "When did you learn how to do stuff like this?" Ali asked.

"I think I've always known. But I didn't realize it...not until a friend of mine told me, 'Morgan, you're a curator at an art museum. You understand color and form and proportion. You can use what you know to work magic.'"

"Your friend was right." Ali looked around the room, awestruck.

Morgan's grin was bashful. "This is only the second time I've ever done it in a major way. The first time was when you weren't with me. When I was all alone. When I decorated my house and made it really pretty." Morgan took a deep breath. "Being away from you put me at the bottom of the pit...and I came out a completely different person."

There was triumph in Morgan's shy smile.

Ali was blinking back tears.

Before the tears could fall, Morgan was wiping them away.

The party was in full swing. Everyone was having a fabulous time. Waiters wearing red ties and black silk shirts served French champagne and broiled Maine lobsters, and tiny portions of lemon sherbet that were as light and cold as snowflakes. In the center of the room, while a man at the piano pounded out a rafter-shaking rendition of "Mustang Sally," more and more dancers were crowding the floor.

The happiness in the room was contagious. And it briefly dimmed Ali's nagging worry about the suitcase, allowed her to enjoy herself. She blew a kiss to Sofie, who was at a nearby table. Perched on Matt's lap. Pretty as a picture. In a little black-velvet dress and white leggings.

Morgan was a few feet away, talking to Quinn Sebelius. Ali heard Quinn tell Morgan, "I've been wanting all night to let you know how pretty you look." But Morgan's thank-you was drowned out by a loud flourish coming from the piano. And Quinn rushed off, saying, "Oops, that's my cue!"

Quinn took her place beside the piano, nervously. Shooting Ali an anxious glance. Ali gave her a thumbs-up, and Quinn, flushed and excited, picked up the microphone. "Thank you, everybody, for coming to celebrate my wonderful husband's thirty-fifth birthday." She waved toward the table where Peter was. "And most of all, thank you, sweetheart, for being mine. I love you like crazy!"

Peter's smile was pure adoration.

"Okay. Enough sappy stuff." Quinn smiled. "We've had a great dinner and great music. And now, before we get to the truly amazing birthday cake Ali whipped up, let's have some really great laughs." The lights dimmed and Quinn announced, "Ladies and gentleman, I give you a video tribute to the life and times of Dr. Peter Sebelius. We'll begin with the early years." A photo of a bald-headed baby splashing in an inflatable wading pool appeared on an overhead monitor.

The room erupted in laughter, and Ali crossed to the table where Matt and Sofie were. She settled into an empty chair beside Matt, telling him, "We're shorthanded in the kitchen. I should help with the setup for the cake and coffee."

"I'll come with you," he said.

"Me, too. Me, too." Sofie was already scrambling off Matt's lap.

As Ali scooped Sofie into a hug, Morgan appeared at Ali's side. "Do you want me to take her home now? It's getting late."

Sofie gave Morgan an adamant shake of her head—then looked up at Ali with a little pixie smile. "I want to sing 'Happy Birthday, Dr. Peter,' 'cause he's nice."

Ali was a mother completely in love with her child. She kissed the tip of Sofie's nose and told her, "I guess we can postpone bedtime until after we cut the cake. Because birthday cake is one of Sofie Easton's favorite things, isn't it?"

Sofie giggled. And happily went into Morgan's open arms.

Ali headed for the kitchen, leaving Sofie snuggled in Morgan's embrace, fascinated by the images of Peter Sebelius that were flashing across the monitor's screen.

"He's nice," Sofie whispered to Morgan.

"Yes," Morgan agreed. "He's very nice."

For that brief span of time, all was right with Ali's world.

Six hundred ninety-three miles from JOY,
under a star-filled sky.

Agony.

Two nights since the brown rabbit darted out of the shadows, and the tip of the man's ski snagged on the tree root, and he was sent flying into the air.

Two nights since he'd landed with his head at a grisly angle, smashed against the snow-covered base of the tree.

Two nights of unwanted images and sense memories flashing through his mind. Shuffling and reshuffling with lightning speed... The smell of night-blooming jasmine and a shred of amber-colored silk... White cotton and a woman's eyes, green, and so very wide open... Droplets of crimson-red blood, in another place and time, falling onto a blanket of snow, and the letter L... Hot sand, the flicking of a lizard's tail against a bare ankle, and a curl of lace the color of a blueberry.

Two nights of lying freezing and paralyzed—straining to hear footsteps, praying for rescue.

Ali

ALI CAUGHT ONLY A FEW GLIMPSES OF QUINN'S VIDEO TRIBUTE to Peter. The presentation of the birthday cake and serving after-dinner drinks had kept Ali moving nonstop between the dining area and the kitchen.

Now, as the party was winding down, she noticed that Morgan was still there, with Sofie in her lap. "You've been at it since dawn," Ali said. "You must be exhausted."

"It's okay. I'm fine." Morgan seemed surprisingly wide awake and energized. "Actually, I have something else to do as soon as the party's over."

"Then go. I'm serious. People are starting to take off. This celebration is pretty much done. Put Sofie to bed in her old nursery in the kitchen. She can sleep there till Matt and I are ready to leave."

"Okay, if you're sure. I really do need to get going." Morgan seemed as if she wanted to say something more. Then she brushed a kiss across Ali's cheek and disappeared, carrying Sofie into the kitchen.

When Morgan's lips had touched Ali's skin, the kiss was rushed, nervous, like Morgan was keeping secrets. Ali wanted to follow Morgan into the kitchen, to talk about it. But she couldn't get away. Matt, Peter, and Quinn were the only people left in the dining room, and Quinn had looped her arm through Ali's—saying, "Come with me. I want you to see Peter's video tribute from beginning to end. And I won't take no for an answer."

The picture of Peter as a baby, in the wading pool, flashed onto the screen, and all four of them—Ali, Matt, Quinn, and Peter—leaned back in their chairs, pleasantly tired. They were gathered around a small table. Several bottles of champagne were on a nearby bar cart. Matt had opened one of the bottles to share with Ali and Quinn. Peter poured himself a glass of mineral water.

While the video tribute unfolded, one of black balloons crowding the ceiling suddenly popped, with a small bang. It distracted Ali for a minute. When she turned back toward the table, she saw Matt struggling to keep his eyes open.

"Are you okay?" she whispered.

"Yeah. I guess it's just being home from Australia for less than forty-eight hours and not getting very much sleep. It's probably jet lag."

Ali leaned toward Matt, rubbed the back of his neck, and then looked up at the screen.

What she saw sent a shock wave through her.

A raucous Christmas party crowded with nurses and doctors, wearing Santa hats. A large banner proclaiming *Docs Rock!* An Asian girl in scrubs at the side of a makeshift stage, shouting, "Pay attention to this friggin' talent show and vote for the winner by stuffing your cash into one of those slot-topped boxes. We're raising money for a toy drive, people!" Five performers were lined up on the stage. A trio of men blowing bubbles the size of beach balls. A pretty woman doing a belly dance. And a tall, muscular man strumming a guitar.

The man was clowning his way through a ridiculous cowboy song. His shirt was satin, the pockets and cuffs edged in black. His belt buckle was big, shaped like a horseshoe. And his ostrich-skin boots were eggplant purple.

Ali was fighting not to pass out. Swaying in her chair. The chair rocking and tipping. She was inches from hitting the ground.

Matt somehow managed to grab her and break her fall.

Peter Sebelius reached in to help.

Ali screamed. Clawing at him like a wild animal.

Quinn shrieked.

Ali saw Matt catch sight of the image on the video screen—the man in the satin shirt and eggplant boots.

The man was Peter Sebelius.

Matt roared and drove his fist into Peter.

Peter slammed into the wrought-iron base of a nearby table.

Quinn shrieked again, louder.

And in this place called JOY, Ali was drowning in a sea of fear and violence.

Six hundred ninety-three miles from JOY,
  under a star-filled sky.
The prelude to death.
  The man, lying in the snow, with his head smashed
  against the trunk of the tree.
  Unbroken silence. No sound of a footstep, or a
  helicopter.
  The images in his mind shifting, changing. Whirling
  like a living hologram.
He's hurrying through a shadow-filled garage. He needs to get back to the street, where his car is. The taste of cheap hospital party booze is sour in his mouth, like day-old piss. He's popping another breath mint. He's in less of a fury than he was when he got here… He's less drunk. Now he's thinking how stupidly conspicuous his clothing is. It might make somebody take notice when he comes out of the garage.

He's upset. And then, all at once, he isn't. He's spotted a scribbled sign—*For Salvation Army*. And there's a brown suitcase, and a pile of discarded clothes. He grabs a T-shirt, khakis, and a pair of flip-flops. Then he ducks into an empty storage room, stripping off the cowboy stuff, pulling on the discards…the T-shirt and khakis.

He's thinking about how easy it was to teach that

bitch her lesson. He didn't even need to duct-
tape her eyes, the way he did with the others so
they couldn't see his face. She already had a towel over her head. And he didn't need to bother
taking panties to remember her by. What for?
She was somebody he saw all the time. She—

The images jump, stop like a piece of broken film.

A noise. Something rustling. The sound of movement.

A snow-laden tree branch breaking and falling.

Burial.

His shroud thick and powdery, icy cold.

Morgan

MORGAN WAS IN THE NURSERY, WATCHING SOFIE SLEEP, WHEN she heard the noise. The muffled, unmistakable sound of screams.

Morgan ran toward the door that separated JOY's kitchen from the dining area. She could hear Ali shouting, "Why did you do it? Why would you hurt me like that?"

As soon as Morgan pushed the door open, she saw Peter Sebelius on the floor—Matt charging toward him, and Peter trying to shove Matt away, asking, "What the hell's going on?"

Ali, swaying and unsteady, was clutching the back of a chair. Staring at Peter, horrified.

Quinn was circling Peter and Matt, screaming, "Stop it! Stop it!"

And Matt pounded Peter with a blood-splattering punch.

Suddenly there was silence.

Then Ali's voice, devastated, telling Peter, "At our housewarming, you said you were leaving to go to the hospital Christmas party. Then, after that, you came back, to the apartment. You came through the sliding door in my bedroom, with this sour smell on your breath, wearing that shirt and those boots. And you *raped* me!"

Out of the corner of her eye, Morgan glimpsed Matt close his hand around the neck of an unopened champagne bottle. Like it was a club. And he was preparing to commit murder.

In that same split second, Morgan caught the ghastly look on Ali's face.

Ali's eyes were locked on the video monitor. Her scream was deafening.

The video's camera angle had widened, showing that Peter Sebelius wasn't alone on stage. He was performing a duet. With a man who was also wearing a satin cowboy shirt, a horseshoe-buckled belt, and eggplant-colored ostrich-skin boots.

It was Logan.

Morgan watched Ali collapse into a chair.

Still gripping the unopened champagne bottle, Matt swung it in Peter's direction, shouting, "What the hell was Logan doing there?"

Peter sounded dazed. "He's a consultant at the hospital. His company sponsored the party. They paid for everything."

Peter looked at Ali, horrified. "That morning, when you were moving, when I came by and the police were at your place...you'd been raped?"

Ali nodded.

"Christ." It was obvious that Peter was in anguish.

"What are all of you talking about?" Quinn asked.

Peter pointed to the video footage, telling Ali, "That was back when I was drinking. I made a fool of myself. I was really loaded that night."

Now Quinn was looking at the footage, too, saying, "Peter was drunk, but he wasn't on duty. A lot of people who weren't on duty were drinking. But the guy Peter's onstage with...your friend's husband? He was ten times more drunk than anybody else. He was coming on to every woman in the place. It was disgusting."

Gasping for air, Ali asked, "What would any of that have to do with him raping me?"

"I don't know exactly." Quinn frowned. "But toward the end of the party—"

A killing wave of guilt raced through Morgan.

"—that's when your friend's husband checked his texts and got really pissed off by one of them. He started cursing and saying the person who sent it was a bitch—" Quinn stopped and corrected herself. "No. Not bitch. He used the *C* word. He said the message this woman sent was 'Fuck you,' 'Screw you,' something like that. He blew out of there looking like he wanted to kill her."

Everything in Morgan went dead. The text Quinn was talking about was the text Morgan sent on the night of Ali's housewarming. When Morgan had gotten Jessica's phone mixed up with Ali's. And the message Morgan intended for Levi was accidentally delivered to Logan.

Morgan was frozen by a single unspeakable thought: *I caused my sister's rape.*

Unaware of Morgan's presence, Ali was wandering the room, saying, "None of this makes sense. What reason would Logan have to hurt me? And how could he hide his clothes in my attic…in a suitcase I gave away to the Salvation Army?"

The agony in Ali's voice sent Morgan's thoughts to the knife she'd taken from Ali's kitchen. She had intended to use it to punish Logan.

But now she was thinking, *The person who deserves to be punished is me.*

Six hundred ninety-three miles from JOY,
under the same star-filled sky.
Last rites.

The man, who a few moments ago thought he was go-
ing to die, remains trapped at the base of the tree,
still hoping for rescue.

His thoughts circle back to where they were just before
the tree branch broke and shrouded him in snow.
He's recalling how easy that particular one was. No
need to blindfold her. No reason to take her un-
derwear. What for? She was his wife's best friend.
He didn't need anything to remember her by. He
could see her, enjoy the misery he'd inflicted on her,
anytime he wanted.

Now he's reliving a specific moment, right after the rape…
He's coming out of the storage room, in the underground garage. He's dumping the cowboy outfit
into the brown suitcase that's on the Salvation
Army pile, knowing it'll be hauled away, lost forever in a load of junk nobody gives a shit about.
Then he's running for his car. Thinking what a
fucked-up left turn this night has taken—a night
that started off sweet and smooth with the story
to Jessica about missing his plane and being stuck
in San Francisco, the easy lie that put him onstage at a party packed with hot young nurses

instead of doing time at a half-assed, suburban housewarming. Then that fucking arrogant "Go screw yourself" text had shown up…and Ali, the haughty cunt, had needed to be put in her place.

He'd been angry enough to kill her when he jumped in his car and went to her house, not really knowing what he'd do when he got there. Then, while he was parked in the dark at the curb, he saw her leaving—alone. And he remembered how she'd told him Matt worked into the wee hours of the morning, and how Jessica said she was always bitching about a broken lock on her goddamn patio door. That's when he shot across town—and arrived at the apartment complex a little ahead of her, just in time to make it to the pool area and see her walking, all by herself, into that empty apartment.

He had really enjoyed bringing her down, teaching her a lesson…just as much as he'd enjoyed bringing all the others down. He'd done her quickly and at night, grabbing her from behind. The only thing different with her was he didn't slap a piece of duct tape over her eyes. Except for that, he did her the same way he'd done all the other women.

There had been so many others. One of the ones he'd liked the best was that time in Rhode Island, right after his wedding. A young rookie cop had refused to let him talk his way out of a ticket, and she'd made him furious. So the next night, when she got off work, he followed her— yanked her off a jogging trail and dragged her into somebody's greenhouse. The air inside was sticky with the smell of night-blooming jasmine, and he'd raped the hell out of her.

That was a good one, but some of his favorites were the ones he'd done in California, while he was traveling on business, all over the state.

There was that green-eyed woman—the hospital emergency room nurse who hadn't given him any respect, hadn't treated him like he was special. He'd flirted with her and charmed her, and she told him to take a number, kept him sitting for an hour and a half before she bandaged the minor injury he'd gotten while playing golf. He'd raped her at the end of her shift, deep in shadow, on the top floor of the hospital's parking garage, as she was getting into her car. And while it was happening, the duct tape came off, and her green eyes had been so wide open.

The droplets of blood on the blanket of snow were from one of the ones he'd done a long time ago—from a college girl named Lynn. A virgin who wore underwear monogrammed with a tiny L. She'd been in a crowded bar, high in the Sierras, at a table near his, and she said he was an asshole, told him to shut up, while he was in the middle of telling his colleagues a loud, raunchy joke—a joke he liked to tell. A few hours later, he followed her and brought her down, after she'd left her friends and was walking alone on the dark, snowy road that led to her rented vacation condo.

And the hot sand had been in a resort town called Rancho Mirage, not far from the corporate office in Palm Springs. While he'd been talking to an attractive hotel clerk about a problem with his bill, he'd seductively run his hand down her thigh. People in the lobby, including his boss, overheard her when she called him an idiot. A couple of weeks later, he returned to the desert and raped her at the sandy edge of a vacant lot. While the tail of a lizard flicked against the bare skin of her ankle.

He had hated every one of the women he raped. They had belittled him and made him feel small. He believed they deserved to be punished for that.

Morgan

A LI REPEATED HER QUESTION: "WHAT DO YOU MEAN...YOU know how that suitcase got into my attic?"

"I put it there." Saying those words took every ounce of courage Morgan had.

Morgan and Ali were in the restaurant's kitchen now, just the two of them, at the long wooden table. Matt had stayed in the dining room with Peter and Quinn.

Morgan died a thousand deaths as she explained the story of the suitcase. "While I was at your apartment complex, when I was helping with the move, I took that brown suitcase off the Salvation Army pile. It was practically brand-new. It seemed like a waste to throw it away. All I was trying to do was—"

"How the hell did it get into my attic?" The question was angry.

There was nothing Morgan could add that would make this right. All she could do was finish the story as quickly as possible. "After I got to your house that night, Ava was unpacking things in the kitchen. While I was waiting for her to finish, I put away stuff I'd brought back from your apartment, the vacuum cleaner and some towels. The suitcase didn't seem like you'd be using it a lot, so I put it in the attic, along with a bunch of empty moving boxes. Ali, it was the suitcase that Dad's stupid wife, Petra, gave you as your wedding present. You always said it was kind of heavy even when there was nothing in it. It never occurred to me that there was anything inside. I thought it was empty when I put it away. I thought—"

The vicious look Ali gave her almost knocked Morgan out of her chair.

"I don't give a shit about your opinion of the suitcase. How did those clothes get inside?"

"Ali, I don't know. I swear."

"But you do know things, things you kept secret. You knew it was Logan who raped me. And you knew it before tonight, didn't you?"

"I only figured it out a couple of days ago. And then—"

Ali kept her eyes locked on Morgan. "Why did Logan attack me, out of nowhere, out of the blue?"

It wasn't out of the blue. For an instant, Morgan was ready to confess. *It happened because of the text I sent from your phone at the housewarming. The "Go screw yourself" message Logan was pissed off about when he left the hospital party.*

But this was information that would make Ali hate Morgan for the rest of their lives, something Morgan couldn't bear. So she skipped over the details and said, "You weren't attacked out of the blue... Logan hurt a lot of women. I figured it out. From the file folder in your closet."

"What does the folder have to do with anything? Logan couldn't have been mentioned in any of those articles. Jessica would have known."

"No, he wasn't mentioned specifically, but—" Morgan stopped talking. She couldn't face it. Didn't want to explain that having sex with Logan was how she'd found the evidence of his crimes. The panties in the drawer and *buttercup.*

Tears were in Ali's eyes. "I don't understand. Why did he choose me? He knew I didn't like him, but how could that be enough? And why that particular night? I didn't even see him that night. He never made it to the housewarming. Jessica said he was out of town. None of it adds up."

Yes it does, Morgan thought. *It makes perfect sense. Logan lied to Jessica about being out of town whenever he was tired of her…or when he was in the mood to go down to his boat and roll some random woman across his black silk sheets.*

The boning knife she'd taken from Ali's house was tucked into a side pocket of Morgan's purse. The purse was lying on the wooden table. Morgan checked the side pocket, telling Ali, "I need to go." Morgan said it just as Ali's phone rang. Ali didn't hear her.

Morgan's fingers slowly traced the outline of the knife's handle. What she had brought into Ali's life was hideous. She needed to right that wrong. And the only way she could think to do it was to hurt Logan as much as he had hurt Ali.

Morgan picked up her purse, getting ready to leave. And was stopped in her tracks by Ali's startled gasp.

Clutching her phone, Ali told Morgan, "The call was from Jess. Logan went to Deer Valley on the men's version of that Perfect Ten ski trip she's always talking about. They got into a big fight before he left. They weren't speaking to each other. He had an accident. He's been lying on the side of a mountain for days and she didn't even know. Another skier, a stranger, found him a few hours ago. If Logan wasn't such a lowlife, help would've gotten to him sooner. The people he went skiing with didn't report him missing because they assumed he was off in a hotel room, fooling around with some woman he'd met."

A beautiful calm came over Morgan. "How badly is he hurt?"

"Head injuries, spinal injuries. Jess said they told her his condition is too gruesome to describe."

Morgan put down her purse, the knife still inside—wondering if she would have been able to go through with shoving that carbon-steel blade into Logan. Now it didn't matter. "I'm glad he got what he deserved," she said.

"I am, too." Ali seemed lost in thought. Then she asked Morgan, "Why didn't you tell me it was Logan who attacked me?"

Morgan opened her mouth to answer. No sound came out.

The "Go screw yourself" text. The appalling reality that she'd slept with a rapist.

They were secrets Morgan didn't know how to tell.

Ali

T HEY WERE STILL ALONE IN THE RESTAURANT KITCHEN.
Ali looked at Morgan, knowing Morgan was keeping secrets
and needing to hear what those secrets were.

The only thing Morgan said was "I'm sorry."

For Ali, *sorry* wasn't enough. It was clear that whatever Morgan
was hiding was connected to Ali's attack. And she wanted to make
Morgan pay for shutting her out.

This impulse to deliberately hurt her sister was a level of rage Ali
had never experienced before.

It felt wrong.

Ali moved away from Morgan. Opened the door to the walled
garden and looked out into the night darkness. Remembering the
feel of Morgan's hand holding tight to hers as they walked, together,
toward their first day of kindergarten.

And Morgan's lovestruck thank-you at their sixth-grade dance
recital, when Ali whispered, "Don't worry. If you fall down at the hard
part, I'll just fall down, too…like it's a joke we made up, together."

Together.

The way they were on the night Ali the homecoming queen rode
onto the football field, and Morgan was waving from the bleachers,
thrilled. Holding up a beautiful handwritten sign: *My sister! The Queen!*

Ali realized that hurting Morgan, or blaming her, for whatever she
was hiding wasn't what Morgan deserved.

In spite of her flaws and weaknesses, there was no part of

Morgan that didn't love Ali. In the same fierce way Ali had always loved Morgan.

They were sisters. Twins. They would always be what they always were—together. Every step of the way.

For the first time in her life, Ali understood what forgiveness was. The place where you don't forget the hurts, but you let go of them, and hold on to the love.

"Come home with me," Ali said. "Spend the night, like you used to, in Rhode Island. Let's go back to being us."

"We can't go back." Morgan's voice had regret in it. But there was also something hopeful.

"Why?" Ali had a feeling she didn't want to hear the answer.

"I'm moving away," Morgan told her.

There was a sudden stillness—as if everything had stopped.

"I leave at the end of next month," Morgan said. "The Getty Museum, in Malibu...they want me to come to work for them."

Ali grabbed Morgan's hand. Tightening her grip on her sister, and understanding it was too late. Their separation had already begun.

"What will I do?" Ali asked. "You'll be so far away."

"Not that far. Only fifty miles or so."

"You can't go," Ali pleaded. "You'll be all alone."

"I won't be alone." Morgan told her. "And neither will you."

Morgan took a small sheet of pearl-colored paper from her pocket and handed it to Ali.

The note, written in Morgan's elegant handwriting, left Ali aching. With love. And joy.

> *Wherever I go, I will never be gone.*
> *Wherever you are, I will always be there.*
> *Whenever you want me, whenever you need me, I will come.*
> *The stranglehold is broken.*
> *What remains is the bond.*

Six hundred ninety-three miles from JOY,
  in the coldest, darkest part of the night.
Perfect justice.
  The man, Logan, being carried down the mountain on
  a stretcher.
  For the first time since this ordeal started, he thinks of
  something other than the rapes. He thinks of his
  wife, Jessica, and the file she put together—and he
  wonders. Did she know? How could she not
  have known? Can a woman be married to a
  man, share his home, and grow his children in
  her belly, and have no idea who he really is?
  His thoughts are interrupted by the sound of his rescu-
  ers' voices.
  They're saying he'll probably die and if, by some mir-
  acle, he survives, he'll be a vegetable. Spending
  the rest of his life mute and paralyzed. His brain
  dangling from its stem like a smashed pumpkin.

Ali

THE GUT-WRENCHING REVELATIONS IN THE PETER SEBELIUS video. The stunning news that Morgan was moving away. Ali thought these things would destroy her.

To her amazement, they made her stronger, more of her own person than she'd ever been.

The party at JOY had ended hours ago. Ali was in bed—with Aidan Blake's face filling the screen on her laptop. Aidan's tone was light as he asked, "Why are you calling me in bloody Australia to talk about this? Why does it matter now?"

Ali's response was brisk, determined. "I'm cleaning up a lot of old business tonight."

Aidan studied her for a beat. "Is everything good with you and Matt?"

"Everything's fine. This has nothing to do with Matt."

"Right, then. You asked for the truth and I'll give it to you. The truth is, you're a gorgeous creature. I'd love to fuck you. You're also the wife of a man I greatly respect. Which means I'd never lay as much as a finger on you."

"Then why did you kiss me, that day in your truck, when you gave me a ride to my friend Jessica's house?"

"Why? Because I was an ass." Aidan seemed uncomfortable. "It happened before I could stop it. Made me feel like a fool then, and it's doing the same now."

"You didn't have the right," Ali told him.

"I'm not suggesting I did. All I can say is, much of the time when

I'm around you, I find myself behaving like a randy schoolboy." Aidan looked away and grinned. "I'm usually better with women than that."

"You had no right to touch me, to touch any part of me."

Aidan's grin vanished. "Point taken. It should never have happened." He came closer to the camera, as if wanting Ali to see he was sincere. "I'm saying it again. I was an ass. I'm begging your pardon, humbly…hoping you'll forget it ever happened."

"I don't know if I can do that."

Aidan seemed surprised. "You can't forget something as simple as a man's uninvited kiss?"

"It's not that simple," Ali told him. Aidan didn't know about the rape and how, for a while, it had left her terrified to be touched, by any man, in any way.

There didn't seem to be anything else to say. Ali closed the laptop and pushed it aside just as Matt came into the room, his hair damp and his skin warm from the shower.

He got into bed and lay close to Ali. "Are you okay?"

Ali nodded.

"What's keeping you so quiet?"

"I was just thinking about this quote I saw somewhere. 'The life of every person is a diary in which they mean to write one story, and write another.'

"I said I wanted a husband who was a good man." Ali was deep in thought. "But what I expected was for you to be perfect. I wanted a restaurant, wanted to turn Grandma MaryJoy's dream into reality. But to do it, I never guessed I'd have to move across the country and work so hard. I wanted our marriage to be strong when I took that vow, 'for better or for worse,' but I never dreamed the better would only come after we'd gone through the worst…after you were out of work, and we were in debt, and I was raped."

Ali stopped. Then said, "I wanted a child and I have Sofie, the most loving little girl in the world, but it's only because I lost the most extraordinary friend I've ever had. And for my whole life, I wanted my sister to be happy and independent, so I could be free of her. And now I'm getting exactly what I wished for, and I don't want to let go of her. How do you make sense of any of that?"

"I don't know if you can." Matt held Ali's hand. "All of us are looking for missing pieces we never quite seem to find."

"What about you?" she asked. "What's the missing piece you're trying to find?"

"Atonement," Matt told her.

"For what?"

"For a lot of things."

"Name one."

"Something I did once, somewhere I went, when I was lonely and needed a friend. I think it might have been wrong, but I'm not sure. I'm still trying to figure it out."

"Do you want to talk about it?"

Matt stayed quiet for a while. "After it was done. Completely finished. I made a conscious decision to shut the door and not tell you about it. Not to shut you out, but to save you from any more hurt. I want to keep us facing forward, Al. I want us together, and strong. I also want you calm and happy."

Ali sensed that if she wanted to know, this was the moment. Matt was ready, willing. It would be easy to make him confess.

She bit her lip, weighed her options.

She was sure that part of Matt's search for atonement was connected to his unfinished business with his mother and his sister. But she understood there was more to it than that—other things, other people. Stories he still hadn't told.

And this was the tipping point, the place where she could demand to know every single detail.

Ali thought about it.

And she said, "Look at me."

She waited till their eyes met. Then she held Matt's gaze. Letting him see that whatever his transgressions had been, they were forgiven.

Ali forgave Matt because she understood what he was dealing with. She had secrets of her own—her relationship with Levi, and the baby she'd miscarried. And she understood that those secrets belonged where they were. In the past.

Ali had no questions for Matt. She knew everything she needed to know. She knew the truth about his soul. It was absolutely pure.

Matt pulled Ali close, his touch tender. "I love you, Al. That's the only thing I know for certain about my life. All the rest of it is a mystery I don't understand."

Listening to the comforting beat of Matt's heart, Ali said, "Maybe the only thing to do is to take it on faith. Live life one day at a time. Knowing that at the end of whatever dark tunnel you're in, there'll always be a light...pointing you toward something new and completely beautiful."

Matt kissed Ali with all the sweetness that was in him. "Do you really believe that, Al?"

"Yes. I'm not sure why, but I do."

Epilogue

TWENTY-THREE HOURS OF LABOR AND A DIFFICULT DELIVERY. IT was the hardest thing Morgan had ever done.

And now she was experiencing pure delight. "I can't believe it. You came!"

"Of course I came. I'll always come."

Morgan heard the caring in her mother's voice, the unwavering devotion. And she was finally able to say what had been bottled up inside her for so long. "I love you, Mom."

Her mother rested a hand on Morgan's shoulder—while Ali lowered the baby into Morgan's arms.

Morgan looked at the sleeping newborn and had a fleeting moment of doubt—the same anxiety that had been with her every minute of this pregnancy. *Can I really trust myself to love this child?*

Ali seemed to have read the question in Morgan's mind. "In a single afternoon on that boat, life threw you a real curve, Morgan. But this baby is as much yours as it is Logan's."

Devoted, tenderhearted Ben Tennoff had been at Morgan's side every step of the journey. He took her hand and held it.

Morgan smiled.

Then she looked down at her baby, knowing that everything would be fine. Her child carried the spirit and promise of truly remarkable people. Morgan's people. Courageous, graceful people like her sister. Strong, faithful people like her mother. And wise, enduring people like her grandfather in Maine.

The baby opened its eyes. They were the color of violets.

And Ali said, "You're the great-grandchild of MaryJoy O'Conner. She believed in the power of celebration. And her dream, when it came true, was a place called JOY."

It was then that Morgan clearly saw her daughter's destiny, and knew her name.

Reading Group Guide

1. Describe the dynamic between Ali and Morgan. Do you think Morgan's jealousy is justified? Do you think Ali's guilt is?

2. Why do you think Morgan turns to the mysterious Sam figure for comfort and companionship? Have you had a person in your life who has been your support system like Sam is for Morgan? Explain that relationship.

3. Why does Morgan get involved with Logan on his wedding night? How do you think that relationship and the continued affair later on make Morgan feel? How does this foreshadow Logan's overall character?

4. Describe the difference between Matt's and Ali's upbringings. How do you think Matt fits in with Ali's family? Do you think Matt recognizes the dysfunction in Ali and Morgan's relationship, or does he idealize Ali's situation?

5. Why do you think Matt keeps his disappearance a secret from Ali? Could you marry someone who did the same to you? How would this affect your relationship?

6. Morgan and Ali have an almost psychic twin connection. Have you ever had someone in your life with whom you felt that

kind of a connection, where you could intuitively sense their feelings? Explain.

7. Why do you think Morgan sells the tract of land her grandmother bought years ago? Is it out of love or revenge?

8. Describe the relationship between Ali and Levi. Why do you think Ali continues their flirtation after marrying Matt and moving to California?

9. Do you think Ali is justified in blaming Matt for her attack? How does she change after that night? How does it affect their marriage?

10. Describe the dynamic between Ava and Ali. How is it different from Ali's relationship with Morgan?

11. Why do you think Matt turns to Danielle for comfort? Describe their affair. Is it physical or purely emotional? Do you think Ali deserves to know?

12. How does owning Ralph change Morgan as a person? Does it affect her relationship with Ali? With herself? With Ben Tennoff? In what ways?

13. How does Ava's baby, Sofie, bring Matt and Ali back together? Ali and Morgan?

14. Why do you think Matt decides to take the movie job in Australia? If you were in his position, would you do the same?

15. How does Ali react when she sees the suitcase in her attic? When Morgan finds out about Ali's rape, how does it affect her feelings toward her sister?

16. How do you feel about the ending of *The Other Sister*? Do you think Morgan and Ali got the lives they deserved? Do you think they each have a happy ending once the book ends? Explain.

17. Imagine having a twin brother or sister. Do you think you'd encounter the same difficulties that Morgan and Ali do? Is there always some level of sibling rivalry? How do you overcome that?

Acknowledgments

Alice Tasman's belief in this book and its writer.

Shana Drehs's world-class ability to make any novel in her care so much better.

Heather Hall's and Diane Dannenfeldt's brilliantly meticulous copyediting skills.

MaryLu Edick's, Jan Winford's, and Gail Schenbaum's unfailing love and support.

Loraine Despres's and Carleton Eastlake's enduring friendships, and their wizardry with crashed-computer, day-before-the-deadline file recovery.

Stephanie Ortale's generosity and enthusiasm.

Josie Assini's contribution of the perfect writing environment.

Gigi Chow's, Tina Mui-Wong's, Denise Sparks's, and Alice Rossiter's kindness and magic.

To these wonderful people, for all of their beautiful gifts...

Thank You!!

About the Author

Dianne Dixon has two Emmy nominations and is a winner of the prestigious Humanitas Prize for outstanding accomplishment in writing for television. She was visiting professor of creative writing at Pitzer College in Claremont, California, and has also taught screenwriting at Chapman University's Dodge College of Film & Media. *The Other Sister* is Dianne's third novel. Her debut novel, *The Language of Secrets*, was named a Top Ten New Fiction title by Amazon. Dianne is an insatiable reader who loves good books, great food, and dark chocolate.